MY NAI
VENUS BLACK

MY NAME IS
VENUS BLACK

MY NAME IS
VENUS BLACK

A NOVEL

Heather Lloyd

THE DIAL PRESS / NEW YORK

Published in the United States by The Dial Press, an imprint of Random House, a division of Penguin Random House LLC, New York.

THE DIAL PRESS and the HOUSE colophon are registered trademarks of Penguin Random House LLC.

Library of Congress Cataloging-in-Publication Data
Names: Lloyd, Heather, author.
Title: My name is Venus Black: a novel / Heather Lloyd.
Description: New York : Dial Press, 2018.
Identifiers: LCCN 2017020823 | ISBN 9780399592188 (hardcover) |
ISBN 9780399592195 (ebook)
Subjects: LCSH: Teenage girls—Fiction. | Domestic fiction. | BISAC: FICTION /
Family Life. | FICTION / Coming of Age. | FICTION / Crime. | GSAFD:
Bildungsromans.
Classification: LCC PS3612.L578 M9 2018 | DDC 813/.6—dc23 LC record
available at https://lccn.loc.gov/2017020823

Printed in the United States of America on acid-free paper

randomhousebooks.com

2 4 6 8 9 7 5 3 1

First Edition

Book design by Victoria Wong

For Noah, as we all knew and loved him

MY NAME IS VENUS BLACK

Prologue

My name is Venus Black because my dad was Joseph Black, and because on March 4, 1966, my very pregnant mother, Inez, just so happened to be watching a TV special about the Space Race when her water broke. I suppose the name Venus sounded better than Mars or Pluto.

If my mother had been reading a novel that night instead, or if she'd gone to the grocery store, I'd have a different name. If she'd had one of her famous migraines on the night I was conceived, I wouldn't have been born in the first place.

We all feel so destined. It had to be me, *we think*. But the truth is, we all just barely made it here. Thousands of other combinations of your mother's egg and your father's sperm just missed their chance to connect, and one small change in circumstance could have wiped you out before you began.

If you ask me, we're all born by accident and there's no such thing as God. We travel through this life with no real trajectory, ricocheted here and there by the consequences of other people's actions. And it works both ways, of course. The stupidest little thing we do can alter the future for so many people.

That means everything you ever did, you almost didn't do.

I think about this a lot lately, trying to figure out how I got *here. I trace my life back in time, looking for all those places in the past where, if I could change one key detail, I would never have seen what I saw or done what I did.*

—*Opening page of journal, Echo Glen Children's Center, Issaquah, Washington, September 12, 1980*

PART ONE

★

Everett, Washington; February 1980

PART ONE

Everett, Washington;
February 1980

1

I could swear I'm in some weird dream or movie, but that can't be true because the burning sensation between my legs is way too real. Now I know how babies feel when they don't get their diaper changed. I'm trying to hide what happened beneath my winter coat, but how long can I last?

A female cop and a cranky older detective in plain clothes are trying to interview me, but I'm sobbing so much it's not going well. They keep saying things like, "Calm down." "Take a deep breath." "We can't understand what you're saying."

But I can't calm down. A bubble of horror has enveloped my brain and left me hysterical.

I make it about five more minutes before pain trumps pride. "I think I wet my pants," I sputter, looking at the female officer.

She's blond and prettier than my idea of a woman cop. She stands up. "Let me take Venus for a few minutes," she says to the man. I don't get up until she is standing by my chair. I feel like a small child as she leads me to a ladies' room and tells me to wait inside for her.

The door locks behind me. I use one of the metal stalls, which remind me of the ones in my junior high. When I'm done, I go to the sink to wash. In the mirror, my face glistens with tears and mucus, my eyes are swollen half shut, and my hair is flying everywhere in an enormous black tangle. Then I remember I've been madly pulling at it.

Pretty soon, the female cop returns, holding a pair of blue pants that look like pajama bottoms with ties in the front. They're way too big, but it's a huge relief to get out of my soaked jeans.

When she leads me back to the interview room, calmer now, I see that Inez is seated off to the side. Has my mother been here the whole time? "I want her out of here," I say, trembling with anger. And then louder, "I want her out! She's the one you should arrest!"

Inez looks white as a sheet, like she's seen a ghost, which I guess isn't too far off. She exchanges whispers with the male cop and then leaves the room.

After she's gone, the police try again. They start out with easy questions about my friends at school. I try to cooperate. I admit what I did. But when they want to know details and *why*, I clam up. "I can't remember," I say.

"You mean you don't want to," says the old guy.

IN THE MORNING, I wake up at Denney Juvenile Justice Center. I've heard of plenty of kids getting sent here, but they were always rough, older, criminal types. The kind who dropped out of school, sold drugs to kids, or stabbed each other and stuff like that. The kind who scare me.

When I learned last night that I'd be locked up here, my knees shook like Mexican jumping beans. "I'm only thirteen," I pleaded. "I get straight A's! I've never gotten drunk, or smoked pot, or even skipped a class. At school I hang out with the smart girls' group." But even my biggest achievement—"Last year I was Citizen of the Week a record six times!"—didn't change anyone's mind about where I belonged.

At Denney, breakfast is served in a small cafeteria that reminds me of our school's. I go through the buffet line and then find the table with the fewest people and try to send out a vibe that says, *Don't even think about sitting here.*

While I eat, random, bizarre details from last night flash in my mind. Like how good it felt when one of the cops gently laid his hand on my head as he guided me into his police car. For a second there, it seemed like he was rescuing me instead of arresting me. And this one: When the car I was riding in pulled away from our house on Rockefeller, I saw the garage door wide open, lit up like a giant TV and neighbors gathered around like someone should make popcorn.

I should be too upset to eat, but I'm starving. The toast is spread with what I'm pretty sure is real butter, not margarine. I wolf down the scrambled eggs even though they come in a square that leaks water.

While I eat, I wonder what my friends are thinking—or if they've heard what happened yet. Who is my best friend, Jackie, going to sit with at lunch today? I'm dying to call her, but I'm sure they won't let me.

Since I might be here for a while, I hope they'll let Jackie pick up all my assignments from school and bring them to me. I don't want to fall behind.

It hurts to think of my teachers, because I know they won't understand. Over the years, I've always been teacher's pet, and now I can just hear them saying, "Venus Black? But she was one of my favorite students! And always such a nice girl."

Inez would probably beg to differ with *nice*. She likes to remind me that *smart* isn't the same as *nice*. She also insists that I have two personalities, one for school, and one for at home. Every time she comes back from a parent-teacher conference, she tells me how surprised she was to hear what a pleasure I am to have in class.

So maybe I'm not a pleasure to have at home. But did she ever think there might be a reason for that?

AFTER BREAKFAST, A guard brings me to a room half-filled with toys. My mother is seated in one of two blue plastic chairs situated next to a messy desk.

Part of me wants to rush into her arms and plead with her to get me out of here. I want her to comfort me and tell me it will be all right. But a bigger part of me wants her to know how much I blame her for what happened.

She must feel the same way, because she doesn't get up or try to hug me. All she says is, "Venus."

"Inez," I say right back.

Before I sit down across from her, I make a big show of scooting my chair farther back from hers. Like she smells bad or something. Right off, I notice how horrible she looks. Her eyes are red and raw, and her face is all puffy like mashed potatoes. She's clutching a white hanky that belonged to her father back in Greece, which she knows I think is super gross. *It's the eighties! Who still uses a handkerchief?*

At first, she is all motherly and worried. She asks how they're treating me, if I'm okay, and if I got breakfast. For a second there, she's my old mom again, and her seemingly genuine concern threatens to crack my anger.

"Aren't you going to talk to me, Venus? Are you really just going to sit there?"

That's when I realize she's suggested a good strategy. Just because you put me in a room with Inez doesn't mean I have to talk to her. Which is something I never thought about before, how you can force people to do a lot of things, but speaking isn't one of them. You can't grab someone's jaw and move it up and down and make words come out.

Eventually I hear her say, "How could you do this, Venus?"

How can she even ask that? She already knows the answer. Clearly she's planning to act like she has no idea, so people won't realize how easily she could have stopped this.

I continue trying to block out her words, but it's hard to miss when she refers to Raymond. She's trying to explain, trying to defend herself. "You didn't give me a chance, Venus."

What is she talking about? I gave her all the chance in the world. I manage to tune her out again for a while, until I can tell she's getting angry. "You better smarten up right now, young lady," she scolds. "Damn it. I can't help you if you won't talk to me."

It's a ridiculous thing to say, because she didn't help me when she could have. I glare at her, hoping she'll guess what I'm thinking, but she's looking down at her hands.

I used to think Inez was pretty, in a Cher sort of way. I was always jealous of her straight black hair because I hated my wild curls. When people said we looked alike, I thought that meant I was beautiful, like her. But now I know it only means we both have black hair, the same Greek nose, and the same darkish eyelids.

Sitting here watching Inez's mouth move, I notice she's been chewing on her lips again. Small pieces of flesh stick up like bits of plastic in her bright-orange lipstick. The lipstick flashes me back to when I was little and she'd ask the Avon lady for lots of those tiny white tubes of lipstick samples so I could play with them later. But that's a happy memory, so I squash it.

"Okay. Be that way, Venus," I hear her say. "That's fine if you're angry at me. But for your own sake, we need to discuss your defense."

I want to scream, My *defense? What is* your *defense?*

How does Leo do it? My little brother is so good at ignoring people that he should be in the *Guinness Book of World Records*. But they'd probably disqualify him, because he has something wrong with him that makes it easy for him to pretend you're not there.

Leo is seven but acts more like he's three or four. He has what Inez calls "developmental issues," probably because he was born too early. My stepdad, Raymond, was super disappointed when Leo didn't turn into a regular little boy. But Leo's always just been

Leo to me. So what if he makes weird noises and doesn't want to be touched? He likes things to stay the same, and sometimes, he throws big tantrums. But really he's the sweetest thing, which is hard to believe when you think about where he came from.

When I trace my life back to make it so Inez never met or married Raymond, I always get stuck here. Because what would I do without Leo?

By this point, Inez is actually crying and pleading with me to talk to her. I'm not used to seeing her this way, and it makes me uncomfortable. It's like I have more power than she does. And in a way, it's true. Here I've gone and done the worst thing in my life and she can't even ground me.

No wonder she's so upset.

After a while, she stops crying and begins staring at me in this weird way. When she gathers her purse off the floor, I think she's getting ready to leave and I'm so relieved because it takes a lot of work not to talk to somebody.

Instead, she leans forward in her chair and whispers to me like it's a secret question, "Venus, are you even a little bit sorry for what you did?"

When I don't answer, she gets this frozen look on her face and makes a strange little gasping sound. Then she stumbles from the room like she's drunk or blind.

Or like she can't wait to get away from me.

LEO WAKES UP in a bed that is not his bed. The bedspread is the wrong color of green. Where is his blue bedspread? He can't stop seeing last night. His mother is crying. She makes him get in a strange truck with the lady called Shirley. He knows Shirley, but this time she has pink plastic things all over her head.

Soon the woman called Shirley comes into the room where Leo is, only now she looks different. The plastic things are gone and her hair is curly and the wrong yellow.

"Good morning, Leo!" she says too loud. "Remember me? From when I came to your house and babysat you."

"I want my mom," Leo says.

"Remember? She had an emergency and asked me to watch you for a while."

Leo doesn't know the word *emergency.* He ignores the lady and her talking until she asks if he needs the bathroom. He does. After he is done, he washes his hands like he's been taught. The towel is the wrong color. Shirley is waiting for him when he comes out.

He goes back to the room with the bed. So does the curly lady.

Leo asks, "Where is Venus? Where is my mom?"

He might have what his mother calls "a big tantrum." He had a big tantrum last night.

"I'm sorry, Leo," the lady says. "You will see your mom soon. She's going to stay here for a while, too. She'll sleep right out there in the living room on the couch. She's not here now, but she will be. And, look, she gave me some of your favorite things. See?" She points to the floor by the bed. Leo sees some of his toys. "Your mom even brought your blanket," she adds, holding out his purple blanket. He needs it to ride in a car or when he wants to be in his closet.

He takes the blanket, sits on the bed, and rocks while the lady keeps talking. He blocks out her voice. He puts his head between his knees because he hears the scary sounds from last night. The fire trucks hurt his ears. So many people were yelling and there were red feelings everywhere.

2

My cell has white cement walls, a plain metal cot, and a small wooden cupboard for clothes. Obviously, someone—a cop, or Inez?—has raided my dresser at home and picked out a small wardrobe for me. Seeing a bra and undies in the mix makes me angry. The thought of someone pawing through my drawers.

When I look for my shoes, I can only find a pair of ugly white sneakers with Velcro, like my little brother, Leo, wears, since he can't tie his shoes. They're the right size, so I put them on.

We're also given a notepad and a few pencils without erasers. I don't know why. Do they think I might want to write home like I'm away at summer camp?

It turns out they let you leave your cell during the day and hang out in what they call the common area, where there are couches, tables, and a TV. I plan to just stay in my room, though. I already know I don't want to make any friends in here.

But instead of sitting in my room all day, all of a sudden it's like I'm this important person with lots of meetings to attend. Everyone wants to talk to me—including a geezer guy with enormous nostrils who is my lawyer, a woman doctor named Barbara, and a young-looking caseworker who asks me to call him Officer Andy.

They all act the same. Just like the police, they start out really friendly, asking about my boring life as if I'm the most fascinating person on earth. But when they start to ask about that night, I throw a white sheet over my brain so I can't see a thing. I'm like a child wearing a ghost costume with no holes cut out for eyes. "I can't remember," I tell them. And it's true.

After that, they stop being so nice.

On the morning of day three, I'm taken down a hall to a small courtroom where my lawyer, Mr. Dutton, makes me plead not guilty, even though I don't deny what they say I did. When the judge announces the charges, I have to stifle a nervous laugh. My lawyer glares at me, nostrils flaring.

But how can I help it if none of this seems real? A few days ago, I was hanging out by my school locker, gossiping about boys with my girlfriends. My biggest worry was how to talk Inez into buying me a new pair of Jordache jeans. Now I'm locked up with junior criminals, I've been labeled a violent offender, and my biggest worry is getting beat up.

No wonder the only time I don't feel like I'm dreaming is when I'm asleep.

And yet at night, when I do finally fall asleep, I get jolted awake by nightmares that leave my nightie and sheets soaked through with sweat. The bed's thin mattress has a plastic cover, probably in case I pee the bed, which of course I would never. But this is like *my entire body* is wetting itself.

After the nightmares, I visit the community bathroom down the hall and use cold water to splash my face and try to dry my body with paper towels. In the mirror my eyes look buggy and wild. I look like a deranged person. Like someone who could do what I did.

Back in my room, I change into regular clothes. I strip the wet sheets and try to sleep on just the plastic. While I lie there shivering, I remember how the planet Venus rotates backward as it orbits the sun, while Earth and most of the other planets rotate forward, in the direction they're going. That's how I feel, like all of a sudden my life is turning in the opposite direction of where I want to go.

HERE'S WHAT I keep thinking. None of this would have happened if my father hadn't died when I was five. It was a freak factory accident, they said, where his belt buckle got caught on a piece of machinery. So if Joseph Black had only worn a different belt to work that day, he'd still be alive. And then Inez would never have taken a job tending bar at the Tyee Lanes. And she would never have met Raymond Miller the night he rolled six strikes in a row and strolled into the bar to celebrate.

In the coming years, Raymond loved to recount how he met Inez—leaving out the fact that my dad's body was barely in the ground. He'd linger on the bowling part of the story, and then he'd pat the cigarettes in his shirt pocket and joke that it was his "Lucky Strikes" that led him to Inez.

Now it's weird to think how it would have been better for everyone if only Raymond had been a little less lucky that night.

The morning after the strikes, Raymond showed up at our crummy place in the projects with flowers for Inez and Pop-Tarts for me. Being only five and having only seen Pop-Tarts on TV—to save money, Inez usually fed me gross hot cereal with powdered milk—I thought Pop-Tarts were amazing, like getting to eat candy for breakfast.

Over the next few weeks, Raymond kept it up, trying to buy us with small gifts. Things like a gold locket for Inez and a Skipper— Barbie's little sister—for me. I can't remember all the other presents, but I'm pretty sure it was the four-holed toaster—*four pieces of bread at a time!*—that sealed the deal for both of us. They got married six weeks later.

That's the problem with being just a kid. You let the littlest things impress you. You have no way of knowing that if this man marries your mother, the gifts will dry up, the Pop-Tarts will stop, the Rainier beer will kick in, and you'll never feel at home in your own home again.

I still don't know Inez's excuse.

Just as soon as I was old enough, I came to hate Raymond with my whole heart, though I couldn't have explained why. At seven, I started biting and clawing and kicking if he tried to spank me. At eight, I made a rule that he couldn't hug me. I think I was nine when I began arranging the cereal boxes on the kitchen table to block my view of him sitting there smoking in the mornings while I ate my Lucky Charms.

After I started middle school, I began mocking him from across the dinner table. I'd copy the way his teeth clicked when he chewed. Or I would imitate his habit of jiggling his pinky finger in his left ear. That would set him off. But how could I help it if my ear just so happened to itch right after his?

Nine times out of ten, Inez took Raymond's side.

At least they never made me call Raymond "Dad." But, then, Inez never taught me to call her "Mom" or "Mommy," either. She swore it was a women's lib–type thing to do at the time— "preserving one's identity," as she put it. Later, she changed her mind and tried to change mine. But it was too late.

Now you couldn't pay me a million dollars to call her "Mom."

3

On the fourth day, I develop a new theory for how I ended up here. What if I never had a choice?

When I was in third grade, our teacher showed us a large wooden frame with fabric stapled over the top. She set it on a table and told us to roll marbles from one end to the other. Easy-peasy, of course. Then she put a heavy stone in the center and asked us to roll the marbles straight again. This time—*duh, Ralph*—they rolled toward the rock.

She was trying to show us how the pull of gravity inside a black hole is so powerful it sucks everything into it and nothing can escape, not even light. I'd been reading astronomy books since I was six, so this was old news to me. But I hadn't yet learned that smart kids shouldn't be show-offs, so I made sure everyone knew this.

Now the concept of black holes sparks a new idea. Up to now, as my life whirled by, I thought I could at least decide where I wanted to go, could choose my next step. But what if all along I was like that second marble and my destiny was like a black hole, sucking me toward recent events, and I was helpless to resist?

It seems like that should make me almost innocent.

Later that morning, when I try to explain this to Officer Andy, he totally doesn't get it. "You don't deny you're guilty, Venus," he says. "So what do you mean you might be innocent?"

"I mean, what if it was just my destiny and there's nothing I could have done to change it?"

"Well," he says. He removes his wire-frame glasses and rubs his eyes like I'm making him tired, when all I'm doing is sitting here. "Maybe that's true in some way," he offers. "I guess we all have a destiny. But it doesn't change the law. And the law says you have to take responsibility."

"Yeah," I agree, annoyed. "I get all that. But the point is, if it is a person's *destiny* to do something they normally would never do, why should they be punished the same as a bad person?"

"Because that's the law," he says.

I sigh heavily and gaze out Officer Andy's small office window at the big yard and the tall cyclone fence in the distance. It doesn't seem fair that my caseworker gets to leave here at the end of the day and I can't, when you can tell just looking at the two of us sitting here that he's not a better person than me.

What I want to tell him but don't is that I really, really want to go home. Most kids who go to Denney get out in a few weeks. Even days. I'm starting to think it will be longer for me.

The weird thing is, I kind of miss my mom. Not my mom now, since what happened is her fault. But I miss having a mom I don't *hate*. It feels like not having one at all.

Of course, I miss my friends, too. I wonder how they're going to treat me when I go back to school.

Thinking of my friends, I decide this is a good time to ask Officer Andy a question that's been burning in my mind. I try to sound casual. "So, hey," I say. "I was just wondering . . . do you think I can see a copy of the local paper? The one that came out right after . . . ?"

I know my story is all over the news, because I've overheard girls talking. And I'm worried about what photo they used. I hope they didn't use my seventh-grade school picture, which is super dorky. Jackie has some way better ones of me on her corkboard at home.

"I'm sorry, Venus," he says. "That's against the rules."

"Don't I have a right to read what people are saying about me?"

"That's just the way it works. Maybe your mother could show the paper to you."

I scowl, because he knows how I feel about her. "Can you at least please tell me what the paper *looked* like?"

"In case you're wondering, there was no picture of you," he says, and I'm embarrassed he guessed what I was worried about. "If I remember correctly," he says, "the *Herald* used a picture of your house with police cars out front. I don't know what the Seattle papers did."

"Oh," I say, thinking about how weird this is and yet strangely appropriate, too—since none of this would have happened if Raymond hadn't moved us to that exact house on Rockefeller.

By now, I realize, the police are probably talking to all my friends, and my teachers, too. They're probably asking questions about my relationship with Raymond or if I ever said I wanted to hurt him. I wonder if Jackie will tell them how I couldn't stand Raymond and if she'll act like she's not surprised by what I did.

None of my friends could ever understand why I hated my stepdad so much. They all thought Raymond was sweet just because he was always inviting them to sleep over or offering to drive us places, like to Davies Beach or to the roller rink or to the movies. Sometimes he'd offer to pay for everybody: "Shhh. Now, don't go telling Inez," he'd say.

Once, when I tried to explain to Jackie how Raymond gave me the creeps, Jackie defended him. "Okay, but what about that time after we were shooting cans in the woods and he stopped at Thirty-one Flavors *without us even asking*?"

Now I want to call up Jackie and yell, "See? You were wrong. I was right about Raymond all along!"

But I know I'll never make that call, because if my friends ever learn the truth about Raymond, they'll wish they'd never met me.

And besides, if I say, "I was right all along," it makes it sound like I knew all along when I really had no idea.

That's another thing that got me here. Nothing is as it appears. It's like that with space. Objects that look round might not be, and stars that look close to each other might be billions of miles apart. And it's the same with people. Only instead of standing too far away to see the truth, you're probably standing too close.

4

That Friday afternoon, I lie on my metal bed and look at the ceiling, thinking of Leo. If he were here, he'd already know exactly how many tiles there are. So I count them, and there are twenty-two, not including partials. Then I notice that each tile has small marks on it, and if you used your imagination, you could think of them as stars. It made me want to get a ladder and a Magic Marker so I could map out some constellations.

Leo would love that, which reminds me of the night our toaster broke. I remember it so clearly because it was one of those bad things that turned into a good thing—in this case, maybe a miracle.

I was probably ten or eleven and Leo was about four or five. At that age, I loved to badger Inez with questions about the universe and tease her when she got them wrong.

On this particular evening, I asked her, "On a clear night, how many stars can you see with the naked eye?"

She was making one of her grossest dinners, creamed tuna on toast. I was in charge of making the toast, which was the only part of this meal I was planning to eat, unless the canned fruit for the night was peaches, not fruit medley, which I think should be outlawed.

"I have no idea," Inez said, opening a can of tuna.

She dumped the tuna into the saucepan and started cranking the can opener on the soup. "I don't care, Venus. I really don't."

"You don't care?" I said accusingly. "You don't care about what your own daughter is learning in school?"

"You're not learning this in school," she said. "You're just reading your books about space."

"So what? How could a mother not be interested in her daughter's favorite subject?"

"Okay, Venus," she finally said, like it was super hard just to talk to me. "Do you mean with the naked eye? And where am I standing? It depends on what part of space I'm looking at."

She was right. The answer I had read in a book was three thousand, but that probably meant the number of stars that are visible in the entire, viewable sky.

"Okay. So yeah," I told her. "With the naked eye and if you could see them all at once."

"Three thousand," she said, turning to look at me with a sly smile, still stirring the junk in the pan behind her.

She was right again. But there's no way she could've known that unless she read it in one of my books, which made me mad. "You're wrong," I told her. "It's not really three thousand, since lots of those stars you think you see already died a long time ago, so all you're looking at is leftover light."

"For God's sake," she said, turning back to the stove. Then she told me to set the table.

I was reaching for the plates when I smelled smoke. One of the pieces of toast was stuck in its slot and burning. I tried to force the lever up, but it wouldn't budge—*clearly, four holes doesn't mean quality.* When the fire alarm started going off, Inez yelled at me to unplug the toaster, while she dragged a kitchen chair out to the hall to stand on so she could reset the alarm. Leo had been sitting at the kitchen table spinning the wheels of a toy car and staring into their turning. But now he was wailing at the top of his lungs like he always did when he heard any kind of loud noise.

I took Leo downstairs to my room to calm him down. I had discovered one of his favorite things was to watch the blue lava lamp I got at Spencer's at the mall. I plopped down on my bed, expecting Leo to go straight to the lamp. But, instead, he lay down next to me—not touching, of course, because Leo hates that. He stared up at the mobile of the solar system hanging from my light fixture. I'd recently bought it when our class took a field trip to the Science Center in Seattle. I also bought dozens of glowing stars, which I stuck to the ceiling.

I didn't realize Leo hadn't seen them yet, so I began to point at each planet and name it for him. "Mercury, Venus, Earth, Mars . . ." Then I said, "Let's count the stars, Leo, starting in the corner." I tried to include him, even though I knew he wouldn't join me. At this point, he hardly talked. Just single words, like *no!*, and our names, and *doughn* for *don't.*

While I counted aloud, Leo continued to calm down. After a while, he was at that stage of a tantrum where the worst is over but your body still has the hiccups. I love that feeling, and it made me wish I could have a big tantrum, too, even though I couldn't decide what I would cry about.

I had just begun counting the stars from zero again, and when I got to *five,* Leo said *five,* too, and then kept counting with me. I was never so shocked in my life. If I hadn't been lying down I might have fainted.

I wanted to race upstairs to tell Inez that Leo could count out loud, but I was scared to interrupt him in case he never did it again. So, instead, I lay there listening to his small, mechanical voice—*sex . . . leven . . . fiffteam . . . wendynime*—as he counted with me across the starry ceiling.

So this is what Leo would sound like if he said more than a word at a time.

When we got to the end of the stars, Leo pointed at the mobile and made his grunting sound that means he wants something. I realized he wanted me to do it all again, so I started to name the planets again, and on the second round, he started to name the planets after me, pausing when we got to Venus to say, "Venus is red!"

He was right. For some reason, Venus was red, even though Mars is supposed to be the red planet. But this was another shock, that Leo knew his colors. It was like all of a sudden something had clicked in his brain. For a long time I'd been trying to teach him colors, using the original box of eight Crayola crayons. After that night, he named them all, like it was easy. But when Inez got him a box of twenty-four Crayola crayons for Christmas later that year, he got so upset. He would only use the original eight primary colors, and every other color he called "wrong."

Leo is funny like that. He cracks me up. And thinking about all this now makes me miss him so much. At home, sometimes I act like he's a big hassle. But now I feel so guilty, because he must be having so many tantrums without me there to do my part in his routines. I wish I could ask Inez to bring him to see me, but she hasn't come back since the first day when I refused to talk. Plus, Leo would have a fit, because he doesn't like to go new places. Only familiar places like McDonald's.

Anyway, after the night the toaster broke, we all realized Leo was smarter than we'd thought. So I started to teach him things like ABCs. Which wasn't that easy, because he only wanted to do it when *he* wanted to. You had to wait for him or he would totally ignore you. And you had to turn everything into a rhyme or chant.

As a rule, I never liked it when any of my family came down to my basement bedroom. At the time, I liked the feeling of being away from everyone else. And though the room had ugly knotty-pine paneling, the attached bath and shower more than made up for that. After Leo fell in love with my mobile and my stars, I didn't mind him coming down at all.

Pretty soon, he didn't even need my help. I could just lie there in the blue light of my lava lamp while Leo counted the stars and chanted the planets. Now and then I'd drift off to sleep, leaving Leo and his naked eyes alone to roam the universe.

LEO PLAYS IN the sandbox. He uses two fingers of one hand to slice through the sand, and then he makes two slices across with the other hand. Each time, the sand glitters and shifts the way Leo likes.

His mother and the curly lady come outside, and he can feel them watching him. He is getting used to the lady with curly hair called Shirley. But he still cries for Venus and his mom. His mom comes to see him and sometimes she stays for a while. But then she leaves again and she won't take him home.

This time, she sits by Leo in the sandbox and says, "Your father is gone now, Leo. I'm so sorry."

"Where?"

"I'm afraid your father is dead, Leo. You won't see him anymore."

Leo doesn't understand *dead*. "What color is dead?"

"Oh, Leo," she says. "Dead means you never wake up again. So maybe it is black. It means he went away and won't come back. But he is in a good place."

Leo grunts. "I want Venus. Where is Venus?"

"She had to go away for a while. You won't see her very soon, but she is not dead."

"She's not black?"

"No, Leo. Venus isn't black."

"Do you like the sandbox, Leo?" She leans closer to him. Her smell is familiar.

"Can I go home?"

"Oh, Leo," she says softly, "I'm sorry, you can't. Just a little longer."

"I want curlers," he says. When his mom's voice is soft this way, she says yes almost every time.

The curly lady laughs and his mother starts talking again. He blocks out their voices. He plays with the sand. When he hears his mom say, "Goodbye, Leo," he almost yells, "Stay!" But his attention is caught by a rock that sparkles like stars.

5

That evening, I decide I might need a friend on my side, because a couple of large Indian girls from Marysville keep looking at me like they want to beat me up. Not for any good reason, but just because they can tell I'm not really like them. Like maybe they think I'm stuck up.

So at dinner I scan the cafeteria for a girl named Truly. When I spot her sitting alone at a table, I walk in her direction, trying my best to look bored. I pick her because she seems harmless and she reminds me a little of Leo. She's super skinny and has fuzzy, short blond hair that shows through to her scalp.

With Leo, unless you keep his blond hair super short, he tugs and pulls on it until his scalp bleeds and gets bald patches. That means every few months we have to give him a buzz cut. The worst part is when Raymond sits him down near the kitchen counter, where the cord will reach. Leo knows exactly what's coming and he screams the whole time like you're killing him.

It's one of my least favorite things about being Leo's big sister. But you have to do your part. So while Raymond holds him tight enough to leave bruises, I use the clippers, trying hard not to nick his pale little head. Inez is the one who insists we go through this. But then she always refuses to help and goes to another room.

That's just like Inez, to want to look the other way.

Now I plop down across from Truly, hoping she'll notice and start talking to me. But she doesn't. She acts like I'm not there, like it's cool to ignore people. She eats her spaghetti super slow, sucking each noodle and then patting her tiny pink lips like she doesn't have a care in the world or she's eating in a fancy restaurant.

I'm tempted to get mad, but I decide to go first instead. In my best casual we're-all-in-jail-together voice, I ask her what "got her in here," which is how I've heard the other girls strike up conversations.

Truly takes another bite of spaghetti and slowly sucks another noodle and I think she's going to ignore me, until she pauses and says in this sweet but husky voice, "Stealing stuff. Stuff I needed."

"Oh. Cool," I answer, not at all sure if it's supposed to be. I have never understood how people can shoplift—because it would feel so scary, and if you got caught, how embarrassing! I go red just thinking about it.

"I already know why you're here," Truly says, finally turning her gold-brown eyes on me. "But, then, everyone does."

I nod, uncertain how to answer. And then it dawns on me that maybe the other girls are more scared of me than I am of them.

6

I've already had one lawyer, Mr. Dutton with the nostrils. Now they have switched it to be a woman lawyer. I bet they changed lawyers because they think I'm more likely to open up to a female. But they're wrong. I'm ready to throw my white sheet over my mind the second she goes near that night.

On the bright side, the first time I meet with Betty, I can tell I'm going to like her. She's heavy and round, wears lots of makeup, and reminds me of a sassy waitress in a southern diner. She pumps my hand with her plump one, and then she asks me to sit down and make myself comfortable.

She tells me to call her Betty. She explains that she's court-appointed, which means I get her for free. I know it's because Inez doesn't have money. And even if she did, I doubt she'd spend it on me now.

At least Betty's office is more impressive than my caseworker's. Her desk is wood instead of metal, the window is way bigger, and there's a big painting of lily pads on one wall. Something about the room reminds me of the time Inez took me to see "a shrink," as Raymond called him, because she said I had anger problems and lacked impulse control.

It's true that I was angry a lot, and it was also true—at least at home—that I had a temper, especially when it came to Raymond. Sometimes, I picked fights with him for no good reason. It was almost like I wanted him to hurt me so I could have some way to explain to myself why I hated him so much.

The shrink was an old guy with a smoker's cough, and I remember being as rude to him as I could. When he lit up, I asked, "How can a doctor who is so dumb that he smokes cigarettes expect to help anybody?" He frowned and snubbed out his cigarette. I don't know what he told Inez, but she never brought me back to see him—or any other shrink—again.

Maybe she shouldn't have given up so easy.

At first, Betty does like the others and asks me easy questions that have nothing to do with what happened. But I get the feeling she cares, like she's not just pretending to be interested so we can get to the real questions. Questions about Raymond. About *why*.

When she asks what I dream of doing with my life, I surprise myself by telling her the truth. I usually don't tell people my dream, because I'm afraid they'll think it's dumb, or that it's just because of my name, which has nothing to do with it. "I want to be the first American woman in space," I tell her, blushing a little. "But now it's probably not going to happen."

"Because of what you did?"

"No, because of that woman Sally Ride," I tell her. "She's going to make it into space any minute. Do you even think that's her real name? It sounds like a name she made up to go with her job. Like a stage name."

Betty reassures me that even if I am the second or third American woman in space, that would still be quite an accomplishment. Maybe I could be the first woman to land on the moon or on Mars or something. I'm relieved she doesn't seem to think what happened will hurt my chances.

I go on to tell her about my friends, especially Jackie and Vanessa, but I don't want to focus on them too much. "Jackie has the best mom," I say, "because she is the opposite of Inez. Mrs. Newton actually packs Jackie's lunches, and she makes dinners that aren't Hamburger Helper and gross stuff like that."

Betty laughs.

When she finally asks about Raymond, she calls him "Ray." Clearly, she's been talking to Inez. From the start, Inez insisted that everyone call Raymond "Ray," because she thought "Raymond" sounded dumb. I call him "Raymond" for the same reason.

"So, Venus," she says. I brace myself, ready with my sheet. "Let's talk about Ray. Tell me how this thing with your stepfather began."

"What *thing*?" I ask, wishing I sounded less snotty.

"Whatever thing it was that made you want to hurt your stepfather."

"There wasn't a thing."

Betty squints at me. Her black eyelashes have so much mascara they look fake. I don't even wear mascara, but I really miss having lip gloss and my Baby Soft perfume.

"I need you to tell me how you felt about your stepfather."

"That's pretty easy. I hated him."

"Okay," says Betty, nodding. "Why did you hate him?"

It was a simple question, but I didn't know where to start. I hated the way he chewed. The way he smelled like motor oil. The way he constantly cracked his stubby fingers. The way he actually combed the thick blond hair on his forearms. I hated the way he watched me load the dishwasher. I hated the way it felt when he touched my back or got sloppy drunk and called me Veenie. I hated when he was mean to me, but I hated even more when he tried to be nice. Like the time he tried to offer me one of his Rainier beers behind Inez's back. He must have known I hated him, but it was like he was always trying to create secrets between us. But most of all, I hated the way he treated Leo.

I go with this last one. "I hated the way he treated Leo."

"How did he treat Leo? Did he hurt him physically?"

"Yeah," I say. "Raymond would shake him when he was already crying. Or he'd box his ears with his fists. Stuff like that. He got mad because Leo refused to act like a regular kid. When I tried to interfere or defend Leo, then Raymond and I would end up in a brawl. Once, he threw me down the stairs."

"Oh my," says Betty. She's been writing things down. "Where was Inez when all this went on?"

"He usually did it when she was at work. He was alone with us a lot because he only worked part-time at an auto shop in town, and the rest of the time he worked on cars at home in the garage."

"What did your mother do when you told her about Ray hurting you or Leo?"

"Sometimes she'd believe me and they'd get in a fight. Other times, she'd think I was making it up or exaggerating. She liked to say that I egged Raymond on. And maybe I did."

"Oh, Venus," Betty says, like my name is a sad thing. She places a hand on her heart, which makes me think of the word *bosom,* which I always love when I come across it in old-fashioned novels. She is quiet for a moment, jotting down more notes. "What kind of relationship did your mother have with your stepfather?"

"They fought a lot. I don't think she really even loved him. I was always rooting for her to kick him out, but she never would. I think she just didn't want to be poor again and go back to the projects."

Betty nods. She's quiet for a moment, and I worry what she'll ask next. "I'm really sorry," she finally says, "but I have to ask. Did Raymond abuse you, Venus?"

I squirm at the question. Sigh heavily. "If what you mean by *abuse* is did he sometimes hurt me, well, yes. Like I already told you."

"Okay, Venus. That's what we call physical abuse. But there's another kind of abuse when a grown-up touches a child in their private parts or makes a child touch theirs. That's called sexual abuse. Did Raymond do this to you?"

"No! Oh my God! Do you realize how gross that is? I would never let him touch me like that!" I realize I'm practically yelling.

Betty holds up a hand. "I'm sorry. But I had to ask. I need to understand what happened that day to make you so angry."

"Why do I have to say it?"

"It's okay to cry, honey," she says in this soft, caring voice.

"No, it's not!" I squeeze my stupid eyes shut, but a few tears spit out anyway, like a sprinkler when you first turn it on.

"Why isn't it okay to cry?"

"Because if I cry, then I might think about it! And I'm not going to talk about it. It's way too embarrassing!" I feel that sheet slipping, and my throat starts to close. And then I'm leaning over and hiding my face in my hands. I can hear Betty rolling her chair out from behind the desk. "It's okay, sweetie," she says, patting my back. "That's a good girl. Just let it all out. That's a good girl."

Let it all out makes me realize I'm sobbing. I can feel my spine shaking under Betty's hand while she pats my back with gentle thumps. It's the same thing I sometimes do to help Leo calm down when he can't on his own. It's the only kind of touching he allows, and I'm the only one, and you have to count the pats out loud or it doesn't work.

But I don't really care about the pats. I just want Betty to keep calling me a good girl.

LEO IS PLAYING with a plastic shovel in the sandbox when he hears a voice. "Leo!" The voice that is trying to come in is a man's voice but not his dad's. Leo hates it when voices try to poke into where he is.

"Leo!" The voice is louder. Brown shoes come into view, and then the man is touching his arm. Leo tries to yell but the man sticks something over his mouth. Scared feelings get stuck in Leo's throat. He is being lifted out of the sandbox, kicking his feet.

The man puts him in the backseat of a car he doesn't know. It is different from the truck he didn't know with the curly lady. He is going to have a tantrum, even though Venus says don't.

Leo needs to blow his nose. *No crying, Leo!* Mother says. *Get a tissue, Leo!*

His mother isn't here. There is no tissue. He curls up on the floor of the car to rock, but there's not enough room. He looks for his purple blanket. He can't ride in a car without it. Where is his blanket?

Leo hears the car start. He can't cover his ears like he always does, because his hands are stuck together in front of him. He tries to yell but nothing comes out. He sees white stitches on the car's brown seat. Some part of his brain begins to count them. He starts to calm down.

At some point, the car stops. The man takes the covering off his mouth. It hurts and Leo cries out. The man's hair is the wrong orange. The man tells Leo, "Stay quiet." When Leo sees scissors, he screams with fear and tries to hide on the other side of the car. But the man pulls on him and then he cuts the tape between Leo's wrists. Now Leo can move his hands again. Then the man gives him a blue race car. He straps him in the seatbelt and says in a mean voice, "Stay." They start driving again and Leo cries. After a while, he stops. He spins the wheels on the car and stares into the turning.

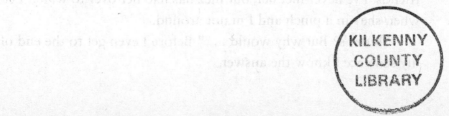

7

On Sunday morning, Inez shows up—and they let her in my room, and it's not visiting hours. I notice something is wrong—more wrong than everything that's already wrong. For one thing, she's not wearing any makeup. Not even lipstick, which is normally the first thing she puts on when she gets in the car. For another thing, she looks wild-eyed, like she just came out of seeing *Jaws*.

"Leo's gone missing," she announces.

"What do you mean, *missing*?"

At first I'm not worried at all, because Leo disappears now and then, but he's always either behind the couch, near the heat vent, or on the floor of his closet, curled up with his purple blanket. He doesn't leave the house except maybe to walk around the block with me, or sometimes to visit McDonald's.

"He's gone!" Inez exclaims angrily.

"Did you check the usual places?" I ask. "The couch—"

"He hasn't been at home, Venus," she interrupts. "Leo and I have been staying at Shirley's. He's been missing since yesterday."

Shirley works with Inez at J. C. Penney, and I guess they're friends. I've never met her, but Inez has had her over to watch Leo when she's in a pinch and I'm not around.

"Shirley's? But why would . . ." Before I even get to the end of my sentence I know the answer.

"Why? Well, let's see," Inez says sarcastically. "Could it be because his home has been turned into a crime scene?"

"But it's been a week! Surely by now . . ."

She looks at me with a mixture of panic and guilt. "Things have been crazy every day—police questioning me, reporters hounding me. And then there's trying to get you out of jail!" She is pacing. "It was just better for us to be at Shirley's, and it seemed like Leo was starting to adjust, so I thought he could stay a little longer. . . ."

Her voice trails off. "He was in the backyard," she says finally. "Yesterday morning. He was playing in a sandbox."

I'm surprised she's actually explaining and defending herself to me this way, like I matter. But then I realize she isn't really talking to me. She's blabbering on because she's so scared and she knows it's her fault.

Pretty soon her fear triggers my own and I realize this is real. "Oh my God!" I yell. "This is so stupid! It's the stupidest thing I ever heard. You can't just put a kid like Leo in a house with people he barely knows!"

"I didn't have a choice," she says, glaring at me.

"Well, then, what are you doing *here*? If Leo is out there lost, you need to go find him. The police need to look for him!" I want to push her out the door.

"Don't you think we're looking, Venus? Everywhere!" She spreads her arms dramatically. "The cops are looking but they say he's not officially a missing person until he's been gone seventy-two hours. Can you believe that? He's seven years old! We've already checked Jimmy's and all the neighbors' and everyone we know."

Jimmy is a weird nineteen-year-old kid who lives nearby and keeps tons of hamsters. Sometimes he watches Leo if Raymond is at the shop and Inez has to leave for work before I get home from school. I think he smokes pot, but Inez doesn't know that.

"At least Leo knows his address," I tell her. "Since *I* taught him that." It took me a long time to teach Leo to say our street address if you asked him. Inez has always left it to me to teach Leo stuff, acted like she's too busy, when really she just doesn't have the patience for it.

"So what about his phone number?" Inez asks hopefully. "Did you teach him that?"

I haven't. Leo doesn't exactly carry on conversations, and so I never pictured him using a phone or needing to call home. It just didn't occur to me.

"Aren't *you* his mother?" I shoot back. "Why didn't *you* teach him his phone number?"

Inez covers her face with her hands, and her shoulders start to shudder. But I am too scared to cry. I keep trying to picture Leo out there, lost, wandering around looking for us. "Someone must have seen him by now," I announce firmly. "It's not like he's going to blend in. A little kid like Leo . . ."

I feel a stinging in my eyes, and my left cheek starts twitching.

"Oh, Venus," Inez says in a softer tone. She dares to reach out as if to touch me, and I slap her hand away.

"No!" I yell. "Don't you touch me! This is all your fault!"

She gives me a wounded look. "No, Venus. If something has happened to Leo, it's because of what *you* did."

After she's gone, I sit on my bed, shivering. I wrap my arms around myself as hard as I can, like I'm freezing. I shut my eyes and talk to Leo, wherever he is. *Go home,* I tell him. *Go home, Leo. Go home!*

Then I remember what happened there, and I realize he might be too scared to come home.

I can't sleep at all that night, terrified of what I will dream if I do. Every time I start to drift off, I hear Leo crying out for me. And then I hear Inez saying, over and over: *It's because of what* you *did. . . .*

8

I wake up Monday in a panic about Leo, adrenaline shooting through my body. I go down to use the communal shower, hoping I didn't sleep too late. I always make sure I'm the first one there, so I'm alone. I'm modest that way. My friends used to make fun of the way I dressed for gym class, maneuvering inside my clothes so no one could see anything.

This morning, I have so much excess energy that I decide to go to the trouble to wash my hair, even though it always takes quite a while, because it is so thick and long. Then I have to untangle it and use a hair pick to comb it out, which is always embarrassing if people see me.

By lunch, when I still haven't heard any more about Leo, I break down and get permission to call Inez. I can't believe it when the phone rings and rings. How many times have I told her we need a stupid answering machine? What if I was someone calling about Leo?

I want to scream at the top of my lungs. What if a car hits him? He doesn't even know how to look both ways. What if he's hiding under someone's porch, afraid to come out? What if he only needs to hear my voice calling for him around the neighborhood?

I have to get out and help look for him. I know if I do, he'll come home. I beg the guards, my caseworker, and anyone who will listen. "You have to let me out. Leo will come to me! He knows my voice! He's probably just scared and hiding under a porch and he'll hear me and come out."

I try to imagine some stranger trying to help Leo—and how Leo would scream if they touched him. I think of the time I was at the kitchen table, working on a school project that involved Popsicle sticks, when Leo joined me. He watched for a few minutes, and then he picked up two sticks and used the glue to make a cross. He must have made ten of them. I was so surprised and proud of him. But when it was time to clean up, every time I tried to pick up one of his crosses, he started to wail like it hurt him.

It took me a while to realize that to his mind they weren't crosses; they were *people*. And in his mind, they were just like him and so they couldn't bear to be touched. I had to wait to clear the table until he was in another room, and for some reason that made me want to cry. The memory stings now, reminds me how sensitive Leo is.

That afternoon, the police come to talk to me. At first I think it's good news. But, no, they're actually there to grill me. They even have the gall to suggest I was somehow involved. They say maybe I was so angry at Inez that I asked friends to steal Leo. . . .

"But I didn't know where he was staying!" I screech. "And I can't talk to my friends because their parents won't let them, which is probably because of you guys."

It's true that when I was finally allowed to call Jackie, Mrs. Newton sounded cold and weird on the phone. She acted like I was some stranger and told me Jackie wasn't home. But I know she was—because I know her exact schedule, and I could hear *The Brady Bunch* in the background, which she watches after school.

WITH LEO MISSING for more than two days, the hours feel like torture. It feels like time is going so slow that I might as well be living on the planet Venus, where it takes 243 Earth days for a single day to pass. That means you get up in the morning with the sun and it won't set again for thousands of hours.

It's weird to think how for regular people, time is just time. But if you're locked up, time is your enemy. Maybe that's why they call it "doing time." They use time's passing—and seemingly *not* passing—to punish you. You wouldn't think it could hurt so much, but it does. And with Leo out there lost, it's excruciating.

Leo would do great at being locked up, because he doesn't really care about time. Sure, he knows that when the hands on his yellow plastic watch point to a certain number, he gets to eat lunch or watch *Gilligan's Island* or whatever. But when Inez gives him a time-out in his room, he doesn't care for how long, he just starts stacking blocks or spinning the wheels of a toy car.

And then there's the loneliness. Leo doesn't mind being alone for long stretches. And if he's upset, he doesn't need or want someone to hug him. If I'm not around to pat his back and count, he simply curls up on his bed and rocks himself until he feels better.

At Denney that night, when I can't sleep and I feel like screaming, I turn on my side, wrap my arms around my knees, and decide to give Leo's rocking thing a try. At first I'm embarrassed even in front of myself. But after a while it starts to feel good, like someone is actually comforting me, even if it's just me.

It gives me hope that someday I really can become more like Leo—unafraid of time, unchanged by my punishment.

9

When I meet with Betty Tuesday morning, I can tell she's worried for me or angry or something. I start out begging her to get me out so I can look for Leo. But her voice takes on a briskness that shuts me down. "I'm really sorry about Leo," she tells me. "But we have to talk about your case. I haven't wanted to push you, Venus. But it's been more than a week now . . ." She pauses to take a breath, like she doesn't like what she has to say. "And, unfortunately, the prosecutor is being pressured to move your case to adult court."

"What do you mean?"

"It means you would be tried as an adult in front of a regular jury. Which is ridiculous. I don't think it will happen. But if it does, you could get sentenced to a lot more time. At eighteen, you'd be transferred from Echo Glen to an adult facility to serve out the rest of your sentence."

I'm confused. "What is Echo Glen?"

"I'm sorry. It's a juvenile facility in Issaquah, where most Snohomish County teens end up serving their time. It's kind of like a school, though. It's really not a terrible place. . . ."

Now she's scaring me. I'd been picturing staying here at Denney. I figured I'd get privileges for being good, so I could get out early.

"I don't want you to worry, Venus," she assures me, as if she's read my mind. "You're way, way too young to be tried as an adult. You're only thirteen!" She bangs her fist on her desk for emphasis, but it doesn't even make me jump like on TV.

"Plus, you're a good student," she continues. "You have no prior arrests, and you're unlikely to re-offend. And since Washington uses specific sentencing standards for juveniles, you're already guaranteed an appropriate sentence."

"So what is appropriate?" I ask. "I wouldn't want to be inappropriate." I know I'm joking to hide my fear.

"I can't say for sure, Venus," Betty admits. "Depending on your disposition—what you're convicted of—at worst, you could be incarcerated anywhere from three and a half years up to when you reach the age of twenty-one, which for you would be more than seven years. If you got convicted in adult court," she adds, "it would mean a longer sentence."

Longer? She must see the confusion and alarm on my face. I feel like my whole body is going numb with novocaine from the dentist.

"But I didn't even mean to do it!" I exclaim.

"It's going to be okay, Venus," she says in a hushed voice. "Given the evidence, I know enough about what happened to know that, at the very least, your case presents a good amount of mitigating circumstances that can help us."

"What does *mitigating* mean?" My brain is still frantically trying to make sense of how any of those numbers—years!—could apply to me. Did she just say I could go to juvenile prison until I'm twenty-one? I'm not even sure *where* Issaquah is, but it has to be pretty far away and a Podunk town, since I've barely heard of it. I can't bear being grounded for a month, so how would I ever survive being locked up for *so long?*

"*Mitigating* means we'll try to show that there are extenuating circumstances that should be considered," Betty explains. "The most important one is probably going to be whatever drove you to do this, Venus. For example, if your stepfather sexually abused you, that would be a serious mitigating circumstance."

"But he didn't sexually abuse me!" I exclaim.

By now I'm distraught and terrified. *Maybe I should just lie? Tell her what she and everyone want to hear.* But I can't bring myself to.

Before I leave Betty's office, she asks if I want to hurt myself.

I tell her no. "Not yet," I add. That's when she mentions that I was on suicide watch my first three days of detention. She explains to me that every fifteen minutes someone was looking in at me through that small glass window in my door.

The news totally freaks me out. "It's a really good thing I didn't know that was happening," I tell her. "It might have had the opposite effect. Did anyone think about that?"

Honestly, suicide hasn't crossed my mind since I got to Denney. And now I feel kind of bad, like I failed to meet expectations. I didn't realize I was supposed to feel so guilty about what happened that it should make me want to die.

This must be the reason for the cheap plastic sneakers with Velcro straps they make us wear—*duh*. They don't want us to hang ourselves with the shoelaces. Same with taking the erasers off the pencils, so we won't use the metal part to slit our wrists. I'm pretty sure no one would have thought of doing these things . . . but it's like they're determined to convince you that you want to kill yourself.

I hate to disappoint everybody, but I'm just not there yet. Maybe down the road if things get bad enough . . . but it's harder than people think to get in the mood to kill yourself.

I know, because I've tried. It was just last week, and here I am, alive.

10

After my latest session with Betty, I don't know who I'm more worried about—Leo or myself. I can't imagine going to a real prison. And I can't just sit here while my little brother is lost and needs me.

By dinner, my mind is made up. I sit by that girl named Truly again. I overheard her brag once that she'd escaped Denney twice. Something about hospitals trying to kill her.

Since I can tell she's not one for small talk, I dive right in. "My brother's gone missing. I might be the only one who can find him. Did you really break out of here before?"

"Yeah," she says casually. "So did your brother run away?"

"No," I tell her. "It's not like that. He's only seven, but it's more like he's three or so, because he has developmental problems. He's not retarded, but close." I want Truly to get the point fast. "It sounds like he is lost or he was taken away from the house where he was staying with a friend of my mom's. . . ."

"Shit, I'm really sorry," she said. "What's his name?"

"Leo. Like the constellation."

"I get it. Your mom's a space freak."

"Actually, she's dumb about space," I tell her, impatient and annoyed.

"This is just shit," says Truly, shoving her plate away. It takes me a second to realize she means the food, not what I'm saying.

"Yeah, it is," I agree. The Salisbury steak sucks, but in an irrational moment I'm tempted to ask Truly if I can have her green peas. Maybe because they remind me of the way Leo always carefully arranges them in a swirl on his plate. He also likes that they are the "right" green.

"I want to break out tonight," I tell Truly. I can't believe I just said that.

"Yeah?" she answers, like no big deal. "Tonight? I could do tonight. I'm pretty much ready to go again. There's lots of ways to get out of here."

And then she outlines an escape plan that makes me want to burst into tears. Truly will ask a girl named Belinda, who works in the kitchen, to jimmy the kitchen door so we can escape out a back entrance in there. We'll climb over the chain-link fence, she says. But since there's barbed wire at the top, we'll use the big bath mats from the girls' showers so we can get over it without cutting ourselves.

Bath mats? Her plan sounds stupid, scary, and dangerous. What if we can't get the mats and ourselves to the top? What if they shoot at us? How bad of a crime is it to try to escape, anyway?

I still haven't totally agreed for sure before a buzzer signals the end of dinner. "You better be ready," she says. "I'll meet you outside the kitchen at eight P.M."

I nod, trembling.

I know Truly can tell I'm scared to do this, because she leans into my ear and says in her husky voice, "You're the one who's looking at years behind bars. Plus, don't forget Leo."

Like I ever would. It's for him that I'm about to do the second-worst thing of my life.

. . .

I AM THERE early, a black rubber shower mat rolled up under one arm. Just around the corner, six girls are watching TV and another two are playing poker, using ripped-up pieces of paper as money.

When Truly shows up with her own bath mat, she hisses, "What's wrong? You look scared, but you should be smiling. We're about to be free. I'm mainly doing this for you, you know."

I shrug my shoulders and try to look relaxed. "Thank you. I really am grateful," I tell her. "I just hate doing stuff where you could get caught—"

"Are you serious? You're in the biggest trouble of anyone in this building! And you're afraid to skip out of juvie? Are you going to bag out on me?"

"No," I say defensively. I can hear the TV in the community room and the other girls talking. This plan seems so stupid, like we aren't being sneaky enough, like we're escaping in broad daylight, even though I know it's dark outside. In Denney, you never get a sense of day or night, because of the lack of windows and all the fluorescent lights.

Truly signals me and then opens the kitchen door, pointing out the latch where Belinda has taped a nickel so it wouldn't automatically lock when the cook left. As we enter the kitchen, I instinctively grip Truly's knobby elbow and she knocks my arm away. "Don't be a sissy!" she hisses.

As we quickly cross the big kitchen, I catch whiffs of tonight's dinner along with the scent of something sour, maybe the dishrags. After we pass the enormous sinks, we come to a huge walk-in pantry.

We drop our mats and hurriedly empty the cupboard of all the dried goods and cans. On the count of three we pull the shelf away, and sure enough, there's an old wooden set of doors back there, secured only by a metal latch. All we have to do is slide a lever and the door swings open.

Before I have time to be afraid, Truly tells me to grab my mat, and then we're both outside, running across the large yard behind Denney to the chain-link fence. It reaches up above our heads a good ten feet.

We rush to take off our Velcro shoes and our socks and begin to climb. But barefoot and lugging the rolled-up mat, scaling that fence proves even harder than I imagined. My toes and fingers scream in pain, and I have to keep switching the mat from one arm to the other, trying all the time not to drop it.

The steady drizzle doesn't help. Neither does the cold.

Truly is lighter than I am, and she reaches the top first. I hear her swearing as she struggles to drape her rubber mat over the strands of rusty barbed wire. Then I see her crawl over fast as a crab. And then she's inching her way down. In seconds, I hear a grunt as she lands in the grass on the other side, safe.

But I'm still going up. When I finally get near the top, I manage to fling the mat over, but it keeps sliding around. How am I going to get myself over?

"Get your feet way up close by your hands," Truly calls from below. I try to take her advice, positioning my feet nearer to my hands, but every time I get close, the mat threatens to slide away.

I get one foot over the top and then manage to heave myself up far enough so that I can straddle the mat. I hug it and the fence for dear life, relieved and euphoric—until I realize my hair is completely tangled in the barbed wire.

"My hair is caught!" I scream to Truly. "I'm stuck!"

I don't have a free hand to work on the mess. I battle with my hair, yanking my head and trying to twist free. But nothing works. I hear myself saying *fuck* over and over, conscious of the fact that I've actually never used this word aloud before. In private, Jackie and I said *shit*, but *fuck* was for the bad kids.

I shout for Truly to come up and help me from the other side. But no one answers. I look under my armpit and there she goes, running toward the lights of the boulevard.

My heart sinks, but I don't really blame her.

I notice I'm shaking in exhaustion and pain. And then I start sobbing like an idiot. But it's my next thought that fills me with horror: How long can a barefoot girl cling to a cyclone fence before her toes and fingers give out and she's scalped by the weight of her own body?

Then I remember that staff will find me missing at bed check. And I can already picture how it will all play out. How the guards will come running across the yard, yelling at me to come down, until they realize I can't. Then they'll have to call the fire department or something. And they'll probably cut off all my hair, which will feel like the worst punishment of all.

I imagine years from now a small chunk of my hair still stuck atop this fence, flying in the wind like a black flag. I wonder if the girls who see it will be inspired by my attempt or if they'll view it as proof that you can't escape your fate.

Soon the rain lets up, but I'm still shivering from the cold. Then I realize that if I crane my head to look under my arm, I can see a small patch of clear sky over by the Boys & Girls Club. I'm able to pick out Venus pretty quick, but it's the wrong time of year for Leo. Then a bright light flashes on in the yard, and I hear voices calling out to one another. *I am rescued! I am caught.*

Moments later, the fence starts to shake and a voice I recognize as a bony, mean older guard named Lucinda screams at me to come down. Then another voice yells, "Are you stuck? Oh my God, I think she's stuck!"

I don't bother confirming the obvious. As the commotion beneath me grows, I try to block it out. Eventually, I hear the distinct wail of a fire truck in the distance—and I remember the sound of Leo's wailing that night.

I curse myself. I curse my life. I take back every wish I ever made on Venus.

PART TWO

★

Everett, Washington; Oakland, California; February–May 1980

11

It's a Sunday night in February and Tinker Miller is sitting on his friend Jerry's front porch, smoking a cigarette. When a wood-paneled truck pulls up across the street, he watches as a lady with curlers grabs a small suitcase from the cab and then takes a small boy from the backseat into the house. The kid has a blond buzz cut, a strange tilt to his head, and Tinker immediately recognizes him as his brother Ray's boy, who everyone knows is a little off.

He's seen Inez at this house before. She and the lady must be friends. Tinker always makes sure to stay out of view, since he had a falling-out with both Inez and Raymond some time ago. After he got out of Monroe prison, he showed up at their house and apologized for burglarizing them, explaining that it wasn't personal, since theirs wasn't the only house he hit.

But Inez is a vengeful bitch and would never forgive him.

The following evening, Tinker is at a tavern with a few buddies, and the TV news is on in the background. When he hears his brother's name, it grabs his attention. The reporter is saying the victim, identified as Raymond Miller, was killed in his home the previous evening.

It takes a second for Tinker's brain to catch up to and believe what he is hearing. "Holy shit!" he exclaims, lowering his beer to the counter. "That's my brother!" Then they show a picture of

Ray's house on Rockefeller Avenue and he knows for sure. "Jesus Christ!" he yells, frantically motioning to his buddies to come look at the small TV near the register. "It's my brother who got killed."

By then the story is almost over, but they say a juvenile girl has been taken into custody. Some people in the bar already saw the story on the morning news. They ask about Ray's family and then they suggest it has to be Ray's stepdaughter who was arrested.

Tinker doesn't know what to do, how to act. People keep telling him how sorry they are and buying him drinks. It dawns on him that having your brother murdered is a pretty big deal.

Truth is, Tinker always resented Ray. It was like Ray got everything Tinker deserved. Tinker had been the one who was so good at tinkering on cars in the garage that his dad dubbed him Tinker— his real name is Thomas—but who got the loan to go to school and become a mechanic? *Ray.* Who ends up as a short-order cook? *Tinker.* Who gets to be a dad? *Ray.*

But Tinker doesn't want to speak ill of the dead. The one to be mad at now is Venus. Last time he visited his brother, he could tell just by looking at her that Venus was a little bitch. Raymond called her "a brat on steroids." In the bar, when Tinker starts calling Venus a murdering bitch, his friends get all riled up. They say stuff like, "Oh man. That's so fucked up, bro."

One person shows Tinker the paper from that morning, but it doesn't add much. As the night wears on and the free drinks flow, Tinker finds himself explaining that Ray was a good man, a great mechanic, and he didn't deserve to die. By closing time, he gets all choked up thinking how close they'd been.

The next morning, Tinker lifts a *Herald* from one of Jerry's neighbors. The story about his brother is on the front page again, this time with Ray's picture. Seeing his brother's face there makes him wonder if he should go down to the 7-Eleven and buy extra copies for souvenirs.

He eagerly reads the story, but they don't mention Ray having a brother. It's mostly just about how the neighbors are all shocked.

"They seemed like a nice family," said one lady. "The daughter seemed like a good girl. She was always babysitting her little brother. Sometimes she would walk him around the block."

Tinker thinks about actually calling Inez to get some juicy details, but she's always hated him for no good reason. She'd probably hang up on him. No one at the bar knows that he did a stint in Monroe, and Tinker doesn't think it should matter.

When Tinker returns to the bar the next evening, everyone still wants to talk about the crime. But since he doesn't have any new information to add, he's embarrassed, like he's letting them down. He gripes loudly about being left out of the loop by Ray's horrible wife, Inez. When not a single person buys him a beer, he feels robbed.

The next day, Tinker is flipping burgers at work when he remembers seeing Leo across the street from Jerry's. And he had a *suitcase*. It makes sense that he'd be staying with a friend of the family. Inez was probably a basket case, and being such a selfish bitch, she must have just pawned him off.

The more Tinker thinks about Leo, the more surprised he is to realize he's his own flesh-and-blood *nephew*. It hadn't ever occurred to him to think of Leo that way. So, shit, as *an uncle*, Tinker should have some kind of rights, shouldn't he?

Leo should be with *family*. And not family like Inez, who obviously has to be a horrible mother since she raised a vicious, murdering bitch like Venus. And since his and Ray's parents are dead, and he's pretty sure that Inez's estranged parents still live back in Greece, this poor kid doesn't even have grandparents to take him.

Tinker always wanted to be a dad, but for some time now, he's been secretly worried that his sperm's no good. None of the girls he ever slept with have gotten pregnant, even though he's never worn protection and he's screwed a lot of women over the years. When he has sex, he pictures his sperm like shriveled up little tadpoles with twisted and deformed tails, which bothers him a lot.

By the time his shift is over, Tinker feels like his destiny has become clear to him. *If* Leo is still at the house across from Jerry, Tinker should rescue him. He and the boy can move to sunny California, and the boy will look up to him like a dad. Besides, Tinker's never been to California, and his welcome on Jerry's couch is wearing out, anyway.

It all happens just like he'd hoped, and it's easy to grab Leo—well, not easy, since the kid doesn't know his uncle, and you can blame Inez for that. After circling round the alley, he spots the boy playing in a sandbox. He quickly slaps duct tape over his mouth and tapes Leo's hands together at the wrists—just to be on the safe side.

While Tinker drives, Leo makes moaning sounds, and Tinker feels guilty about the tape—he isn't an actual kidnapper, after all. And so at the first exit, he pulls off I-5 and takes the tapes off. To see what will happen. In case the kid still goes banshee in the car, he straps him into a rusty seatbelt that's hard to open or close.

"I want my mom," Leo wails, crying. "Where's my mom?"

"Your mom is busy," Tinker explains.

"I want Venus!"

"Trust me, you don't want her. She's dangerous," he says. "Can you be a good boy and just sit tight in the seatbelt? Later we'll get some ice cream." Leo doesn't say anything, and Tinker takes that as a good sign.

Then he remembers the model car in his pocket he stole from Jerry's vintage collection—probably worth something. He'd thought of it at the last second and picked out the coolest one. When that is all it takes to make Leo stop screaming for his mother and Venus, Tinker feels like a genius.

LEO WAKES UP in a strange bed with a scratchy cover that is not the right blue. He gets out of bed and looks at his yellow watch. The short line points at the nine. He was supposed to get breakfast when it pointed at the eight. But Venus isn't here. His mother isn't here.

He hears the sound of someone in the bathroom. He remembers riding in the car, counting the white stitches, and the man with the orange hair.

When the man comes out of the bathroom, Leo goes in. But after he tinkles, there is not the right soap on the counter. This soap is shaped like a circle. And the sink is not the wrong pink like at home. It's the right white, though. So he washes his hands.

When he comes out, the man is there. He tries to hand Leo a banana. "Want a banana, kid?" Leo loves bananas. But Venus has to peel it. She cuts it in ten pieces.

When the man keeps trying to hand him the banana, Leo gets angry and makes angry noises. He wants his purple blanket. He wants his mother. He knows she isn't here, because this is not home. It is different from the wrong place that had the sand.

Everything is wrong.

He goes over to the corner of the room and sits on the floor and begins bumping his head on the wall. When he senses the man coming toward him again, he bumps harder, because he can't help it. Leo sees the man's brown shoe right next to him. The man touches his shoulder, and Leo screams, "No touching! No touching!"

"Okay! No touching. I won't touch you." The man sets a toy car on the floor. It is the same blue car from yesterday. The man says, "You sure you don't want the banana, kid? You gotta be hungry."

Leo ignores the man.

"You're a real whack job, aren't you?" says the voice. "Your daddy never told me."

After a while, the man goes away. Leo reaches for the blue car and spins each wheel, one at a time. Just like at home, he stares into the turning.

AFTER ONE NIGHT in a Motel 6, Tinker is pissed that his brother wasn't up-front about how bad off his kid was. He can't quite remember, but last time he visited Ray, didn't Leo eat food and talk? Plus, he can't get the kid to stop making these weird noises and rocking and shit.

Talk about conspicuous. Tinker feels proud of himself for knowing that word. Leo is *conspicuous,* and Tinker is worried about being caught with him. A regular kid would blend in. But what if folks are on the lookout for a baldish kid who is six or seven but acts like he's two?

And if Leo doesn't start eating soon, what's Tinker supposed to do?

Last night, Leo refused to eat any of the snack foods Tinker picked up at a gas station. This morning, he offered Leo a banana, in case he is used to healthy shit. Plus, don't most kids like bananas?

But Leo wouldn't even touch it.

On the bright side, Tinker has discovered by testing him that Leo won't try to run or get away if he's left in the car. He stays when Tinker says, "Stay." And he comes when Tinker says, "Come." On this point, he's like a well-trained dog, which is a huge relief.

Worst-case scenario—Tinker could always just drop the kid near a hospital or church somewhere. It's not like Leo could identify him. Or draw a picture of him. Tinker laughs at the thought as he drives down I-5 toward California. He's never even been to the state, which he would never admit to anyone. He reaches over on the seat to grab the banana. "More for me, kid," he calls out. He peels it using his teeth while steering with one hand.

LEO IS RIDING in the wrong car again. His neck hurts. He uncurls himself and climbs up onto the seat. His stomach is making a funny noise. He looks at his watch. It is almost time for his lunch. But his mother isn't here.

His eyes are drawn to the shiny mirror in the front of the car.

The man's eyes are there. Leo doesn't like for other people's eyes to look at his eyes. But it's not like that now, because the man is staring ahead.

The eyes are squinting. Three lines come out of each eye on the outside corners. The eyebrows are furry and not the right orange. The eyes glance at Leo and he quickly looks away. But he saw that the man's eyes are the wrong blue. His dad's eyes are the right blue, like the toy car.

Leo won't look at the man again. He looks at the doorknob, which is shiny metal, which is not a color. Leo knows that if he pulls on the handle, the door could open. That has happened before. The loud noise scared him. His mother yelled at him for a long time.

Leo gently presses his thumb on the door handle and then pulls it away. The thumbprint slowly fades. He does this again and again. He discovers a metal pocket, too. It opens and shuts. It smells just like his father.

When the car stops, Leo looks up. He sees the *M* that is the right color yellow on the right color red. He is excited. He goes here with his mother and Venus.

He is surprised when the man gets out and says, "Stay." His mother always said, "Come." He stares at the big yellow *M*. He feels excited because he smells the right smells.

He startles when the door next to him suddenly opens. The man hands him a bag. The bag is familiar. But what's inside is wrong.

He yells, "No! No!" But the man has gotten back in the front seat.

"Don't tell me you don't like McDonald's," he says. He doesn't start the car. He is eating something. "I thought all kids like McDonald's."

Then Leo smells something that makes him stop. He looks up and sees that the man has the red box with the yellow *M*!

"Fries!" Leo yells. "Fries!"

"What the hell!" The man turns around in his seat. Leo's eyes are on the box in the man's hand.

"You want my damn fries?" says the man. He reaches over the seat with the box. "Here you go, kid. Knock yourself out."

Leo takes the fries. He begins to count each one aloud before it goes into his mouth. "One," he says, and then eats a fry. "Two . . ." He keeps on counting, pausing in between to chew.

"So you can count!" says the man. "What else can you say besides crying for your mommy and Venus? *Hello? Goodbye?* How about, *Thank you for the fries, Tinker.* That would be nice."

When Leo says twenty-four, the box is empty. He licks his fingers one at a time, starting from his left pinky. The man has been laughing. Leo knows the sound, but he's never made it. He doesn't know how.

12

Tinker had just about been ready to ditch the boy. Who knew that French fries were the key?

Tinker thinks that next he'll try Pop-Tarts, because he himself loves chocolate Pop-Tarts, but he always feels kind of embarrassed in the checkout line when he's buying them. Like people can tell he doesn't have a kid at home.

Tinker takes Leo to the bathroom whenever he can. Thank God the kid is at least potty-trained. No accidents so far.

The next time he stops for gas, there's a little market where Tinker gets Leo a carton of milk. He's been giving him cups of water, but he's gratified when Leo steadily gulps the milk until it's gone.

When Tinker sees a cop car on the freeway and gets paranoid, he reminds himself that even if he did get caught with Leo, surely he wouldn't go back to prison. For Christ's sake, the boy is his very own flesh-and-blood nephew. They can't call it kidnapping if you're related, right?

He realizes then that if he can't get the kid to stop crying for his mother and Venus every two hours, it's going to be a problem. Finally he yells back at Leo, "What about your dad? Why don't you cry for your dad?"

Leo doesn't answer, of course. Finally, Tinker pulls off at an exit and finds an isolated place to park. He gets the duct tape out of the glove box. He gets in the backseat next to Leo. When Leo sees the tape, he screams, "No! No!" and hunkers down on the floor of the car as far from Tinker as he can get.

Tinker thunders at him, "Don't say *Mommy*. Don't say *Venus*. Don't say *Mommy*. Don't say *Venus*! Do you understand, Leo? If you say the word *Mommy* or the word *Venus,* I will put this tape on your mouth again."

He shoves the tape down by Leo's head and yells again. "No more crying for Mommy. No crying for Venus. Do you understand, Leo?"

The boy seems to be nodding his head, though it's hard to tell. Tinker can only hope this will work. Back on the freeway, he feels kind of bad. He's never been mean to a kid before.

They arrive in Oakland in late afternoon. By now Leo has settled down and is sitting up on the seat again. Inside a Safeway, Tinker purchases an *Oakland Tribune*. When he comes back out, he is gratified all over again that Leo is still just waiting in the car. He can be such a good kid; it's too bad about the crying and the other weird shit.

Tinker locates the cheapest furnished rental in the listings.

"Two hundred big ones, Leo," he says. "Was hoping we wouldn't have to spend our wad so quick."

Tinker had a wife once. Her name was Kimberly, and they lived in an apartment in Olympia for only a hundred fifty dollars a month. Kimberly was a real beauty, with long legs, big boobs, and doll eyes. She had the whole package except for the one arm. She'd lost her left arm in a car accident when she was twelve.

But Tinker didn't mind. Scoring Kimberly was like buying a really cool car that was maybe missing a window or a bumper. It still ran, though, and people looked at you with envy when you drove past. Plus, for all anyone knew, Tinker had married Kimberly before she ever lost her arm, which might make people think Tinker was a great guy for sticking around.

Or, if they knew he married her with one arm, that didn't look too bad, either. He always knew he had a big heart, and Kimberly proved it.

The marriage lasted over two years, which was almost a success in Tinker's mind. Kimberly divorced him when he got arrested for the burglaries. She'd been fine knowing he did them. But when he got caught and the money ended, so did the love.

Tinker still misses Kimberly sometimes. And who knows, they might have worked things out after he got out of Monroe if he hadn't yelled as she was leaving that day, "Who else is going to want a one-armed wife?"

He regrets that now. Not just because it was mean, but also because he knows he was probably wrong. He's pretty sure plenty of guys don't give a rat's ass about shit like arms and legs.

13

Tessa Herrera is sitting on the steps in front of her dad's tattoo shop, playing jacks in the sun. She's on foursies when a beat-up white Impala pulls up at the curb. She watches a man with reddish-blond hair, a large belly, and big sweat circles under the arms of his green T-shirt get out of the car and head toward her.

She scoots to the side of the steps and politely asks, "Tattoo appointment?"

But the man says no, he's looking for the apartment for rent, but maybe he has the wrong address.

"Oh no," she says, turning to point. "There's two apartments above the shop—we live in one and rent the other one out. My dad's inside. He'll tell you all about it."

"Why, thank you, little lady," he says with a small bow. Tessa feels like he's making fun of her for being young. She's eleven, but her dad says she's "petite" for her age, which she knows means small.

A few minutes later, the man comes back out of the shop with her dad and they head up the stairs. The guy is talking and laughing too loud, and Tessa can tell he is trying too hard to impress her father.

Tessa's dad says that she might be shy but she's "good at reading people," and sometimes he even asks Tessa's opinion about whether or not they should rent to a person.

She's about to resume her jacks when she notices a blond boy with a buzz cut in the backseat of the car. The kid seems to be looking her direction, so she smiles and waves. When the boy doesn't smile or wave back, she feels dumb for trying.

Obviously the boy in the car belongs to the guy looking at the apartment. But they've never rented to anyone with a kid before, probably because the apartment has only one bed. Usually it was just a single older person, or else a couple.

When she finally looks up again, the boy is still openly staring in her direction. He must be about seven, she decides. She doesn't wave again, but she is too polite not to smile. When the boy doesn't smile back, just keeps staring, she's embarrassed. What a jerk!

The phone starts ringing from inside the shop and she jumps to her feet. Her dad has a thing about always grabbing the phone in case it's a tattoo client. This time, Tessa hopes it's someone who wants to rent the apartment, who doesn't have a totally rude kid who won't stop staring.

TINKER HAD TO walk away from the first two apartments because they wanted a background check and references. When the third address turns out to be an apartment above a shop called Tattoos by Tony he gets his hopes up.

He leaves the kid in the car, since he doesn't want Leo to ruin his chances by acting all weird and shit. He's convinced they look like any dad and son—he's pretty sure there's even a family resemblance. But if people are looking for a blond kid with a buzz cut who acts like a whack job, Leo fits the bill. Totally *conspicuous*.

A pretty, young Mexican girl with black braids is sitting on the front steps, and she directs Tinker into the shop, where her dad introduces himself as Tony. He's got long black hair in a ponytail. Tinker shakes his hand. "I'm Phil," he offers. "Phil Brown."

While they climb the wooden stairs on the side of the building, Tinker makes small talk, turns on his natural charm. Inside the apartment, he notices a big front window that looks out onto the street. "Nice big window!" Tinker exclaims. On the opposite wall is a small white stove, fridge, sink, and about a foot of counter space. He motions toward it. "Everything I need," he says.

The Tony guy explains that the tweed couch is a pullout.

"A hideaway?" says Tinker. "That's fabulous. More than I was expecting." He hopes he doesn't sound too enthusiastic. The rest of the furniture is odds and ends. There's a card table and folding chairs for a kitchen table. There's also a small TV with rabbit ears, which is a big bonus. Tinker likes TV, because it keeps him out of trouble.

When Tony waves him toward the bedroom and bathroom, Tinker pretends to inspect them. The bed is a full size with no headboard. He hopes the bedding is included, but he doesn't want to ask in case it isn't. The bathroom needs new grout and smells a little funny, but it's probably bug spray or something, which Tinker chooses to take as a positive.

Back in the front room, he reaches for his wallet. "This is perfect," he says. "I'll take it." Maybe if Tinker pulls out cash, the guy won't bother to ask for references.

"Just you?" Tony asks, waving away the cash.

Tinker's heart sinks. What if no kids are allowed? "It's just me and my boy, sir," he says, with what he hopes is obvious sadness. "He's got some issues with his thinking, so he's kind of immature. But he's a sweet kid. I only got him recently, after his mom got a heroin habit and ran off. I don't do any of that shit. So you don't need to worry."

Tony is looking out the front window down at Tinker's car. "Is that your boy?"

"Yeah, that's Leo," says Tinker, trying to sound proud of his son.

"How old is Leo?"

Hearing the kid's name come out of Tony's mouth, he realizes his mistake. Shit. Goddamn. Holy Mother of Fuckups. Why didn't Tinker come up with a fake name for Leo? He's about to say he thinks Leo is around six or seven, when he catches his stupid self. *Dads know how old their kids are!* He takes a guess. "Leo's six years old," says Tinker. "But you'll notice he seems a lot younger."

"So where do you work, Phil?"

More with the questions. This Tony is scrutinizing him in a way that makes Tinker nervous. "Well, I'm just relocating from Redding," says Tinker. "But I got plenty of money until I find something."

Tinker notices that Tony is probably what the ladies think is good-looking. The girls all go for that pretty shit. Tinker knows his gut is kind of pudgy, so he sucks in his stomach while he's thinking about it. "It's a deal, then?"

When Tony doesn't answer right away, Tinker regrets he never bothered to get a tat, because needles scare him. What an idiot! Having a great tattoo could've really helped him out here. "I'm planning to be one of your next customers," Tinker offers, spur of the moment.

"Yeah?" says Tony. "I look forward to that."

"So I got the apartment, right?" Once again, Tinker extends his small stack of cash. "First and last, fifty-dollar deposit. It's all there."

Tony takes the cash this time and Tinker sighs with relief.

"When would you two move in?" he asks.

"Right away, sir. Or whenever you want." Tinker realizes he should probably have more stuff, like a truck or something. All he has is a huge duffel. He should have tried harder to look more . . . He fumbles for the word. It starts with an *L*.

"Okay, Phil," says Tony. "Move in whenever you want."

Tinker notices how weird it feels to be called Phil. He took the name from a best friend in high school. And brown is the color of his shoes.

"Dad!" a girl's voice calls up the stairs. "Marco's on the phone."

"You'll have to fill out an application later," Tony tells him hurriedly. "Rent's due by the fifth of each month. Sorry, I gotta go get this."

Tinker smiles, hardly able to contain his relief. "No problem at all," he says in his best no-big-deal voice. He doubts his brother, Ray, could have swung this deal so quickly.

Left alone in the apartment, Tinker realizes his bladder is about to burst. It thrills him to think he has his own bathroom to use. He's almost done whizzing when the word he was looking for earlier finally comes to him. He should have tried harder to look *legitimate*. He shakes himself, flushes, and lets out a small hoot.

14

Leo watches the girl get up and leave. He sees the things that look like stars and the small ball. He wants the sparkling things and the red ball. He gets out of the car and quickly snatches them up.

Back in the car, he counts ten metal stars. The red ball is one. The man comes back to the car and tells Leo to come. "Where did you get those?" asks the man. Leo ignores him. He follows the man up some stairs and into another place that is not his house. His mother isn't here. Venus isn't here. He wants to cry for his mom, but the man yelled, *No!*

He sits on the floor by the window in a patch of sun. He folds his legs like he saw the girl do. He tosses the metal things. They glitter in the light. After a while, he picks up the red ball. He bounces it and catches it. He does this over and over.

Now the man's voice is poking him again. "Did you steal those, Leo?" Leo blocks out the sound. Eventually the man quits talking and goes away. When Leo feels hungry, he looks at his yellow watch. The short line is on the eight. He has dinner on the six.

The man isn't here. Leo stands up and walks over to the TV. The show is not *Gilligan*. Leo wants to touch the metal sticks on top of the TV. But he hears his dad yell, *No, Leo. Don't touch the TV!*

He goes into the room with the bed. He sees a closet with a

door, like at home. But it's the wrong closet. He wants his purple blanket, but he knows it isn't here. He curls up on the floor in the closet. He checks his watch again. Where is Venus? Where is his mother? He wants dinner.

He cries and rocks and counts until he is asleep. When he wakes up, he is not in bed. He is in the wrong closet. His neck hurts. He remembers the man with the orange hair. He smells bacon. Bacon is what his father ate.

AFTER SCHOOL, TESSA sits at the little white desk her dad got her for her tenth birthday. Sitting here doing her homework always makes her feel more like a grown-up. Every now and then, she glances at the framed picture of her mother on the corner of the desk. She's known since she was very little that her mother died when Tessa was born.

Her father says it's not her fault, but Tessa has never felt sure.

Right next to the picture of her mother is the small statue of the Virgin Mary that belonged to her mom. Her dad says it was her favorite thing. "She was strong in her faith," her father liked to say. Tessa wishes he talked more about stuff like the dates they went on.

A half hour later, she is deep in thought, doing work for math class, when she hears a strange knocking sound. She quickly decides it's coming from the other apartment. They share a wall and sometimes Tessa hears noise from the neighbors, so she isn't surprised. The father and son moved in last night, but she had to go babysit at the Smiths' house, so she missed it.

Now she decides they must be hanging a picture, even though the dad didn't look like the type. She wonders if the boy sleeps in the same bed with his father or if he has to sleep on the hide-a-bed in the front room. She hopes the boy doesn't find out the Herreras' apartment is way bigger and nicer than theirs.

After dinner, Tessa's father tells her he has to work late again, which is always a disappointment to her. He went right back down to the shop after he finished the spaghetti Tessa had cooked for him. "You're such a good girl, Tess," he tells her, pulling her in for a hug. He always says this whenever he works at night.

Tonight, while she fills the sink with soapy water, she feels a little lonely. Her dad might be right about her needing more friends. She has her best friend, Kelly, at school, and sometimes Tessa spends the night over at Kelly's house. But she doesn't really like to have friends stay over at her house, since there's no mom to make things feel homey or like a family.

After Tessa has cleaned the kitchen, including the Ragú sauce stuck under the stove burner, she sits down on the couch in the front room and looks at her book of horses for a long time. Then she goes to her room to study spelling for tomorrow's test, even though she knows she'll get an A. But before she starts to study, she hears the same steady knocking sound she heard earlier. The neighbors must have a lot of pictures to hang—but how many pictures can you hang on one wall?

At 8:00 P.M., she turns the TV on to watch *Little House on the Prairie*. She loves this show so much it usually makes her cry. Not because it's sad, but because she wants to be part of the Ingalls family. Of course, Tessa never cries if her dad is around. He might think she's not mature, after all.

The show ends at 9:00 P.M., which is when she thinks her mother might want her to go to bed if she were alive. She does that a lot, tries to imagine her mom's wishes, in case she's watching from heaven. After she prays on her knees and climbs into her carefully made bed, the pounding noise starts in again. She sits up and looks around the room. The moon has come out and the walls look bluish, even though they're plain white.

She gets out of bed and goes over to the wall and puts her ear to it. The nailing is coming from behind her dresser, way down low on the wall, not where you'd hang a picture. She moves her dresser out, scraping it along the wood floor. She kneels down and listens. Before she can think why, she impulsively knocks on the wall. The knocking stops. She knocks again, softly. Three times. And three knocks come back. She smiles but feels confused. It must be the bratty boy knocking, but why would he do that?

She sees herself squatting there, her white nightgown pooling around her on the floor in the blue light. Silence. Suddenly she's embarrassed. She decides not to knock again and climbs back in bed.

The silence lasts.

15

The man with the wrong orange hair is not here. Leo doesn't know when he left. It was after Leo was watching the TV for a long time. Not *Gilligan* or *Speed Racer*, but a show with fuzzy white and black and gray squiggles. Leo liked staring at it. The man had stood near him and said something. Once, the man changed the channel. But when Leo started yelling, he changed it back.

Now Leo goes to the room where there is a closet. He curls up on the floor and starts to rock. He wants Venus. Why won't she come? He sees her in his head like at night when he sleeps. He sees her room, and he hears her voice counting stars and saying the planets.

He wants his mother. She always gets his purple blanket for him. She never yells at Leo for being in the closet. But sometimes his father opens the door and yells, "Goddamn it, Leo!"

Leo knows the word *damn*. It's a red feeling. And when his father says it, Leo gets scared his father might hurt him.

TINKER FINDS A job the first day out. Not surprising, since he is a skilled fry cook. One of the few good things that came out of his stint in prison. Whenever he wants a job, he finds a place that needs a short-order cook and offers to work three nights for free. They always keep him, despite the huge gaps in his application.

It works again, this time at the Burger Bar on Catalina Avenue, where they were advertising for a swing-shift cook. It means that he'll have to leave Leo alone in the afternoon and evening, but so far the kid seems surprisingly self-sufficient. He even puts himself to bed, and Tinker's starting to think it's the same time every night. The kid is always looking at his yellow plastic watch.

Tinker lets Leo take the bed, since the boy seems to assume it's his. He doesn't mind the pullout, especially since he likes to stay up and drink beer and fall asleep in front of the TV. Pretty soon he's going to get one of the waitresses to bed, and he can only hope the boy sleeps hard.

After a couple of days in the new apartment, he's made a little progress on the food with Leo. He ate the bologna that Tinker brought home one night. He carefully removed the edges, but he didn't count the bites. He rolled up each piece into a tube, put it to his eye and looked through it, then ate it.

It made Tinker laugh, but the boy was dead serious. Tinker thinks how proud Ray would be to see his brother taking such good care of Leo. He's pretty sure Ray's looking down from heaven and cheering him on.

Next he tries to get Leo to eat peanut butter, but something about the jar upsets him. He shoves it away with a grunt. Maybe it's creamy instead of chunky, or the wrong brand, or the wrong color. Damn, who'd raise a kid to be so damn picky? Inez. Inez would.

He's seen a commercial that said, "Choosy mothers choose Jif," so next time he tries that kind. As soon as Leo spots the Jif, he grabs the jar and takes two slices of the Wonder bread, as if he wants to make the sandwich himself. Tinker reluctantly offers him a butter knife. Starting in the middle of each piece, Leo makes perfect swirls of Jif outward until none of the bread shows, then he slaps the two slices together.

Tinker is surprised but relieved to discover the boy can make his own sandwich. But he's annoyed, too. Choosy mothers make choosy kids, and then look what happens. They turn out like Leo.

After a few nights, Tinker realizes that the boy should probably have a bath. But he knows better than to think he can touch Leo, so how's he going to get him in the water? He pictures all kinds of screaming and crying and rocking shit.

But as soon as Tinker turns on the water and starts to run the bath, Leo comes to the door. He begins to strip off his clothes himself, which is a huge relief. Tinker makes a mental note that he needs to buy the boy some changes of clothes.

THURSDAY AFTERNOON, TESSA comes home from school, bakes some oatmeal cookies, and arranges half of them on a paper plate. She never would have tried this with the grouchy old man who last lived in the apartment, but she's curious to meet the new boy next door.

Maybe all the knocking he does is his way of apologizing to her for staring. Weird, but you never know with boys. She's been watching for him to come out of the apartment, but if he does, it's when she's at school. While she was baking cookies, though, the fat-belly man—her dad says his name is Phil—drove away in the white Impala. The boy wasn't with him, and so she figures he's in the apartment alone.

But what if he thinks the cookies are stupid? Or what if he's rude to her again? To be on the safe side, Tessa decides she'll act like she thought his dad was at home. When he answers the door, she'll say *Is your father around?*

And if he's mean about the cookies, maybe she'll be mean right back and say *I made them for your father, not for you.*

Tessa is working up the courage to knock when she hears a faint sound coming from inside the apartment. It sounds like hard raindrops hitting the window, but that can't be. Finally, she knocks three times. The intermittent sound of rain continues but nothing else. She knocks again, harder, and the tinkling stops. She pictures the boy. Alone, trying to decide.

"Hello?" she calls. "Anyone home?"

Moments later, she hears a knock on the other side of the door. She is flustered. What's that supposed to mean? She knocks again, two raps. She hears two raps in return. She gets it now: It's a game, like the other night. But what is she supposed to do? Stand here and play knock-knock all afternoon?

"Hello!" she says loudly to the door. "Do you want to answer the door?"

Silence. She waits. She smells the warm cookies she's holding in her left hand. She wishes they had chocolate chips in them. She is about to knock again when she hears the tinkling sound resume.

She can't even believe it! Why would he knock back and then ignore her?

Made bolder by frustration, she puts her hand on the knob—not to open the door, she assures herself. Just to see if it's locked, which it is.

Finally, she makes up her mind. She sets the cookies on the ground and darts back down the stairs to the shop. She knows her father keeps the master key to the apartments on a ring in the back of a desk drawer.

Moments later, she's standing at the boy's door again, master key in hand. She pictures how much trouble she could get in if her dad found out she broke in to someone's apartment. But she's not breaking in, is she? She's just worried about the boy. That's it! What if the boy needs help?

She feels her face burning with shame even as she forces herself to slide the key in the lock. She tells herself she doesn't really mean to turn the knob and push the door. But, of course, she knows better. She always knows better, even when she doesn't want to.

The door cracks open a few inches and Tessa peers in. She sees the boy, kneeling at the window, his back to her.

"Hello?" she calls. But the boy acts like she's not there. And then she realizes what he's doing. Throwing *her* jacks against the window. That was the sound she'd been hearing. She knew she left them on the stoop that day.

What a little thief! But she's not prepared to accuse him, in case she's wrong. She makes a throat-clearing sound, the kind you make to get someone's attention. The boy doesn't react at all, which is when she realizes he must be deaf. That would explain a lot.

She steps into the living room and says loudly, "Hello! Can you tell me your name?"

"My name is Leo," he says in a slightly mechanical way, his attention still on the jacks.

Clearly he's not deaf. "Hi, Leo. I'm Tessa," she says in a kind voice. "I live next door."

Nothing.

"I brought you cookies."

She walks over and sets the cookies on a small gray card table that serves as the kitchen table. She'll take them with her when she goes so Leo's dad won't know she was here. She notes the unmade pullout bed in front of the TV. The beer bottles that line the kitchen counter.

"Would those happen to be my jacks?" she asks in a friendly way. He doesn't answer, so she walks over and stands right near him. His face is delicate for a boy, his nose a little snubbed, and his eyebrows are arched and thin. He's also weirdly skinny.

That's when it hits her. The kid probably wasn't staring at her from the car that first day but at the jacks. And now he isn't being rude; he's just got something wrong with him. That has to be it. Leo probably belongs with those kids at her school who are in special ed.

She notices that the little red ball that goes with the jacks is lying nearby. She retrieves it and then gets on her knees at the wide windowsill next to Leo. When she starts to bounce the ball and catch it, the boy stops throwing the jacks. Starts watching the ball.

"Do you want the ball?" She holds it out to him on her open palm. He stares at it and then takes it from her. His eyes are metal gray and they skitter, like he might be trying to look at her but he can't.

He begins to bounce the ball on the sill, exactly the way Tessa did, and she feels her heart fill up. "Do you know when your dad will be home?" she asks.

Nothing.

She asks how old he is. "I'm seven," he says, in his small, robotic voice. She thought her dad had said the boy was six. She's not sure how long she sits there watching him bounce the ball, but it's long enough to be totally amazed that he isn't growing bored.

He makes her think of her friend Kelly's kitten, how it is so easily distracted by toys and loses interest in her and Kelly. She wishes Leo could at least look at her. Or talk to her.

When she reaches out to touch the boy's shoulder, he yelps and jerks away as if she's hurt him.

"Okay, no touching!" she says quickly.

She thinks again about the special-ed kids at her school. They rarely cross paths with the regular kids. Tessa always wants to feel sorry for them, but she can't, because they always seem so happy. Maybe Leo is happy, too.

"Leo," she says. "Leo is a good name."

Suddenly, Leo stops rolling the small red ball and holds it up, turning it. He gets a look on his face like he's just realized something. "Venus!" he says. "Venus is red."

16

Leo becomes Tessa's after-school secret. She has never had such a big secret before, and she worries it might be the same as a lie.

She's always careful to make sure the Impala is gone before she borrows the master key and visits Leo. She's figured out by now that Leo's dad works afternoons and evenings. Her father doesn't notice she's gone, just assumes she's doing her usual routine or visiting her friend Kelly, who lives nearby.

Because Tessa is also doing volunteer work at the old-folks home down the street, she's busier than she would be. But every time Tessa visits Leo, he's lying on his side, spinning the wheels on his car. Or sometimes he's watching the TV without really seeming to watch.

Sometimes she finds him sitting quietly on the floor in a patch of sun that's coming from the big front window. She wonders if kids like Leo get lonely, and she hopes not. Often, she brings a new toy or some other item to see if it will interest Leo or get him to speak again. She's always careful not to leave anything behind, so Phil won't know she was there.

So far, Leo doesn't respond to her horse book. He shows no interest in the handheld plastic pinball machine she brought him. She tries different foods, too. No to lollipops. No to Velveeta. And then one day Leo responds to a bag of Cheetos, with strange grunting sounds that make Tessa think he's upset, until she realizes he is excited.

"You like Cheetos, Leo?" She hands him the bag and he gently dumps its contents onto the table. Carefully, in a way that makes Tessa know he's done it before, he arranges the Cheetos into three horizontal lines. He eats the first of the Cheetos from the left top row. "One," he says. Then he eats the next and says, "Two."

"Leo, you can count!" she exclaims. His voice is a little nasal, but it also sounds sweet to her. When he finally eats the last of the Cheetos, he says, "Twenty-six." Then he carefully licks the orange dust from each finger, starting with his left pinky and ending on his right thumb.

When he's done, Tessa bursts into clapping but stops when Leo clamps his hands on his ears. He clearly hates loud noises. But then she gets an idea. If Leo can count, maybe he can do the ABCs? She begins to sing the ABC song, and sure enough, Leo joins in. The way he sounds singing makes Tessa want to laugh, but she holds it back. When they finish the song, she doesn't clap.

She just says, "Leo, you can sing the ABCs."

She leaves the apartment that afternoon thrilled by her discoveries. Three big successes in one day—Cheetos, counting, and ABCs!

Tessa is dying to tell someone about Leo, but there's no one to tell but her mom. So she lets herself whisper out loud, "Mom, can you believe it?"

That night, as she cuts the fat off the chicken breasts she's using to make chicken and dumplings, she worries about Leo in a new way. If Leo can count and talk, shouldn't he be in school? Her dad says Phil teaches Leo at home. But Tessa knows better—there's no evidence of anything like that in the apartment.

She does see evidence of Leo's father, though. There are beer bottles. Clothes lying all over the floor. Food left out and, often, dirty dishes in the sink. But there's a lot missing, too. No pictures on the walls. No photos anywhere. No signs, really, of a family.

She debates telling her dad everything, confessing to what she's pretty sure is called "breaking and entering." But she just can't bring herself. Usually, she and her father talk a lot while they eat dinner. He asks her about her day. About her homework. He tells her how grateful he is that she is such a good girl. Sometimes he tells her funny stories about the people who come for tattoos.

But tonight she can't think of anything to talk about, because she can't talk about Leo. So, in near silence, they eat the chicken and dumplings and canned green beans she made. "Are you working tonight?" Tessa finally asks.

"Nope," says her father. "But guess what? It's figure skating on the Olympics tonight."

"Oh, that's my favorite!" Tessa says, and she means it. Plus, she loves to watch any kind of sports with her father. She likes to lean up against him. She likes to study the tattoo of her name on his left arm. Sometimes he puts his arm around her. She likes to wait on him as if she's a waitress. *Do you want a beer? Can I get you some potato chips?*

During a commercial, Tessa checks out the front window to see if Leo's dad has gotten home yet, but there's still no sign of the Impala. She wishes again that she could tell her dad about the boy. She could lie and say he let her in, but lying is a bad sin, and her mother would see it happening.

She brings her dad some potato chips and ranch dip, his favorite. He puts one arm around her shoulder, which makes her realize Leo must never get hugs, since he won't allow touching. What would that feel like, to live without ever getting hugged?

Maybe someday Leo will let her. At every commercial break, she checks her bedroom for the sound of knocking. She can't bear the idea of him knocking and her not being there to knock back.

ONE DAY TESSA is in the grocery store with her dad, when she spots a huge metal bin full of plastic balls in various swirly colors. She thinks of Leo and the red ball he calls Venus. Surely he'd like another ball.

The next day is Saturday, so when she sees Phil's car leave earlier than usual, she figures he has errands to run on his way to work. She takes her gift to Leo, and just like she'd hoped, he clearly likes it. She watches Leo spin the swirly purple ball in one place. Then she teaches him how to roll it on the floor back and forth with her. She finally tires of the game and stands, ready to go. Just then, the door to the apartment opens. Phil is standing there with a bag of groceries, looking surprised and angry. "What the hell is going on?" he says.

"I'm sorry," Tessa stammers. "Remember me? I'm Tony's daughter, Tessa. I'm just visiting Leo. We're friends."

For a moment, she can see that Phil is wavering, trying to decide something. Then he forces his mouth into a smile. "Well, isn't that nice. Did Leo let you in?"

Tessa ignores his question.

"I actually need to go home now," she says. "Goodbye, Leo!"

She races from the apartment, down the long back hall and around the corner to her own door. Why didn't she watch for the Impala? Why wasn't she more careful?

ONCE THE GIRL is gone, Tinker's anger spikes. "How the hell did that girl get in here?" he demands of Leo. "Did you unlock the door, Leo?"

Of course, the kid won't answer. He is lying on the ground, twirling a purple ball that Tinker's never seen before. "God damn it, answer me!" Tinker says. He strides over and kicks the ball as hard as he can against the wall. He's gratified when it bounces back and hits Leo in the face.

When Leo starts to wail, Tinker wishes he could hit the kid. Spank him or something. But, God damn it to hell, he's too good a person. Instead, he grabs Leo by the arm, and of course he starts screaming, "No touching! No touching!" Still, Tinker drags him into the bedroom and roughly shoves him onto the floor of the closet.

Let him knock his head all he wants.

He returns to the living room and looks around. The girl left behind a bag of Cheetos, on the kitchen counter. What the hell has been going on?

He angrily grabs the bag and starts eating the Cheetos. Turns on the TV to drown out Leo's banging. After Tinker has a few beers, he feels bad. He goes to the closet and opens the door. For a moment, he watches the kid hitting his head and making his moaning sounds.

"Shit, kid, I'm sorry," Tinker says. "Do you want some bologna?"

BACK IN HER apartment, Tessa hears Leo knocking his head on the wall of his closet. She's figured out by now that this is where he does it. She knows it means Leo is upset, and she feels terrible. The guilt eats at her the rest of the afternoon, so much that she plans to tell her dad that night what she's been doing. But instead of coming up for dinner, he calls her from the shop and asks her to bring dinner down so he can eat between customers. "Got a long night, baby," he says. "You deserve better."

It's one of her father's favorite phrases. "You deserve better." Which Tessa knows is her father's way of saying, *You deserve a mother*.

Over the next two days, Tessa stays completely away from Leo's apartment. She half-hopes that Phil will tell her dad she's been sneaking into his apartment, because she doesn't have the courage to do it herself. But for some weird reason, Leo's dad doesn't rat on her.

In the meantime, what if Leo is missing her? What if he thinks she left him all alone and isn't coming back?

By the third day, she can't bear it, and she goes to Leo's door. But even before she goes to unlock it, she sees that a shiny new bolt lock has been installed.

To keep her out, she's sure.

Her only hope of seeing Leo now is getting him to open the door.

SPOTS ON THE wall. Yellow. Leo puts his hands on the warm spot. He feels the yellow warm on the backs of them. He watches his fingers. He is still and watching. Eventually, the yellow moves. And he moves his hand again. Then the yellow is gone.

Leo looks at his watch and turns on the TV. It is time for *Gilligan's Island*. But Venus is not here. He hears knocking. Three raps.

A voice is calling. It is interrupting! He blocks it out. The voice calls louder. Someone is shouting his name. It is the girl with the Cheetos. The girl who sings ABCs. He hears five raps on the door. The raps touch only a tiny part of his mind. He's buzzing comfortably. He's unwilling to break away. The knocks keep coming.

"Leo!" the girl calls. "I have Cheetos."

Leo sees the bag in his mind. It is the right orange. He wants Cheetos.

"Open the door!" she calls.

Leo hears his father's loud voice in his head. His father's face is red. He remembers touching and pain. *Never. Open. The. Door.*

He sees the man with the orange hair. He says the same thing. *Never. Open. The. Door.*

The girl keeps knocking. She has black hair that is the right black. Her hands are the wrong brown. Sometimes she has a blue shirt that is the right blue. She brings him things. She doesn't touch. She never yells. Leo wants her to come inside. Why won't she come?

17

One sunny day in late March, Tinker stands in the supermarket, trying to think like a retard. After weeks of trying, he still hasn't conquered breakfast. Once, he even cooked for the kid—made him a damn fine omelet—and Leo refused to take a single bite. It's not like the kid is going to starve or get sick from eating bologna for breakfast. But feeding Leo is like trying to crack a code, and Tinker wants to win.

So far, Leo hates eggs, and bacon, too. He's already tried two cereals—Apple Jacks and Trix. "Other kids love this shit," he'd told Leo, digging into a bowl of Trix himself, milk dribbling down his chin. "What's wrong with you, kid? It's got round things and fun colors!"

Now he scans the cereal aisle and notices the Cheerios. They aren't sweet, but Cheerios make sense, because you'd start eating those when you're still in your high chair, before you got spoiled rotten by Inez. He's about to grab a box, when he spots the Rice Krispies. *Wait a second,* he thinks. *Snap! Crackle! Pop!* And Leo likes rice. He says, "Rice is the right white!"

Tinker reaches for the box. "I got you this time, kid!" he says. He doesn't even care that he's startled an elderly woman reaching for Grape-Nuts. He can hardly wait to get home and see if he's right.

As soon as he gets back to the apartment, he realizes Leo already had lunch. And he doubts Leo will eat breakfast in the middle of the afternoon.

Leo is spinning his plastic ball from the Mexican brat, when Tinker calls out to him, "Come here, Leo! Come right now!"

Usually, Leo obeys him. But this time Tinker has to take away the ball in order to get Leo to come to the table. Leo is starting to get upset, when Tinker shows him the box. "Rice Krispies, Leo! You want some Rice Krispies?"

Leo freezes. "Rice Krispies," he repeats.

Tinker is always surprised when Leo speaks. Clearly, he has the kid's full attention. But then Leo startles Tinker with loud grunts and squawking sounds. It takes Tinker a few moments to realize they mean Leo is excited.

"Yes, Leo," Tinker says. "It's Rice Krispies. You want some?" He brings a bowl and spoon to the table, where Leo has already positioned himself. He pours the milk on the cereal and watches Leo tilt his ear above the bowl to listen. Then he takes a bite. For the next five minutes, Tinker sits still and quietly watches Leo eat. With each bite, Leo tilts his head to listen, then eats a spoonful. Tilts, eats a spoonful. He isn't smiling—he never smiles—but there's a look on his face that makes Phil think he is happy.

When the cereal is gone, Leo lifts the bowl and drinks the milk. Tinker dabs at his eyes with pudgy fingers. Goddamn kid is really messing with his mind.

LEO DREAMS OF his sister. The stars on her ceiling. The planets in a row. He is lying on her bed, and Venus is counting. Her voice is soft. It doesn't hurt him.

When he wakes up, he thinks he is in the closet with his purple blanket. But he is not. He is here in the strange bed. The man with the orange hair is out there with the TV. He misses his purple blanket. He smells bacon. Bacon is what his father ate. Where is his father? Leo sees his angry face and flinches.

Leo goes out to where the man is. He sees a spot of yellow on the floor. Warm. He squats and puts his hand there. When the yellow moves, he moves his hand again. Suddenly he sees a flash. The man has something silver. It's the loud, terrible thing! It is his father's *never ever touch*. Leo freezes in terror. It is going to be loud. He starts to scream about Venus.

The man gets up. He is yelling at Leo to stop screaming. Leo puts his hands on his ears. He remembers the terrible sound. He remembers his sister from before. He waits for the terrible loud to come.

It doesn't come. The man is still yelling at him. Then it is dark. The blanket from his bed is on his head. He can't see the silver. He starts to rock. He counts to calm down. He counts his fingers over and over like his mother taught him.

When Leo gets hot, he stops counting. He hears quiet. He knows the man left. He comes out of the blanket, and the room is empty.

TESSA IS ANGRY with herself that she didn't think of it sooner. She knows it was her guilt that made her dumb. Obviously, the best way to deal with Phil might be to simply ask permission to play with Leo. She can offer to help Leo with his schoolwork, even though she knows for a fact he doesn't do anything. She could show up with some alphabet magnets or some books for teaching Leo. How could he say no? Maybe he would jump at the chance!

Because of Phil's and her schedule, Tessa didn't see an opportunity until Sunday morning. "I'm going to go say hi to the neighbors," she tells her dad. "See if Phil needs any help with his son."

Her father looks up with surprise, but of course he's perfectly fine with this idea, since she knows he worries she is too shy. "Good for you, Tess," he says, winking at her.

Now she's standing at Phil's door, feeling nervous. She has put in her pink barrettes, one on each side at eye level. She has put on her new training bra, too—even though her breasts are just nubs.

And she's wearing her favorite shirt, the one with all the drawings of Holly Hobbie on it.

She is about to knock on the door when she hears Leo begin to scream and wail. And then his father is yelling, "It's just a gun, Leo! It's okay!"

Tessa freezes. Leo's father has a gun. Should she run to tell her father?

"Venus!" Leo yells. "A gun!"

"Yes, Leo. Venus had a gun," says Phil. "But Venus isn't here. Look! I was just cleaning it, Leo! I put the gun away." He is yelling but trying not to yell too loud, Tessa can tell. After that, Leo's wails sound muffled, like he's under a blanket.

Tessa guesses he is probably rocking. He is going to be okay. She hurries back to her own apartment, where she holds her statue of the Virgin Mary next to her heart. She says Hail Marys as she replays in her mind what she heard at the door. She knows something important now that she didn't know before. She whispers partly to herself and partly to the Virgin, "Venus is a person."

18

Tinker is startled to hear a knock on the door. He paid April's rent already. He hasn't given his address to anybody—not even the waitress Wendy yet. He nervously unlocks the door and opens it a crack. It's the snoopy girl from next door.

"Good morning," she says. "How are you today?"

"I'm fine," says Tinker. He glances back into the apartment, making a quick survey of how messy it is. He needs to be friendly, but he doesn't want Miss Snoopy to come in.

"I'm kind of busy right now," he says. "Do you need something?"

"Is Leo around?"

Tinker chuckles. "Yeah, he's here. He's just playing," he says, which is true. Leo is sitting on the floor on the other side of the pullout bed. He's found a spot of sun and he's tossing the jacks on the floor.

"My father wants to invite you and Leo to Easter dinner," she announces.

At first, Tinker is too shocked to make what she said compute. He's barely talked to Tony since he moved in. He still hasn't gotten that tattoo he promised he'd get from Tony.

"Well, problem is, I work nights," answers Tinker, relieved that this is absolutely true.

"Even on Easter Sunday?" she asks. "They don't let you off?"

"Sorry, sweetie," Tinker tells her. "Where I work, we put on a special Easter dinner for anyone in need. Not everybody has a big family or relatives to come over." He can't believe he was smart enough to think of this lie so fast.

The girl doesn't answer. Tinker sees her try to peer around him into the apartment.

"What about Leo?" she asks.

"What about him?"

"Well, it's Easter. Maybe he could come even if you can't."

Tinker bursts out laughing. This girl has no idea, which is kind of reassuring. Clearly, she doesn't know Leo.

"Um, I don't think you want Leo," he manages, grinning. "That boy's one picky eater. Probably doesn't like turkey—"

"We're having ham."

"And I also gotta warn you, he doesn't talk much; he's not much of a . . . what do you call it?"

The girl waits. It's on the tip of his tongue. "A conversation-ist," finishes Tinker proudly. He bets this girl doesn't know such a big word.

"Conversationalist, you mean?" she asks. Before Tinker can agree, she adds, "But we don't mind at all! Are you planning on leaving Leo here alone on Easter?"

Shit. Now Tinker feels stuck. If they think Leo is being ne-glected or something, it will raise red flags. Maybe the best thing is to just let Leo go. What can it hurt? It's not like Leo can tell them anything.

"Tell you what," he says, like he's doing the girl a favor. "I'll ask Leo. He's not much for strangers. But if he wants to come, then I'll let him." This is good. This makes him sound like a real father. A good father.

"How about three o'clock?" she says, acting as if Tinker said yes. "You can drop him off at our door on your way to work."

And the snoopy little bitch knows his routine! "You got a deal," says Tinker with a broad smile. "But only if he wants to."

IT HAD TAKEN some perseverance from Tessa to get her father to say yes to inviting Leo and Phil. She can tell he's not a big fan of Phil. But she knew he'd say yes in the end, because how could he say no to inviting people to Easter dinner who might not have family around?

"If it means that much to you," he finally told her, which is what he always says when she wins an argument. And this time, it really *does* mean that much to her. She is hoping, hoping, hoping that Leo will come. *Please,* she prays at night, *let Leo come to dinner.*

It's not until later, when she's looking for hamburger in the freezer, that she remembers Phil calling Leo "that boy." She can't picture her dad calling her "that girl." And Phil said Leo probably wouldn't like turkey. Wouldn't a dad know if his own son likes turkey or not?

THE MAN IS doing something to Leo's head. Leo fights him. He feels wet on his head. "I just want to comb your damn hair, now that you have hair to comb!" the man says. He is holding something. Leo recognizes the comb. His dad had a comb. His comb was black. The man's comb is the wrong brown. Leo liked to play with his dad's comb.

"Fine," the man says. "I give up!"

Leo picks up the comb. He runs his fingers on the points. The man says to come. Leo comes with the comb in his hand. He follows the man out the door and down a hall. The man knocks on the door three times. So Leo knocks three times, too.

The door opens. It is the girl who has Cheetos. She is wearing a purple dress that's the right purple. Leo likes looking at the dress. He hears voices. The man is talking to the girl. "Go on in," he tells

Leo. Leo waits. When the girls says, "Leo, come," he follows her into a place that he doesn't know. It smells good.

The couch is the right brown. A man and a woman are sitting on it. Then he sees the rug. It has a lot of colors that are the wrong colors. But it has rows and rows of Vs and Xs. Leo sits down to look. He traces the patterns they make with the comb.

The girl's brown hands are holding something out to him. It is a red fire truck. It makes him think of his sister from before. The gun. The terrible screaming. But then the girl turns it over. It has very large wheels. She spins them with a finger and hands it to Leo. He feels her sit down near him. He spins the wheels, stares into the turning.

19

Before Leo arrived—in case he did—Tessa warned her dad, Marco, and Marco's fiancée, Maureen, that Leo is special. "He's not normal," she explained. "He's, like, special ed." She went down the list. "Don't try to touch him. He hates that. Don't expect him to say anything. He might, but he probably won't. He stares at things a lot, and sometimes he rocks—"

"Tessa," her dad had interrupted. "How do you know all this? I thought you'd only met him a few times."

Tessa blushed. "I know from seeing the other kids like him at school," she said dismissively. "He just seemed like a kid at school in special ed, and so I'm thinking that Leo is the same."

Her father's eyes lingered on her long enough to make her nervous that he didn't believe her. The timer going off in the kitchen for the potatoes saved her.

Ten minutes later, Phil dropped Leo off. Tessa couldn't believe it. She was so worried he might not come.

At first, Leo sat on the floor and traced the patterns in the rug with a comb he brought. "He seems like a sweetie," Maureen offered. Maureen is super short, and her long dark hair has maroon stripes in it. She met Marco when he stopped by while Tony was giving her a tattoo. Tessa likes her because she is talkative. She's like the opposite of shy, and Tessa thinks her dad would call her "sassy."

Then she remembers the gift she has for Leo. It's a toy fire engine with big wheels. At first he acts afraid of it, which is weird. He won't touch it, and Tessa can tell he's getting upset. Quickly, Tessa turns it over and sets the big wheels spinning, because she knows Leo likes that. Finally, Leo takes it and starts spinning the wheels himself.

Tessa chats with Maureen and watches Leo until Marco announces it's time for everyone to come to the table.

"It's time for dinner, Leo," she tells him. When he doesn't respond, she reaches down and gently tugs on the fire engine. "Come here, Leo," she says firmly. "It's time to eat."

To her great relief, he lets the truck go and stands to follow her. She leads him over to the dining table and pulls out a chair. "Sit, Leo," she says. It feels like she is ordering him around like a dog, but she knows it's the only way to get him to do what you want.

Tessa sits down next to Leo, nervous about how this will go. She hopes he'll eat something and not make weird sounds.

Then Marco, who's more religious than her dad, says grace. Instead of closing her eyes all the way, Tessa watches Leo, who is staring at the bowl of peas in a way she knows.

As soon as Marco says "Amen," Tessa asks her dad to pass the peas.

"The peas? You hate peas," her father says.

"I know, but I have a feeling that Leo likes them." She's about to add that he might count them but catches herself. She dishes a good-sized mound onto Leo's plate. He begins to touch them, gently spreading them out. Everyone is watching. "I think it's okay if he uses his fingers," she says.

Marco starts asking for people to pass the food, and it's a relief. She always liked Uncle Marco. Not just because he looks so much like her father, except with short hair, but because he is always joking. Compared to him, her dad seems sad.

Tessa glances at Leo's plate. He's working on putting the peas in a swirl pattern that starts with one pea in the center and goes around in circles outward. "Look at what Leo is making," she says proudly.

"Why, he's a regular Einstein," says Marco, laughing.

"Not so sure I'd put it that way," her father counters.

They all watch to see what will happen when the design is finished, the last pea placed. Leo picks up the pea in the center and pops it in his mouth, quickly following it with the next in line. He doesn't count them. Tessa isn't sure if she's disappointed or glad.

The rest of the meal proceeds pretty normally. The only other thing Leo eats is the ham—three slices, in fact, which is way more than Tessa expected. Of course, he wouldn't eat it until after she had cut it into small pieces.

But now Tessa feels warm and happy. Marco tells jokes. Maureen talks a lot about movies. She goes on and on about *Coal Miner's Daughter.* Her father keeps the food moving, and now and then Tessa sees him quietly watching Leo.

Tessa can't wait for dinner to be over so she can get Leo alone and ask him about Venus.

TINKER DECIDED TO let the boy go for Easter in the hopes he might look like a regular dad. But that doesn't keep him from worrying during his entire shift at the Burger Bar.

He feels like he's taking unnecessary chances. But it also seems like the smart thing to do. Act regular. Let Leo have a friend. When he thinks about what could go wrong, he's grateful in some ways that he kidnapped such a weirdo. A normal kid might still be asking for his mom.

It's not Leo who worries him. It's that girl. She's a smart one, you can tell. She has that same look Venus used to get whenever he went round there, like she knows what you're thinking and she's sure it's bad.

He arrives home at a little after eleven. The apartment looks the same, all tidy like he left it. The girl or her father had promised to bring Leo home by 8:00 P.M. He wishes he'd had a hidden camera hooked up to make sure that no snooping went on. Not that there'd be much to find.

He checks on the boy. Sees the familiar lump and is relieved. He lingers for a moment and then approaches the bed. Leo's holding something in his hand. A red fire truck. The Herreras must have given it to him. He feels a pang of jealousy. There's nothing wrong with the blue car Leo already has.

He watches the boy breathing evenly. He looks different when he's sleeping, more like a normal kid. Tinker wonders if his brother kissed his boy good night. He bets he did, because that's the only time you can ever touch the kid without him acting like you're hurting him. Tinker never thought about stuff like that before. Like what Leo might be missing from not being at home.

Maybe he should kiss the boy good night for his poor dead brother. For a second, he feels embarrassed at the idea. But finally he leans over to Leo's head and his lips quickly brush the blond hair. He smells like Johnson's Baby Shampoo, the only kind Tinker buys, ever since Kimberly told him it might help him not lose more hair.

Then it's over. The boy has no idea. Tinker gently pulls the blankets up a little higher over his bony shoulders. He shuts the door behind him. He knows that in the morning, at around eight, the boy will emerge looking soft and sweet. If Tinker is up early, he'll say "Morning, Leo." And Leo will ignore him.

More likely, though, the boy will get up first. And since the pullout is right next to the card table, Tinker will wake to the sound of a spoon scraping in a bowl. It's something he's come to count on. Snap! Crackle! Pop!

AFTER EASTER, TINKER is more nervous than ever that the Mexican girl is onto him. She keeps asking to visit Leo, and Tinker keeps putting her off. When Tinker goes to the shop to pay for

May's rent, Tony brings up the tattoo. "Hey, you still want that tat you mentioned?"

Tinker is stuck. He doesn't want the tat, but he can't see how to squirm out of it. "You bet," he says with fake enthusiasm.

"What kind of design do you have in mind?" Tony asks. "Maybe Leo? I could do a cool lion image with his name."

"That sounds great," Tinker answers. "I'm kind of busy lately, though, so maybe in a few weeks?"

He wishes he could say *years*. When Tony suggests a day and time in late May, Tinker agrees. It will give him enough time to think of a way to get out of it.

Instead, he finds himself in Tony's shop on the designated day and time. He figures he might as well get it over with. He tells himself he's only a little nervous, but the truth is that he is terrified. He knows that getting a tattoo is no big deal for most dudes. But Tinker hates pain. He hates needles. What if it's so painful he runs crying from the room?

A few days earlier, Tony had knocked on the door and showed him a drawing of a lion's mane with the word *Leo* inside it. Tinker had acted as if he liked it, but what kind of idiot gets a tattoo of the name of the kid he kidnapped? At least it will be hidden on his chest. He can cover it up.

And now the time has come. When Tony directs him to take off his T-shirt, Tinker hesitates. What had he been thinking? He'd wanted to make sure he could hide the tat. But he hadn't thought about having to take off his shirt. The last thing he wants is for anyone to see his jelly belly or his man boobs.

He tries to act like it's no big deal, whipping his shirt off in a flash. But he feels totally naked and can't help crossing his arms over his chest. Tony directs him to lean back on a padded contraption that reminds Tinker of something they'd have in a gym.

He's sitting there shirtless when the daughter comes in and takes a nearby stool. Tinker can't believe it. He waits for Tony to throw her out. Instead, he asks, "Okay if Tessa watches?"

Are you kidding? It's the last thing he wants, but he can also tell Tony isn't really asking. "Fine by me," he says. "Promise you won't tell if I cry?"

But the girl doesn't even laugh. "It happens," she says, serious-like. And then she smirks at her dad.

Tony is swabbing Tinker's chest with something. Cleaning it, probably, which makes sense, he supposes. This is sort of like getting a shot, needles and all. Then Tony applies some kind of cream and Tinker spots a razor on a tray.

"You gotta shave me?"

"Oh yeah," says Tony. "But just this one spot. It'll grow back, don't worry," he says.

Tony explains that the first part of getting the tattoo is the most painful. Then Tony asks about his music preference.

"Got any Van Halen?"

"Sure do. Tessa, you want to put that on?" Tinker sees that the girl doesn't like his choice. Good. Maybe she'll go away.

"Runnin' with the Devil" comes on, but it's not nearly loud enough. When the girl asks about Leo, Tinker's not surprised at all. But why is some girl who's almost a teenager so interested in a kid like Leo?

"Leo's good," says Tinker. "He likes the fire truck you gave him at Easter."

"Great," she says. "It was so fun to have him."

Ha! Tinker resists the urge to snort.

"Do you think I could go up and say hi to him while you're getting the tattoo?"

Tinker stalls. He can't see a way to say no. "Sure, you can pop in for just a few minutes," he says. "But Leo probably needs his nap soon."

"So does Leo have any friends around here?" she asks.

"Not really," he says. "He doesn't like to play with other kids."

The girl falls silent then, but Tinker can tell her mind is loaded and aimed right at him.

"Did Leo ever have siblings? At Easter he mentioned a sister named Venus."

Tinker panics at the mention of Venus. "Venus?" he asks. "Well, that's a strange name. But, no, Leo's mom and I never did have another baby. You can't take what Leo says seriously. As you know, he's not right in the head."

Tinker's thoughts are racing. *How'd she find that out? Little snoop!* Now he's more desperate than ever to get the girl off his back. *Why doesn't her dad make her shut up?* Instead, he seems perfectly fine to have his daughter torment a customer while he gets ready to stick him with a needle gun.

How did Tinker let this happen? What did he ever do?

Finally, the girl hops down from the stool by Tinker's head. "So I'll go check in on Leo," she says. Tinker pulls out his apartment key and hands it to Tessa.

"I'll see you later," she says. "Good luck with the tattoo."

Soon, the pain comes. Tinker shuts his eyes—he can't watch. There's the needle. Maybe more than one needle. He suspects that Tony hates him, so he's probably using the thickest needles he has.

But Tinker doesn't cry. Instead, he gets really angry with himself, because he's almost certain now this nosy Tessa girl is onto him. Why was she asking about Venus? He thinks about how stupid he is. How stupid to take Leo. How stupid to get a tattoo. How stupid to think he could turn his life around. How stupid to think all this could end up any other way than bad.

By the time he stumbles up to his apartment to drink beer and pass out, he knows what he has to do. It's time to get rid of Leo.

PART THREE

★

Seattle, Washington; September 1985– February 1986

20

Somehow, I thought that five and a half years would be enough time to make the damn reporters forget. But I was wrong. I'm standing on a corner at the Seattle Metro bus stop in downtown Issaquah when I spot several reporter types rushing down the sidewalk in my direction. They probably followed the Echo Glen van from the parking lot.

I fight the urge to run—to the tire store across the street, or the grocery on the other corner. Maybe I could lose them out a back door. Or maybe not. I don't want to risk missing the bus I've been waiting to board for years.

So I stand my ground, gripping my suitcase in my left hand, hiding my face in the crook of my right arm, my big hair helping to shield me. The news people gather around me anyway, snapping pictures like birds pecking at the same worm. Shouldn't there be a law against this?

Just then, to my relief, I hear the bus approaching. One of the reporters offers me a ride. The others fire questions without waiting for answers:

"What are your plans, Venus?"

"Do you think your sentence was fair?"

"Why isn't your family here to pick you up?"

"How does it feel to be nineteen and free?"

"Do you know what happened to Leo?"

This last one catches me off guard. I should have known they'd bring up Leo, but it's been a couple of years since I've spoken his name aloud. Everyone at Echo Glen knew better than to bring up the subject of my missing brother.

Finally the bus screeches to a stop in front of me and the doors gasp open. Without turning around, I scramble onto the bottom step. "Quick! Close the doors," I tell the driver. He looks at me strangely.

"Can't you see? They're fucking *reporters*!"

The driver glances over my shoulder, shrugs, and pulls a lever. I hear the doors snap shut behind me.

"Thank you!" I say, finally allowing myself to exhale. I step up to pay, and as I dig in my pocket for the fare, I venture a glance outside. The reporters are casually walking away. Clearly none of them ever planned to board.

Embarrassed, I carry my case down the aisle toward the back, where perhaps there are some passengers who didn't witness my stupid little scene. I stash the case, then slide into an empty row and do my best to slouch from view. Which isn't as easy as it used to be. Despite the shitty food at Echo, I've grown three inches, to a gangly five foot nine.

Inez always said I took after her mother's side—most of them tall.

After a while, I realize I'm suffocating. *Duh*—I have on several T-shirts and tops, plus a sweater. When you leave Echo Glen, they let you raid the charity bin. But since we each get only one suitcase, we pile on the layers. I'm also wearing shorts beneath my high-water jeans.

I peel off the purse strapped across my chest, then the sweater and two other shirts. It still feels weird to carry a purse. After I bought it on a group excursion to Kmart, I had no idea what to put inside. Now it holds a self-help paperback, a "graduation" gift from my counselor, Sharon. There's also a beautiful hand-tooled journal from Diane, the president of Echo Glen. And a few other items, like an Afro hair pick and a cheap wallet I bought to hold the fortune I had made on work release.

Okay, it isn't a fortune, but three hundred dollars looks pretty good in there. I picked a billion damn berries and shoveled a million tons of horseshit to get that rich.

My original transition plan from Echo had me living and working at the YMCA in Seattle, helping out in their after-school program. My worst nightmare, in other words. I might as well have stayed at Echo Glen. All I want is a room of my own. Privacy. And a decent job until I can save enough to buy a car and move to California.

Doug, the guy who ran the transition program, repeatedly emphasized how hard it can be for a felon to get a job straight out of lockup, even if you're a juvenile.

I know he's right, especially since in Washington State, violent crimes like mine stay on your record forever and can never be sealed.

Which means any prospective employers who do any checking will quickly discover the truth about me. Which is exactly why I'm done being me. What Doug doesn't know is that I'm not planning to look for work as Venus Black, the thirteen-year-old girl who got a gun and blah, blah, blah. I'm dumping that girl to begin all over again as Annette Higgman. That's the name on a Washington State driver's license I filched from a girl I met picking berries.

I would have preferred a softer name. A *Sarah* or a *Holly,* maybe. I've noticed that girls with easy, breezy names don't end up at places like Echo Glen. My theory is that if you have a nice name, people are nicer to you, and so you become a nicer person than someone with a hard, mean name like Venus.

At least Annette, with her dark curly hair and noticeable nose, looks like me. Kind of. I don't know how to drive, so I won't be using the license for that. And she's only a year older than me, so I can't use it to drink. But it might come in handy if I need it for a job or a hotel room.

Which is my first assignment, I remind myself. My hands are growing more and more clammy with excitement and nerves as the Metro bus rumbles on and off the highway, making its way toward the city through a seemingly endless number of stops. Finally, we roll across a long bridge and into a tunnel. And after the tunnel, we are suddenly in downtown Seattle.

I watch out the window for the Capitol Hill area of Seattle because a newbie at Echo named Carla told me it would be a good place to find restaurant work. She also suggested I list my last place of employment as the Crab Pot in Renton, since they recently went out of busines. I exit the bus and march up Madison Street, checking out any hotel that doesn't look too much like a flophouse or too nice for a felon.

By now I've put my hair in a big thick braid down my back. Seeing those reporters was a wake-up call. If I don't want to be Venus Black, I better disguise myself a little. It would be smarter to just hack off my hair and dye it blond, but I can't bring myself to even consider that. Apart from an occasional trim, I haven't cut my hair since the night of my failed escape from Denney.

Every time I think of going short, I remember the look on the fireman's face when I asked him, sobbing, "Will you at least please cut it straight?" I think he really tried. And ever since, I've had this silly fantasy that someday I'd go find him and thank him for being kind—and if my hair was short, it would kind of ruin the moment. Or maybe it's just a point of pride. Either way, the braid is my best option.

After exhausting myself checking hotel prices, I settle for the only-partly disgusting St. James Hotel. At the registration desk, a guy smoking a pipe asks for my ID. *Thank you, Annette Higgman.* And just as I suspect he'll do, he barely glances at it. Or maybe through the cloud of smoke he can't read that I'm supposed to be three inches shorter with brown eyes.

I have a theory about photographs. If you have a prominent nose, no one notices anything else.

My room is on the third floor, and so naturally the elevator says it's broken. It probably hasn't worked in years. The carpet on the wide stairs is dirty and worn, and at my door, it takes a while to get the key to work. Clearly, the room was a steal because it is a dump. I gaze at the crummy floral bedspread, the cracked, filthy window, and the old-fashioned steam radiator like the ones we had on Rockefeller—and I feel ridiculously happy. Because it's *my* room. All mine.

For a second, I think I might burst into tears of joy, which scares the impulse right out of me. After not being able to cry for so long, I'm afraid that if I ever do, my tears will take me back to places and memories I never want to visit again. At this point, years of counseling have put way too many holes in that sheet I used to wear.

I am bummed to notice there isn't a TV. The phone on the side table is accompanied by a card warning of charges for local calls. Seriously? I shouldn't care, since I have no one to call, but nevertheless I feel an overwhelming urge to phone a friend and shout: "I'm free! I'm out! It's over!"

I sprawl on the bed to think about my plan. I have the numbers of a couple of friends who got released from Echo Glen about a year ago. I really liked one of them, Carmen. But calling her up right now would make me feel like I was going backward. Like I'm still Venus Black.

Of course, I know the number of the house on Rockefeller, but I can't imagine Inez is still living there. Not that I would call her, anyway. I haven't seen my mother since a few years ago, when I finally agreed to do some counseling with her. She tried to convince me how sorry she was for dismissing and ridiculing my suspicions about Ray. For a second there, I almost believed her. But then the next time I saw her she asked if she could sell the rights to our story to some woman named Anna Weir in California. "She's a great writer and she promises to be fair. If Anna's book did well, maybe there'd be a movie. . . ."

I haven't spoken to her since. She and Anna Weir can go . . . well, you know.

I didn't exactly keep in touch with old friends, either. Jackie wrote me once during the first year. Her handwriting—curvy and round like cartoon words—looked the same as when we passed notes in junior high. She apologized that her mother wouldn't let her talk to me or visit me at Denney or Echo Glen. She wrote about the latest gossip, like who made out with whom at a dance. What teachers she got for winter semester.

I never wrote her back. But once in a while I would pull out her letter and read it again, marveling that I used to live in that world, that I was once a girl like her.

Most of the time, I worked hard not to think about the life I almost had. Like whom I might have dated. How popular I might have been. On my sixteenth birthday, though, I couldn't help wondering what it would have felt like to get a driver's license, celebrate with friends at 31 Flavors, and finally get to cruise Colby Avenue.

Now, though, my having such a life or doing such normal schoolgirl things seems so far-fetched it strikes me as absurd.

After using the rusty hotel bathroom down the hall, I unpack my small suitcase into an old wooden dresser. That takes about one minute. Now what? I'm anxious to look for work, but it's only 2:00 P.M., and Carla said the best time to check at restaurants is between 4:00 and 6:00 P.M.

I wish I could take a nap, but I'm way too wound up. I could read the paperback I got from my counselor. *You Can Heal Your Life*. Sharon knows I think such books are full of shit and have nothing to do with my life. But I flip through a few pages to make sure it's the same old easy solutions and sentimental crap I hate. Sure enough, my eyes immediately fall on a page, some of which is in all caps:

When we really love and accept and APPROVE OF OUR-
SELVES EXACTLY AS WE ARE, then everything in life
works. It's as if little miracles are everywhere.

Seriously? I imagine little miracles like butterflies floating
around my head as I trip along through my easy life where everything works, all because I love myself. Then my eye falls on another sentence on the same page:

The very person you find it hardest to forgive is the one YOU
NEED TO LET GO OF THE MOST.

Oh, really? I'm tempted to throw the book across the room, but
I don't. Partly because it was a gift from Sharon, and partly because it's still my fondest secret hope that someday I'll become the
kind of person who can believe this shit and make it work for me.

I'm way too restless to read, anyway. It almost feels like I'm
waiting for something huge to happen—but supposedly it already
has. I got released from Echo Glen. So why does it feel like my
happy balloon got popped seconds after it was full?

I'm already at loose ends and I've only been free less than three
hours. I could go to eat somewhere. But earlier at my going-away
party, I ate a bunch of cake along with lunch, so I'm not at all
hungry.

I set the book aside and get up and try to open the one window,
but it has been painted shut. I finger the crumbling windowpane
and look out at the sunny afternoon, trying to recapture the wave
of joy I felt earlier. But all I feel is empty, which I just can't understand. I gaze down at the heads of people on the street directly
below me. I can't see their faces, but I can tell by the purposeful
way they walk that they know where they're going. They have
things to do and people to see.

Eventually, it dawns on me, the reason I feel this way. The transition program at Echo Glen taught me all kinds of practical life

skills for when I was free. Like how to type. How to keep a check-book. How to cook a roast. But clearly they forgot to teach me the most important thing, which is how to get a life in the first place.

AFTER A WHILE, I realize that I do have somewhere to go. I need dress clothes—especially if I am going to look nice for what Doug called "job-seeking." I can't remember the last time I wore a dress.

By the time I locate the nearest Goodwill in the phone book and trek there on foot, I'm sweaty and irritable. Inside, it smells musty, like stale perfume and old ladies. The clothes are organized by color. I start in the purple to magenta section. One of the first dresses I find that fits me is a high-collared belted dress of scratchy fabric. Once I have it on, I realize it's reminiscent of one Inez used to wear.

Wouldn't it be funny if I bought a dress my mother donated?

I have more luck in the blue section, where I find a plain navy Brass Plum shift dress in a size 6. It's sleeveless with a scoop neck, and the material is light enough for the warm weather. When I try it on, it's a little short—because my legs are a little long. I also real-ize that I will need to buy a razor. There wasn't a reason to shave much at Echo Glen. But Annette Higgman is going to be the type who probably shaves almost every day. And uses skin lotion, too.

In order for the dress not to be too short, I need some dressy but flat shoes. The selection in my large size is dismal, but I finally settle on a pair of black patent-leather sandals that are a little tight but will go with a lot.

Obviously, I should look for a restaurant that provides uni-forms—or I'll go broke buying clothes.

By the time I get back to my hotel room to change, it's past time to hit the streets. As I walk down Broadway, I pass a couple of taverns—but the dark windows and seedy atmosphere keep me away. And the men. I know I don't want to work around a bunch of beer-bellied, leering men.

At Echo, I endured a lot of unwanted male attention. I got so sick of the ogling, the comments, the jokes about my body. Granted, I didn't have to share a room with the boys, but I had to attend school with them. Eat with them. I got so tired of glaring that my eyeballs ached.

Eventually I come to a Mexican restaurant and go in the front door. A Mexican woman at the hostess stand asks, *"Uno?"* A quick glance around the restaurant confirms the servers are all dark-skinned. I turn around and walk back out, my face flushed with embarrassment.

In the next hour, I visit an all-night diner, a loud steak house, a fancy restaurant with a French name, and a casual Italian restaurant with blue-checked tablecloths. No one is hiring, but the steak house allows me to fill out an application.

Under "job history," I'm tempted to list my kitchen duty and extensive experience with an industrial-sized dishwasher at Echo, but I'm pretty sure that wouldn't impress anybody. So I take Carla's advice and list the restaurant in Renton, claiming to have worked there as a busser for six months.

When I answer the question about felonies, I put "None." Where it asks about schooling, I find myself stuck again. While at Echo, I graduated high school with straight A's and then went on to complete enough credits for almost a year of college. But I wasn't about to list Echo Glen High School. I realize I should have figured out in advance where Annette Higgman went to high school. Based on the address, I take a stab and list Snohomish High.

Answering this question is painful because it reminds me of everything that stands in the way of my fondest dream. I desperately want to go to college and study science and astronomy, but even with financial aid, I couldn't afford it. And even if I could, since my GED and other transcripts are under the name of Venus Black, I'd have to go as myself, which I'm not about to do.

I turn in the application, feeling deflated. After getting turned down at a few more places, I can feel a terrible blister forming on my heel from the Goodwill dress shoes. On the way back to the hotel, several men whistle or make comments. I flip each one off—until one of them starts to follow me, saying, "Yes! I will fuck you!"

After that, I realize the best way to handle this kind of thing is to look strong and unafraid and just keep walking. This is what I learn on my first night of freedom and the first day of my life as Annette Higgman: Men on the outside can be just as disgusting as boys on the inside.

21

The next morning, I wake up amazed. I stretch out my arms and legs like a snow angel and roll all around the enormous queen-sized bed, making happy groaning sounds. Even though this bed is lumpy and old, it feels pretty wonderful after sleeping on a hard, narrow single for more than five years.

As I lie there, I still can't believe I'm *never* going to wake up at Echo Glen again. I'm never going to hear morning call, never going to file into the pistachio-green cafeteria for runny eggs and soggy toast. Never going to tromp through the rain to morning classes.

Not that Echo Glen was near as bad as I anticipated. Most of the time it didn't feel like a prison but more like a super-strict boarding school stripped of frills and fun. We were treated like students, stayed in cottages, six to a building—separated by gender, of course. We all wore regular clothes, most of them donated.

Despite my bitterness at being there, I liked most of the staff, as well as the teachers. There was a lot of turnover among the employees, but thankfully it was usually the mean ones who didn't last long.

At first, I couldn't believe it when I found myself doing the same old thing—excelling academically, trying to impress my teachers, and making sure most people liked me. Sharon told me once that she thought I needed adult approval I never got at home.

But I disagreed. I never cared about getting Inez's approval, and it was the last thing I wanted from Raymond. I think I got on well with teachers and staff because when you live with mini-criminals, it only makes sense to be friendly and cooperate with the few people not in that category.

It felt weird last night to walk around not knowing who is good or bad, kind or dangerous. Twice I was pretty sure that people did double takes or looked at me funny. Not necessarily because they recognized me, but perhaps because I was so conspicuously alone. How come being all by myself felt somehow weird or wrong, like something to be ashamed of?

Oh yeah. *Shame.* Why am I lying here in bed when there is potentially so much more shame to be had?

I jump out of bed and throw on some clothes before I race downstairs. There's a newsstand just outside the hotel—the morning paper, the *Post-Intelligencer.* As I insert my quarter, I note with some relief that I'm not on the cover.

This probably means I won't be front-page news when *The Seattle Times* comes out later this afternoon, either. I'm sure Everett's *Herald* will put me front and center, though. One of their reporters has asked me so many times over the years for an interview; she was probably there at the bus stop yesterday.

I decide not to look at the paper on the street. I go back to my room, grab my purse, and walk to a bakery I noticed yesterday when I got off the bus. It stood out because of the name, the Big Dipper. Even though the logo is a doughnut being dipped in coffee, naturally my mind went to the constellation.

The place is kind of funky inside, with bright-orange walls and turquoise upholstered booths. They have a large selection of baked goods in a glass case, but there's also a small breakfast and lunch menu.

I order an omelet—unheard of at Echo, by the way. And then I can't resist adding a bear claw, along with coffee and cream.

After I pay, the girl at the counter hands me a number on a

stick. I take it, but my confusion must show. "We bring it to you when it's ready," she explains. She has long blond lashes and no mascara.

"Oh!" I say, feeling so dumb. Before Echo, most of my eating out happened at Herfy's or McDonald's. I take my number 23 to a corner booth and sit on the side facing the wall. Then I wonder if I'm making myself even more obvious by trying not to be.

I remind myself that I need to act like a normal person, not someone in hiding. Then again, normal people aren't reading the morning paper to make sure they're not in it. Taking a deep, nervous breath, I open the front page and quickly scan the spread. Nothing. I keep turning pages until I get to the "Local News" section, and there I am: RELEASE OF TEENAGE KILLER REIGNITES CONTROVERSY.

Shit.

Under the headline there's a picture of me standing at the bus stop in Issaquah yesterday before I spotted the reporters and before I got my hair in a braid. It's a full-body shot, showing off my high-water jeans, which makes me cringe. Next to that picture is the original mug shot from my arrest at thirteen.

I look surprisingly the same in both pictures, except in this new one, my hair—by far my most prominent feature—is blowing in the wind, so I look even more . . . scary? That's how it hits me. I look like a tall, skinny, scary person.

The other thing that jumps out is the thickness of my eyebrows, which seem to take up half my face. I make a mental note to buy some tweezers. I've never plucked my eyebrows in my life, and now I realize that doing so might do a lot to change the way my face looks.

Out of nowhere, a waitress is at my table, and I quickly slap the newspaper shut. She sets my food down, and I notice it's the same girl who took my order. Her name tag says JULIE. She seems in a hurry, so maybe she didn't notice my overreaction.

Once she's gone, I dig into the omelet, which tastes amazing. I scan the *P-I* story, which holds no surprises. There's mention of Leo and the mystery surrounding his disappearance. As usual, there's an inference that I was somehow involved, because of the timing, so close to my crime. Otherwise, it's mainly an overview of the controversies my case stirred up at the time. A lot of folks got upset when the prosecutor tried to have my case moved to adult court. They accused him of grandstanding for the media, and they shared Betty's contention that I was way too young to be tried outside the juvenile system.

While the judge kept my case in juvenile court, I was still convicted of murder one because my crime was determined to be premeditated. But rather than receiving the maximum sentence—thanks to Betty and all the mitigating circumstances—I got five and a half years when I could have been locked up till I was twenty-one. Some folks in the legal world questioned the legitimacy of the mitigating factors in my case. A small but vocal camp insisted that I should serve more-serious time. They worried if I wasn't punished severely, it would send the wrong message to other kids: *If your parents piss you off enough, it's okay to kill them.*

I'm guessing a number of asshole stepdads were shaking in their J. C. Penney slippers.

Others wrote editorials in the opposite direction, and a bunch of women's-rights types practically made me their hero. They used my story to raise awareness—outraged that what Raymond did wasn't technically a crime at the time.

But did anyone ever consider that *I* might not want more attention brought to my case?

Of course, I didn't know about most of this until much later, when my counselor, Sharon, told me about it. She reassured me that justice had been done, and she emphasized over and over that I shouldn't feel guilt about what Raymond had done to me. What I never heard her say once, though, is that I shouldn't feel guilt about what *I* did to *him.*

Which, of course, I did. Even as I raged against him, I was horrified that I had killed a man. Even at my young age, I knew Raymond deserved to be punished but he didn't deserve to die. To her credit, Sharon helped me see that I could take responsibility for killing Raymond—without letting Inez off the hook for her part. And I could admit the enormous guilt I felt—without wishing Raymond were still alive.

Taking a bite of my bear claw, I look for the section with the funnies, and my eyes slip over to the horoscopes. I don't actually believe in astrology, but I always read it, anyway. The one for Pisces says "your career will take a positive turn today." Great news if I had a career.

My eyes drop down to the entry for Leo—and guess what? If he's alive somewhere, "a financial venture may prove lucrative." Why do I bother reading these things?

When I first arrived at Echo Glen, all I could talk about was Leo and what could have happened to him. I clung to the hope that he was still alive and badgered the staff for news. I even begged random people like the maintenance man to make the police do their job and find him.

At night, I'd lay awake, imagining all kinds of dark scenarios—scenarios that seemed increasingly possible now that I went to school with a good number of young pervs and violent offenders. Once I finally got to sleep, I'd have nightmares where Leo was in great danger and pain and begging me to rescue him but I couldn't because I was locked up.

It was a bad dream that always came true.

I thought I was going to die of missing Leo and wondering about him, until one day something clicked. I remembered the epiphany I had back at Denney about doing time and how being anxious for it to pass is how they punish you. And everyone knows nothing makes time drag more slowly than hoping and waiting for something.

That meant if I wanted to survive my sentence with my sanity intact, I couldn't afford to keep hoping for Leo. But hope is hard to kill, so the best I could do was *pretend* to give up on Leo so other people would shut up about him.

In the meantime, I never really bought the idea that Raymond's brother took him, which was one of the early theories the police went on. They named Tinker a person of interest, partly because he was an ex-con—he'd done time in Monroe for burglary—and because he seemed to have left the Everett area shortly after Leo disappeared.

But what would a guy like Tinker want with Leo? The idea that Tinker might be a pedophile or want to sell Leo to one—it's possible, but it just felt wrong. The few times I met him—he and Raymond never got along, so he wasn't around much—he struck me as kind of an idiot, not evil. Plus, he had showed zero interest in Leo.

While I couldn't bear to keep hope alive for Leo's safe return, Inez dealt with losing him in the opposite way. She kept badgering the press all the time to do follow-up stories—at least that's what Sharon told me. Come to think of it, Inez is probably to blame for the fact that there's even a story about *me* in the paper today. She's been so determined to keep Leo's story alive, she's kept mine alive, too.

The realization is like an unexpected gift—something new I can blame on Inez.

Done eating, I force myself to turn to the "Help Wanted" section. Why didn't I start here last night? I find postings for a lot of dishwashers, cooks, and bussers. The one that pops out is a hostess job at what sounds like a fancy seafood place. I like the idea of being a hostess. But then I think about the hostesses I met last night, and I realize they were all beautiful, bubbly types who were practically jubilant to see you.

The opposite of me, in other words. Plus, greeting every single customer would only raise my odds of getting recognized.

"Ma'am?" It's Julie the waitress again, and she's holding a coffeepot. "Can I give you a refill?"

"Sure," I say, trying to seem relaxed this time. It feels so strange to be waited on like this. It's also weird just to be allowed to have a second cup of coffee. At Echo we couldn't drink coffee until we were sixteen, and then we were allowed only one cup—but you can see why, since most of those kids needed to calm down, not rev up.

While Julie fills my cup, I look at her face, knowing that will lessen the likelihood of her looking at mine. She seems about my age, slightly plump, with feathered strawberry-blond hair and long bangs.

After she's gone, I realize I've probably been sitting here too long. I glance around and see that all the other booths and tables are taken. I guiltily gulp the coffee as quickly as I can and then head for the exit, located by the crowded order counter.

I have to say, "Excuse me," several times in order to squeeze past people in line. When they glance at me, I'm newly conscious of my never-before-plucked eyebrows, which all of a sudden feel like enormous hairy caterpillars plastered on my forehead, screaming, *It's me! Venus Black, that girl you saw in the paper!*

I'm so worried about being recognized, I almost miss the small sign on the door as I close it behind me: HELP WANTED.

Hilarious. I think my career just took a positive turn. And maybe Leo is somewhere getting rich.

22

Turns out Julie put up the HELP WANTED sign just this morning when another employee failed to show and called in fake sick for the umpteenth time. When I tell her I'm looking for work, she immediately says, "You're hired!" Next thing I know I'm wearing a turquoise Big Dipper apron.

The next four hours pass in a blur. I simply do whatever Julie tells me to, learning to use the till during breaks in the action.

Later, Julie asks me to fill out an application. "Not that you're not hired," she says. "But my mom, June, is the one who owns the shop, and she'll want that."

I put down my new address and name—hoping they won't recognize that the address is actually a hotel. I put the Crab Pot down as a reference, even though it doesn't appear I need one. But who knows what Julie's mom will think of her daughter hiring me on the spot like this. When it comes to my Social Security number, I go ahead and make one up. My guess is it won't get noticed until Julie's mom does her taxes next spring. I can only hope that by the time the IRS finally catches it, I'll have saved enough to move to California.

After a few days, I have learned the ropes and been assigned a schedule. I'll work Tuesday through Saturday from 5:30 A.M. to 2:00 P.M. Inwardly, I gasp at the early start time. But it's a full-time job—with a tip jar we split. Maybe once I get a real apartment or room somewhere, my life will start to feel like a life.

After a couple weeks at the Big Dipper, I already know at least ten regulars by name. The place is a constant swirl of activity. A whole world unto itself—and I feel grateful to work there. But I still feel like I'm on the outside somehow, perhaps because I am so reluctant to be friendly or talk to folks. I feel like a marble rolling around a Chinese checker game that can't find an empty hole to slip into.

Eventually, Julie invites me to hang out with her and her friends. But after giving it a couple of tries, I just can't get comfortable and I resist further invitations. It's hard to have fun when you constantly have to lie. Plus, even though Julie is twenty and most of her friends are probably older than me, they seem so immature.

It's like I came out of Echo Glen knowing both too much and too little to come off as anything but *weird*. I feel like a tall, scary person people don't want to get to know. But inside I feel as insecure as a ten-year-old who lost track of her mother in the big city.

I quickly fall into the habit of being alone a lot. I'm desperate for books, so even though it feels risky, I get myself a Seattle Public Library card for "Annette." As usual, I stick to old-time comforting novels like *Gone with the Wind* and *A Girl of the Limberlost*. Or else interesting biographies of amazing women of science like Marie Curie. When I'm not reading, I go walking. It turns out that Seattle is good for that, and it's fascinating to me. I learn to navigate buses and go all over—even visiting the park at the Space Needle.

By early October, I've settled in at the St. James quite nicely. I am loath to leave. But I also know my money is going to run out if I don't find a cheaper room. On the second Saturday in October, I vow to look for and find a place.

After work, I take the *P-I* and a map of Seattle over to Volunteer Park, where I can sit on a bench while I look at the rental listings. After ruling out a bunch of apartments and rooms that I either can't afford or are too far away from the Dipper . . . I end up with only two options—both single rooms inside other people's houses.

Things are so expensive! Both of the rooms list for one hundred fifty dollars a month. I consult my map and decide to check out the closest house first. As I walk away from the hubbub of the city, things get more residential and there are some really nice houses. But when I get into the right neighborhood, things get junkier. Up ahead, I notice a ghastly lavender house with pink trim. *Let it not be that one,* I plead.

But of course it is. As I walk by, I try not to be obvious about glancing into the windows through the thin curtains. It's dark inside, and I can't see anything. I notice the cement driveway is crumbled and uneven. It appears no one is home, but a pink bicycle has been tossed against the small front porch.

I pass similar but less ugly houses before reaching the end of the block, where I cross the street and turn around so I can pass the lavender house again on the way back. This time, a little girl appears on the front steps of the porch. She looks to be maybe nine or ten. "Take a picture, it'll last longer!" she shouts at me.

I'm so surprised, it takes me a second to realize her mean remark is aimed at me. Inexplicably, it hurts my feelings. I ignore her, stare straight ahead, and walk faster. I've put the incident behind me when, a block or so later, I hear a noise at my back and turn to find the girl on her bike. I stop and step aside, giving her plenty of room to pass on the sidewalk.

But she stops instead. "Where you going?" she asks. She is missing a front tooth and chewing a large wad of blue gum.

"I'm just walking," I tell her. I wave my hand again for her to pass, but she doesn't budge. In the bike basket is a blond baby doll whose hair has been dyed purple.

"No, you go ahead," she says. I can smell her gum in the air and it reminds me of Jackie, who often chewed Bubblicious. I was a Bazooka girl all the way—partly because each piece came with a comic.

I take the girl at her word and start walking again, way faster than I was before. I can hear her pedaling right behind me. If I were to stop or slow down, she'd ride right up my ankles. Once again, I step aside and motion for her to pass. When she stops, too, I ask, "Do you mind?"

"You don't own this sidewalk, lady," she says.

"And neither do you. How about if you leave me alone? Maybe you should go home."

"You're not the boss of me," she says.

What a brat! "You're right," I tell her. "So go home to whoever is the boss of you and quit following me." I decide to cross to the other side of the street, but the girl sticks to me like gum.

"It's rude to ignore people, you know."

I can't believe it. Is this how little kids who aren't locked up act these days? I suddenly whirl around, hoping to scare her. "What is your name!" I practically shout.

She stops her bike just shy of my knee. She's startled, for sure. The chewing stops. "Why do you want to know?" she asks in a noticeably smaller voice.

"Because maybe your mother should know what you're doing. Following a stranger down the road."

"I don't have a mother," she says, her attitude back. "So you can't tell her because she doesn't exist." I notice her hair is a little greasy, her brown bangs unevenly cut.

"How old are you?"

"I'm nine," she says proudly.

"Do you want to quit following me?"

"No," she says, looking into my face. "I don't have anything else to do. I'm bored."

Her honest answer softens me despite myself, because I relate to bored and alone. "What's your doll's name?"

"Smelly Shelly," she says. "I don't really like her, though. I'm way too big for dolls." She picks up the doll by its purple hair and smacks it in the belly.

"Really?" I ask. "You like to hit your dolls?" I can see Echo Glen in her future.

She shrugs and looks away.

"I'm done talking now," I announce. "Do. Not. Follow. Me."

I walk on, and I can feel that she's finally stopped following. After a half block or so, I glance back to make sure. She's sitting on her bike where I left her. "You looked!" she screams, laughing. "Lookers are hookers!"

I turn around quickly to hide my smile and keep walking. At least I know where I'm *not* renting a room.

INSTEAD OF RETURNING to the hotel, I go straight to the nearest phone booth to call about the other room. I'm worried I've missed my chance while wasting time on the lavender house with the horrible girl.

I reach a woman named Josie, who tells me the room is still available and I should come right over. When I find the house, it's a really nice Victorian painted a soft yellow—and no bratty kids in sight. Josie greets me at the door before I can even knock. She looks maybe forty and is wearing a cool bohemian dress—elegant, not hippie-ish.

The house is immaculate and airy. The room I would rent is even better than I had hoped for. It has a dormer with slanted ceilings; the walls and old-fashioned furniture are all painted a bright clean white. The double bed, covered by a quilt of yellow flowers and blue diamonds, makes me want to lie on it and reread *Jane Eyre*.

I want the room so badly I can hardly breathe.

The interview with Josie seems to go well. I eagerly tell her about my job at the Dipper and that I recently moved here from Portland. I explain that I have the first month's rent and the fifty-dollar security deposit. I think I sound smart and responsible, and I can tell she does, too.

Then she ruins everything. "Do you have references?" she asks.

"References?" Just to rent a stupid room?

I must have a blank look on my face, because she tries to help me out. "I would just need the phone number of your previous landlord," she says. "Or were you living at home? I could always talk to your parents."

"Oh no. There was a landlord," I say quickly, sounding even to myself like an over-eager liar.

But Josie doesn't seem to see through my act. I can tell she likes me and wants to give me this room. I imagine she's thinking how *swimmingly* we'd get along—and she is exactly the kind of woman who would use that word.

And if I lived here in that room, I feel sure I could become that kind of woman, too.

I beam at her, promising to call her later with my landlord's number. "I just have to check my address book," I say.

But of course I don't have one to check, and I'll never see Josie or that room again.

ON SUNDAY, I check the paper for new listings, but there's nothing. Reluctantly, I call the owner of the house with the horrible girl. The guy's name is Mike, and he confirms the room is still available, which I'd been half-hoping it wouldn't be.

He asks about my situation, what I'm looking for, and how soon I could move in. He sounds super friendly, like he's been waiting his whole life for me to call.

I should have known there was a catch. When he asks what hours I usually work, it seems like he is getting too personal. I'm about to object when he finally admits why it matters: He is looking for a renter who could also watch his niece for a couple of hours after school.

"You mean you want me to *babysit*?"

"Well, I wouldn't call it that. It's really just someone to kind of be around until I get home from work. We're talking a couple hours a day."

"Oh man. I'm sorry. But I can't do that," I say automatically.

"When do you get off work?" he asks. I can't believe the gall of this guy.

"I work until two. But that doesn't mean—"

"That will be perfect!" he says. "My niece doesn't get home from school until around three."

I don't respond, and for a second he's quiet, too. "Okay, Annette. Here's the deal. If I meet you and think you're responsible enough, I'd cut the rent in half because of the babysitting."

In *half*? That would make a huge difference in how fast I could save up to buy a car and move away.

"Would you need a reference?"

"I guess not," he says, hesitating only briefly. "I would just need to meet you."

A few hours later, I'm knocking on the door of the lavender house. When no one answers, I clang the knocker as hard as I can. Someone is home—I can hear cartoons coming from inside.

Finally, the familiar little girl opens the door and sticks her head out.

"Is Mike home?" I ask.

She shakes her head. "Why do you want to know?" She sounds wary, the bravado of yesterday nowhere in sight.

"Didn't he tell you I was coming? I'm here to see your room for rent."

"Oh!" she says, clearly relieved. I realize then that she'd actually thought I'd come back to her house to tattle on her. Too funny.

She opens the door all the way. "You can come in. Mike is at the store."

I hesitate, annoyed that this Mike guy isn't here. He'd made it sound like he'd be around all afternoon.

"It's okay," she encourages. "C'mon! I'll show you." She has a spattering of freckles across her face and a spot of dried milk on the corner of her lip.

I step inside and shut the door. "This is the living room," she says uncertainly, waving her arms like a game-show lady. She is wearing dirty white Keds sneakers, a wrinkled polka-dot T-shirt, and grass-stained jeans.

I gaze around the living room. Wood floors, worn throw rugs, and cheap but usable furniture. A large TV is blaring Tweety Bird, the volume painfully loud.

"Can we turn that down?" I ask.

She stomps dramatically to the TV and shuts it off. "There. Are you happy now?"

I take a deep breath and exhale. What a total brat. I'm tempted to leave, but I know from dealing with younger kids at Echo Glen that you can't tell how a kid really is until you try to be nice to them at the same time as they're being mean to you.

"Do you want to tell me your name now?" I ask, my tone friendly.

"Piper Porter."

"Piper?" I ask, not sure I'm hearing right, since I've never heard of such a name.

"Yes," she says defensively. "Piper. *P-I-P-E-R.* You got a problem with my name?"

"Of course not," I tell her. "I think it's a nice name. It goes well with your last name." I extend my hand, and she reaches out shyly to shake it. "I'm Annette. Annette Higgman," I add. "Do you want to show me your bedroom?"

She giggles. "Sounds like Pig Man," she says.

"Yeah, I got teased a lot in school," I tell her, realizing that poor Annette probably did get teased.

She abruptly turns away and scrambles up the uncarpeted wooden stairs. "C'mon!" she calls. "The room is up here." At the landing, we turn in to the first door on the left. "This is my room," she announces. I watch her gaze around, as if seeing her own bedroom for the first time.

It's a small plain room. There're an unmade single bed and a small white dresser with a few scruffy stuffed animals on top. I note a cracked window and a torn screen. The doll with the dyed hair is lying on the bed, and the floor is littered with clothes and toys.

"What a nice room," I say. "Do you like it?"

"It's okay," she says.

I decide to risk her wrath and sit on the edge of the bed without asking. "So what do you like to play?"

"I don't know," she says, looking around as if the answer might be in view. I pick up Smelly Shelly and absently stroke the doll's purple hair. "What happened here?"

"Kool-Aid," she says with a smirk giving way to a giggle.

"Grape?" I ask with a smile, and she nods and smiles back. She has the greenest eyes—like a cat's. If you fixed the gap in her teeth and cut her crooked bangs, she could be kind of cute.

"Let me show you the rest," Piper says. I get up from the bed and follow her to the next room, on the right. "This is where Mike and Jackson sleep. I'm not allowed to go in. So you're probably not, either. But Jackson is leaving, I think. They had a big fight."

"That's fine," I assure her. Uncle Mike must be gay. As far as I'm concerned, this is a good thing, since it means he for sure won't be hitting on me. The door is cracked open about three inches, and I catch a glimpse of a large unmade water bed with a mirrored headboard. There's a faint scent of incense or cologne.

Next up is the bathroom. Piper flips on a light, but it would have been better had she not.

I doubt I'll be luxuriating in bubble baths.

"There's one other room," says Piper. "This is the one for sale."

"You mean for rent."

"Okay," she says with a huff. "For rent." She opens the door to a small room filled with junk. Amid the piles of dusty odds and ends, I notice an ironing board, a skateboard, and box after box of albums. The bed is a single with no headboard, and the mattress looks worn, but at least it's not pee-stained.

The room doesn't have a window. Seriously, it's everything I never wanted in a room.

I can feel Piper studying my face. "This is great," I lie. "Once it gets cleaned out."

"I can clean it!" Piper declares, clearly motivated. "I can help Mike or Jackson do it."

"That's great, Piper," I agree, not meeting her eyes. "*If* I take the room, I'm sure we can spiff it up in no time."

"I can tell you don't like it," she says accusingly.

"I like it just fine," I lie again.

I head back downstairs, Piper at my heels. "But, wait!" she says with excitement. "I didn't show you the kitchen." As if it will make all the difference. I follow her through an old-fashioned alcove, past a small dining-room table covered in clutter, and into the small kitchen. The linoleum floor is cracked but clean; the cupboards are metal and half of them are open.

Piper must suddenly see the kitchen with fresh eyes. "Well, I guess it's a little messy and stuff," she blurts out.

"But I love the chairs!" I exclaim. The chairs at the kitchen table have chrome legs and red vinyl seats that sparkle. They're fun in a fifties retro kind of way.

Piper looks at the chairs uncertainly.

"And look at that. You have so much light in here." It's true. Big windows above the sink and a sliding glass door that leads outside let in a lot of sunshine.

"I'm sorry I called you a hooker," Piper says. In this light, her eyes are a muddy green. I think of alligators.

"You didn't think you'd ever see me again, did you?"

She shakes her head and puts her finger in the gap where her front tooth is missing. It hits me then that it had to be an adult tooth that got knocked out, because she's too old for it to have been a baby tooth.

"Let's just pretend today is the first time we ever met," I suggest.

"Okay," she agrees.

By now I worry I've gotten her hopes up too much. I don't really want this room and I don't want to be her babysitter. I wonder if she even realizes that's part of the deal. At least a few hours of every day, I would be "the boss of her."

From the kitchen I head back to the living room. "Tell your uncle Mike that Ve—*Annette* came by. I'll call him about the room."

"Okay," she says. "Are you walking?"

"Yes."

"Don't you have a car?"

"No." I can tell she's disappointed.

"How do you go places?"

"Sometimes I might take the bus. But mostly I walk."

"Oh," she says, chewing the thumbnail on her right hand.

"So, maybe I'll see you sometime soon," I say, moving toward the door. "Thank you for showing me the house."

I'm already stepping onto the porch when Piper says to my back, "You're not even going to come live here, are you? You are just acting like you are."

Mother of God, I wish she were right.

BACK AT THE St. James, I lie on my bed for a while with a wet washcloth over my face. I had no idea it would be so hard to find a reasonably priced room near the Big Dipper. And I'm not about to quit that job and have to look for another.

Times like this, I almost miss Echo Glen. Not the place itself, but the way everything was already figured out for you. You might not like the plan for the day, but at least you didn't have to make one up and then make everything happen all by yourself. Your meals, housing, and even a few pseudo friends came as part of the deal.

After a while, I throw the washcloth on the floor and grab the journal from Diane off the nightstand. When I open it, I realize I forgot to read the card tucked in the pages. It says:

Dear Venus,

I came across this little story, which has been adapted from Loren Eiseley's Star Thrower. I thought of how you are being "tossed" back into the outside world for a second chance at life. I believe you will experience the "welcoming sea." I hope all of us here at Echo have been star throwers for you.

Rooting for you,
Diane Tamworth

Once, on ancient Earth, there was a human boy walking along a beach. There had just been a storm, and starfish had been scattered along the sands. The boy knew the fish would die, so he began to fling the fish to the sea. But every time he threw a starfish, another would wash ashore.

An old Earth man happened along and saw what the child was doing. He called out, "Boy, what are you doing?"

"Saving the starfish!" replied the boy.

"But your attempts are useless, child! Every time you save one, another one returns, often the same one! You can't save them all, so why bother trying? Why does it matter, anyway?" called the old man.

The boy thought about this for a while, a starfish in his hand; he answered, "Well, it matters to this one." And then he flung the starfish into the welcoming sea.

The story affects me in the weirdest way. I think I relate so much to the poor starfish, flung onto a hostile landscape it can't possibly survive. I wonder about its underside, that tender, pink, and fleshy part that had always found safety in darkness—now suddenly exposed to air and light. I feel the terror and shock of that.

I continue to think about the starfish while I use the bathroom down the hall. I don't have a mirror in my room, so I use the chipped one on the medicine cabinet. By now the red puffiness of my newly plucked eyebrows has healed and smoothed—just in time for tiny caterpillar follicles to start to grow back. Shit.

I wash my hands, and then for some reason I catch my own eye in the mirror. Not the usual way, to check my appearance—but I look into my face to wonder who this woman really is and why she's on the planet. I think again of the starfish, only this time I wonder why the boy assumed it *wanted* to be saved. What if it had been crawling across the dark ocean floor forever and it was weary and tired? Maybe it only wanted to rest for a while on the warm sand before it died.

23

It takes me a while to settle into the Porter household and figure out how things work. From what I can gather, Mike and his boyfriend, Jackson, have recently broken up, freeing up the third bedroom—the one filled with Jackson's extra junk—for a tenant.

Mike himself is a contradiction in terms, a hefty, muscle-bound guy who makes me think of Rocky—but he works as a photographer at Olan Mills. He's the most cheerful person I've ever met, perhaps because he has to make people smile all day long—which would have the opposite effect on me.

When Mike isn't at work, he spends a lot of time pumping weights out in the small garage, in front of a full-length mirror. At first this seemed vain to me, but now I go out there a lot myself to check my clothes.

I don't know if it has anything to do with being gay, but Mike likes to cook. Nothing super fancy—but nothing like the food at Echo Glen or Inez's cooking, either. He even grocery shops twice a week. It's almost enough to make up for the lumpy single bed, the bratty niece, the housework, and the way Mike snores through the wall next to me.

One afternoon in late October, I'm tidying the living room when I find a worn copy of *People* magazine in a large pocket on

Mike's recliner. It's from August, and the cover story is about Rock Hudson, who recently died from AIDS. The article talks about how people in Hollywood are so scared of the disease, they're afraid to use public bathrooms and swimming pools. They've quit inviting gay men to parties and have started to blow air kisses instead of actually kissing their friends on the cheek or mouth.

This last part gives me pause. First, I can't imagine having a friend of my own close enough to air kiss, much less *kiss* kiss. Second, it reminds me of how Raymond used to make mean jokes about gay people, calling them "homos" and "fruiters." At the time, I thought "fruiters" was funny. Now it doesn't seem funny at all.

Especially given what Mike told me about Piper. How she has so few friends because all the parents in the neighborhood know that Mike is gay. So far, Mike has never said whether he has AIDS. But since he doesn't seem sick, I'm not about to ask.

This is another thing I like about Mike. He doesn't ask me personal questions. He rarely refers to my past or expresses curiosity about my life. Even though he makes no bones about being gay, I wonder if he can sense it when others want to keep part of their lives secret.

At some point, I feel comfortable enough to ask about Piper's parents. He tells me they died in a fiery accident on a mountain pass in Oregon on their way to ski.

"Holy crap," I say, horrified. My heart goes out to Piper. "So was her mom your sister or was her dad your brother?"

"It was my brother, Peter, and his wife, Nan," he explains. "Nan has a sister named Sue, though, and technically she has custody of Piper. But she lives in Spokane and she asked me to keep her here."

"So how long has it been that Piper is living with you?"

"Just a year or so," he says. "Sue got pregnant with twins and wanted me to keep Piper for a while, but she's so overwhelmed—she also works as a nurse—I don't see her taking Piper back anytime soon, if ever. She and Piper never gelled to begin with," he adds.

I can only imagine.

IN EARLY NOVEMBER, we start drowning in the famous Seattle rain, which of course is a lot like Issaquah rain. But now, instead of a daily sloppy trudge to the school building from my cottage, I make a mile-long walk to the Dipper. One time, I forgot an umbrella and showed up at work drenched to the bone. "You need an umbrella!" shrieked Julie.

"No, I just need to *remember* my umbrella," I told her. "It's weird, because it was nice when I first left the house. But wow. It's really coming down, isn't it?"

"Yeah," Julie replied. And then she explained her theories on rain and customers. "There's this certain kind of foggy rain that's misty and romantic—and it brings customers in droves. Plain rain tends to keep customers away. But surprisingly, this kind of rain, where it is dumping buckets, can also really draw the crowds, because it's exciting and it feels sort of celebratory. People gather and stay for hours, almost like men watching a game in a bar."

This morning's rain is the bucket kind, and we are very busy. I notice that cheerful atmosphere Julie mentioned. I also notice people seem more likely to order breakfast or a Danish or a doughnut to go along with their coffee—probably so they can linger longer.

In the middle of the rush, at about 9:00 A.M., I look up to see a familiar customer with a big grin on his face. He's already introduced himself to me as Danny. He's wearing a Rainier beer baseball cap like the one Raymond wore. It's a huge strike against him, but of course how could he know that?

I've noticed he often shows up on Tuesdays and Thursdays at around 10:00 A.M., and he tries to talk me up while he orders. I've already let him know in every way possible, short of being mean, that I am not interested in flirting—not that I would even know how to. But he doesn't seem to get it—he's as relentless as Piper.

"Hi there," I say, smiling.

"She smiles at the sight of me!" he declares, as if surprised.

"You're a customer is all," I answer. "I smile at everyone. So, how can I help you?"

"Well, you might be able to help with this problem I have."

"Yes?"

"There's a pretty girl who works at the Big Dipper, and I can't get her to give me the time of day."

Oh man. Seriously? "I'm sorry, I don't have time to joke around today," I tell him in a stern voice. "We're pretty busy. Do you want a Danish or something?"

"I'm really sorry," he says, clearly taken aback. "I'd like some black coffee please. And some of that coffee cake."

When I hand over his order, he tips his baseball cap at me and I feel a little swoop inside. He really is kind of cute and I'm flattered that he's attracted to me, especially given my big ugly braid. After he's gone, my eyes spark and try to water. I have to wonder, what if he knew the truth?

I'm nineteen and I've never been kissed.

As THE WEEKS pass, I come to appreciate Mike's dinners and his bright outlook. His greatest fault, though, is that he doesn't parent Piper. And Piper is hard to deal with. She's bratty, bossy, and starved for attention. Every afternoon, and for a couple of hours after dinner, she shadows me. If I don't let her, she gets surly and sour.

Part of me wants to be mean and insist she give me my privacy. But the other part of me feels sorry for her and wants to take care of her. I find myself asking her if she has homework and making her do it. Ordering her to take baths and brush her teeth. I even try to make sure she doesn't watch too much TV.

On some evenings, I resent having to do all this and I give up and totally ignore her. I shut the door to my room and wish it had a lock. Piper knows better than to come in—I told her absolutely not—so she knocks on my bedroom door all evening with silly questions. She's determined to engage me—perhaps all the more because she can't understand why I'd want to spend so much time reading books.

To her, reading is the same as doing schoolwork. "Why don't you want to do something fun?" she asks through the door.

In a way, Piper's right. In Echo Glen, reading was everything to me. It was how I escaped reality, how I coped with the sameness and sadness of juvenile prison. Now that I'm out, you'd think I'd be having all kinds of adventures and have better things to do with my time than read. But ironically, now that I'm free, my need to escape reality is as strong as ever.

Back in Echo Glen, *Little Women* was my favorite novel. I must have read it at least three times, drawing hope from the stories of the March sisters, dreaming of the day when I'd get out of Echo and be the same kind of smart and brave as Jo.

And yet one chapter never fails to make me angry. It's the one where Jo's younger sister Amy gets mad at Jo for something dumb and so she burns all of Jo's precious writing. There is no second copy. My fury on behalf of Jo is always so great that when Amy falls through some ice, I almost want Jo to just let her drown. Instead, Jo helps to save her and then goes ahead and totally forgives her before the chapter is even over.

Maybe if I had a sister I'd understand. Maybe if I'd had a mother like Mrs. March, I'd be a kinder, more forgiving person.

One Saturday, after I get off from the Dipper, I take Piper on the bus with me to the library. I have this harebrained idea that if she gets the right books in her hands, she'll fall in love with them the same way I did at her age. I get her to check out *The Boxcar Children* and *A Wrinkle in Time*.

She pretends to read them, sometimes lying on my bed next to me. But after a while I figure out they're just too advanced for her. She admits she can't read that well, and I can tell she thinks she's dumb, which couldn't be further from the truth. But her aversion to reading means that now she's constantly begging me to read to her aloud. Something I should be happy to do but often resist.

Inez read plenty of books to me when I was little; I'll give her that. But once I could read by myself, she stopped. I think I was six when Raymond decided to pick up where she left off. Inez thought it was the sweetest thing. And Raymond acted like it was required, kind of like brushing my teeth before bed. But even at that young age, I didn't like Raymond sitting on my bed, especially when his words sounded mushy and his breath reeked of beer. Those nights, I picked out the shortest books I could find in my collection. Even if I liked a story, I couldn't wait for it to be over.

THANKSGIVING IS A quiet affair at the Porter household. Mike has a new friend named Curtis—and the two of them make a traditional meal with turkey and gravy and all the usual fixings. I enjoy their banter and the old-fashioned music they play on a boom box in the kitchen.

I don't see it coming until Piper refuses the peas. For some reason, the memory of how Leo would arrange his peas on his plate comes smashing down on me. Grief barely ever caught me off guard this way at Echo Glen, perhaps because the place didn't resemble a home in any way. Now that I'm part of a pseudo family, it seems I'm getting more flashes of the past.

The same thing happened recently when I was helping Piper clean her room. I came across one of those xylophone toys with the bright-colored keys you hit with a stick to make music. Leo was obsessed with that thing one Christmas. He loved it because all the colors were the "right" colors.

Both the peas and the xylophone are happy memories of Leo. What I can't figure out is why good memories hurt as much as bad ones. Maybe it's because you're not on guard against them, so they hit full force, like a slap from a wave.

. . .

IT HAD TO happen sooner or later, or at least that's what I tell myself. I'm in the middle of a shift at the Dipper when I look up from the register and realize I'm peering into a very familiar face.

Shit. Gloria Crocker. She once owned a beauty school back in Everett, and our family used to go there to get our haircuts. I wish it were anyone but Gloria, because Inez might still be going to her salon, and Gloria is exactly the type of person to look up Inez and tell her where I'm working.

She's obviously as startled to see me as I am to see her. "Well, Venus!" she says, sputtering with surprise. "I knew you were . . . but I didn't expect . . ."

"Out? Yes, I am. How can I help you today?" I quickly note with relief that Julie is out of earshot.

"Um . . . just a large coffee," she says. I can see the wheels spinning madly in her coiffed blond head.

"To go or to stay?" I ask matter-of-factly.

"To stay."

I know she only wants to stay because she's curious. I turn away to get her coffee and in a single quick motion unclip my ANNETTE name tag and stick it in my apron pocket.

"Cream or sugar?" I ask, setting her cup on the counter.

"No, thank you. Black is fine," she says with a big false smile.

I tell her the price and watch as she fumbles with her wallet.

When I hand her the change for her five-dollar bill, I say with a deadpan face, "It was so nice to see you, Gloria." And then I look past her to the next person in line.

For the next ten minutes, I watch her out of the corner of my eye and she watches me.

Eventually she leaves, waving in my direction, which I ignore.

Unfortunately, just after Gloria came in, so did Danny, and Julie waited on him. I'm sorry I missed him. Something about his silly persistence in trying to flirt with me feels like a safe way to practice. Kind of like third grade.

"He left a note," Julie whispers in my ear, and I whirl around.

"Who?"

"That guy. The cute guy."

"Danny? You think he's cute?"

"He's a doll. Since you started working here, I see him all the time, and don't think I don't notice him flirting with you. Here," she says, handing me one of our Big Dipper napkins. Under the logo he's written, "Annette. Is there a friendship in the stars? Call me." And there was a number.

Of course I wasn't going to call him! The idea that I would just call him up—or that he'd think I would—knocks the breath out of me. And then I realize it probably shouldn't, probably *wouldn't,* if I were any normal girl.

Danny's handwriting is cramped and small, which makes me smile. I like that he associated the Big Dipper with space despite the doughnut logo. The fact that he mentions stars makes me wish it wasn't addressed to Annette.

I can't help but wonder if he'd like my real name.

24

As I continue trying to get Piper to do a few things around the house, I notice how much I nag or scold. I sound just like Inez used to. It alarms me enough that I search for a better tactic to get Piper to cooperate. It turns out she's highly susceptible to bribery.

Gum works. Cookies work. Money works miracles.

One night I offer her twenty-five cents to help me do the dishes, and I can tell she thinks she's struck it rich. Actually, I kind of like washing dishes by hand. I enjoy the warm soapy water and the basic idea of washing something clean. You don't get that from piling dirty dishes in a machine.

While I wash and rinse, Piper stands on a stool and dries. As the two of us work at the sink, we can see our reflections in the window as clear as if it were a mirror. Piper looks so much better since I took her in for a real haircut.

"Stop staring at me!" she says.

"I'm not staring, Piper. I'm just looking. Because you're a pretty little girl."

"Don't look," she says, shaking her head and flicking some bubbles at my face in the window.

"Okay, I'll stop looking," I say, laughing. "But I was wondering if I can ask about your front tooth."

"What about it?" she says defensively, automatically lifting a soapy finger to the gap.

"What happened to the tooth?"

"Why do you want to know?" she asks my reflection in the window.

"Just curious. It must have happened after you were six or seven, right?"

She considers. "Yeah. I was seven."

"Did you fall off your bike?"

"No."

"Did you bite a rock?"

She giggles. "No."

"Did you trip and fall face-first on the sidewalk?"

"No."

"I give up," I tell her.

"I broke it in an accident," she says. "When I was in a car."

Oh my God. I'm such an idiot! Why didn't I think of the accident? I couldn't decide whether to pretend I didn't know about her parents or just admit that Mike told me about the accident.

"I'm sorry, Piper," I say, looking down at the sink and the pan I'm washing.

"*You* didn't do anything." The way she says it makes me wonder if she thinks it was somehow her fault.

After that, we wash and dry in silence for a while. The mood has dampened. The kitchen radio, on KJR, is playing Elton John's "Goodbye Yellow Brick Road," so I decide to get us out of our funk. I turn it up loud and begin to sing along, botching most of the lyrics.

Piper smiles at me and I can tell she likes it when I act silly.

"Annette?"

"Yeah, Piper."

"How much longer do you think it will take before my tooth grows back in?"

Oh my God. She doesn't know it won't. Why hasn't someone

explained to her the difference between losing baby teeth and losing adult teeth?

Never is such a terrible word. And because I'm a coward, I tell
her, "I bet it will grow back soon."

I immediately regret the lie and add, "I really hope it never
grows back, because having that gap makes you special. You look
way prettier without a tooth there. It makes you unique."

She looks doubtful.

AFTER DINNER, MIKE usually settles in front of the TV in the rat-
tier of the two recliners. But he watches news or a sports show that
bores Piper, making me the prime bait. Tonight I decide to take her
for a walk, even though it's pretty cold out.

"A walk?"

"Yeah. Let's go for a walk."

"To where?"

"I don't know. Haven't you ever just gone on a walk?"

Her blank expression tells me that she hasn't.

We put on our coats and set out heading south. Piper is quiet.

"So tell me about your friend Penny. The one you said likes you
but moved too far away."

"She was nice," says Piper. "We went together because of our
*P*s. Piper and Penny."

"I get it."

She suddenly turns around and walks backward. "Tell me if
I'm going to hit something."

I'm jolted by memory. Jackie and I used to do this. We'd see
who could take the most steps backward before they freaked out.
Once, I purposely steered her into a bush. It didn't hurt her, but she
got so mad. "You should have known I'd do something like that,"
I told her, laughing.

"Do you have a boyfriend?" Piper asks. She is walking forward
again.

"Have you seen one?" I ask. This is the kind of sarcastic answer she's always giving me.

She smiles. "Nope. But you must have before. How old are you again?"

"I'm nineteen," I tell her.

"Oh," she says. "So you *have* to have had a boyfriend."

"Oh, a few," I lie. "But each one is a secret. You have to do something special to get me to tell you."

"Like what?"

"Let me think about it."

We cross Broadway and turn toward the Sound.

"Annette!" a male voice calls from behind us. But I still don't automatically respond to that name. Then I hear again, "Annette," right behind us. I turn. It's Danny from the coffee shop, on a bike.

"Hey," he says, grinning as he sidles up to us. "I've been looking for you."

I keep walking, but faster. I take Piper's hand. "I have not been looking for you."

He gets off his bike and walks it to keep pace with us. "Who's your little friend?"

"None of your business."

"Piper!" Piper volunteers. She's working hard to keep up with our new pace, trying to look across me at this guy.

"So, Piper, Annette. Where are you headed in such a hurry?"

I slow the pace a bit, for Piper's sake.

"We're on a walk," says Piper. "Haven't you ever just gone on a walk before?"

"Oh, a walk. Of course I have. And it's a beautiful evening for a walk."

"What's your name?" asks Piper.

"Danny," he says. "And what a pretty lady you are."

"Watch out, Piper," I say. "You know how your uncle Mike taught you not to talk to strangers? He was thinking of this guy."

"How about an ice cream? Let me buy you each a cone."

"Yes!" says Piper.

"No thanks!" I say.

Piper ignores me. "The answer is yes!"

"The answer is no," I tell him. "Besides, it's too cold for ice cream."

He doesn't say anything for a minute but keeps pace. "Can I just ask you one last thing and then I'll leave you alone?"

I jerk to a stop.

"Yes. Ask us one last thing," says Piper. She is smiling up at him with her single front tooth.

"Do you like chocolate ice cream or strawberry?"

"Chocolate!" says Piper.

I shake my head. I'm trying hard not to smile. "Strawberry."

In a booth at Dairy Queen, I learn that Danny is twenty-four, older than I thought. And, given his occupation, the last person in the world I would date, if I knew how to date: Halfway through with our cones he tells me he's in narcotics.

"What are narcotics?" Piper asks.

"Drugs," he says.

"But drugs are bad!" she practically yells. "You shouldn't take drugs."

"No, silly. I help catch the guys who are selling bad drugs."

"You mean you're a cop," I state. I can't believe it. What are the odds? Plus, he doesn't *seem* like a cop. I expected him to work in construction or something.

"You say 'cop' like it's something terrible. You don't like police?"

"I didn't mean it that way. Police are great."

Piper's big green eyes grow large. "You're the police?" You'd think he said he was the president.

"Yes, but a special kind."

"Like you arrest people and put them in jail?"

"Sometimes," he tells her. "But only really bad people."

That's me, I think. *A really bad person.* "You're dripping ice cream on your shirt, Piper."

She looks down at her Mickey Mouse T-shirt. Mickey's left ear has been hit. She lifts up her shirt and puts that part in her mouth to lick it off. "Use a napkin, sweetie," I say, a little embarrassed.

A moment later, Piper is dabbing at her shirt with the napkin when she quietly announces, "I went to a police place once."

I'm surprised. "Like on a field trip?" I offer.

"No," she says. She looks back and forth at us. "I don't want to say."

Danny and I exchange a glance. "That's okay," I tell her. "No problem.

"I just met Piper a few months ago," I explain to Danny. "I rent a room from her uncle Mike."

"Well, lucky you, Piper!" says Danny with enthusiasm. "I'm jealous."

"Jealous of what?"

I redden. "Oh, nothing, kiddo," he says, smiling at me.

I don't want a boyfriend. I am not interested in men. I am especially not interested in a man who is a cop. After five more minutes of chitchat and cone-licking, I wrap things up as quickly as possible. I stand. Tell him thanks. Tell him I need to get Piper home; it's a school night.

"Will I see you again?" he asks.

"I have no idea," I say, tossing the rest of my soggy cone into the trash. "You know where I work."

"Ouch," he says, and I immediately regret the brush-off.

After we say goodbye, Piper scolds me all the way home. "I don't think he thinks you like him now. He looked sad when we said goodbye."

"Don't worry, Piper. I'll see him again." I grab her hand and start to swing it between us, forcing myself to seem happy.

When I guide Piper toward bed at nine o'clock, she still has chocolate smears around her lips. "Go wash your face," I tell her.

"Why?"

"Because you've got chocolate on it."

"So?"

"So. You don't want to get chocolate on your sheets."

She hesitates. She is wearing the same pink nightgown for the umpteenth night in a row now, and I realize it must be only one of two she owns.

"Fine," I say. "Go to bed with ice cream on your face."

She wipes her arm on her mouth and climbs in bed. I shut off her light on my way out. "Good night," I say.

"Good night, John-Boy," she says. She does this every night and for some reason thinks it's funny. Clearly she's seen too many reruns of *The Waltons*.

She begs me to answer, "Good night, Mary Ellen," but I won't.

"You're a weird little girl," I tell her. And I shut the door.

Once I climb into bed, I can't sleep, because I keep thinking about cops, about being arrested, about people knowing who I am. I remember the distinct feeling of metal around my wrists. The way I split myself off from myself. How I started orbiting my life instead of living it.

I'M TIRED OF seeing Piper in rags, so I ask Mike if she ever got new school clothes. Clearly he doesn't understand the concept, but he offers to give me twenty-five dollars to take her shopping. On Sunday, I tell Piper our plan. But I don't quite know how to tell her that twenty-five dollars won't go far.

Then genius strikes. "Would you rather shop at used-clothes stores and get lots of cool stuff," I ask her, "or would you like to shop for new clothes at regular stores like Sears but get a lot less—and everyone will be wearing the same thing?"

Piper thinks about this. "What do you think?"

"Well . . ." I hesitate. "I like thrift-store clothes a lot. You can be more creative. Here's what I would do," I explain. "I know where there's a pretty decent Goodwill store we can walk to. If we don't like what we find, we can take a bus to the mall."

She nods. "Okay." Today she has put her hair in pigtails using green rubber bands—an idea of mine that I now regret. She looks silly. Her face is too serious for pigtails. The hair pulled tight makes her chin look sharp.

We spend the afternoon in the same Goodwill I visited on my first day of freedom. Piper is not exactly a picky shopper. In fact, she doesn't seem to know where to start or to have a clue about what she likes. I flip through the racks, growing uneasy. Fourth grade. Doesn't it start to get important right about then, what you wear? I rack my brain. I have no idea what is in style these days. I randomly flip through the racks in her size. She says she's a girls' size 12. I find a couple pairs of stone-washed jeans that are the right size. Piper nods approval. Slowly I begin to fill my right arm with clothes. Among them, a plaid shirt that has pink and green. A blue crew-neck sweater. A green V-neck sweater vest. A pair of brown corduroy pants. We also find her a couple of pairs of shoes, one of them suede Hush Puppies that don't seem practical but Piper loves. I steer her away from the neon colors she repeatedly gravitates toward. After an hour of looking, Piper steps into a cur-tained dressing room and tries everything on.

Most of it fits. Piper is too tall for all the pants besides the jeans. They look cute on her. All the shirts fit, and a couple of jumpers I grabbed last minute also work. As we head to the counter, I spot a bin of bandannas, barrettes, and hair scrunchies. I remember how I was going to buy a bandanna back when I was even more para-noid about being recognized.

I spot a bright-green one with white and black. "Try this on, Piper," I tell her, shaking it open.

"How?"

"Let me do it." I fold it into a triangle shape and turn her around. I lay the longest straight side over her forehead and tie the two ends behind her neck beneath the pigtails.

"Turn around," I tell her.

She wheels around. "What do you think?"

The green in the bandanna brings out the green of her eyes. "It's perfect, Piper!"

But she's skeptical. "Do you think other girls will have bandannas?"

"Well, if they don't, I bet once they see you, everyone will want one."

"Okay," she says.

"If you decide you don't like it, I'll buy it from you," I say with a wink.

I add up the purchases in my mind before we get to the counter. We're spending more than twenty-five dollars. I have the envelope of money from Mike. When the cashier starts to ring up our stuff, I tell Piper, "Honey, go out front of the store and see if there's a newspaper machine, okay?"

"Why?"

"Just do it." After she's gone I take the extra money we'll need from my wallet. It's only ten bucks, I reason. Maybe Mike will let me take it off this month's rent. Then I also remember that Piper's birthday is coming right up. I already know what I want to get her, but I need to talk to Mike.

Piper comes up as the cashier is putting the receipt in the bag. "There's no paper box," she says.

"I'll take that," I say, and put the receipt in my wallet. Piper looks at me suspiciously. When we get outside she says, "We spent too much, didn't we?"

"No, we didn't. We spent just enough."

WHEN PIPER AND I get home from shopping, Mike and Curtis are in the middle of a romantic steak dinner. They even have a candle going. Piper and I say hurried hellos, grab peanut butter sandwiches and some potato chips, and disappear upstairs.

"Do you like Curtis?" she asks me after we're done eating. I think we were both starved from shopping.

"He seems nice enough," I say. Curtis looks Japanese to me, though I can't be sure. "Mike told me he's a pharmacist."

"What's a farmist?" asks Piper.

"A pharmacist. It starts with a *ph*. They fill your prescriptions when your doctor gives you medicine."

"Oh. Do you want to play crazy eights?"

I think about it. "Actually, Piper, I'm tired. If you don't mind."

Later, when I go to tuck her in, she's wearing the green bandanna. "Oh my gosh, it's so cute!" I screech. "It makes your eyes as green as a lizard."

"A lizard? No!"

"A leaf?"

"No!"

"Okay, how about as green as apple-flavored Jolly Ranchers?"

"Yeah!" she says. "That's it!"

She wears the bandanna for the next four days, until we have a little talk about matching and what colors go together. I can't help but think of Leo. He would say Piper's bandanna is the wrong green.

A FEW DAYS later, while Piper and I are doing dishes, I mention Leo. I might not have if Piper hadn't been talking about her twin cousins—baby Abel and baby Asher.

"I have a brother," I announce.

She stops in the middle of drying a plate to turn and look at my face. "Really?"

"Yes. Really."

"Where is he? Where does he live?"

"To be honest, he's been missing for a long time."

"What do you mean, *missing*?"

I should never have brought Leo up. What was I thinking? "We're not sure if someone took him from a house he was staying at or if he ran away."

"What's his name?"

"Leo," I say. For some reason it feels good to say his name to Piper. "Leo is thirteen now."

Piper looks thoughtful. She wipes a fork. "Are you sad?"

Am I sad? "I miss him a lot," I tell her.

"But why did he run away?"

"He got lost, Piper. He wasn't as smart as normal kids, and one day he got lost and then we couldn't find him." Oh my God. Saying this so matter-of-factly to Piper makes it sound so awful. "But I like to think he's in a good place," I hurry to add. "I'm almost *positive* that a good mother found him and she took him home and she is taking good care of him."

I can see Piper processing all this while she stares at my reflection in the window.

"Leo," she says softly, like she has a new possession.

25

One thing about working at the Big Dipper is that I've gotten totally addicted to coffee. I try to limit myself to two cups in the morning and one after lunch—but sometimes I sneak in a bit more. I always eat my lunch sitting in a booth by the window. I people-watch or sometimes read the paper or a celebrity magazine.

I'm doing just that—wrapped up in an article about Rod Stewart—when Inez sits down across from me.

Gloria certainly wasted no time, did she? But it feels like an enormous stroke of luck that I'm on break—and Julie is busy with customers.

I gaze at Inez flatly, trying to muster a glare, but a glare seems premature—and immature. "Gloria, I suppose," I state matter-of-factly.

"Yes," she says, brushing rain off the shoulders of her tan trench coat. "Gloria told me where you work."

"Are you here to cause problems?"

"Of course not, Venus." The creases around her eyes are deeper. Her damp hair is still black, long, and straight, but gray roots show along her part.

"What do you want?"

"I just wanted to see you, Venus." She speaks softly, like she's approaching a dangerous animal.

"Okay. See me?" I say. "Now you've seen me, now you can go." I realize I sound more like Piper than a grown woman.

"Can I have coffee with you? Actually, I'd like to talk to you about something important."

She sounds so sad that I instantly go to Leo. "Is it Leo?" I ask hopefully.

"No, it's not Leo," she says wistfully. "It's about you. . . ."

"What about me?"

She looks out the window, and the dark metal flecks in her gray eyes match the rain outside. "It's nice here," she says, glancing around. "I'm so glad you found a job—Annette?" She chuckles softly, nodding at my name tag.

"I like it here, too," I say. "And I'd appreciate it if you didn't tell anyone that I'm trying to start a new life with a new name." The front door jingles, signaling a new customer.

"Good for you, Venus," she says with meaning. "I don't care what you call yourself, as long as it makes you happy. But there's something else," she says. She opens her purse and pulls out her ChapStick. Same old nervous habit.

"I want you to know something," she says, rubbing the wax on her lips over the top of her orange-ish lipstick.

"Yeah? What should I know?"

"I'm going to have money for you to go to college."

Immediately my blood pounds. "From where? Did you get it from selling my story to that Anna person?"

"Oh no! I never followed through with that, since you clearly . . . Actually, the money will be coming from the sale of the house on Rockefeller. I'm going to move into something smaller, and there's some equity—"

"I don't want any blood money from that horrible house," I tell her.

"I understand, Venus. But you're so smart. And I want to see you go to college if you want to."

Her seeming generosity surprises me but only a little less than the fact that she's continued to live in that house all these years. I take a gulp of coffee and look outside.

"I'm not going to college, anyway, at least not anytime soon."

Inez's hopeful expression collapses. "But, Venus—"

"Not just because I can't afford to," I continue. "I can't possibly go to college without using my transcripts and risking the whole school learning who I am. And can you imagine the looks I would get? The way people would treat me once they knew the truth?"

She hesitates for a moment. "I understand. It's painful to be you. But hiding isn't going to help, sweetie."

"Please don't call me 'sweetie.' And I'm not hiding. It's called 'starting over.'"

She looks at me, shakes her head like it's a sad thing I'm doing. "You can't run from the past, Venus," she whispers.

"Just watch me," I say.

We fall silent and I can smell her perfume. Charlie. It was always Charlie, and now the scent makes me sick. I bet she even has a hanky somewhere in that purse.

I notice that her hand is shaking and realize she's really nervous. She puts her ChapStick back in her purse and looks at me in this pleading way. "I meant what I said about being sorry, Venus. I don't know what else to do. I'm so sorry I—"

"Don't!" I interrupt her. "Don't even try." I don't want to hear her apologies. For a moment, we're both quiet and looking out the window. Rain on puddles. Rain on rain. The rain is getting rained on.

After she quietly gets up and leaves, I feel deflated and angry. Her attempt to apologize annoys the hell out of me because it doesn't match up with the story in my head.

That afternoon, I'm not in the mood for Piper, but she is waiting for me as always on the front steps. I wish she would just play outside like other kids and give me some space.

"Why don't you ride your bike anymore?" I ask.

"It's winter, doofus," she says.

"It's Seattle, not Alaska," I reply. "And you're not allowed to call me 'doofus,' remember? It's stopped raining, and it's really not that cold, as long as you wear a jacket."

"It's a dumb bike."

"What about it is dumb?"

"Other kids have ten speeds, not banana seats. It's a baby bike."

I doubt this, but I wouldn't know. I turn on the TV, hoping that MTV will distract Piper and she'll leave me alone. That's another thing that happened while I was away. When I went into Echo, music was just music, not these weird videos.

When Piper seems glued to Madonna, I sneak up to my bedroom, shut the door, and lie down on my back, perfectly flat, as if being still will take away the pain. Kind of like when you're sick and it helps to lie on the cold kitchen floor.

I shut my eyes and try to make my mind go blank, but all I can think about is Inez. How painful our meeting was. How much I wish I had a mother to help me navigate this new life of mine—and I know Inez would be happy to. But at times I think the only thing that's held me together all these years is my anger at Inez. If I forgave her, it would mean facing the past, feeling those feelings. I'm afraid I'd fall apart. Plus, what if she betrays me again?

Back at Echo, Sharon once said that maybe I needed to blame my mom to survive, like a coping mechanism—but that someday the opposite might be true. What if she was right?

"What's wrong?"

I open my eyes to see Piper's apple green ones staring down at me. Up close they always look brighter, even greener.

"Nothing," I say.

"Are you sick?"

"No. Just tired."

"You're lying," she says.

"You're being a pest."

She sits on the edge of my bed. "Scoot over," she demands, like it's her bed, too. I grudgingly roll over, and she lies down next to me.

Her presence there reminds me of Leo and me lying on my bed, naming planets and counting stars. The memory hurts, so I turn my attention to Piper. "What did you do at school today?"

"Nothing. I played solitaire at recess." I taught her how a week ago.

"Did you win?"

"Only when I cheated."

We are quiet for a while, staring at the ceiling. Elton John's "Levon" is playing on KJR on my clock radio, and it makes me want to cry. I can't do that with Piper here, so I try to hold back tears.

"What's really wrong with you? I can tell you're sad," Piper says.

"I saw my mother today."

"Really?"

"Yeah."

"Your mother?" She says it like it's such a surprise that I have a mother. I think she's seen me as belonging only to her and to the here and now. "Is she pretty?"

I think about this. "I guess so. But she's kind of old now, like forty-two or something."

"Where did you see her?"

"At the Big Dipper."

"Why are you sad?"

I sigh. "It's hard to explain." Then I gently ask, "Do you want to talk about your mom?"

"I don't know," Piper says. I smell bubble gum on her breath and I suspect she's been spending her milk money on gum and candy. I always spent my milk money that way, too, so I let it go.

"Piper, do you miss your mom?" I've never before directly asked Piper about her mom.

"Of course!" she says, as if I've insulted her.

"Sor-rry," I reply. "Not everyone loves their mom, you know."

"Don't you?" she asked.

"I don't know about that anymore. I used to. But I've been mad at her a long time." *Why did I go down this road?*

Piper turns onto her side and props up her head to look at my face. "Really? How come?"

"She made some big mistakes," I tell her. "You're not old enough to understand."

Piper huffs. "I am old enough to understand. If I had my mom, I would be soooooo nice to her. I would love her even if she made big mistakes. Everyone makes mistakes, right?"

I sigh again. "You're right, Piper. But some are just harder to forgive."

"So if I make a big mistake, you might not forgive me and then you won't love me anymore?"

"Oh, Piper! For God's sake, no. That's not what I'm saying." Since when did Piper decide that I *love* her?

I sit up and climb over Piper's body on the bed. "Let's go make cookies," I say, which is actually one of the few motherly things Inez did with me. We always made the peanut butter kind, and I loved making the crosshatch in the dough with the fork.

26

On December 12, we celebrate Piper's tenth birthday at Farrell's Ice Cream Parlour. It's Mike, Curtis, a new friend of Piper's named Amy, and myself. Amy's a funny, quiet little thing with chunky brown hair and a tiny face. But I'm so glad Piper has a new friend.

After we get home from Farrell's, I sneak out into the garage to retrieve Piper's present.

The kitten is black with green eyes. If it were up to me, I'd name him Spooky. But I already suspect his name is going to be Felix. It's one of Piper's favorite old cartoons. She likes to sing the jingle about the wonderful, wonderful cat and laughing so hard your sides ache.

I have Spooky-soon-to-be-Felix in a cardboard box with an old towel. I tell Piper to sit down at the kitchen table and cover her eyes. When she opens them, she stares dumbly at the box.

"Open it!" I say. She lifts the lid. Peeks in. Squeals, "It's a kitty! Oh my gosh, it's a kitty!" She gingerly lifts out the kitten, which appears to have been sleeping. He's supposedly eight weeks old. "He's so cute! He's perfect!"

I am smiling so wide. We had a kitten once when I was four. After I purposely dropped him in a full bathtub, I planned to put him in the dryer. Fortunately, Inez caught me in the act, and Toby lived to die another day, courtesy of a car.

"You like him?" I ask.

"I love him!" she exclaims. She hugs me around the waist and won't let go. "Thank you, Annette. Thank you!"

"What are you going to name him?" I ask, gently unwinding her arms.

"I don't know," she says, her green eyes going serious.

"What about Spooky?" I ask.

She thinks about this. "Spooky," she says. "Like he's scary?"

"No, but since he's black—"

"I know, I know!" she screeches. "Felix! Felix the wonderful cat." And she goes off into the cartoon jingle.

I have this girl nailed.

THE FOLLOWING MORNING, it's totally dead at the Dipper when Danny sidles up to the pastry window. "Hey. It's the only girl in the world who doesn't like me."

"That's not true," I say. "I'm sure there are plenty of others."

"Ouch!" he says. Danny has a largish nose—something we share. He also has broad shoulders and long lashes that would suit a girl fine. He reminds me a little of Tad Martin from *All My Children*. Sometimes I watch that soap on Mondays when I'm off work.

"What can I get you?" I ask him.

He pretends to scan the pastries. "What is that one with yellow?"

"Lemon filling."

"Is it good?"

"I like it," I say. "I think you've had it before."

"Oh wow," he exclaims. "So she remembers what I like."

Clearly, us going out for ice cream with Danny got his hopes up all over again. And maybe for just a second it had gotten mine up, too—until I found out he was a cop. Who could discover the truth about me faster or more easily?

Now I don't really have a choice but to get him to move on. And the sooner the better.

Julie has finished with her own customer and now she comes over to join us. "You gotta try our new brownie," she tells Danny.

"Really?"

"It's awesome. Perfect mix of moist and chewy. I'm recommending it to all my favorite customers." She's smiling at Danny in a way that makes me realize she's flirting. It's my customer, so why is she butting in?

Danny doesn't seem to notice, though. "I'm trying to talk Annette here into having a cup of coffee with me on her next break," he tells Julie.

I frown. "No, he's not."

"Well, don't be rude, Annette," says Julie slyly. "Remember, the customer comes first. And you can take that break anytime you want."

"Thanks a lot," I tell her.

"So, why don't you like me?" Danny asks after Julie's walked away. "Is it the nose?"

I shake my head, smiling. "No, of course not," I tell him. "I like your nose fine. And it's not that I don't like you. But I'm not . . . How come you don't just give up?"

"Give up?" He seems to think about this for a moment. "Maybe I'm not convinced there's no hope," he says.

An awkward moment passes and he tries again. "What if we were just friends? I promise on a holy stack of flapjacks that I won't make a move on you."

"'A holy stack of flapjacks'?" I bust out laughing. "That's a weird one."

"So what's your answer?"

I sigh heavily. "It's not you; it's only that I heard the whole let's-just-be-friends thing doesn't work, at least not for the guy, anyway."

"What? You think you're so damn irresistible? Like I can't resist your charms? What if *I'm* only looking for a friend, too?"

"*Touché,*" I concede. "You have me there."

"I wish I did," he says wistfully, and I feel myself blushing hard. Now it feels like we really *are* flirting. *What am I doing?* This poor guy has no idea how screwed up I am. And as much as I like him, the way he glances at my body makes me feel something close to panic.

"So it's decided," he declares out of nowhere. "Dinner. Movie. Tomorrow night. Just friends. Simple as that." He pauses to put a napkin to his mouth to catch a bit of brownie.

"Really? You think it's that simple?" I ask. "You *are* a pushy guy," I say.

Of course, when I don't outright say no, Danny takes this for a yes. Then he turns into a gentleman and insists I don't have to come if I don't want to, which instinctively makes me reassure him that I do.

How did he do that?

PIPER IS BESIDE herself excited that I am going on a date. "You're going to wet your pants if you don't stop prancing around," I tell her.

The idea of wetting one's pants triggers that memory of when I wet my pants the night of my arrest. It seems like just yesterday and also like a hundred years ago.

When Danny picks me up at the house, it's all a blur of my quiet nervousness and Piper's constant yapping. Once inside the movie theater, I admit that popcorn would be good. Not only because I love popcorn, but also it will give me a way to occupy my hands in case he has any ideas about holding one of them. While Danny gets in the concession line, I find us seats.

When the lights finally go down, I feel a small thrill. Danny has bought himself Jujubes, that awful gummy candy that sticks in your teeth. He smells good, though I can't decide if it's from cologne or a musky deodorant or soap. On the way here in the car, I noticed that his hair still looked a little damp. He's more handsome without the cap.

During the previews, I watch his hands out of the corner of my eye. He has long fingers, smooth nails. I wonder what he looks like when he's up close enough to kiss. If you would still notice his nose so much.

At dinner, there's an awkward moment when Danny orders wine for us and the waiter cards me. I don't want to use Annette's license, since she's not twenty-one—and I told Danny that I was. Thinking quickly, I volunteer that I lost my license and hadn't bothered getting a new one yet since I don't own a car. The waiter lets me order wine anyway, which I barely sip.

In order to deflect the conversation away from me, I ask Danny questions about his family, background, and hobbies. I learn that his mom and dad are both realtors. He's got two sisters, both of whom live in Los Angeles. He's crazy about college basketball, though he never played himself. He grew up in Springfield, Oregon, until he was eighteen. After graduating from the University of Washington, he enrolled at the police academy. He likes Bob Marley. He likes Jujubes. And, apparently—he likes me.

I still wonder why. What do we have in common? I guess he thinks I'm pretty. And we do have an easy way of bantering. Our senses of humor seem to go together, and he says I make him laugh. When I admitted I love astronomy, he claimed that on any clear night he can find every constellation in view.

Of course, I didn't offer up my astronaut dream. What a joke.

I should have realized that by asking him all those "get to know you" questions, he'd do the same to me. Sweating and awkward, I tell him a series of small (big) lies, like that I'm an only child. I graduated from Snohomish High School. I went to Everett Community College until I ran out of money. The being-poor part there's no hiding, so why lie?

Once, I catch Danny looking at me in a gentle, probing way that makes me wonder what he's thinking. At the Porters' door, I'm nervous he'll try to kiss me. Instead, he bows, reaching up to tip his hat—which isn't there—and we both laugh.

OF COURSE, PIPER is waiting up for me and accosts me as soon as I shut the front door.

"So how fun was it?" she asks. She has on her same pink nightgown. "What movie did you see?"

"It was called *Runaway Train*," I tell her.

"About a train?" she asks. "Did people kiss and stuff like that?"

"No, silly. It was a movie about criminals who escape prison and end up on a train that is out of control."

"Oh," she says. I can see the wheels turning. "Was it good?"

"Actually, I really liked it," which is true. I wish I could tell Piper about the time I tried to escape juvie and failed—only I'd give her the funny version. She would love that story, especially the part where the fireman cuts off my hair.

I go to the kitchen and open the fridge, looking for milk. The wine at dinner has left my tummy feeling funny.

"Did you kiss?" She is right behind me.

"Piper! I told you we are just friends." She looks disappointed. I pour a glass of milk and sit at the table.

"Did you hold hands?"

I laugh. "Piper, you're a romantic, aren't you?"

"What's that?"

"Oh, nothing. No, we didn't hold hands." I take a gulp of milk. "We went to a movie and then for a bite."

"What restaurant?"

"A place called Thirteen Coins." I see her mind still working. She wants details but doesn't know how to get at them.

"Are you going out again on another date? Is he your boy-friend now?"

I sigh heavily. "I don't know, Piper. I think we will just be friends."

As Piper and I make our way upstairs, I realize something. I had told Piper about Leo. And if I keep seeing Danny, someday the subject of Leo will come up. Then I'll have to make a really embarrassing apology about not being an only child. How would I explain? That alone should be reason enough not to go out with Danny again.

A COUPLE NIGHTS later, I have the run of the house. Mike, in a highly unusual move, has taken Piper, along with Curtis, to see an early showing of *Pinocchio*. Maybe Curtis has some parental instincts Mike seems to lack. I hope so, for Piper's sake.

I'm determined to maximize my Piper-free time, but instead I'm restless and there's not much on TV. Around eight, the phone rings. When it turns out to be Danny, I'm surprised he called me so soon after our "date."

"Annette," he says. "How's it going?"

"Okay, I guess." *Does he just want to chat? I feel like I don't know how.*

"Have you recovered from our date? I know I left you swooning."

I let out a small laugh. "Not exactly," I tell him.

"You're hurting my feelings," he jokes.

"No, really," I assure him. "It was a lot of fun."

"That's great," he says. "I can't wait to get together again. How about this Friday? Do you want to bring Piper?"

"No, I don't want to bring Piper! I want to escape Piper!" Then I realize he's done it again, drawn out a yes from me, this time by implication.

"What grade is she in?" he asks.

"Fourth."

"Ah yes, he says. "Fourth grade, Marcy Mayhew."

"Marcy who?" I nervously curl the phone cord round my finger.

"Mayhew. I used to chase her around the playground. Sometimes I got close. But then I'd panic. I mean, what would I do if I actually caught her?"

"I remember that," I tell him. "The chasing thing."

"Did a boy ever catch you?"

"Yeah," I answer truthfully.

"What happened?"

"I punched him in the mouth. I didn't mean to. But I didn't know what to do. I was afraid he was going to try to kiss me."

"Uh-oh. I'll keep that in mind."

"Very funny," I tell him. "But, about Friday . . ." I'm about to worm out of that date when he quickly cuts in.

"I'll pick you up at six. I have something special planned."

"Oh?" I say, curious.

"It'll be fun. I'll see you then." He hangs up before I can object. I sigh as I place the receiver back in the cradle. I'm tempted to call back and cancel, but that seems so rude. Or is Danny the one who is rude? He's pushy, for sure, but he also seems genuinely kind and, yeah, maybe a little desperate.

I wander over to the fridge and, for some reason, grab one of Mike's beers and snap it open. The sound reminds me of Raymond, who was always demanding someone bring him a beer. Raymond, with his stinky socks, the TV remote plastered to his hand, his ass planted in his La-Z-Boy. Raymond with his eyes growing lazy and bloodshot as they followed me. Raymond getting all goopy and sweet, calling me Veenie.

I shudder. And then I realize the reason I'm thinking of Raymond is that I've been thinking about Danny. It's almost like the two subconsciously overlap in my mind in a bizarre, unfair way. Suddenly feeling sick, I pour the beer down the sink.

27

The next evening, I overhear Mike talking on the phone to a friend about how it's strangely balmy outside. I step onto the back porch to check, and he's right. The rain has left everything damp but clean. What surprises me more than the mild temperature is the clear night sky. The two don't usually go together in Seattle in the winter. Suddenly I feel Piper at my side, looking up with me.

"Do you see Venus?" I ask, pointing it out to her.

"It's such a pretty star," she says. "Like you," she adds with a self-conscious giggle.

"You think I'm pretty?"

"Of course!" she says. "You're as pretty as one of *Charlie's Angels*."

"Yeah, right," I say. "But thank you, Piper." I sit down on one of the crumbling cement steps and she joins me. "Actually, Venus isn't a star," I tell her. "It's a planet. But lots of people call it a star—the Morning Star."

"Why can't it be both?"

"It kind of is," I say, enjoying her interest. "The only thing that shines brighter than Venus in the night sky is our moon."

Piper tells me she's been learning about space at school. She wants to talk about the Space Shuttle *Challenger* and how that one teacher was going to get to go into space even though she wasn't an astronaut, just a teacher.

"If it happens when we're at school, we might get to watch it on TV," she says.

"Wow, Piper. That would be so great. I'll probably be at work, unless it happens on a Monday." I don't bother sharing with Piper how I used to want to be an astronaut. I know now that they don't send people like me into space. Still, I'm so jealous of that teacher—Christa McAuliffe—that I'm not even sure I'll watch the launch.

"So can you find the Big Dipper, Piper?" I ask.

"You work there, silly!" she says. "It's not in the sky." Then she laughs and I suspect she knows better.

"You're right," I tell her. "But it's in the sky, too. You know that. The real Big Dipper is a constellation of stars."

"What is a con-sul—"

"A *constellation* is a group of stars that make a picture in the sky," I explain, trying to keep the science on her level. "Like Taurus is a group of stars shaped like a bull. Or at least that's how it looks to us. But the stars themselves aren't actually related to one another; they just look like they belong together."

"Kind of like our family," she says.

"What do you mean?"

She takes a second to swallow a bite of cookie, which she snuck after I cut her off hours ago. "You said the stars aren't really related, they just belong together. That's just like us."

I smile in the shadows. "You're a smart girl, Piper."

I DON'T PLAN it, don't even realize I'm going to do it until Danny shows up on Thursday at the Dipper. He begins to flirt with me first thing—and I stiffen. "I'm sorry," I tell him. "About tomorrow night . . . I can't."

"Okay, so how about the next night?" he says, trying to humor me along.

"I'm sorry, but I can't," I blurt out. "I appreciate the movie and dinner. That date was great. But I was only being nice. I think it's probably time for you to give up, you know? Would it help if I tell you there's no hope?" I can hear a hint of disdain in my voice, which I totally didn't mean to be there. By the surprised look on his face, I can tell he heard it, too.

"Okay," he says. He doesn't stay to order anything. Just walks out the door. For the rest of my shift, I feel sick to my stomach and totally devastated. I can hardly plaster a smile on my face for customers. By the time I get home, I want to cry or scream or punch something, because I'm so disappointed and embarrassed, too. I was so rude!

What does it mean for my future that I just shot down a guy I really like? I had hoped that once I was free, if I met a guy I felt attracted to and liked, I'd be able to have a boyfriend. But my reaction to Danny seems to prove true one of my worst fears—that I'll never be able to really be with a guy.

Of course, part of the issue is that I'm terrified of being discovered as Venus Black. But even worse than being recognized, I fear being *known*. I'm almost positive that if I date Danny, one thing will to lead to another—until it won't. Because I can't bear to have the tender, secret parts of my body exposed to the light of a man's gaze. Like a starfish belly-up on the beach, I'd shrivel and die.

Which means I'd eventually hurt Danny worse than I just hurt him now. In time, he'd discover that I'm not unlike the planet I'm named for. At a great distance, Venus is beautiful, the brightest of stars in the sky. But what NASA discovered when they orbited her is that she's actually an inhospitable planet, a boiling cauldron of poisonous gases.

Come too close and you'd fry.

28

When Christmas comes around, I convince Piper I don't need a gift and tell her I'm not giving her one, either. But, of course, I hide a new Barbie under the tree at the last minute.

Recently, Piper has lost interest in tormenting Smelly Shelly and wants a Barbie instead. Personally, I don't like Barbies, because when they are naked, even without genitalia, they make it so you can't help but think of sex. Once when I was young, a girl came over with a Ken doll and wanted to play nasty. I never played with her again.

Christmas morning, Mike is sick and can't join us. "The flu," he says from his bed. "All I want for Christmas is some Pepto-Bismol. I like it cold, so it's in the back of the fridge."

So Piper and I open presents alone. Piper is ecstatic about the Barbie. I make her promise to keep Barbie dressed.

And, of course, Piper has a present for me, too. It's a Polaroid instant camera—"So you can take pictures of me!" she announces. I can tell she's not even joking.

"Remember when I told you to take a picture because it will last longer?" she asks.

I smile and nod.

"Well, now you really can!" She literally grabs the camera from my hand and loads the film. "Uncle Mike showed me how," she says, handing it back to me. Obviously Mike was in on this gift and must have given her the money, too. It couldn't have been cheap, and I feel bad that I didn't buy him anything but a Bruce Springsteen album.

Piper sits in front of the rather pathetic Christmas tree. "I'm ready now!" she declares. I raise the camera and frame her in the tiny window. Her lips are slightly blue, her single front tooth looms large, and she's wearing the new Christmas nightgown she got from Mike, which she opened last night. "C'mon, Annette! Hurry up!"

I snap the shutter, and then we both watch as the black film slowly slides out. We lie on the floor and lean over it, waiting for Piper to emerge. Gradually, she comes into focus.

"You're so pretty, Piper," I tell her. "Merry Christmas."

She quietly studies the picture for a long time, which makes me wonder if Mike—working at Olan Mills, for God's sake—has ever taken her picture. Watching her stare at her ten-year-old self, I get a lump in my throat. I hope she never has a reason to shy away from cameras, hope she'll always feel confident and beautiful.

Piper spends the rest of the morning ignoring her new Barbie and taking pictures of *me* with what is supposedly *my* camera. At one point, for fun, I pull out my braid and shake my hair loose and wild, which delights Piper no end. I kneel down on the ground and let Felix play with my hair. Piper tries to do the same, but her hair doesn't interest Felix as much as mine.

I wear my hair down like that for the rest of the day, reveling in the familiar feeling of having it loose. We force Mike to open his gift from Piper and me from bed. We dance around all morning to "Born to Run," laughing.

Between Piper taking pictures of Felix and me and asking me to take more pictures of her, we waste a whole package of film.

NOT SURPRISINGLY, DANNY never comes back. When Piper grills me about him, I finally admit that I told him I couldn't go on any more dates.

"But you like him!" she squeals.

"I know. You're right that I like him. It's just that . . ." How can I explain to Piper that I'm screwed up when it comes to guys?

"What?" she wails. "Why? How could you be so mean?"

It's a good question and one that I've asked myself. But somehow I hadn't expected Piper to be so upset about Danny. Then again, I hadn't expected to be so upset myself, either. The whole thing is only made worse by the abrupt, stupid way I handled it. I know I hurt his feelings and probably embarrassed him, too—and he must hate me now.

Ever since it happened, my mood has grown dark. The days are so short—it's dark by four-thirty now. Plus, I am more and more at a loss about how to keep Piper both entertained and on task with schoolwork. Meanwhile, I worry about how close we've become. What will happen when I want to move on? Clearly she thinks we're some kind of family. Sweet but scary.

At times, I debate calling Danny to apologize, but I can't see how to do that without changing my position. *I'm sorry I dumped you so rudely, and by the way, I still can't go out with you.*

Sometimes the stupid irony of my situation is just too much. I begin to practically drown in my sadness—only to get angry at myself, because it's all of my own creation. It's no one's fault but mine that instead of having a boyfriend to possibly plan a future with, I have skipped right to being a pseudo parent to a bratty fourth-grader.

Then I realize I have made progress. I'm not blaming Raymond or Inez. Sharon would be so proud.

ONE WEDNESDAY IN early January, Julie goes home sick and I get off work extra late. When I get home, it's almost four. I call out for Piper, but there's no answer. She's supposed to leave me a note on the front door if she goes somewhere—to her friend Amy's, or out riding her bike.

I strip off my wet windbreaker. My hands are red. I wish we

had a fireplace. The house is too cold. The wood floors too bare. I wish we could find a huge, warm rug at a garage sale.

Felix follows me, rubbing up against my legs. Curtis has left his coat here. It's hanging on the back of the couch. I pick it up and put both it and mine in the coat closet just inside the front door. For some reason, the closet looks less full than usual.

I go into the kitchen and I'm getting a drink of water when I notice that the side door to the garage is open. It's flapping in the wind. I go out and shut it. When I come back in, I feel like something is wrong. I go upstairs to double-check for Piper, and her room looks bare. The few stuffed animals on her dresser are gone. I open a drawer—it's empty. I open the closet door—the few dresses Piper owns are missing.

I fly down the stairs and call Mike at work. He sounds like he's expecting my call. "I'm sorry, Annette. It's about Piper."

"Duh!" I say. "Where the hell is she?" My legs grow weak, and my mind races.

"I'll explain when I get home."

"What the hell?"

But he hangs up. By the time he gets home, I'm stalking around the house, swearing, conjuring worst-case scenarios.

"You need to sit down," he says. I stubbornly refuse.

Despite his Rocky Balboa build, Mike suddenly looks shrunken, diminished. And it scares me to death. There is no sign of the cheerful Olan Mills photographer.

"Is Piper okay?" I can hear the fear in my voice. "What's going on?"

"Sit on the couch, Annette," he orders.

This time, I obediently sit down. He pulls his recliner halfway across the room so he can sit across from me, which is somehow the scariest thing he could have done. "I was going to tell you sooner," he starts. "I just didn't expect . . . I thought she'd give me a few more days. At least a heads-up. I'm so sorry that you didn't get to—"

"What the fuck, Mike?" Now I'm angry as well as scaréd. "What are you telling me?"

"Piper is gone. She went to live with her aunt Sue, in Spokane. I couldn't help it. I told Sue that you two were attached now and Piper seemed happy here. It wasn't supposed to happen until *next* Saturday, and I was going to tell you, but then Sue had business in Seattle today and she didn't want to make the drive twice. . . ."

"Oh my God!" I screech. "For how long? What are you saying?"

Mike looks up at me, his eyes full of tears. "You don't get it. Didn't you hear when I told you Sue has custody? This whole arrangement was never going to be permanent. I told you that when you first moved in here. I guess I didn't make it clear to you. And maybe not clear enough to Piper, either."

I stand up, because I'm way too upset to stay sitting. I can't take this in. "So you're telling me Piper has *already* moved to Spokane, so my services as her babysitter are no longer necessary and who knows if or when I'll ever see her again? *And I don't even get to say goodbye?*" I yell this last line, because I can't imagine this could be true.

Mike keeps talking. "Sue came early. She didn't care about you because she doesn't understand your connection to Piper. You don't have to move out. You can still stay here. And Piper will come visit me on some weekends and you can see her then. She'll be back, I promise. And I won't even raise the rent back up."

"Oh my God! How generous of you." I slam out the front door and start walking, tears streaming, trying to absorb what just happened. With every step, I remember the sound of Piper pedaling behind me.

AFTER PIPER GOES, I am too furious to stay at Mike's, but I'm too cheap to move right away—not with rent being so reasonable. I decide to stay until I can save enough to put down money on a junky car and move to California. That's always been the plan anyway, right? To be in a warm place where the chance of being recognized would be so much slimmer.

Of course, I talk to Piper on the phone several times a week. The first time, she cried a lot, because she missed Mike and me. Plus, she was devastated when Aunt Sue refused to let her bring Felix. "Cats and babies don't mix," she'd told Piper. After a few weeks pass, though, Piper begins to sound like she's adjusting, partly because she is so in love with her twin baby cousins. Isn't that every girl's dream? To have real babies to take care of?

Every time we talk, she tells me she is praying for Leo. Apparently, Aunt Sue is some kind of Christian. "I'm praying for Leo to come home so you won't be alone," she says. I want him to come home, too. But the surprising truth is that Piper left a space in my heart only she can fill. *Why did I let that happen? I should have seen this coming.*

Meanwhile, Mike is wrapped up with Curtis, so he's rarely ever home. Which means I rarely ever eat dinner, and now I'm so skinny I look freakish—yes, even spider-like. I spend my afternoons and evenings lying on the couch like I'm sick, watching TV to numb my brain. I know I'm in trouble when I start to watch really dumb game shows.

On my day off on Monday, I get to watch soaps. Amazing how you can still follow the story watching just one day a week. My favorite is *All My Children*, perhaps because Tad Martin makes me think of Danny. The quirky confidence, the flirty sense of humor.

I still fantasize about finding a way to fix myself.

After a while, I feel guilty just lying around the house all the time, so I set up a system to survive my own lethargy. Every commercial break, I force myself to get up and do something useful, like wash the dishes, or make my bed, or make progress on a cleaning project around the house. And there are so many of those. I put new Con-Tact paper down in the kitchen drawers and under the sink. I find paint in the garage to patch up all the dings and marks on the walls. I ask Mike for money to replace the ratty drapes in the living room, but he says he doesn't have it.

Bumping around that house alone, looking for projects, I keep thinking of Inez. She was always trying to find a new, cheap way to decorate. Because my bedroom was in the basement, it didn't have a rug, so she used small carpet samples and double-sided tape to create a patchwork rug. Leo would only step on the squares that were solid colors and avoided the ones with shag mixes.

One of the worst ideas Inez ever had was when she covered an entire wall in the foyer with a mural—basically a giant photograph you paste on like wallpaper. It featured a small waterfall among ferns.

"I don't get it," I told her. "Is this supposed to look real? So people will think you have a waterfall just inside the house?"

She frowned at me. "It's okay if you hate it, Venus," she said. "I think it's really nice. It's supposed to make you feel refreshed and happy to see nature."

"But isn't nature supposed to be outside?"

She blew. "For God's sake, Venus! Would you prefer blank walls everywhere?"

Ha. It's funny now to think how her suggestion totally came true at Echo Glen. Five and a half years of blank walls without a single fucking waterfall has brought me around to her point of view.

29

It's January 28 and I'm at work when it happens. I'm filling an enormous order for a woman who is angry that we are out of maple bars. "It's only eight-thirty!" she declares. "How can you already be out of such a basic, important thing?"

I explain that we are just a little behind and more maple bars will come out from the oven soon, if she wants to wait. In the kitchen, we have a portable TV that's rarely turned on, but this morning Julie and Gus, the baker, want to watch the launch of the *Challenger* shuttle. I'm too bitter about my own life to care.

The angry maple-bar woman continues to frown at me while I wait on other customers. When I get the chance, I go check on her maple bars—and happen to glance at the TV. A news anchor is reporting that the *Challenger* blew up shortly after takeoff. All day, every channel keeps showing the astronauts, the launch, and the sickening explosion. Over and over, the teacher Christa McAuliffe and the astronaut Judith Resnik and all the others explode into thin air.

All day, I feel a small worm of guilt about the jealousy I harbored toward the women on that crew. It strikes me as the saddest kind of tragedy possible. To have your big dream come true—only to have it turn into your worst nightmare. Not that they even knew what hit them.

. . .

BY EARLY FEBRUARY, I'm so depressed that I struggle to see a future, much less want it. Sunny California seems closer at hand than ever before, given my savings. But with Piper gone, and with Danny out of my life—I feel so alone it aches as if a heavy stone is hanging from my rib cage.

I think of Anita and Arabella, two spiders NASA sent to space in 1973. It was an experiment to see if they could spin webs without gravity. It seems Arabella had trouble at first, and she spun sloppy webs. However, by the third day, both she and Anita were spinning webs just like those back home. Today, both of their spider bodies are on display at the Smithsonian.

When I first learned of the spiders back in grade school, their determination struck me as magical. Now I wonder what would have happened if there'd only been one spider in the first place. Would Arabella have gotten her groove back without Anita spinning next to her?

That's kind of how I feel with Piper gone. Without her by my side, it's harder to breathe, the air feels heavy, and I struggle for a reason to keep going through the motions of life.

One morning, I come downstairs in the dark and grab the Cheerios from the cupboard. I go to the fridge for milk and I'm pouring it over my cereal when I freeze. I set the carton down, disbelieving my eyes. The room begins to spin as I read what it says under Leo's picture:

Missing: Leo Miller
From: Everett, Washington, February 9, 1980
DOB: August 7, 1972
Hair: blond
Eyes: gray
Estimated Height: 5'0"
Note: mentally handicapped

I think I might be sick or faint. None of this information is new, but still, here is proof that people who don't even know us think there's still a good-enough reason to hope that Leo is alive to go to all this effort.

The picture of Leo is painfully familiar. He is sitting among piles of wrapping paper the Christmas before it all happened. You can't tell from his face that he's happy, since Leo never smiled. But I know he had just opened up a new Lincoln Logs set that was the "right" brown and he was making his happy humming sound.

Then I realize something else. Mike bought this milk two days ago at least. How could I have picked it up and not even noticed my own brother's picture on it?

Because I wasn't looking for it, of course. Because I *haven't* been looking for Leo. I've been out of jail for months now, and I haven't once been brave enough to check up on his case or do a damn thing to help look for him, just in case he's alive.

The Cheerios sit there, getting soggy. When I try to put the milk back in the refrigerator, I can't. Instead, I empty the carton into a pitcher. Then I rinse the carton, open it out flat, and take it upstairs, where I put it in my bottom dresser drawer.

At work, I somehow manage to get through the Dipper's morning rush. During my break, though, when I take a minute to catch my breath, Inez's words from six years ago ring in my ears again: *If something has happened to Leo, it's because of what you did.*

It's a truth I've been working hard all these years to avoid: If I hadn't killed Raymond, Leo would still have a father. And he would never have been at Shirley's house to begin with. All those years in Echo Glen when I worked so hard to pretend Leo was dead—it wasn't because I couldn't afford to hope, it was because I couldn't afford the guilt.

My mood grows blacker after that. I feel darker and more depressed every day that goes by. Sometimes I laugh to myself like a crazy person, recalling how I honestly thought that after I got out of jail, I would be so happy. Instead, I'm so unhappy that Julie asks me if I can try harder to be friendly toward customers.

Maybe I'm feeling reckless or want to sabotage my life that isn't a life. Or maybe I do it for Piper, in her memory. But one day out of the blue, I reach behind my back and pull the band from my braid. At work, I have to at least tie it back loosely because of food-safety rules. But otherwise I wear it loose every day. I tell myself it's safe now, because after all these months at the Dipper, no one has come close to recognizing me—except Gloria, who doesn't count.

But, of course, I should have known better. I should have known I couldn't trust my hair not to betray me all over again. This time, it was through a Polaroid that Piper took at Christmas.

I learned only later that some of the pictures she'd snapped of us had traveled to school for a holiday show-and-tell. Since Piper never even got the chance to clean out her desk, she'd left several behind, tucked in a spelling book. Weeks later, a teacher's assistant tasked with emptying Piper's desk found them. She thought the woman with wild black hair in Piper's photo looked a lot like that crazy girl who killed her stepfather in Everett.

I guess she grilled the teacher about whether she knew anything about the woman in the picture. Since I had donated doughnuts to the class more than once, the teacher just so happened to know where Piper's "babysitter" worked. The nosy mother excitedly informed a reporter friend.

And so one cold Tuesday in February a reporter shows up. At first, I'm not positive she's with the press. But I notice her studying my face in a way that sets off alarms in my brain. She's wearing black slacks and pumps, a gray blazer, and she has a thin briefcase with her. She takes her coffee and sits where she can watch me.

After a while, I realize she's waiting for me to go on a break or finish my shift. My hands start to sweat and I beg the God who doesn't exist to help me. Of course, I might as well be praying to a chair. This woman isn't going anywhere.

But then, to my great surprise, it dawns on me that I'm not going to run, slip out the back door, or try to avoid this confrontation. Maybe I'm sick of hiding. Or maybe I am too depressed to care. Or maybe I've finally realized that a fake ID will never set me free of being me.

I take some deep breaths. I decide this won't go down like before—with me acting scared and hiding my face in my hair. It's going to happen on my terms. I think about Piper—how she's so brave and bossy. Piper would never run from a reporter.

As soon as the order counter is empty of customers, I tell Julie I need to take a break. I calmly hang up my apron and approach the woman. She is petite, has her brown hair in a top bun. Because she is sitting, I feel like a giant looming over her. "You've been sitting here for quite a while," I say. "Is there something more you want?"

"Yes, *Venus*," she says with an apologetic smile. "And I'm really sorry it's not a doughnut."

"Why do you guys have to hound me like this?"

"Why do you assume you're being hounded?" she replies. "No one is *hounding* you, Venus. I would just like to have a friendly conversation."

"Yeah, right," I say. "I'm guessing it's not about movies, boys, or books."

"It might be."

"Can you wait until I get off work? I'll meet you at the bottom of the tower in Volunteer Park at two-thirty."

She looks doubtful. I can tell she doesn't think I'll show. But what is she going to do? Follow me when I get off work? Continue to chase me around? I doubt a picture of me hiding my face again is enough to make a story.

I don't wait for an answer. "I'll see you there, bottom of the stairs," and then I go put my apron back on. Julie says nothing about how I cut my break so short. But I can feel her watching me for the rest of my shift.

A few minutes before I'm off, she approaches me. "Did I hear that woman call you Venus?"

I nod.

"Was she a reporter?"

"I guess so," I say. "You heard the conversation?" I must have been so distracted by the reporter that I hadn't registered Julie's whereabouts.

"I heard enough," she says in a soft voice, cocking her head. "So, are there going to be a bunch of people coming in here to get a look at you? Are you Venus *Black*?"

"Yeah," I admit. "I can't fucking believe it, but I am." I tear off my apron and hang it up for the last time. "I'm sorry I didn't say so sooner," I tell Julie, pulling on my coat and readying to leave. "I'm sorry I lied. I was trying to start over. I understand you'll want to fire me."

Julie gets a shocked look on her face. "Oh no!" She puts an arm around my shoulder, which makes me realize I'm shaking. "Fire you?" she says. "That's the last thing my mom or I would do. Don't take this wrong, but it might even bring more customers in."

"Oh. Great," I say, letting out a half laugh. "Customers can come look at me like a monkey in the zoo. But, hey, I guess it will mean more tips for everyone, right?" I can't hold back the tears that threaten. I hurry off to use the bathroom before I go.

Looking at myself in the mirror, I can see my future. For the rest of my life I'll plaster a smile on my face and fill breakfast orders for rude people. I will never have friends. I'll never have a real boyfriend, much less get married. I'll never go to college or pursue any of the old dreams. I'll die a broken, bitter old spinster fondly remembered by no one, famous for being the nice, straight-A kid who put a bullet in her stepdad's brain.

PART FOUR

★

Oakland, California;
Everett, Washington;
February 1986

30

Leo is thirteen now, and he likes to tell people this. Thirteen is really old, Tessa says. Now he waits at the bus stop next to Tessa for his bus to come. He is wearing his blue backpack and carrying his cello. Every day he takes these two things to school. He wishes he could wear his backpack all the time, but Mrs. Langhorne says no.

The bus that is the wrong yellow comes two minutes after it is supposed to. Leo says goodbye to Tessa, like he's been taught. Then he boards the bus and sits in the spot where he always sits. Once, another boy sat in his seat and Leo got mad. Then the driver got mad and there were red feelings everywhere.

On the way to school, he looks for blue things and names them aloud. Mr. Taft, his speech therapist who makes him talk a lot, wants Leo to make sentences with blue things in them, but he mostly just likes to find blue things. He looks out the window and sees a blue car in the next lane. "A blue car goes fast," he begins. Then, "I like blue houses."

Leo hears the boy sitting behind him saying the same blue things he says and then laughing. Leo doesn't mind if other people say blue things.

After a while, he forgets about looking for blue and stares at the ribbon in the hair of the girl in front of him. It is just like Tessa's. It is yellow and purple stripes. Purple and yellow are his new favorite colors. Leo sees these colors a lot when he's at school. Tessa says they're the school colors, even though the school is brown.

When the bus stops, Leo makes sure he has the two things before he stands up. Backpack. Cello case. Inside the school, he goes to the classroom where he belongs. He puts his cello in the back corner. He takes off his coat and hangs it on a knob. Then he slides his backpack under his desk and sits down.

His teacher says, "Good morning, Leo."

He says back, "Good morning, Mrs. Langhorne." He likes his teacher because she smells like lemons, and lemons are the right yellow and they even smell like yellow. But not to eat! One time, Leo took a bite of lemon and he spit it out. Tony laughed and Tessa got mad at Tony.

While he waits, Leo plays his cello in his head until the other kids make too much noise. The one called Stan talks too much and he gets to ride around in a silver chair with really big wheels. Leo is jealous of his chair and he wants one just like it, but Tessa says no. Mrs. Langhorne says no, too. Leo doesn't like when people say no.

Mrs. Langhorne says it's time for spelling. Leo looks at his watch. It is 8:32. Spelling should not start until 8:35, but he won't get upset. He is learning not to get upset as much. But no matter when it starts, Leo hates spelling, because the words always break the rules.

After spelling comes science. This week they are on a chapter about the stars and planets. When he looks at the solar system in his book, he gets upset. He shakes his hand, like he's been taught.

His teacher says, "Yes, Leo?" And Leo shouts, "Venus is not yellow. Venus is red!"

"Okay, Leo," she says. "If you want Venus to be red, it can be red. I'll even let you fix it in your book."

While Leo uses a colored pencil to make Venus red, he names the planets like he used to with Venus.

"Well, that is very good, Leo!" she says. "You already know all the planets' names and their order from the sun."

When Leo continues to say them, Mrs. Langhorne wants him to stop. She shushes him and asks him to remember the other students. People at school always interrupt you. They want you to answer questions, and then when you are asking questions or talking, they tell you to stop.

TESSA STABS THREE potatoes with a fork, placing them in the microwave on a paper towel. She should have started dinner sooner.

She goes to tell Leo it's almost time. He's watching bowling, his longish blond hair hanging across his face. Tessa thinks, as she often does, that at a glance you would never know about Leo's differentness. You'd just think he was a handsome thirteen-year-old boy.

After six years, she still has moments like this—where, for just a second, it doesn't seem far-fetched that Leo should look up and smile and ask if he can help make dinner.

"Leo," she says.

He grunts.

"Ten minutes."

He grunts again. The ten-minute warning is a fairly new routine. She blames herself. With Leo, you have to be very careful not to do the same thing the same way too many times in a row, or he's bound to notice and then turn it into yet another requirement.

She goes out to the back porch to check the steaks on the hibachi. Now that they have an actual private deck, it's her favorite way to make dinner.

They rented this house—a humble rancher in a so-so Oakland neighborhood—shortly after Leo came to stay. They needed another bedroom, and with rental rates skyrocketing, her dad realized he could afford to let out both apartments above the tattoo shop and rent a small house for them.

She lifts the lid and checks the steaks, but they're thicker than usual and not near done.

Leo won't be happy if she's late getting them on the table. But at least he doesn't throw tantrums all the time anymore. He's really matured in the last six years.

Still, all the routines and demands have made her life harder. Whenever she resents this, she reminds herself how sad it was before he came. How she and her dad were just two lonely people and their biggest connection was the shared gap where her mother should be. Adding Leo made it three, more like a real family.

For a long time, Tessa thought if she just loved Leo hard enough, he would get better—all the way better, meaning he would be more like a regular boy. She used to pray to Mary for a miracle, too, but it never came. He still makes a strange humming sound when he's happy, but she's never actually seen him smile or heard him laugh. She wishes he would look her in the eye and share his feelings. But no matter what special gifts Leo has or what he learns to do—converse, follow directions, read, and even play music—part of him is still trapped somewhere Tessa can't reach.

What hurts most is that Leo doesn't seem to care.

Yet she knows that in his own strange way, Leo does care about people. Whenever she—or anyone, really—is upset or sad, if Leo is nearby, he will start to gently rock. Her dad says Leo has empathy.

Tessa turns the steaks, sees they still need time. She absently thinks about a boy she wishes would ask her out. She's seventeen now, and she's been allowed to date since she was sixteen. It's beginning to embarrass her that she hasn't gone on a single date. At the same time, she's pretty sure her dad isn't going to like it if she gets too busy with a boyfriend, because he still needs her at home a lot.

A breeze comes up and she zips her sweatshirt, grateful for the small rise of her breasts. Because she was a late bloomer, she's still getting used to the idea of looking and feeling like an actual woman. It makes her feel closer to her mother, almost like she's becoming her.

As she continues to wait for the steaks, she notices a single star in the dusky sky. She guesses it's probably Venus.

Sometimes she still feels a twinge of guilt about not telling her father that Leo might have a sister named Venus somewhere. That first Easter, when Phil had let Leo come to their apartment for dinner, Tessa had been anxious to get Leo alone and learn more. Leo had said, "My sister is Venus. Venus is red." But he had refused to answer her questions about Venus—or, for that matter, anything in the past. To this day, he's made it clear that nothing makes him madder than being asked to "remember."

He always blurts out, "I don't know before."

But Tessa does know. And as hard as she tries to pretend it doesn't matter, the truth is like a tiny splinter lodged in her conscience that hurts when she touches it.

TONY IS STANDING in the doorway, waiting for dinner to be ready. He should go help Tessa, at least set the table, but a patch of winter sun is slanting through the front window onto his face and he can't make himself move. He studies Leo, who is watching bowling on TV. With Leo, you can do that, watch him. Tessa would never allow it.

As usual, Leo is tipping his head to the left. The doctor says there's nothing wrong with his neck, it's just a quirk of Leo's. But at least they eventually managed to break him of pulling on his hair. Now it's long and blond and hangs in his eyes. Tony thinks a man pony is a good idea—like father, like son. But Tessa says it makes him look like a girl. "His face is too pretty," she says.

On a whim, Tony asks Leo if he remembers when he took him bowling.

Leo just grunts, which usually means yes.

Tony is always looking for father-son types of things to do with

Leo. He discovered early on that Leo liked to play catch with a ball. Leo wasn't good at throwing, but Tony always made sure he threw catchable balls. They started with a baseball and then later moved to a football. Tony wishes Leo could actually play sports at school, but he knows Leo couldn't do that. Sports are complicated, and it would seem to Leo that people weren't following the rules.

Once, Tony had mistakenly assumed that since Leo liked to watch bowling on TV—something they discovered when his brother, Marco, had it on at Christmas—he might like to learn how to bowl.

It was a nightmare. Every time Leo heard the sound of pins crashing, he covered his ears and moaned. Still, Tony had been determined, because with Leo you have to be. He can learn new things, but it takes repetition and a lot of patience. Which Tony had in spades, or so he thought.

Finally, when it became apparent that his gentle wrestling with Leo to try to get him to roll the ball was upsetting other patrons—the shoe guy kept glaring at him—Tony had given up. And Leo had continued to love watching bowling on TV.

31

Leo has a secret. He knows what a secret is because Tessa explained it once. Keeping a secret means you don't tell anyone about something you know.

At the time, Leo didn't understand why a person would do that. But now he's pretty sure that's what he is doing. Once, Tony told Leo about sex. And about how his body is changing and girls' bodies change, too. So that's not a secret, because Tony knows. But what feels like a secret is that Leo likes a girl at school. She is older than him. Her name is Sarah, and she has blond hair and she stutters. It used to upset Leo a lot every time she got stuck. He wanted her words to come out so bad that sometimes he would yell out the word she was trying to say. But this made the teacher mad. Leo couldn't understand. He was trying to help.

Now it seems like Sarah stutters less. And she has grown what Leo knows are called "breasts." He gets a weird feeling when he thinks of Sarah's breasts or when he looks at them at school. He wishes he could sit by her in class, but the teacher says no.

Leo wants to tell Tessa about his secret. But if he tells her, then it won't be a secret anymore. And maybe Tessa won't like it that Leo likes Sarah's breasts.

Leo decides he doesn't like secrets at all. He hopes he never gets another one.

. . .

THE FOLLOWING EVENING, Tony sits in his truck, his heart beating out of his chest. He stares at the milk carton on the seat next to him. It features Leo's face under the heading MISSING. He slams his fists on his steering wheel, saying, "Fuck! Fuck! Fuck!"

The name on the carton says Leo Miller, not Brown, but the date of his disappearance matches the time frame—he can't remember the exact date—when Phil moved into the apartment. In this photo, Leo is much younger and his hair is buzzed short. Tony remembers when he looked like that. Now Leo's hair has grown long, because he hates to have it cut.

So if you saw this picture, would you even make the connection? You might, he decides, for the simple reasons that the name is Leo, his strongly arched brows make his face distinctive, and he's described as mentally handicapped. They turned his last name to Herrera to avoid questions, but they never changed Leo's first name because it would have upset him. Plus, he might make mistakes when asked his name.

It stuns him to think that, after all these years, someone is *looking* for Leo. Someone *misses* him. And now Tony looks like a kidnapper. And who knows how many laws he broke when he asked a shady client to get him a fake Social Security number and birth certificate for Leo so they could enroll him in school.

Thank God Tony saw this carton, not Tessa! Since shopping requires a car, it's always been one of the few chores Tony does, and it's the one he likes to mention in case people think he lets Tessa do everything.

After Phil left, Tony suspected that Phil wasn't actually Leo's dad, or else how could he just abandon him? By now, Tony has come to love Leo as if he were his own son. But that still doesn't explain the series of crazy decisions he made almost six years ago.

It started with a bizarre phone call from Phil, a couple of days after Tony had finished his tattoo. Phil thanked him and said it was healing up fine. Then he added, "But, yeah, man. There's something else I gotta tell you. I was calling to let you know . . . Well, you know how you guys like Leo so much? I was hoping you could keep an eye on the kid for me . . . just for a while."

"What do you mean, 'for a while'?"

"Well, he's been there a day and a half; I'm sure he's doing fine. But I'm gonna be out of town a few weeks—"

"What? You left him alone? I'm sorry, but that's not—"

"I'll call back in a couple days to check in," said Phil, and then he simply hung up.

Tony was so stunned it took him a moment to put together this call with the fact that he hadn't seen Phil's white Impala out front the last of couple days. He raced upstairs to Phil's apartment and found the door unlocked. Inside, Leo was calmly watching TV, an open jar of Jif on the counter, along with a half-empty bag of Wonder bread.

Tony's first instinct had been to immediately call the police. The only reason he hesitated—his first mistake—was because Tessa would be home from school in fifteen minutes. He didn't want her to panic at the sight of police cars, especially if they took Leo away in one.

When Tessa got home and saw Leo on their couch watching TV, she acted more guilty than surprised. Then Tony took her into his den and gently explained what had happened with Phil. "We have to call the police right away, honey."

He knew she wouldn't like it, but he hadn't anticipated how upset she'd become. "Daddy, you can't call the police!" she wailed. Then she barraged him with questions about what would happen to Leo. Tony admitted he'd most likely get put in foster care, at least until they could locate Phil.

"But Phil didn't *abandon* him," Tessa argued. "He asked us to babysit! And his mother was a drug addict and didn't even want him. So Leo has no one!" she screeched. "You know it's true, because why else would Phil leave him here? He said he would call. I'm sure he'll come back like he said. Just a few weeks."

Tony pointed out that parents aren't allowed to do what Phil had done and that authorities have people who know how to handle kids like Leo who have special problems.

"But they'll be strangers! And Leo will start having a tantrum and hitting his head . . . and they won't know what to feed him or what he likes to play! I know what he needs even better than Phil. . . ." Tessa trailed off, realizing she'd given herself away.

"What do you mean? How could that be?"

Tessa confessed she'd been secretly visiting Leo for months. Tony could tell she thought she was going to be in big trouble for using the master key to trespass. But of course that didn't matter now. "If you found a way to help Leo and figure out what he likes, so would the professionals," he had argued. "Plus, they may even let you pass on key information."

But Tessa wouldn't see it. "I promise I'll take care of him, Dad!" she pleaded. "You won't have to do anything. I'll do everything."

"He's not a stray dog, Tessa! He's a little boy."

"If he's not a dog," she yelled, "then why do you want to treat him like one and call the pound?"

Tony had never been in this kind of fight with his daughter before—and he saw flashes of her mother Maria's stubbornness. Which made him weaken. Made him say what he should have never said. "He can stay two weeks maximum, and then we call the police if there's no word from Phil."

Tessa was jubilant and set about turning their large laundry room into a small bedroom for Leo. She decorated it and used her allowance to buy things she knew he liked. Tony could see her becoming more and more attached to Leo.

After fourteen days, Tony sat her down, planning to be firm. Two weeks ago he had told Tessa it was non-negotiable. They would call the police and she had agreed. How could she argue with him now?

Easily, it turned out. Having heard nothing from Phil, they'd agreed it was hard to believe he was ever coming back for Leo. Now Tessa's case was simple. They should make Leo part of the family.

She pointed out that no one else was even aware of Leo's existence, other than Tony's brother, Marco, and his fiancée, Maureen. "And you know M and M would think it was the right thing to do, too!" she insisted. "You know they would. And we could get Leo in school and just say that he's my cousin and his parents died and he's come to live with us."

This was the moment when Tony should have laid down the law. Remembered that he was the adult, the parent. Explained to Tessa that her idea was madness. He should have let Tessa go ahead and hate him for an evening, or a week, or whatever it would have been.

But something kept Tony from acting. At the time, he thought he simply couldn't bear to watch Tessa suffer such a big loss when she was already growing up without a mother.

Now he realizes it was also guilt that drove him. Tessa had already been deprived of a normal family life, and he'd made things worse by letting Tessa do too much for him around the house so he could work insane hours at his tat shop, all so they could afford this whole setup.

Taking on Leo would only double the pressure on Tessa. But she deserved to have something she wanted so deeply, and Tony had never seen her as happy as she was with Leo.

And so he said the stupidest words of his life: "Okay, Tessa. We'll give it a try."

Tessa threw her arms around him like he'd handed her the moon.

If he could have, he would have handed her the stars, too.

But now—sitting outside Sye's Market in his truck—he realizes the sky is about to fall on all of them. It's started to rain. Enormous splats of water slap his filthy windshield, then slide down the pane in rivulets.

Leo would like watching that, he thinks. He looks again at the information under Leo's picture:

Missing: Leo Miller
From: Everett, Washington, February 9, 1980
DOB: August 7, 1972
Hair: blond
Eyes: gray
Estimated Height: 5'0"
Note: mentally handicapped

He can't believe this is happening. What will Tessa do if he goes to prison and Leo is taken away? She could lose her entire family in one fell swoop. The realization is too terrible to take in.

So what the hell is he doing just sitting here in his truck? He needs to call Marco, who's always been smarter than him. He'll know exactly what to do—once he gets done with all his I-told-you-so's. Tessa had been wrong about what M and M would think. But, of course, they eventually came to love Leo, too.

After talking to Marco from the phone booth outside the market, Tony calls Tessa. He makes up a story about how the truck won't start and now he's waiting for a mechanic friend to come take a look. "Tell Leo I'm sorry for missing dinner," he says.

"Of course, Dad," she says, "but Leo's not going to be happy."

Tony wants to laugh when she says that. Tessa has no idea how *not happy* Leo is going to be pretty soon. Because *of course* Tony plans to turn Leo over. But even Marco—after yelling and swearing about how Tony should have listened to him all those years ago—agreed they should get legal advice first and come up with a plan.

In the meantime, as dumb as it seems to both men, the best way to buy time might be to buy milk. So Maureen is already making a list of all the grocery stores and markets within the boundaries of their school district, since people who shop there are most likely to have had contact with Leo. But even if all three of them rotate stores, checkers, and different times of day, all they can hope to do is to improve their odds until . . . well, until Tony figures out *how* to break the news to Tessa and turn Leo over to the authorities.

Just last night, Tessa was talking to Tony about Leo. "Kids at school like to try to get him to look at them, and when he tries hard to make eye contact, they get excited. Or sometimes they like to toss him a ball because he can catch it without seeming to ever look at it. It's really kind of weird, Dad," she said. "But everyone loves Leo."

Yeah, Tony thinks now. *And everyone drinks milk, too.*

32

That night, Tony lies in bed and doesn't sleep a wink. Once he got past his initial shock and fear for himself and Tessa and Leo, he realized the most important question of all was *who* exactly is looking for Leo? Leo is like a son to him, and he's not about to hand him over to strangers without knowing more. Where would he live? What kind of a home environment would it be?

The next day at noon, Tony sits in his small den and has some heated discussion with Marco. His brother looks like Tony feels—sweaty, panicked, and short of breath. He's been buying milk all morning, so that could be part of it. But since Marco is normally the calm one, the guy who has it together, it scares Tony to see his brother—a clean-cut, tattoo-free professional—so rattled.

Marco explains that he has spoken with a lawyer friend. "I gotta warn you, buddy. This guy is a lawyer, but he doesn't seem to know this part of the law very well."

"Still, he's a lawyer. So what did he say?"

"He said that if the police find the hypothetical missing child before his 'friend' voluntarily turns him over, it will definitely *look* worse, though he's not sure it will change the outcome."

"Define *worse*," Tony says, feeling his heart beat a little faster.

"Either way, no matter how or when you hand Leo over,

charges against you could range anywhere from kidnapping to simple interference with custody."

"Okay," says Tony, standing up from his chair to pace around. "But why wouldn't it count in my favor if I was arrested while trying to find answers? Surely, they'd understand my need to know who's claiming my son. How could any good parent just hand over their kid without knowing more?"

The plan he and Marco finally arrive at sounds crazy, but it seems like their best shot. Tony will cancel all his appointments for several days, beginning tomorrow—Friday. In the morning he'll drive to Everett, Washington. Marco pointed out that surely, when Leo first went missing in 1980, there had to be a story in the local newspaper. Tony should start with that. From there, he should be able to get a name and scope out the situation.

He'd rather not go. He wishes he knew someone in Everett or that he had access to Everett newspapers from 1980.

After Marco leaves, his eyes fall on Tessa's junior-year school photo. She framed it in a green ceramic frame for him. What will Tessa do if they have to give up Leo? What will she do if Tony goes to prison? He can't imagine it.

As he ate his dinner last night, Tony had felt Tessa studying him. She has some kind of radar for sensing when he's troubled about something. For the umpteenth time, he worries that he relies on her way too much. He wonders if he would try harder to find a wife instead of dating casually if Tessa didn't take such great care of everything.

He's also concerned that Tessa is so devoted to Leo and himself that it's gotten in the way of her having other friendships and acting like a normal adolescent. Tony isn't sure, but isn't she supposed to be having sleepovers, and shouldn't she be begging to date boys by now? Tony always insisted she had to wait until she was sixteen, but he's secretly disappointed she hasn't seemed to care.

If there's one thing he's sure of, it's that Tessa has to go to college. She's smart as a whip, like her mother, even if she's way less outgoing and not quite as driven. Tessa doesn't seem to mind an occasional B or even a C. Tony can't decide if this is a good thing or if he should push her hard just in case she could get a scholarship, because he has no idea how he could afford college.

He glances at his clock radio. He has a customer in five minutes, but he's reluctant to move from his spot. Tony doesn't use his den very often, but he likes the idea of it. It makes him feel like there's more to him than being a tattoo artist. He bought a bookshelf, and now and then he goes into the den to read a novel.

Now he reaches for a big green atlas he got at a garage sale. It takes him a few minutes to locate the map of Washington State. He's never been to Seattle, but he's heard that all it does is rain. He scans the map and there it is. Everett is located about thirty miles north of Seattle, right on the waters of Puget Sound.

Who knew a single black dot could seem so ominous?

WHEN TESSA DOES laundry, she always checks Leo's pockets for crayons—he still likes to draw with them. She checks her dad's, too—because she gets half of any money she finds. Usually it's only some change, but today it feels like dollars. It turns out to be an old tire-store receipt with something jotted on the back: "Miss 2-80 Born 8-7-72."

Who is "Miss"? It would be great if this was about a woman, but it's obviously not a phone number. She's always regretted that her father doesn't date more, especially when she realizes it's partly her fault—her fault and Leo's. Between the tat shop and being a parent, he probably doesn't have time to chase women, as he'd say.

She puts the receipt in her pocket to ask her dad about later.

By the time her father comes home from work, she's forgotten about the receipt. Tessa loves Thursday nights, because they always have pizza, and they take turns choosing the toppings. Since Leo always orders the same thing—Canadian bacon and pineapple—and removes all the toppings when it's not his turn, that's often what Tessa orders, too, even though she hates Canadian bacon and pineapple.

But not tonight. She's still bugged by something her best friend, Kelly, said to her today. "You need to stop being so nice, Tessa. Guys don't like girls who don't have personality or stick up for themselves." The comment surprised Tessa and hurt her feelings, but she didn't say so.

Now she realizes that her reaction only proves Kelly's point. If she was the kind of girl guys would like, she would have told Kelly that what she said wasn't nice. It's all so confusing. How can someone be too nice? Maybe what Kelly really means is that Tessa is too shy, which is something she's heard all of her life.

She goes to the door of her dad's den and asks, "How about mushrooms and green peppers tonight?"

"Sure," he says. But she can tell he's not listening. "Tess, actually, can you wait for a sec on the pizza? I need to talk to you."

She takes a seat on the only other chair in the room. It always makes her nervous when her dad says he wants to talk, perhaps because he does it so rarely and it's usually an awkward conversation about boys or sex or something like that.

"I need to leave town for a few days," he says. "There's a big tattoo convention I want to go to. I can learn some new techniques, check out some of the latest equipment. That kind of thing."

"Really?" she asks. Her dad never went anywhere. She can't remember the last time he left the Oakland area, besides the couple of times a year he takes her to visit her grandparents on her mother's side in L.A. "Where's it being held?"

"It's in Seattle, Washington."

"Oh," she says. "That's pretty far. What are the dates?"

"I'd be leaving tomorrow."

"Tomorrow?" She couldn't be more surprised.

"I'm sorry, Tessa," her dad says. "I know it's really sudden.

And I'm not going to leave you and Leo alone. Your aunt Maureen is going to come and stay while I'm gone."

"I don't need a babysitter!" she objects. "Dad, I'm seventeen!"

"Just barely," he reminds her.

"Still, I'm more than old enough to babysit *other* people's kids, so why not Leo?"

"Not overnight. I'm not going to leave you alone overnight."

She can tell her dad's not going to change his mind on this one. "Will she be here all the time, the whole time?" Tessa can't bear the thought. She likes Maureen, but she wants to be treated like she can handle being alone.

"I don't know. Maybe she could just come in the evenings and sleep over."

"That'd be better," Tessa says.

Her father takes a deep breath and Tessa realizes he's upset about something. He's shaking his knee, a telltale sign that he is nervous. What's he so nervous about? And why did he decide at the last minute to go to a conference in Seattle? It just seems weird.

"So you're flying?" she asks. If he's flying, she's going to be jealous. Neither of them has ever been on a plane before—which right there might explain her dad's anxiety. Maybe he's scared of flying.

"No," he says. "I'll actually just be driving. And that's part of why I need to be gone for at least three or four days."

Tessa gets an idea. "What if Leo and I come with you? It could be fun! And we'd only miss a couple days of school."

"I'm sorry, sweetie. It's not a place for kids."

Her dad gets up abruptly. "Call me when the pizza gets here, okay? After we eat, I need to go out for a while. That okay?"

Something keeps her from asking him where. It's like she can tell he doesn't want to be bothered. "Sure, Dad," she says, feeling a little miffed. She'd been hoping they could all play a game tonight. Leo has learned to love playing the game Trouble. She watches her dad get up and leave the room, notices his ponytail is getting some gray hairs.

She stays awhile after her father's gone, feeling left out and somehow abandoned. She can't remember now what toppings she wanted on the pizza and she no longer cares. She uses the phone on her dad's desk to order Canadian bacon and pineapple.

LEO CAREFULLY REMOVES the pineapple and Canadian bacon from his piece of pizza so he can eat them separately. He is sitting at the kitchen table with Tessa and Tony. Tony is talking to Leo. He is saying that he is going to be out of town. "Do you understand, Leo? Leo, please look at me."

Leo forces himself to see Tony's eyes. "Do you understand?"

"No," says Leo.

"I'm not going to be here for a few days. Maureen will come spend the nights while I'm gone. Tessa will still be here."

"Where are you going?"

"Seattle, Washington."

"The Space Needle?"

"Well, I'm not going there, but, yes, that's where it's located. Good for you, Leo, knowing about the Space Needle."

"I'm not dumb," he says, something he's just started saying this past year. "I went up to the top there," he says. "Before."

He can feel Tony and Tessa stiffen. This is why he doesn't talk about before. Before makes Tessa unhappy.

"So Tessa will watch you while I'm gone and Maureen will spend the night. Do you understand, Leo?"

"Tessa will stay here," he says.

"Yes," says Tony. "Tessa will be here."

Leo takes a bite of pizza. It is good. He has liked pizza for a while now.

Leo drinks his milk, too. He hears Tessa talking about Maureen. Maureen is the one who always wears black. And she smells like his mother smelled before.

Leo hears the phone ring. He hates the phone, because it doesn't ring the same number of times before Tessa or Tony answers. He used to yell if they let it ring more than three, but now he doesn't. He hears Tony say Marco's name and then, "I'll take it in the den."

Tessa gets up to hold the phone. Leo does not like it when they stand up and leave during dinner. "No leaving!" he shouts. All three of them are supposed to stay at the table until Leo is done eating.

"Just a minute, Leo," Tessa says.

"No minutes! You have to stay." She hangs up the kitchen phone and sits back down by him. "I'm staying. Eat your pizza."

He won't eat his pizza until Tony is at the table. He starts to rock, but just rocking one. Tessa says he can't rock number two unless he asks. And rocking three is only for an emergency. But Leo still doesn't understand *emergency.*

Tessa is not eating her pizza, either. She is not talking. She is sitting very still, which to Leo seems the same as rocking.

TONY FOLLOWS LEO to his room and waits while Leo gets in his jammies, brushes his teeth, and climbs in bed. "Good night, Leo," Tony says.

"Good night, Tony," Leo says.

After Tony shuts the door, he hears Leo begin his counting.

He and Tessa have talked lately about trying to change Leo's bedtime pattern so it doesn't require Tony's supervising. But after several traumatic evenings, they finally caved in. Tony doesn't even remember how the routine came about. Those early months with Leo were so difficult. When to give in to Leo and when to force an issue? Now, almost six years later, there's little that hasn't been reduced to a routine.

He passes Tessa's door and hears her radio playing. He pokes his head in. "Headed to bed, sweetie?"

"Yeah, in a minute." She is lying on top of her bed with her lamp on, reading a book. How can she read and listen to music at the same time?

She looks like her mother. The older she gets, the more Tony thinks she resembles Maria. The thick dark hair, the penetrating, serious eyes that don't seem to blink as often as they should. And her nose, the perfection of its angles.

Is she a beauty or is Tony just prejudiced? He goes to her. Kisses her forehead. "I'll be leaving before you get up."

"You will?" She looks alarmed.

"It's a long drive," Tony says. He strokes her hair. "You will be okay?"

"I will be okay," says Tessa. "And so will Leo." She smiles reassuringly. Always, she is reassuring him when he knows he should be reassuring her.

Now he can't believe what a cruel thing God is asking him to do to his children. He tries to remember which saint he should pray to. He's pretty sure Saint Anthony is the saint for finding lost things. But what if you don't want to find what you're looking for?

TESSA WAKES UP before her alarm goes off. Her father is already gone. She feels his absence in a way that is different from when she knows he's just gone to the shop early. She pictures him on the highway, driving to Seattle. She worries that he'll get lonely. Or that his truck will break down.

In a few moments, she hears Leo getting in the shower. He doesn't need an alarm. He always wakes up in time to get in the shower at 7:00 A.M.

As she dresses for school, Tessa thinks that sometimes she envies Leo. She doesn't think he ever worries about other people. She's often asked herself if Leo loves her. If he's capable. Sometimes she tells him, "I love you." But he never answers.

She knows they could teach him to—just like they've taught him a whole bunch of other responses, like "you're welcome" and "thank you" and even "I forgive you." But it wouldn't be the same, wouldn't seem right, if you taught him to say, "I love you, too."

At breakfast, Leo is difficult. He is upset that the milk is not the same brand her father always buys. They must have been out, because her dad knows better than to change anything. "Milk is milk, Leo," she says firmly.

"It's the wrong kind," Leo insists.

Tessa is almost tempted to swear. She wonders if she should start swearing, if that would make boys like her more. "Darn it, Leo! Not this morning," she says.

"Why not this morning?"

Tessa sighs. "Leo, would you like me to make you eggs instead? They're the right kind, I'm sure."

Leo considers. "No! I want my Rice Krispies."

Tessa pours milk on her own cereal. "See, Leo? It's exactly the same milk. The milk is the right white. That's what matters, not the name on the carton." She begins to take bites. "It tastes exactly the same."

Leo pours the milk. Looks at it. Takes a bite. Tessa is relieved, because she didn't want to make eggs.

DURING ART, THE teacher lets Leo's class draw whatever they want. Today, Leo draws the strange building from Seattle called the Space Needle. In his mind he sees it from a car window. But he also sees it when he's close and looking up at it. His mother from before asks, "Do you want to go to the top?"

Venus says that she wants to go up. He follows when they tell him to come. They go into a small room with windows. Other people are in the room, too. It jerks and starts moving up in a scary way. Leo cries and hits his head on the windows, and his mother says, "Stop, Leo! How embarrassing." Leo doesn't know *embarrassing*.

"What's that, Leo?" asks his teacher. She is leaning over him. She is interrupting. He ignores her. He is unsure how many windows to draw in the part that is like an upside-down bowl at the top.

"Is that the Space Needle, Leo?" his teacher is interrupting again. But Leo knows those words. *Space Needle*. From before. He nods his head and hopes she will go away.

"Have you been to the Space Needle, Leo?"

He ignores her. He doesn't want to talk. She is interrupting!

When he is finished with his drawing, he puts his pencils away. The teacher comes by and tries to take the drawing. Leo doesn't want her to. He holds it away from her and says, "No!"

She finally passes by. He opens his science book. He finds the right page with the planets. He folds his drawing in half. He puts it in the book next to Venus.

33

Tony is glad that Everett is pretty much a straight shot up I-5. He makes good time until he hits snow in the Siskiyous. Then his driving slows to a crawl and he can no longer find a radio station. Alone with his thoughts, his mind goes to Maria and what she'd think of the mess he's in.

Would she be angry that he'd compromised Tessa's happiness by taking in Leo? Tony doubts it. There was no one more compassionate than Maria Delgado. He was convinced she'd have done the same.

Tony never could understand why such a wonderful girl would marry a bozo like him to begin with. He and Maria had met in high school, where she was a star student. And Tony . . . Apart from secretly loving art class, he excelled at nothing, except maybe baseball. Even there, he'd been an alternate pitcher, not the star. But he could run like the wind and he could hit, too. By his senior year, though, drugs and alcohol had started to get in the way.

It was Maria who helped him turn a corner. He still wonders where he'd be now—one of the strung-out addicts he sees on the street—if he hadn't married her. And yet, falling in love with a Mexican girl brought challenges. Maria's parents were strict Catholics and had immigrated to the United States when Maria was young. They vehemently opposed the match, perhaps because he was neither Catholic nor Mexican. But now he realizes it was more than an issue of religion or race. He had no plan, no real means of securing a future.

And yet, blinded by love, he'd felt no guilt marrying Maria. He was young enough to think life would naturally bring what a family needed to grow. Looking back, he'd been so in love that he couldn't imagine a future without Maria—or a version of life that wouldn't be kind to her.

Maria wasn't perfect, of course. She had a tendency to overspend and she loved to gossip with her girlfriends. She hated housework, but she was always impeccably dressed—in fact, ironing her clothes had been the only housework she had the heart for. When someone would stop by the apartment unexpectedly, she'd race around the house, picking up. Once, he heard her actually scrubbing the toilet while he got their guest a drink.

And they had fought. They had had terrible fights about her family and about the fact that, no matter what Maria said or did, he was convinced that she felt embarrassed in front of them for marrying him; he also suspected she was grateful when he opted out of family gatherings.

Given that strict Catholics had raised Maria, she didn't believe in birth control, and she became pregnant within months of their marriage. They'd both been delighted by the news, and apart from morning sickness during the first trimester, Maria's pregnancy seemed to go smoothly.

Tony was in the delivery room to see Tessa born. But then he was alarmed to realize something wasn't right with Maria. He was ushered from the room and told to wait in the hall. Shortly, their doctor returned to give him the bad news. "I'm so sorry, Tony," he said. "Maria suffered a retained placenta and hemorrhaged. . . . She lost too much blood. She didn't make it, Mr. Herrera."

After Maria died, Tony had been so shocked, overwrought,

and inconsolable that her family had taken the baby, and he'd actually let them. For a few months, he couldn't see a way to go on and he figured Tessa was better off with a rich, if snooty, family.

He was also ashamed. Clearly he hadn't caused Maria's death, but every time he thought of her family and their disdain for him, he was overcome by the certainty that if she'd only married someone Catholic, someone better, she'd still be alive.

It was his older brother, Marco, who saved him next. Marco once had aspirations of going to law school. He never went, but he did graduate from UCLA and he did have a corporate job where he made pretty good money. It was Marco who helped Tony find the will—and the finances—to fight hard to reclaim Tessa.

The law was on his side, thank God. By then Tony had opened his first tattoo shop—a hole-in-the-wall off Beacon Street. He no longer took drugs, though he did still drink on occasion. Once in a while, he smoked pot—which in retrospect seems an irresponsible thing for a father to do.

Once the Delgados were forced to return Tessa—she was five months at the time—they threatened further legal action to prove that Tony wasn't a fit father.

But that never happened. Instead, Maria's mother, Mary, must have finally talked some sense into Maria's father, Gerardo—because they turned on a dime. Tony was pretty sure they realized if they wanted access to Tessa and a chance to act as grandparents, they had to be nice to Tony. Had to at least pretend to accept him.

At the time, it was in Tony's interest to involve them. After all, what did he know about taking care of a baby? His own parents lived too far away to help. So Tony was grateful when Mary offered to babysit her granddaughter. Marco helped, too—and so did a neighbor Tony trusted.

Somehow, they made it through. As Tessa got older and she and Tony bonded more deeply, the Delgados loosened their grip.

They had half a dozen other grandchildren to focus on. And since they moved to L.A., the visits had dwindled to a few per year.

When Tony took in Leo, the Delgados had been his greatest concern. How to explain the sudden appearance of a blond, gray-eyed boy Tony claimed as family? In the end, he concocted a story wherein Tony had a cousin who had adopted the boy as a child but then the cousin died—and no one wanted Leo because he was de-velopmentally disabled.

The ruse could never have worked if Leo hadn't been Leo. At that age, he wasn't interested in or able to contradict the convo-luted tale of his origin. Tony knows Leo must have memories of his life before, but he gets angry when Tony or Tessa tries to probe the mystery.

Tony wishes he could say he has no regrets about Leo, but over the years the enormity of what he's done by keeping Leo has kept him awake nights.

At one point, when he pulls off for gas, he decides to call home. Tessa would be home from school. After two rings, she picks up—only she won't speak. There is simply silence on the other end. "Tessa? Is that you?" He can hear breathing. "Leo? Leo, did you answer the phone?"

Leo grunts yes in reply, and Tony starts to laugh. Leo has never picked up the phone before. When Tony and Tessa had tried to coax him to use the phone—they thought he should know how, for safety's sake—he had refused.

Now Tony is shaking his head in wonder. "Where are you?" Leo asks.

"Remember? I went on a trip to Seattle," Tony says. "Is Tessa home? Does she know you answered the phone?"

"She's in the bathroom."

"Oh," says Tony. "How is everything going?" he asks Leo.

"Fine." Fine is one of Leo's favorite words.

"That's great. How was school today?"

"Fine. Goodbye," says Leo. And then he hangs up. Tony can't stop laughing and shaking his head. God, he loves that kid. Hearing his voice just now gives him the boost he needs to keep hope alive. Hope for a miracle. Hope that whoever is looking for Leo isn't fit to care for him. Or, better yet, doesn't really want him back.

34

Tony spends Friday night in a ratty Motel 6 somewhere in northern Oregon, drives away before dawn, and arrives in Everett on Saturday by late morning.

The library is easy to find. But he feels conspicuous, especially with his tattoos and ponytail. A reference librarian leads him to a desk with a microfiche reader. Then she brings over film for the Everett *Daily Herald* newspaper for February 1980. She shows him how to load the film and press the right button to make it go one frame at a time; another button makes it go very fast. Sitting in the wooden chair taking directions makes Tony feel like he is back at school.

When the librarian leaves him alone, he begins to flip slowly through the pages for each day. Everett definitely has its share of crime. What is wrong with this world? Then he finds it, on the lower right corner of the front page for February 13.

SON OF SLAIN MAN MISSING.

And there, looking blankly up from the screen, is Leo. The same boy he's come to love as his own. The same photograph that's now plastered on milk cartons from here to California—and maybe the whole country.

Tony starts reading, barely breathing.

The son is identified as Leo Miller, seven years old. The paper reports that he is mentally disabled, small for his age, with cropped blond hair. Apparently, Leo went missing not from home but from the house of a friend of the family. It wasn't known whether the boy was abducted or if he ran away.

At the end, the piece quotes his mother, Inez Miller of Everett, pleading for his safe return. The public is encouraged to join the search or report any tips.

But what about "Slain Man"? A related article reveals that less than a week earlier, a thirteen-year-old female related to the missing child was arrested for the murder of Raymond F. Miller, the missing boy's father.

What? Tony scrolls back carefully through the pages until he finds the first mention of the crime. The headline is blazoned in all caps across the top of the February 4 edition: TEEN ARRESTED IN DEATH OF STEPFATHER.

Tony shakes his head in surprised disbelief as he reads about the crime and its aftermath. He plunges ahead, following the trail through February. Almost every day, there's news coverage of the crime and its investigation. Apparently, it was a shooting. Often, it takes top billing over the mysterious disappearance of the boy. Clearly the double tragedies had put the family's story in the full glare of media attention.

After a couple hours hunched over at the machine, bleary with eyestrain, Tony finally quits. He has printed out a small stack of articles.

By now he's starving, so he finds a McDonald's and orders two Big Macs and a large coffee with cream. Seated at a small table by a window, he lays the photocopies in front of him and tries to sort it all out before he finds a phone and calls Marco.

It doesn't take Tony long to realize that "Phil Brown" was actually Leo's uncle, and his name wasn't Phil. According to one of the articles and an accompanying photo, his name was Thomas Miller, a.k.a. Tinker Miller. Tinker was an ex-convict and a person of interest in Leo's abduction, but at the time of these news reports, his whereabouts remained unknown.

But why would this guy abduct his own nephew, only to abandon him in California? That part still makes no sense. The other question is the status of Leo's family. What happened to the girl, and where is the mother, Inez Miller? The paper lists an address on Rockefeller as the scene of the crime, but Tony can't imagine the mom would still live there. At some point, he'll drive by and scope it out.

He's guessing the thirteen-year-old was Leo's sister. Had she been convicted of the crime? If so, where was she locked up? By now, she must be nineteen. Tony had been too exhausted to read all the way through to the conclusion of her case—he was more interested in the mother. Surely it was the mother, Inez Miller, who was looking for Leo. She had lost so much—her husband, most likely her daughter, and her son in the space of a week. He can't even imagine such a thing.

The more he pieces together what must have happened, the more awful it seems. He thinks of Leo back home in Oakland, playing his cello or maybe watching TV in that absent way he has. All his protective instincts rise to the surface. Where was the mother when the sister pulled the trigger? Where was Leo? How could a thirteen-year-old girl do such a thing?

AFTER HE LEAVES McDonald's, Tony drives by the address on Rockefeller. It's an ordinary house on a corner lot, painted blue. There's obviously a basement level, where the garage sits. And then if you turn and drive up the alley, there's a carport, too, and a back-door entrance.

There's no car visible and it appears no one is home.

It's not until he circles the block and drives by the front that he notices the COMING SOON sign in the yard. Whoever lives here now is moving. If it's not Inez Miller, maybe the seller could tell him about the previous owner. How would you go about that? Knock on the door and start asking? Wouldn't that raise red flags?

It's raining as he drives up to Broadway Avenue, a busy, non-residential street, and searches until he finds a small market with a pay phone. Why can't they put the damn things inside instead of outside?

It takes Tony twenty minutes to update Marco and make a plan. In the meantime, his fingers are frozen stiff. It's stopped raining, but a hellacious wind has picked up, and he keeps losing pages of photocopies. Each time, he drops the phone and chases them down, because what could be more suspicious than his obvious interest in this case?

Marco suggests that Tony look up all the Millers in the Everett phone book and try to find Inez. Standing there with the open Everett phone book, he sees pages and pages of Millers—but no I or Inez to speak of. "I can't possibly call all these Millers," he tells Marco. "And even if I find her, then what am I supposed to say? *I think I have your kid, by the way?*"

In the end, Marco comes up with what is probably the best idea. "Forget the Millers," he tells Tony. "Find out the mother's *maiden* name, in case she's gone back to it. And don't waste time on the phone book; everyone in Everett must know this story. Go to a bar, get someone talking—but don't be obvious about it! See if you can't find out what name she goes by now and if she's still around."

The idea of a warm bar sounds like heaven to Tony, and the plan is worth a shot.

Before they hang up, Marco has another good idea. "Pretend to be looking for this Tinker Miller—and you'll have a better shot at talking about the family without mentioning Leo directly."

Tony gets back in his truck and scours his messy glove box for his work gloves—which of course aren't there. The atlas back home had said nothing of this kind of cold in Everett. He begins to drive down Broadway slowly, looking for a bar that seems crowded but not new. He doesn't want to find a bunch of young people too interested in one another to notice him. He's after geezers and bar-flies, the kind who love a story and like to gossip.

It takes some driving around to find a bar that looks like a fit. The Pine Tavern smells like a mix of musty carpet, beer, and sweaty men. There are maybe twelve people in the place, mostly men, sitting up at the bar. Tony takes a seat at the bar near the middle. The bartender is male, pasty-faced, thirties. He's already working on a beer gut.

Tony immediately overhears a customer call him Gary.

"Want a menu?" Gary asks. Tony can tell he hopes not.

"No thanks," says Tony. "Let's just start with a beer. Budweiser. Damn, it's cold out there . . . so make it a warm one," he adds.

Gary doesn't even smile.

Tony decides he should be direct. "Can I ask you something?" he says when Gary places his beer in front of him.

"I suppose," the guy replies, like he's already bored.

"I'm looking for a guy who used to live around here and might have worked as a cook in a tavern or restaurant."

"I've been here for ten years," Gary says. "So shoot. What's his name?"

"Name's Tinker Miller."

"Doesn't ring a bell. Sounds like a fairy. Tinker Bell."

"Sometimes he goes by Phil Brown," Tony explains. "His real first name is Thomas."

The bartender pretends to think. Shakes his head. "Can't help you there."

"I think he was related to that same Miller guy who got shot some years back by a teenaged girl," Tony blurts out. *Was that too much too soon?*

But the reference grabs Gary's attention. He grins. "Shit, yeah," he says, suddenly animated. "That was fucked up." Tony notices Gary's got a big lump behind his lower lip. A plug of chewing tobacco.

"Yeah?" Tony is hoping for more without having to pry. He also wishes Gary would turn down the Kiss song that's blaring from an overhead speaker.

"Take it you're not from around here."

Tony shakes his head. "From California. Tony's my name," he says, extending his hand like he would to a customer of his own.

Gary shakes it, but Tony can tell he thinks it's weird.

Before Tony can think of how to get more details, Gary proudly offers them on a platter. "Yeah. Man, when word got out what happened—the town went crazy with gossip. Story was the step-daughter shot her stepfather, blew his brains out all over their garage."

"Aw, c'mon," complains a guy sitting two down from Tony. "Some of us are trying to drink here."

"She claimed he was abusive, so some people think she did a good thing. I think she should have fried for it."

"Wow. So what happened to her?" Tony wishes now that he'd taken the time to wade through the microfiche to see what eventually happened to the unnamed thirteen-year-old.

"Hell, they just sent her to some kiddie prison, is what I heard. She's already out, too. Was a big article in the *Herald* a while back. Lots of folks still think she should have got tried as an adult, locked up a lot longer."

This is interesting. Maybe tomorrow, Tony can go back to the library and read more-recent stories.

For now he tries to steer things toward Leo's mother. "What about the Miller mother? Any chance you know what happened to her?"

"I know their kid went missing. I doubt she stuck around." Gary pauses then and cocks his head at Tony. "You got a lot of questions, fellow. For being new to town." Then he goes around a corner, and Tony hears him spit.

"Just trying to find my man," Tony calls out. He gulps at his beer. It's time to back off. When Gary reappears, he asks, "Motel around here where I can land?"

"Lots of bedbug traps," offers Gary. "But the Pacific Hotel is nice, and not too far from here." He gives Tony brief directions. At first, Tony worries it will be too expensive, but once he flirts with the desk clerk, the price isn't as bad as he feared. The last thing he needs is something itching. He hadn't even realized bedbugs were real.

35

Inez wakes up on Friday wishing she could sleep in for once. Her work starts at 9:00 A.M. but she's always awake by 6:00. It looks nice outside, but she knows it's probably freezing, at least in the low thirties. When she opens the front door to get the Everett *Herald*, a blast of frigid air cuts right through her robe.

She grabs the newspaper off the porch steps and hurries back inside. She turns up the heat, sets the paper on the kitchen counter, and proceeds to make coffee. While she waits for it to brew, she allows herself to read only the front page. The rest must wait until she takes her coffee to her reading spot in the living room.

This is just one of many routines Inez has developed for herself since she lost her family. She likes to think that in this small way she's become more like Leo. She understands better now the comfort of having a few small things you can count on to stay the same.

Leo is always on her mind, but this week more than ever. It's been a week now since his face was first featured on milk cartons across the country. She's been told not to put too much hope in the project, but they needn't have cautioned her. After six years of searching, waiting, and wondering, Inez isn't easily carried away. She was both gratified and angry when Congress passed the Missing Children Act of 1982, which did away with the seventy-two-hour wait to declare a child missing.

The law was a no-brainer. But it left Inez wondering how differently things might have gone for Leo had it been in place sooner.

She's grateful for the milk-carton project, an initiative of the National Center for Missing & Exploited Children, established in 1984. But she doubts a six-year-old grainy photo of Leo at age seven is going to do much good. She didn't even rush out to get a carton of her own, figuring that would make it one less carton circulating. But if she's honest, another reason might be that she hates seeing the word MISSING above Leo's face. Even back when she was plastering the state of Washington with MISSING posters, the word made her feel exposed and ashamed, like she had misplaced her child the way you might lose your car keys.

She has gone over that night in her head so many times. If only she'd insisted on keeping Leo with her. If only she hadn't become so hysterical. If only she had called a neighbor. But most of their neighbors resented the Miller family, because Ray kept the junky cars he was working on out front of the house. And so, under threat of having Leo put in the care of children's services, Inez had phoned Shirley Cavanaugh, a friend from work who'd watched Leo a few times. She had rushed right over with curlers in her hair to get Leo.

Later that night Inez had packed a bag for herself, too—and eventually joined Leo. Her home was a crime scene and they couldn't stay there. Of course, she now regrets choosing Shirley's. And not being there when Leo disappeared. According to Shirley, he'd been happily playing in the sandbox just outside her glass slider while she was watching TV. "He was so happy in the sand. But I could see him—he was right there!"

Inez should have wanted to strangle this woman, but for reasons she can't explain, she's never held Shirley personally responsible for "losing" Leo. Maybe there was already so much hate and blame going around that she couldn't deal with more. Eventually, she found herself accepting Shirley's desperate pleas to help her look for Leo.

She still thinks it was a smart move, since Shirley's enormous guilt made her more motivated to find Leo than anyone else in the world—apart from Inez, of course. But Shirley did more than help her hang a zillion MISSING posters of Leo. When Inez was immobilized by grief and depression, it was Shirley who kept her from disappearing into her couch. It was Shirley who visited several evenings a week and knocked on her door until Inez opened it.

Still, given Shirley's culpability, Inez was as surprised as anyone when their casual friendship deepened. It was as though working in tandem to find Leo forged a bond between them strong enough to save them both. Inez still thinks of Shirley and herself as the *guilt sisters*.

At times, she knew Shirley was worried Inez would take her own life, but the option of suicide was never on the table, a fact Inez almost resented. She had no choice but to go on—just in case Leo came home. When people told her she was brave, or wondered aloud how she managed to keep going in the face of so much heartache and loss, she wanted to scream. Brave had nothing to do with it. It was hope that held her hostage.

Her coffee ready, Inez pours a cup and takes the paper to the couch in the living room, where one cushion is noticeably sunken and worn. She reads several pages but doesn't get far before her phone rings. Who would be calling so early on a Friday morning? She won't even let herself believe someone has reported seeing Leo.

Her heart is racing as she sets her coffee on the side table and rushes to the kitchen. When it's only Shirley, Inez is annoyed. "Seriously? You're calling me at seven in the morning on a Friday?"

"Well, I knew today meant a week without hearing . . . I just wanted to check in with you. The carton and all."

"I'm fine," she tells Shirley.

"Have you finally got one? A carton?" she asks.

"No," Inez says. "I told you I'm not sure I even want to see it."

"I understand," Shirley quickly replies. "And if you don't want to see it, there's nothing wrong with that. It doesn't mean you aren't glad they're out there or that you can't hope it works."

"I'm just trying *not* to get my hopes up. It's such an old picture. And after all these years . . ."

"Well, I'm worried they're not doing a good job, Inez. Yesterday I had to go to several stores to find a carton with Leo on it. Albertsons had it. But why doesn't everyone?"

Inez sighs heavily. "It's not all brands, you know that, Shirley." She can't help sounding exasperated.

"Yeah, honey. We don't have to talk about it if you don't want."

Shirley almost always says the right thing.

"What I actually need to focus on is getting the house ready," says Inez.

"There's no hurry," says Shirley.

"Yeah, but in a way there is. That realtor, Melissa Lansing? She's kind of pushy. I came home last night and found a Century Twenty-one COMING SOON sign in my yard."

"Are you shitting me? Didn't you tell her you weren't a hundred percent sure?"

Inez hesitates. "I don't know. Maybe I acted more certain than I feel."

"I get it," says Shirley. "It's a huge, scary thing to consider. But just keep in mind that you don't have to do anything in a hurry. And Melissa Lansing is not in charge when it comes to your house."

"Everyone thinks I should move."

"I think it's a great idea, but I'm not responsible for your decisions. You know that, right?"

Inez has taken a lot of flak over the years from people who

worry or act alarmed about her staying at the Rockefeller house. Even Shirley asks why she doesn't move and why she keeps Leo's room exactly as he left it. "Are you sure that's healthy for you?"

Inez couldn't understand it. How could people think she'd take apart Leo's room or move away when any minute she could get a call telling her Leo had been found safe and alive? And so she stayed, tracking each year by Leo's age, assuming she wouldn't move until he was eighteen.

What has changed Inez's mind is that she wants to get the equity out of the house so Venus can go to college. Although Venus turned her down, Inez hopes that someday she'll change her mind and want the money. Once she realizes how hard it is to make a life for yourself from scratch.

After chatting a few more minutes with Shirley, Inez is restless, her routine blown. "I need to go, Shirley," she announces. "My coffee is probably cold by now, and you know how I am about—"

"No problem," Shirley interjects. "Call me if you need anything today. Seriously."

Inez hangs up, retrieves her coffee from the living room, and puts it in the microwave to reheat it. Every morning she makes only two cups, so she can't afford to just dump the cold one.

While she waits, she gazes at the photo of Leo she keeps on the counter near the sink. It was near impossible to get Leo to make eye contact, so all the pictures of him appear spontaneous. You'd never guess she was begging him to look up at her.

Ever since Venus got released, Inez has become more conscious of the fact that there aren't any photos of her daughter anywhere. It's not that she doesn't love Venus as much as Leo. It's just that given how much Venus still hates and blames her, she can't bear to see her face every day.

She stupidly allowed herself to hope that once Venus was out of jail, she might soften, might even forgive her. Maybe she'd find it in her heart to have some semblance of a relationship. But what happened at the doughnut shop snuffed out any hope of that. With her hair pulled back in that braid, Venus's angry blue eyes had eviscerated Inez like a knife.

But there was no knife sharp enough to make her not love Venus.

Their encounter brought back memories of the first time she saw Venus after the shooting, when she was still at Denney. Venus had refused to speak a word, and it had seemed to Inez like her little girl had turned overnight into some kind of monster, which had made it hard for Inez to remember that Venus was also a victim in all this. She may have killed Ray, but she was still a thirteen-year-old girl, terrified and lashing out.

Two years into her sentence, Venus had agreed to do some counseling with Inez and her counselor, Sharon. At the time, it seemed like they were making progress. Inez begged Venus's forgiveness for all the ways she screwed up in regard to Ray. She also apologized for telling Venus it was her fault about Leo. "What a terrible thing that was for me to do!" she'd admitted.

She thought Venus was finally softening. But then Inez made the dumbest move ever. She suggested they sell their story to a writer named Anna Weir. And that's when all hell broke loose and Venus stood up and swore her head off at Inez, declaring she didn't want her blood money and that she should never, ever come back.

Venus's eruption had stunned Inez. After that session, Sharon took Inez aside and suggested that perhaps Venus's refusal to reconcile was a coping mechanism. If she were to forgive Inez, then she'd have to face her own guilt in ways she just wasn't yet prepared to do. "In other words," she said, "Venus needs a scapegoat, and unfortunately you're it."

Inez suspected Sharon was right. And so she'd let go. She quit pushing to see Venus, not as a way to give up on her but as a way to love her. But it was hard. She understood that Venus needed more time to heal and she should take as long as she needed. As Shirley put it, "It takes what it takes."

But what if it takes forever?

The microwave beeps, and Inez brings her coffee back to the living room. But it's no use. She's not interested in the paper any longer, so she goes to the utility cupboard and finds her bran flakes. It's also her ritual to eat while sitting at the kitchen table reading the funnies and the horoscopes.

She turns to the comics, but her mind is still stuck on Venus. How much she misses her. What she wouldn't give to be forgiven, and how unlikely that still seems. She wonders for the hundredth time why she was spared in the first place, why Venus didn't just shoot her, too.

36

Saturday morning, Inez gets an update from the folks at the center. Though they've taken lots of calls, so far there's nothing "actionable," meaning no strong leads or suspects. Turns out a lot of phone calls have come in from children who are scared of disappearing or becoming missing. Hearing this makes her feel horrible.

She spends the morning in a funk, watching old movies, unable to get off the couch. Earlier, when Shirley called to tell her that bowling practice had been canceled—because three people, including her, had the flu—Inez wanted to scream. She had really been looking forward to it.

Next to Shirley, bowling is what Inez credits with helping to save her sanity. Shirley was already in a bowling league when they met, and eventually she convinced Inez to join. After a while, Inez came to see the benefits. It gave her something to do when she got off work. And, unlike so many other sports or pastimes, you could actually drink *while doing it*.

Not long after Leo was finally declared missing, it came out that Shirley was a bad drunk—even had a reputation for making scenes in bars. But Shirley swore she hadn't been drinking the day Leo went missing, claiming over and over that she only drank at night. Since Inez drank the same way, she was inclined to believe her.

A few weeks later, Shirley told Inez she'd joined A.A. Inez figured guilt drove her there, but she supposed she was glad for her. In time, she noticed positive changes in Shirley's outlook and energy level. But, still, Inez wouldn't be caught dead walking into an A.A. meeting. Unlike those folks, Inez mainly drinks wine and just enough—in her opinion—to wind down from her current job as a secretary in the administration offices for the Everett School District.

The irony that she doesn't have a child enrolled in school isn't lost on her. She regrets now that she didn't do more to see about getting Leo into special-ed classes. Shirley has it easy because she continues to work only part-time at Penneys because of her late husband's pension. Inez forgives her this, since Shirley does so much for her—including driving her to and from the Tyee several nights a week, allowing Inez to drink as much as she wants.

She can only imagine Venus's disgust if she knew Inez hangs out at the Tyee Lanes. She was always so embarrassed that her mother had met Ray while working at a "disgusting bowling-alley bar." But truth be told, Inez has found a sense of community down at the old Tyee. The people in her league are caring and funny. They never bring up the past or ask questions about her children.

Secretly, Inez is convinced she bowls better when she's a little tipsy.

BY NOON, INEZ is tired of watching Shirley Temple movies and decides to venture out. It's been years since she visited Mukilteo and walked the beach. It's a stupid thing to do in winter, she knows. She's going to freeze her ass off. But something compels her to go anyway.

She wears a heavy coat and brings a blanket, along with some wine and a goblet.

As one would expect, the beach itself is pretty much deserted. But despite the cold temperature, she abandons her shoes. She wants to feel the hard sand—wet but firm—against her feet. Maybe the cold air and waves and the familiar smells of the Sound will give her some kind of peace or courage.

For tomorrow. Tomorrow is the day she plans to go into Venus's room and clean, pack it up, and make sure it's ready to show on Monday. Melissa Lansing has remarked several times that a basement bedroom with a three-quarter bath could be a big selling point. But she's been wise—or maybe sensitive—enough not to ask to tour the basement herself.

As Inez continues to walk the shore, dozens of seagulls squawk overhead. She pays them little notice. Their sound is as much a part of Everett as the sulfur stench that belches from its troubled lumber plants.

The story she's heard is that John D. Rockefeller and other investors thought the Great Northern Railroad would end here in Everett. Instead, Seattle got that honor. At some point Rockefeller pulled out. And now Everett isn't famous for much but smelling bad. Still, when Inez married Raymond and he bought the house on Rockefeller Avenue, it had sounded rich to her.

Inez has to watch her step, since here and there the shore is littered with the remnants of cigarettes, beer bottles, and other garbage. For a public beach, though, it's actually pretty clean. The tides have left their own litter, too—dead jellyfish, an occasional dried-up starfish, and a lot of purple mussel shells.

Inez spies some kelp—giant pieces of seaweed that resemble snakes. Venus always managed to find a long slimy strand of kelp to bring home and use as a whip to scare neighborhood kids. Until it would start to stink and Inez made her throw it out. Oh God, she misses that Venus—the bratty but funny girl who could have matured into an amazing young woman.

She thinks of Venus's father, Joe, and how different their story would have gone if he hadn't died. In retrospect, it seems to Inez like she hardly took time to properly mourn Joe. Perhaps because Venus demanded so much of her energy. Or perhaps because she met Ray so soon after.

Venus had been five at the time, and she looked a lot like Joe. Even though she had Inez's strong nose, she got Joe's wild black curls and starry blue eyes.

Of course, Joe adored Venus, doted on her, never resented getting up in the night with her. Inez had been a bit jealous at times of his devotion to his baby girl, the way his tolerance for her spread out beneath every cranky mood or tantrum like an enormous blanket of love that Venus could never crawl far enough away to escape.

It had hurt her more than once to be the brunt of Joe's irritation or on the receiving end of his annoyance—only to witness him moments later gently shushing their screaming toddler with the kind of ridiculous tenderness that meant Venus could do no wrong.

Ha. *Venus could do no wrong.* Oh, the irony. And how impossible it seems to her now that Joe's little princess could so quickly morph into such a difficult child and then an angry teen and then . . . And then Inez was nobody's mother.

When she reaches a large piece of driftwood, she sits down on it and runs her fingers through the sand, which is soft this far from the water. It brings to mind the sandbox Leo disappeared from. Tears threaten, but Inez holds them at bay. It's too cold to cry.

She zips her coat higher and settles in to watch the waves. The monotony of the tide is somehow reassuring. She closes her eyes and prays for Venus to forgive her. Prays for Leo to come home. She recalls how the Inez of six years ago wouldn't have been caught dead praying—for anyone.

It wasn't that she'd been some kind of committed atheist. Or that she'd had some terrible experience at church, although her dad's Greek Orthodoxy had left her cold. It was simply that she never thought the concept of God had much going for it. She figured religious people just wanted to feel superior.

But all that changed in the space of a week when she lost everything that mattered to her. Even in the early throes of grief, Inez had understood that when you lose as much as she had—her entire family—you also lose your chance to enjoy the kind of casual disregard for God that regular people can enjoy.

Almost immediately, all the questions about life and death and God and meaning crowd in—the ones that have no real answers and yet you can't stop asking them over and over, like how could a good God let this happen? But, then again, how could she turn her back on God when—if he existed—he might guide Leo home if she prayed hard enough?

At first, anger at God seemed the only way forward. But it takes a lot of energy to keep your dukes up against an invisible being who won't fight back. So while Inez often mocked Shirley's simple faith in God as a loving "higher power," she came to envy it, too. Not because she thought Shirley's trust was necessarily well placed, but because it seemed to bring her so much comfort.

Soon, the question for Inez became: What does one do with a God you are exhausted from hating but can never forgive?

And then one morning Inez thought she got her answer. She awoke from a dream about Leo. In it, Leo seemed happy and was talking to her about God. She got out of bed feeling strange, dazed. When she went to shut her bedroom window, before she could lower the pane, a waft of soft, sweet air swept through the screen and into her face. Her soul seemed to let out a small cry as something heavy inside fell away.

She stood there for a while, breathing deeply, feeling relief. Staring out at her blue hydrangeas, damp with dew, she suddenly knew as surely as she knew anything that *God didn't mind if she couldn't forgive him*. He didn't expect her to. And it didn't change how he felt about her.

Given this small but stupendous revelation, Inez's rage began to lessen. She didn't become religious or start going to church. But she did start praying. She never once gets on her knees—God forbid. She never prays when she doesn't feel like it—because why bother? She never prays for herself, because fuck herself. But she prays for Leo and Venus many times a day.

It's not that she trusts God to answer. That jig is up. But she prays as a way to hang on to hope.

WHEN INEZ FINALLY twists around to check on her things—the blanket and wine she left down the beach—she spots what appear to be several teens eyeing her stuff. She remembers her wine, and she worries they'll grab it and run. That's what she would have done at their age. She stands up and casually waves at them, hoping a friendly approach will save her pinot noir.

The idea of the kids stealing her wine panics her more than she knows it should. Even though she doesn't usually drink during the day, today—maybe tomorrow, too—she plans to make an exception.

She quickly strides back down the beach, hoping to seem relaxed. The boys appear to argue and then finally walk away from her spot. As soon as she reaches her blanket, she sees with relief that the wine is still there. She plops down, grateful she remembered an opener, ashamed to realize that if she hadn't, she would have broken the bottle open on the rocks.

She pulls the cork and revels in that lovely, familiar puff of air being released. As she fills her ruby goblet, she's conscious of the fact that classy people drink wine from clear wineglasses. But Inez has had these scalloped goblets since before she married Joe. By now they're like dear friends who have stuck with her through the worst moments of her life.

And tomorrow is guaranteed to bring plenty of those. Shirley and her bowling partner, Marianne, are the only ones aware of her Sunday plans—and they both begged her to let them help. "It is going to be traumatic," Shirley insisted. "You shouldn't do something like that alone."

Of course, Inez knows Shirley is right—it's probably unwise to tackle something like this without support. But for reasons that are hard to explain, she feels like she owes it to herself, or maybe to Venus, to face the basement alone.

All these years—except for once when the water heater broke, and a few times when she had to retrieve some gardening tools— she has lived as though the lower part of the house doesn't exist.

But tomorrow it will exist, won't it? The forthcoming sale makes it so. She'll unlock and open the door at the end of the kitchen, descend the basement steps, and finally come face-to-face with what she let happen.

37

Since Tony is hungry and wired and it's still way too early for bed, he gets directions from the desk clerk to a nearby Denny's. Afterward, he is driving back to the hotel when he spots a hair salon that looks cheap. He can't explain why, but he has the sudden urge to lose his pony. Maybe it's because he wants to look as clean-cut and as innocent as possible when he's arrested.

The salon looks closed, but there's one light on and he can see a woman still in there, talking on the phone. He knocks until she opens the door. "We're closed," she says.

"But it's just a quick thing," Tony says. "And I bet it would be fun for you to cut off this pony." He turns his head to show it to her. "I'd tip you really, really well." He is suddenly desperate to get this done, afraid if he waits another hour he'll lose his courage.

"Well, I'd get in trouble. . . ."

"Who's gonna know?" says Tony. He winks at her. "You'd be doing me such a huge favor."

She finally relents. While Tony loses several years' worth of his hair, he wonders if this girl could be a source. She says her name is Pamela. She looks too young to be familiar with the case, but he decides to give it a go, because aren't hairstylists famous for gossip?

When she's cut off the pony but hasn't started styling yet, Tony takes a stab. "Remember that case where the stepdaughter shot the stepfather, oh, maybe six years ago?"

"Of course. You're talking about Venus Black?"

Tony's blood rushes to his face. So lucky so quickly! "Yeah. That one. I'm looking for her mother, actually. Used to go to high school with her," he adds, guessing they're probably near the same age.

"Oh," says Pamela, grinning. "It's like that, like maybe you were high school sweethearts?"

"Something like that," he answers.

"She might still be around," she says. "I know because I have a friend who used to live nearby and she kept seeing the mom out front, pulling weeds in the rockery. Can you imagine staying after what happened in that house?"

"No," says Tony, "I can't."

To hide his excitement, he compliments Pamela on how well she is doing with his hair. He'd bet his whole wallet that the mother is going by Inez Black.

Now all he needs is an address and phone number. Then he remembers that he doesn't really *want* to find her. Why would he be in a hurry to find the key to his family's undoing?

When Tony gets back to his hotel room, he reluctantly opens a drawer in the bedside table. He's almost disappointed that there's a phone book. There's also a listing for "I. Black." No address, just a number.

His hands feel sweaty on the phone. He dials the number, feeling like he might throw up. *Let it be Ida. Or Inga. Or . . .* It rings four times. Then a machine picks up. "This is Inez; please leave a message."

Now he knows it's her for sure. Inez Miller went back to Inez Black.

After talking to Pamela, he realizes there's a good chance Inez stayed in the house on Rockefeller. When he calls Marco to tell him the news, his brother suggests the obvious. "Why don't you just assume that she stayed in the house? Call first thing in the morning, pretending to be an interested buyer. It could be the perfect excuse to meet her—if it's her."

After he hangs up with Marco, Tony feels kind of sick inside. When he sees his reflection in the hotel window, he's stunned by the transformation. He knows he looks good—but is this really him? He tries to imagine Tessa's shock and surprise. He guesses she will love it, since he's always suspected she wished he were a bit more traditional. None of her friends' dads have ponies, tattoos, or play with needle guns all day.

He imagines home, thinks of the dishwasher humming and Tessa getting Leo ready for bed. *Oh dear God.* That world, that predictable, wonderful world of normal problems and family stuff and worrying about Tessa going on dates—and not going on dates—he was about to blow it all apart.

Unless. Unless he meets the mother and she is obviously not a good person—say, a drug addict or someone who looks like she's hiding a criminal record. It feels cruel to hope for such a thing to be true, but Tony can't help himself. If she's a bad-enough character, maybe they could apply to be the foster parents of Leo.

But right now what he needs is to hear the voice of innocence, to know that somewhere in the world life still works the way it should. It's kind of late, but Tessa will still be up. He sits on the hotel bed by the phone and reads the directions for long-distance calls. She answers on the third ring.

"Hey, sweetie. How's it going?"

"Dad! It's going good. I'm so glad you called!" she says, clearly elated to hear from him. "How's the conference?"

"Well, it doesn't really get into full swing until tomorrow, Sunday. But I'm sure it will be great. How's everything going there?"

"Fine, Dad. You've only been gone one night. Maureen came over like you said. We watched TV. Leo was upset that you weren't here, but he didn't throw that big of a fit. I did your part in the routine. He wouldn't let Maureen come in his room, said she wasn't allowed."

"You're never going to believe what happened yesterday," he tells her. "I called you, and Leo answered the phone. You were in the bathroom, he said. And then he just said goodbye and hung up on me. It was hilarious."

"Oh my gosh! Really? Leo answered the phone?"

"Guess he thought it might be me," he says. "Pretty amazing, huh?"

"Yeah. But you missed some other big news about Leo," says Tessa.

"I did?" For a second, he panics.

"Yeah. Leo brought home a note from the orchestra teacher. He wants Leo to play a solo in a concert with the rest of the kids two weeks from Monday."

So that's all. Leo has had private lessons for years but never joined the regular kids. "But how will that work?"

"The note says that he's going to start having Leo come to the class on Monday and practice with them to see if he can get used to it."

"That's so cool, honey."

"Yeah. I think it's really cool, too."

"So, what did you have for dinner?"

"Some country fried steak."

"Mmm. That sounds good. I wish I were there."

"Me, too. It's weird when you're gone."

"Yeah, I agree. I sure love you, Tessa."

"Love you, too."

"Tell Leo I love him."

"I will," she says. "Do you think he understands what love is?" Tony is surprised. She's never asked this before.

"I mean, he doesn't ever say he loves us," she presses. "Do you think he does?"

"Yes, Tessa. I think he does a whole lot."

"Me, too," she says. But Tony can hear the faint doubt in her voice.

After he hangs up, Tony thinks about Leo. Thinks about love. Realizes how little he knows about anything.

38

Sunday morning, Inez is rinsing her cereal bowl in the sink when the phone rings. Probably it's Shirley, probably still sick, asking again if she can help today.

She picks up. "Hello?"

"Is this Inez Black?" It's a man.

"Yes, it is. Can I help you?" *What if it's about Leo?*

"I hope so. My name's Tony, and I'm calling about your house. It's for sale, right?"

"Well, yes," she says, let down it's not about Leo. "But it's not on the market yet."

"I understand, but is there any way I could possibly come by today and just take a quick look?"

"I don't think so," Inez says. "You need to go through my realtor. It doesn't officially go on the market until next week."

"I understand," he says again, sounding a bit hurried. "But the thing is, I have to head back home to California tomorrow, and it will be a couple months before I can make it back up to Washington."

Inez thinks, *California.* That's a good thing. *He probably won't know the story.* And what if she doesn't get any other people who are interested, especially since February is a really dumb time to put a house on the market?

The man continues, "My work down in Oakland is transferring me up here soon, so I'm anxious to find a place for my daughter and me."

"Oh," says Inez. *A daughter. He's single.* She suspects both these facts would delight Melissa. She claims men are way less picky about dumb stuff like outdated pink bathroom tile.

"Well, then," she says, trying to stall. "Let me think . . ." How quickly could she get Venus's room packed up? For now she could just hang a picture over the hole.

"I suppose I could let you look," she says. "But it's not quite as clean as I want it to be. I'm not really ready. . . ."

"I don't care about clean," the man says. "Trust me, I can see past that."

She looks at the kitchen clock. It's almost 9:00 A.M. If he doesn't come until late this afternoon . . . And it might actually help her stay on task and avoid the drama. It will *force* her to proceed in an industrious, non-emotional way.

"Okay," she says, her voice shaky. "How about four o' clock?"

Great," he says. "Four P.M. I'll be there. I appreciate this, ma'am."

After she hangs up, Inez tries to call Melissa but only gets her answering machine.

Then Inez has a terrible thought. What if this guy is a reporter or just a neighbor with a sick curiosity who can't wait to tour the house where it all happened?

But if this guy really *is* from California, Inez is going to have a hard time not *begging* him to buy the house. To avoid the torture of showing it, and before it could even go on the market? That would be such a great thing.

She hurriedly dresses in old jeans and a T-shirt. She puts her long hair in a ponytail. She gathers boxes and cleaning supplies in a bucket. At the end of the kitchen, she stands at the basement door, hesitant to put the skeleton key in the lock. When she finally does, the door swings open with a long squeak, *like you'd hear in a horror movie,* she thinks.

She flips on the light and tosses several empty boxes ahead of her down the wooden stairs. At the last second, she remembers to grab several large trash bags for garbage.

Inez begins to descend the stairs when a memory hits, and it's not the kind she's expecting. She remembers how Venus used to love to call for Inez to come downstairs and then she'd hide in the space under the stairs and jump out and scare her. She made Inez wet her pants once doing that.

She finds the door to Venus's room hanging partly open. Inez swings her arm inside to flip the light switch before she enters. Everything is covered in dust, of course. But she hadn't anticipated so much of it or that the moist basement air would have turned it to layers of scum.

Her plan is probably cowardly. But there's a difference between being willing to face something and being willing to see it up close.

The plan is simple. *Do not look. Don't look. Don't look. Don't look at the hole,* she tells herself. *Whatever you do, don't look at that wall. Don't let your gaze fall on it. There is plenty else to see,* she reminds herself. *There is no reason to glance in that direction.*

Part of the plenty to see is the giant mobile and all the pasted stars on the ceiling. How could she have forgotten?

Well, pretty easily, she realizes. Even before the shooting, she rarely went down to Venus's room. She often set her laundry near the top step. Hard to miss, you'd think, but how many times had Venus chosen to not pick it up?

She decides to start with the dresser, a garage-sale find that Venus hated until Inez suggested she spray-paint it whatever color she wanted. Venus went for orange and added decals to the drawers. Inez opens the top one to find socks and a jumble of panties for a young teen—labeled by days of the week. The second drawer contains nighties and a couple of bras. Venus had taken after Inez and was a solid B cup by the time she was twelve.

It is this, the sight of Venus's bras, that makes Inez catch her breath and become aware of the hole in an entirely new way. She imagines Venus coming in from the shower, dropping her towel. Opening her dresser drawer to get her bra. And feeling watched without knowing why.

Over the years, Inez has often tried to put herself in Venus's shoes. But now, standing in her room, imagining her own husband's eye at that hole, she feels a visceral sense of horror on a whole new level.

With a sinking heart, she realizes it's going to be like this the entire time she packs up and cleans down here. She will get to know what it's like. The hole will follow her every move around the room. And it will demand that she remember.

BY THE TIME Venus found the hole so cleverly disguised in the knotted wood, Inez already had some niggling concerns. A few months earlier, she'd had some reason to go to Venus's door and was surprised to discover she'd stopped using her skeleton key to lock it—and had stuffed the keyhole with gum instead.

She never asked Venus why, even though it seemed odd to her that Venus—who guarded her privacy so much—would rather have gum in her lock than be able to lock people out. Now it would seem that Venus must have suspected something but thought she had solved the problem.

Why didn't she say something? Or maybe she had, but Inez had brushed it off. Could it be? Over the years, Venus's complaints about Ray had come to seem like the constant whine of a mosquito. Bothersome but not alarming. Yes, Venus had made accusations of Ray creeping around, trying to be too close to her. Sometimes she claimed he hurt her and Leo physically. But she also complained that Ray was *too* nice to her and her friends.

Once, Inez told Venus to make up her mind. Was Ray a brute or was he way too nice?

Done with the dresser, Inez decides to remove the stars from the ceiling. For that, she'll have to get a chair to stand on. While upstairs, she pours herself two glasses of wine and steadily gulps them down.

But, of course, the wine can't keep the truth at bay. As she stands on the chair and slowly peels the stars from Venus's ceiling, she's confronted with another damning memory. The time Inez had gotten off work early and, pulling into the carport off the alley, she'd almost run right over Ray. He'd been lying facedown on the cement, looking through the basement window into Venus's bedroom. Ray's explanation had been that he'd come out the back door and dropped a screw. It had fallen into the window well, and he'd been looking for it.

She had chosen to believe him. But did she? No, she had chosen to *pretend* she did.

Oh my God. How could she explain to Venus now—or ever—the blinding power of denial. How could she expect her to understand that sometimes the hardest truths to see are the ones staring right at you?

Now she takes some solace—not that she deserves any—in the fact that she is absolutely certain the discovery of the hole that terrible day *would* have been the final straw. It *had been* the end, in Inez's mind. Even as she put Venus off, even as she struggled to breathe through the terror at her throat, she *knew* it was true. *Her marriage was over, and Ray had been exposed as a pervert.*

She *would* have kicked him out on his ass. That day, as Venus hysterically sobbed over the perfectly drilled hole in the knotty pine, Inez could already see herself confronting Ray.

But for God's sake! She needed time to come to terms, to figure out what to do next, to talk to someone. You can't process such a monstrous truth in one afternoon. Venus didn't even give her one day!

This was the heart of her defense—what she screamed at Venus in her mind but would never say to her face: *You didn't give me enough time! You didn't wait for me to figure out how to handle it! You should never have taken my immediate reaction as my true and entire and timeless last word!*

Now Inez knows better. Never assume you can take back anything. Never assume you have time to face facts later. And never underestimate the power of a parent's betrayal.

As Inez moves on to Venus's bathroom, the sight of the pink bottle of Love's Baby Soft perfume makes her want to rush back upstairs and guzzle the rest of that bottle of wine. She doesn't have to open the bottle or spray a drop in order to smell Venus—or to imagine Ray ogling her innocent daughter.

Somewhere deep in her little-girl heart, Venus had known it, hadn't she? And no wonder she'd hated Ray so much all those years. And then to hear the prosecutor archly point out, "But there's no proof he even touched her. You can't claim sexual abuse as a mitigating factor if she was only peeped at."

Only peeped at?

The memory of his disdain fills Inez with rage now. But at the time, it had filled her with something much more like relief. She did not take up Venus's defense. She did not scream at the top of her lungs that *of course* voyeurism is sexual abuse. She had left that to others, then and since.

Now, as Inez stands on Venus's bed to take down the mobile of planets, she sees herself emptying her daughter's sky of dreams, and she sees, coming down with them, her last defense against the truth: Worse than not sticking up for Venus is the *reason* she refused. At the time, she'd been desperate to minimize what Ray did—what *she* allowed to happen—because it lessened her own awful guilt. And it kept her from feeling like she'd been part of a dirty secret.

How could she have been so selfish?

She realizes she is sobbing. Why had she thought she could get through this cleanup without a major breakdown? If only she had taken that guy's phone number, she could have canceled this stupid showing. She could have run from the room. Could have forgotten about moving, and never opened the basement door again.

Suddenly, the thought of calling Shirley and Marianne and begging them to do this for her sounds genius. Of course this is too much for any mother! Of course she can't bear it!

But, in the end, love makes her stay.

39

Tony arrives at the house a few minutes early. It's begun to rain. He parks his truck right behind a red Honda. He is nervous.

He has carefully rehearsed how he hopes this conversation will unfold. He's hoping Inez is not suspicious or closemouthed. He climbs the few steps to the front door and knocks. He'd rather not ring the bell.

He's about to knock again when she answers. He's surprised that she's so pretty. Long black hair, a narrow sculpted face. She's thin, seems fragile, and it looks like she's been crying. What had Tony been expecting?

A woman who looked like she would marry an abuser and raise a homicidal daughter.

"Are you here for the house?" she asks. Her voice is fairly low, like maybe she's a smoker.

"Yes," Tony says, extending his hand. "I'm Tony."

She shakes his hand very lightly. Her small hands remind him of Leo's hands. He's startled by the idea that he's looking at Leo's mother.

"Come on in," she says, standing back.

Upon entering the house's foyer, Tony notices a giant photograph of a waterfall in the woods covering one small wall. He follows her down a single step into the living room. He looks around him. It's nice, but plain. The walls are pale yellow, and there's some kind of rust-colored flower border that runs along the wall just below the ceiling. A small fireplace sits on the west wall. A burgundy plaid living room set looks a bit tired. Then he spots a picture of Leo on an end table. It is so obviously Leo that Tony's throat catches. Shit. Fuck. There goes his last hope of being wrong.

He looks away quickly. "You've got nice light in here," he says.

"Thanks." She hesitates, seeming uncertain. "Do you want me to just let you wander around, or do you want a tour?"

"I'd love a tour," he says. He'd normally rather snoop alone, but he's here to learn what he can about this woman.

She smiles, and he sees that her top teeth are slightly crooked. "Well, this is the living room. Obviously." She walks through it, past a hallway to the right, into a small alcove that is a dining area and past it to a galley kitchen. "This is the kitchen," she says, almost apologetic.

Tony goes over to the bank of windows on the other side of the dining-room table and looks out. He turns back to face her. "How's the neighborhood?" he asks. "Any trouble?"

She flinches, and Tony is almost sorry for the question.

"No," she says. "The neighbors are good."

"So, are you moving across town or farther away?" asks Tony. "If you don't mind my asking."

"Probably not far," she says with a girlish shrug. "Mainly I want to downsize." She is fidgeting with her fingers. No rings. Her nails are unpainted. She seems almost as nervous as he is.

When Tony scans the kitchen, he notices that the appliances are all outdated. He also sees yet another picture of Leo, on the windowsill above the sink. At the end of the kitchen is a back door that leads to a carport. And, catty corner from it, a door that must lead to a basement.

"Let me show you the upstairs bedrooms first," Inez says. She leads him back to the hallway. The first door on the left is a bathroom. He peeks in. Ordinary. Clean. Pink porcelain tub and toilet, cheap fixtures, and a plastic shower door with that bubble glass you can't see through.

At the end of the hall she opens a door to what is clearly a boy's room. Leo's. Tony's gut tightens. He walks in, looks around. Shit. Obviously she hasn't changed this room since Leo went missing, but it's clean and dusted. A red toy car sits on the floor by the bed; a blue plastic ball is in the corner. The curtains are decorated with spaceships. The rug is the "right" blue.

Oh dear God. She has been waiting and hoping for Leo to come home for six years. For a second, he feels dizzy. He puts a hand on a dresser to steady himself.

"I see you have a son," he says with a catch in his voice.

"Yeah," she says. "He's out with friends right now." Tony could swear that she knows he knows she is lying. Her face is flushed and she quickly leaves the room.

"This is the master," she says, turning toward the door opposite the bathroom. Tony follows her in. "I'm afraid there's no adjoining master bath. Just the one across the hall. But there's another bathroom—no tub but a shower and sink and toilet downstairs. I think they call it a three-quarter bath?"

"Great," says Tony.

"So, you said you have a daughter?" she asks. Tony is totally taken aback by the question. He forgot he'd said that. "Sure do. She's seventeen."

"And your wife?"

"She passed when my daughter was born," he says. He's remembering the old advice that when you have to lie, use the truth whenever possible.

"Oh, I'm sorry!" she says, combing a hand through her hair. "That must be hard. Being a single parent."

"Yeah," says Tony. "But we get by."

"I know what that's like," she says. "I've been widowed for a while."

Tony hadn't expected for the conversation to get this personal.

His eyes quickly dart around her bedroom. The bed is plain, a white nubby bedspread. A painted white headboard. Two pieces of art that look like garage-sale buys. On the nightstand, yet another photo of Leo.

Tony thinks it is weird that there are no photos of the daughter, Venus. Then again, given what happened, maybe it's not weird at all.

Pretending to be serious about looking hard at the house, he opens her closet door. When he sees the jumble within, he quickly shuts it.

"I'm sorry, I'm kind of a slob!" she says, with a laugh.

"So am I," says Tony. "I like to think it's a sign of creativity, so maybe you're creative, too."

"I don't know about that." She shrugs. "Are you an artist?"

"Kind of," he says, shaking his head. "So, when was the house built?" *These* are the kinds of questions he needs to be asking.

"You know, I think around the late forties. But I'm not positive."

"Let's go downstairs," she offers. "It's a basement but partly finished."

For the rest of the tour, he sticks to buyer-oriented questions. Downstairs, he compliments the knotty-pine paneling in the bedroom. It contains a stripped bed, small furniture, and packed boxes.

After she shows him the bathroom, which opens right off the bedroom, Tony takes a big breath. "Well, I think I've bothered you enough," he says.

"No bother," she says. But he can tell this whole tour has been a torture for her. She doesn't offer to show the garage and he doesn't ask, just turns away and starts upstairs, desperate to get out.

At the door, Inez says, "I just have a question."

"Yes?"

"How did you know my phone number?"

Tony is caught off guard. "Well . . . I got it off the COMING SOON sign out there."

She nods. "Oh. I didn't even know it was on there."

Tony turns back to her at the door, realizing he screwed up. "I really like the place. I'll probably give your realtor a call once I'm back home and see what we can do."

"Sure," she says. "Thanks." She moves toward him and awkwardly extends her hand. He shakes it. Their eyes meet briefly. Sad gray eyes with brows shaped exactly like Leo's.

PART FIVE

★

Everett, Washington; Oakland, California; February 1986

40

It's a Sunday evening in February, and I can tell Inez is startled to see me on her porch.

"Venus," she says.

"Yeah," I answer, like I'm disappointed it's me, too.

She lets me in and I shut the door behind me. For a second we both stand there, shivering from the blast of cold air we let in. I set my heavy suitcase down, my arm burning with relief. Her arms are wrapped around her body, and she's wearing a thick gray cardigan I don't recognize.

"You could at least offer to take my coat," I say. "Or is this a bad time?"

"Oh no!" she says, looking stricken. "I'm sorry! I'm just surprised. But glad surprised." She reaches for my coat and I raise my hand to stop her. I shrug out of the parka I got from Goodwill and hand it to her.

While she hangs it in the small coat closet, I notice how strongly the house smells like the past, and it makes me want to run for my life. I also notice a glass of wine on the coffee table. "You could offer me some wine, too," I say, surprising myself. "Since I see you're already at it," I add.

I hadn't planned to sound so bratty, much less to ask for a drink.

She looks embarrassed about the wine, and I wonder if she still drinks too much. I can see her debating whether to act like a mother and remind me I'm not old enough to drink—or go with the flow. I kind of enjoy her fluster.

"Okay," she says in a shaky voice. "I've got a good bottle of red, if that's okay . . ."

"That's fine."

While she heads into the kitchen, I take a seat on the bizarrely familiar plaid couch and survey the living room. A black faux-leather recliner has replaced Raymond's shabby olive-green one—but otherwise it all looks creepily the same. How could she stay here?

I hear the pop of a cork from the kitchen just as I notice the framed photo of Leo on the side table. There used to be a picture of me there, too—in a matching frame. I can't help wondering whether she threw it in the garbage or packed it away.

This trip to Everett was never my plan—until that reporter wrote a feature for *The Seattle Times* about my story, including where I work. Julie had turned out to be right about people's curiosity, and pretty soon I felt the way I'd thought I would. Like a monkey in a zoo.

I never liked monkeys anyway. In fifth grade, we took a field trip to the Woodland Park Zoo and there was a sign on the monkey enclosure saying not to knock on the window—so of course I had to. I knocked really hard and the monkeys went nuts. It's one of the few times I ever got in trouble at school. But it seemed worth it at the time and still does now. I've a mind to go do it again.

Inez returns with an open bottle of wine and a ruby-colored goblet like the one she's already using. The glasses are so familiar, and it seems bizarre that after all these years I'm going to get to drink from one. Inez sets it down on the oak coffee table, which is also weirdly familiar. I could have told the story of every water ring I made because I didn't use a coaster.

It seems that while I've spent the last six years going out of my way not to trigger old memories, Inez has found a way to be at home among them.

She turns the black recliner so it's facing more in my direction. In the awkward silence, I watch her fill my glass and top off her own. She sits in the chair, takes off her ratty slippers, and pulls her bare feet onto the seat, curling up like she's trying to feel safe. "I'm so glad you're here, Venus," she says.

"I'm not glad to be here," I tell her. "And I'm not really here to see you."

Given her pained expression, I might as well have slapped her face. I know I shouldn't be so mean, especially since I'm here to ask for money.

"Okay," she says softly. "That's fine. So how can I help you?"

"I changed my mind."

"About . . . ?"

"About the money. I want to take you up on your offer."

"That's great," she says with a genuine smile. "Does this mean you're going to enroll in college?"

"I already told you why I can't go to college, especially around here," I answer.

I take a sip of the wine. It's probably really cheap, but I wouldn't know. The extent of my drinking at Echo Glen was a few gulps of contraband liquor someone snuck in—and I hated it. I never drank, because I didn't want to be like Raymond and Inez, who both drank too much.

"But I want to get a car and move to California. And that takes money," I continue.

"Oh. California," Inez says, clearly disappointed. She's wearing absolutely no makeup, but she is still pretty for her age.

"Where are *you* moving?" I ask. "I saw the COMING SOON sign out front."

"Yes. That. I don't know where I'll land. Here in Everett, most likely. In a smaller place. I have friends here. . . ."

She finally reaches for her glass and takes a couple of swallows.

"So, are you going to make me ask how much you can . . . ?" I wasn't about to say *give to me*. I figure she *owes* me this money.

"Oh. I'm sorry. I hadn't really thought about it yet—"

"It seems like five grand is the least you can do," I say.

I can tell by her face that she's taken aback. "I can't do that, at least not yet," she says. "First I have to sell the house. . . ."

"Surely you have some savings," I prod. "And since you never had to pay a single dime to raise me from the age of thirteen up, I would think you could spare at least a thousand?"

That was a low blow. I gulp some wine so I don't have to see her reaction.

"I can probably give you around eight hundred right away," she says. "Every month I put some money in savings. I could go to the bank tomorrow. Is that enough for now and I'll give you more when I sell the house?"

Of course it is. It's actually more than I'd hoped for—I was bluffing by demanding so much.

I set my glass on the coffee table, reaching for a coaster at the last second. The coasters are painted with seagulls, and I bought them in a shop in Mukilteo to give Inez for Mother's Day one year. Why on earth hasn't she tossed them?

"I guess I can make that work," I say. As soon as the words are out of my mouth, they sound stingy and ungrateful. Damn. I wanted to come off more dignified and mature. But when she acts all meek it brings out my mean.

Now I'm anxious to go. I get to my feet, saying, "I'll come back tomorrow for the money. I can get my own coat."

"But you just got here!" she exclaims. "Please don't leave yet." She is still sitting in her chair, as if by not standing up she can make me stay.

"Why not?" I ask. "What else do we have to talk about?"

"Can't you stay for a while, Venus?" She gazes up at me with familiar gray eyes, and for a brief flash I see my mother as I used to—more of an annoyance than the source of all evil—and I soften in spite of myself.

"I won't smoke," she promises. "I'm trying to quit. I have to," she adds with a nervous laugh. "Did you know that pretty soon you won't even be able to smoke in bowling alleys? Isn't that ridiculous?"

What is she babbling about? Smoking was never the issue. I stand there for a second too long, and she takes that for hope and launches into a speech about how she knows I'm still angry, but she loves me, and who knows when we'll ever see each other if I move to California. She seems desperate, on the verge of tears—and I'm so scared that she'll cry and I'll feel sorry for her that I sit back down. "Okay, I'll stay for a few more minutes."

I settle back into the couch and try to pretend Inez is not Inez. I ask about her friends, the only safe subject I can think of at the moment. As she rattles on about Shirley—the woman she should hate for losing Leo!—I continue to sip on the wine. I decide I like the way it tastes and the way it feels to be sitting here drinking.

"What about your job?" I prompt, which seems like another safe topic. She complains about it, but not too much. It's a boring job at the school-district administration office.

Just hearing about her dull life makes me want to stick a fork in my eye. I've decided by now that I really like red wine, especially the way the color of it perfectly matches the bitter berry taste. I think of Leo and how he likes food that is the "right" color. I wonder if he also likes food that tastes like the color it is. Like rice tastes white and peas taste green.

Inez continues to rattle on, clearly desperate to keep me here. As she talks, she keeps refilling my glass when it's half empty. With each sip, it gets harder to resent her or keep a hostile attitude. Soon, my lips feel both numb and buzzy.

We finish the bottle, but Inez keeps up a nervous stream of chatter. She tells me more about Shirley—clearly her only real friend—and how Shirley loves dumb-blonde jokes even though she's a natural blonde herself. "She must know at least two hundred of them," Inez says, smiling.

"Tell me one," I challenge.

"A dumb-blonde joke?"

"Yeah. Why not?" I'm only half serious, but to my surprise she says, "Okay. Let me think for a minute."

I'm starting to realize I could ask Inez to do just about anything tonight and she'd say yes. She tucks her hair behind her right ear, a habit she's always had. "Okay," she says, smiling. I see the familiar crooked incisor that always looks too sharp. She sits up straighter, tucking her feet beneath her like this is going to be a performance. "I guess this is a good one."

"Okay, so tell it already!"

"Okay," she says again, wiping her hands on her jeans like she's nervous. "Okay. It goes something like: Why did the blonde stare at the can of orange juice for such a long time?"

I couldn't think of an answer. "I give up," I say. "Tell me."

"Because the can said, 'Concentrate.'"

The joke is so lame that I smile and shake my head. I take another drink of what's left in my glass. "Try again. Another one."

"Oh no," she says. "I don't even know if I can remember any more. Shirley is the one who—"

"C'mon!" I encourage. "One more. If we can't go after blondes, what else are we going to talk about?" It's an awkward moment, because I just pointed out how much is off-limits between us.

"Okay!" she agrees. "Okay, I thought of another one: How come blondes always like to wear their hair up?" She suddenly gets out of her chair. "You think about it while I get another bottle."

Another bottle? She's that desperate to keep me here. Or else she's truly turned into a drunk. While she's gone, I realize two things: I must be what you call tipsy, and I've heard the joke before. Inez returns with the open bottle.

"So they can catch all the stuff that goes over their heads?" I ask.

"Yes!" cries Inez, actually laughing, which makes me laugh, too.

It must be true that alcohol will make you do things you normally wouldn't do, since that's the only possible explanation for what happens next, which is that I agree to stay and eat dinner with the person I'm supposed to hate most.

INEZ TELLS ME to relax while she makes spaghetti. She turns on the TV for me and then heads down the hall to the bathroom, and I realize my own bladder is about to burst, too. The nightly news is on, but I'm not the slightest bit interested.

When Inez emerges from the hall, I take my turn in the pink-tiled bathroom. After I'm done, I can't resist the urge to peek into Leo's old room. I don't flip on the light, but in the dim glow from a streetlamp, I can see it looks exactly the same, like Inez has found a way to freeze the past in place. If I didn't know better—aromas can't possibly last six years—I'd swear it still smells like Leo. A combination of sweaty sleep, Ritz crackers, and the faint tang of a mattress wet one too many times.

As my eyes adjust to the low light, I walk over and touch his painted-blue dresser. It reminds me how I used to open these drawers every morning and pick out Leo's clothes for the day, which were all as close to primary blue as possible.

For a fleeting moment, I wonder what happened to my planets, if they're still hanging downstairs in my room. Or did Inez clean my room all out?

I pick up one of Leo's cars from his shelf. I spin the wheels; I'm still amazed how long Leo could be content to stare at them.

On impulse, I open the door to his small closet. His favorite blanket, the purple one, is lying on the floor. I hear Inez in the kitchen, making noise with pots and pans. I think of Inez passing

Leo's empty room night after night, and an unexpected wave of horror and sadness washes over me—on her behalf.

It must be the wine, or maybe it's that I worked so hard to hate Inez I never allowed myself to imagine what it would feel like to lose a child into thin air.

Now, because of Piper, I almost can. And it's just too much.

I make my way into the kitchen, afraid to be alone. As if on autopilot, I offer to set the table, since that was always my job. "Sure thing," she says.

It freaks me out a little that I know exactly where the plates are, where the silverware drawer is. And the bouquet pattern on the flatware I could have drawn by heart. I'm careful to ignore the door at the end of the kitchen, the one to the basement stairs.

When I go to the freezer for ice, I find the same blue cracked ice trays from before. Probably lots of people keep ice trays this long, but it just seems wrong somehow.

I decide I need more wine.

41

It's time to sit down to the familiar meal of tossed garden salad and Inez's idea of spaghetti—Ragú sauce mixed with hamburger and onions over pasta. As I awkwardly dig in, I notice the familiar painting of a sad old man praying with folded hands over his soup and bread. It has always hung on this wall. Inez was never a religious person, but it must have seemed to her like the kind of art that one *should* hang near a kitchen table.

Once, when I was ten or so, I asked her why we had to eat near such a depressing painting. She said, "He is praying over his food because he is *grateful*."

"Well, we don't pray over our food," I challenged.

"You're right, Venus," she said. "Maybe we should."

"No thanks," I told her. "Besides, I don't think he is grateful for his bread; I think he's praying for some butter and jam to put on it." I remember this detail because Inez laughed so hard, and she often repeated the story to friends.

"I see our man is still praying for jam," I say now, nodding toward the art.

She turns to see and breaks out laughing. "Oh my God!" she exclaims, "I almost forgot about that."

I almost forgot how much I used to love her laugh. "Have you had any bites on the house?" I ask.

"Not really," she says. "It's not even for sale yet. Officially. But actually, I did show it for the first time this afternoon. Right before you showed up. You practically passed each other on the porch."

"Really? How did it go? Pretty cool if you get a buyer before you even have it on the market."

"It went okay," she says thoughtfully. "But it was kind of weird, too. Normally my realtor would show it. You remember Melissa Lansing? She went into real estate."

"I think so." I vaguely remember a brassy friend of Inez's who had a large mole above her lip, and not the pretty kind.

"I wouldn't have showed the house without Melissa, but this guy said he was from California and going back tomorrow and it would be his only chance."

"Well, how did it go? Did he like the house?"

"I suppose so, but he acted kind of weird about it."

"What do you mean, weird?"

She thinks for a second. "One weird thing is that he didn't ask to look at the garage. And don't most men really care about that? Then again, I didn't offer . . . and maybe by then he knew he didn't want it, so it didn't matter."

"What else was weird?"

"Now that you ask," she says, "he was weird about Leo's room. Like it made him really sad."

I feel a flutter of alarm. "Keep talking," I say, setting down my fork and moving the wine bottle out of reach.

"He said he got my phone number off the sign in the yard, but I don't think it's on there—I haven't checked."

"Seriously?" I ask.

"I didn't have a chance, because you showed up!"

"Please excuse me for a minute."

I go to the closet, grab my coat, and go out the front door to check the sign. When I sit down again at the table, I tell her, "The only number on there is the realtor's."

"Why would he lie?"

Okay, now I'm getting a little mad. "So you've got a strange guy from California who gets your number from somewhere and takes a tour of the house and doesn't look at the garage and acts sad in Leo's room. Doesn't that all add up to super suspicious to you?"

Inez looks hurt. "Now that you say it that way," she says.

I couldn't believe it, but then again I could. "What did he look like? What was his last name—surely you got that," I pressed.

Her hand went to cover her mouth, and I knew she didn't. "I got his first name! It was Tony. He seemed so nice. His name was Tony and he was really handsome."

"Okay. You got a first name. Handsome. Didn't it occur to you that maybe he's related to Leo's disappearance? What if the milk carton flushed him out?"

Our eyes meet and something sparks in the air. I can tell she feels it, too. We both know what I just suggested could so easily be true.

Who knew I was such a great detective? God knows I've been grilled enough times in my life, but now I turn every instinct I have toward getting what I can out of Inez.

"What about a phone number? Did you get it?"

"It never occurred to me. He said he'd call. . . ."

I heave a sigh of frustration. "What kind of car did he drive?" I demand.

She thought for a second. "It was a black truck, and there was a business logo on the side—but it wasn't just letters; there was a fancy design."

"What did it say?"

"It was too far away to read out the window, but I recall it being all scrolly and pretty, like the words were part of the art."

"What make or model of truck? Like a Ford?"

She looks at me blankly. "I don't pay attention to stuff like that. It was a plain truck, older model, I'd guess. Not huge, only one-seat-up-front type. I think . . ."

"What about *him*? What did he look like besides handsome? Did he have any distinctive things about him?"

She perks up, relieved to have something more to add. "He had dark hair cut short and styled all nice. He definitely had tattoos. I saw one on his wrist when we shook hands goodbye. And one peeking out above his collar. But he wasn't the kind of guy you normally associate with tattoos."

"Tattoos of what? What did they look like?"

"I have no idea," Inez says, shaking her shoulders. "It was just brief flashes of color I noticed."

"Okay," I say, frustrated. "So what else? What about his hands? Were they rough or dirty like a labor person or soft like a desk job?"

"His hands were nice," she says. "Normal. I don't think he had any rings on, either. He wasn't like some biker dude."

"Didn't you ask what he did for a living down in California?"

Inez takes a deep breath. Clearly the answer is no. "I'm sorry, Venus. I didn't think of it. I didn't want to be nosy because I didn't want him to get nosy."

She looks so sheepish, I almost feel bad for her.

"But wait! Oh my God, Venus! I remember in the bedroom when he saw my messy closet, he mentioned something about being creative. He said he was some kind of artist, or maybe he said he was *kind of* an artist."

"That's good!" I exclaim. "We're putting together a lot here. We are calling the police. Right now."

"And I can already tell you what they'll say," she says. "Without a license plate or a last name or anything to go on other than an artist in California named Tony— Wait!" she screeches. "Oakland! He was from Oakland!"

That helps, knowing the city, assuming the guy was being honest. But then Inez admits how many goose chases she's sent the cops on over the years. "I can already hear Detective Pete saying, *It's too bad you don't have a license plate to go on. Or even a last name. There's a lot of Tonys in Oakland. And why would a kidnapper tell the truth about where he's from?"*

I sigh heavily and sit back.

"We can still call the police if you want," she says. "We can call right now."

Thank God I came when I did, because we haven't lost much time. "But I don't trust the police to get right on this," I tell her. "Here's what we'll do. Tonight you'll call the police and fill them in. But in the meantime, I'm going to Oakland. I came here to get bus fare for California, anyway. But a bus isn't going to help me with the search. I see you still have your Honda."

Inez's eyes go wide with surprise. "You want to take my car?"

"Yes," I tell her. "Don't you have a friend who has a second car?"

"Shirley still has her late husband's truck. . . . I'm sure she'd let me borrow it."

A plan is forming in my head. And within a few minutes, I can already see myself hunting down this asshole.

"But you'd go alone?" Inez asks, concern in her voice. I realize she's gotten older, more cautious in the last six years.

"Yes." I don't want Inez along for the ride. She'd only slow me down. I remind myself that we're still estranged. "You have to work anyway, right?"

She nods.

"I saw the milk carton, and you need to be here in case something turns up. You can't be driving around California."

"I guess you're right," she says.

"It's not as hard as you think to find people," I tell her. "Look how quickly you found me."

She begins insisting I stay the night and go to the bank with her in the morning. I balk at first, but it makes some sense. I have no car and by now it's raining like hell. What with all the transfers, it took me almost three hours to get here from Capitol Hill.

"You can sleep in Leo's bed," she offers, tentative.

"No way," I tell her. "I could never." So she makes up the couch for me. Funny how neither of us acknowledges my old room downstairs.

Even if it had never been a crime scene, I doubt she would keep my room the way she's kept Leo's—like it's a memorial. I know this in my gut the same way I know she wishes it were me instead of Leo who went missing.

DESPITE ALL THE wine she drank with her daughter, Inez doubts she'll sleep a wink. She still can't believe that Venus showed up. That she stayed. What does this mean? She'd swear Venus is softening toward her, but she doesn't want to get her hopes up.

Now she pictures Venus on her couch in the living room, and it seems too good to be true. Even with the blinds closed, she knows the streetlamps make it bright enough to see out there. All of a sudden she's tempted to go steal a look at Venus sleeping. Surely she must be knocked out by now, given how much wine they drank. Her tolerance would be so low, compared to Inez's.

She debates herself, but in the end she simply can't resist the chance to look at her daughter without fear of saying the wrong thing or otherwise arousing her anger. She glances at her bedside clock and sees it's almost 1:00 A.M. She slips from her bed, feeling strangely giddy and nervous.

At the end of the hall, she peeks into the living room and sees Venus lying still, sleeping on her back, softly snoring. The wine, perhaps. Inez tiptoes closer and pauses. She gets on her hands and knees and crawls around the coffee table in her nightgown, aware of how ridiculous she must look. To whom? God?

No. God would understand. Who knows? Maybe God does something similar when we're mad as hell at him.

And, ah, there she is. Inez notices that Venus's eyebrows are plucked, which makes her face look somehow softer, more open. Her prominent, sculpted nose is a thing of beauty, though Inez knows Venus doesn't like it. Her lashes are thick and long—she probably doesn't even wear mascara. Doesn't need to. As always, her hair is like Medusa's—an enormous tangle of black curls spread out on the pillow.

For several moments, Inez continues to ponder the miracle of her daughter's presence in her home. She wishes she could touch her face, stroke her cheek at least. Instead, she prays for Venus, that she will find peace. That she will come to forgive Inez. That she will find her way to a happy life despite all that's gone so horribly wrong.

Before she's done, it dawns on her that she's finally praying on her knees.

42

The next morning, I wake up early with an excruciating headache and a sore neck because the couch is too small for me.

I sit up and get reoriented before I go to the kitchen to start some coffee. I open the blinds and see that it's drizzly and miserable again. I can't wait to get out of Everett, out of the rain, away from the smell of rotten eggs that can come from the city's pulp and paper mills.

It was a small sawmill on the Everett waterfront that took the life of my father. Inez tried to sue, but I guess my father had violated too many safety rules—so nada. *Sorry, ma'am.*

After using the bathroom and getting my cup of coffee, I sit down in the living room on the side of the couch that isn't sunken from Inez's bottom. I still can't believe what happened last night. That I got drunk with my mother, for one. That I signed up to be a detective, for two.

When Inez gets up, I hear her call in sick to work. After a quick breakfast, we go to the bank, where she withdraws eight hundred dollars. The teller stares at me instead of at Inez. She obviously knows the story and exactly who I am. I look away, wishing I had just stayed in the car. What was I thinking? Of course being with Inez is a dead giveaway.

I remember Piper saying "Take a picture, it'll last longer," and wish I could be so childish toward the teller. Thinking of Piper, I feel a familiar stab of loss. Piper. Where is she right now? We agreed to phone calls twice a week and when her aunt brings her to visit her uncle Mike in Seattle—of course I'll be there.

How I'll do that after I move to California, I have no idea.

After Inez and I get back in the car, she says, "I'm giving you the Honda. To keep. I plan to buy a new car when I sell the house anyway."

"No way," I reply. "I don't want it."

"Why? You need a car, for Christ's sake."

"After all this, I'm not taking a car from you. It's too much."

She is quiet the rest of the way home, and "after all this" hangs in the air.

"Please take it."

Once we're back at the house, she asks again.

"I'll think about it," I tell her. "But to be honest, I would want a way better car." I laugh at my own mean joke.

"So when are you leaving?" she asks, opening the dishwasher. I can hear the worry in her voice.

"Not as soon as you think," I tell her. "We still have a big problem. You're forgetting something very important," I say with mock sternness.

She looks stricken. "What?"

"I don't know how to drive a car!" The look of relief on her face cracks me up. "Lucky for you, I just happen to have a phony license. And you're gonna teach me how to drive in one day."

"How fun!" she says, genuinely excited.

I'm tempted to make a smart remark about how this—her teaching me to drive—should have happened years ago. But I hate to dampen the mood.

A few minutes later, we're back in the Honda. Only this time, I'm the one in the driver's seat.

AFTER A FEW hours of Inez's direction, it's painfully apparent that I'm not yet ready to drive alone to California. We stop at Herfy's Burgers for lunch, and I can barely choke down the burger for the good memories that come with it—my friends and I after soccer games, a gang of girls lining up at the order window, starving, our knees bruised, our bodies sweaty, our faces happy—even if we'd lost.

Damn if those good memories aren't the worst.

On the way home, I can tell Inez is thinking hard about something. It bothers me to still know her so well.

"I really want you to stay for one more night," she says. "I'll work with you on learning to drive the rest of the afternoon—into the evening. I don't care how long it takes. And you need to leave early, because I don't want you to drive at night."

I almost make a joke that this—*I don't want you to drive at night*—is precisely the kind of thing I was supposed to hear from her when I got my license at sixteen. But I stop myself. I wait for further arguments or emotional manipulations. When none come, I meet her eyes and I can tell she's just being practical. Shit. Damn.

"Okay," I say. "One more night. But we get to call in Chinese for dinner."

"Oh, so you like Chinese now?" she asks.

"I have absolutely no idea," I tell her. Which is the point, I guess.

ON TUESDAY MORNING, as soon as I pull away from the house, I notice that even without Inez in it, the Honda smells like her Charlie perfume. The first time I stop for gas, I buy a tree-shaped air freshener and a map of California.

Traveling south on I-5, I'm careful to drive the speed limit or just below. I never try to pass anyone, nervous about being pulled over. *My name is Annette Higgman. I live on Federal Drive Boulevard.*

I drive and drive, and keep on driving. I can't decide if I'm on a fool's errand—or if I really have a chance. Perhaps what matters most to me is that I make the effort. For Leo. For all of us.

Inez warned me that Oakland is massive—not some small town where people all know one another or you can find someone by just asking around. I try not to let her doubts—and mine—get to me.

It's pretty late when I finally stop at a cheap hotel in Redding, California. But I'm so excited just to be in California I can hardly sleep. Plus, the adrenaline must really have me going. In that half-sleep state, I dream of my real father, his black curly hair and sparkly blue eyes—even though I can't recall them exactly. I dream of Leo and Echo Glen. I dream of my childhood best friend, Jackie. I dream of Truly, who died of cancer (the reason for her wispy, barely there hair) a year after her great escape from Denney. I dream of my whole life—and yet I swear I never slept.

At first light, I drive through a McDonald's for an Egg McMuffin and a greasy hunk of hash browns. Almost four hours later, I roll into Oakland. I take a random exit and find a pay phone to call Inez to tell her that I made it here. It's so bizarre to dial the number for home after all these years. She fills me in on her conversations with the Everett police. They suggested she phone the police in Oakland. Duh. We should have thought of that!

I've decided to start with art galleries. I open the phone book. There are five pages of listings. Shit. I rip out all those pages. It takes me an hour to whittle it down to the five galleries that seem most promising because they feature numerous artists—and there are a few Anthonys in the bunch. I make a list of addresses to visit and I use my map.

As I travel around Oakland, I am startled by how different it feels from Everett. The streets—and a lot of the people—seem rough, unfriendly. Phone poles are covered with bills advertising who-knows-what. I spot graffiti everywhere.

At the end of the day, I've only managed to find four galleries—mostly because I have to keep stopping and looking at my map.

Usually, the artist isn't around at the gallery and so I inquire with staff, giving them a description of the artist I'm looking for. No one recognizes our guy.

On day two, I continue my quest, but it feels stupid. After the last gallery leads nowhere, I drive up and down busy retail strips, trying to keep an eye out for a black truck with pretty doors—which is a dangerous way to drive and an act of foolishness, given the size of Oakland.

By the end of the second day, I know how to park a lot better. I've been honked at for going slow, and I've made several errors at complicated intersections. But I have to congratulate myself that I haven't had an accident. As soon as it's dark, I eat dinner at a diner and then fall into bed at the Holiday Inn I checked in to that morning. Tomorrow will be better, I tell myself.

Yeah, sure.

At least I sleep well that night, and I wake up ready to go again at 7:00 A.M. I eat breakfast from a snack machine at the hotel and hit the streets with forced optimism. But by noon, I start to flag, ready to quit. I've seen a lot of art, some of it good. I've found dozens and dozens of black trucks but none with a design on the door that looks like art.

Starving and discouraged, I stop for lunch at a pizza place in a run-down strip mall. As I'm heading inside, I notice a yellow Mustang in the parking lot, because it is decorated on the side with an advertisement: TATTOOS TO DIE FOR, surrounded by an image of razor wire and skeletons. As I approach the pizza place, I notice that next door is the tattoo parlor being advertised. Suddenly I stop in my tracks. My stomach flutters. What if Tony is a *tattoo* artist? What if, just like this guy, he advertises on his truck? That might explain why Inez called it "pretty." Plus, what kind of guy, especially one who wears tattoos, would want something remotely pretty on the side of his truck unless it was an advertisement? It's not any dumber a theory than the one I've been following.

I skip the pizza place and instead enter the fine establishment called Tattoos to Die For. As I push open the door, I'm greeted by a guy with a long beard and a big belly. Business is obviously slow.

"Looking for a tat, pretty lady?" he asks. "Name's Bart." He extends a beefy hand and I shake it.

"I'm sorry. No. I'm looking for a tattoo artist, though. Maybe you know the guy. His name is Tony and he drives a black truck."

Bart pauses to think. "Nope. Don't know him. But there's a lot of tattoo parlors in this city."

I'm disappointed but still intrigued by this new idea. After leaving Bart, I find a phone booth and look up the tattoo section. Bart was right—just a glance tells me there are tons of tattoo parlors in and around Oakland. It will take some time to phone each one and ask if there's a Tony who works there.

I call Inez and run the idea past her. "Could he be a tattoo artist?"

"Well, like I said, he had tattoos. And I guess they might think they're artists. And he did say, 'Kind of.' But still, I don't think . . ."

"Why not?"

"He just didn't have that vibe," says Inez. "Apart from the bits of tattoo peeking out, he seemed so clean-cut. No piercings or weird stuff."

"Maybe you're thinking in stereotypes," I tell her.

"Yeah, I guess," she agrees. "Totally. But I hate to waste time going in the wrong direction."

"You mean you hate for me to waste time."

"Sorry, you're right," she says. "No luck at the galleries?"

"Don't you think I'd have said so? Geez, Inez."

"Any word from the police?" I ask, knowing the answer.

"Nothing yet," Inez says.

"When you think about it, we don't have much to go on," I say. "The guy didn't ask to see the garage and seemed sad in Leo's room. That could mean a lot of things. Maybe he'd decided by then he didn't want the house, so he didn't need to see the garage. And maybe it was your imagination that he seemed sad in Leo's room. What if we're on a really stupid goose chase?"

Inez doesn't answer for a moment. "I'm sorry, Venus," she says. "I'm sorry about everything."

Oh shit. I can tell she's about to cry. "Don't start with that," I tell her. "Not now. We need to focus on finding Leo."

After we hang up, I am so discouraged. I go back to have pizza at the place next to Bart's Tattoos to Die For. I sit at a table facing the parking lot and force myself to finish the extra-large slice of pepperoni. Afterward, I return to the phone book and rip out all the pages for tattoo shops.

A clerk at a nearby market grudgingly lets me buy a roll of quarters from her.

Back at the phone booth, I take a deep breath and start calling shops, beginning at *A*. "Is there a Tony who works there?" I ask. I get all no's, most of them gruff. I run out of quarters way too quickly. Plus, it seems this is a popular phone booth. I have to stop several times to let a lineup of shady-looking people take their own sweet time.

I get more quarters from the market and go back to the phone booth. Once, I call a shop where the woman who answers says, yes, they have a Tony who works there. "He's not in today, though," she adds.

"Does your Tony have short dark hair? Is he handsome?"

The woman on the other end cackles. "Tony—handsome? He'd get a kick out of that!"

WHILE I'M WAITING for an old lady who pulled up in a large Buick to finish using the pay phone, I glance through all the pages I have yet to get to. And there it is. My heart drops. Tattoos by Tony. Why didn't I just start at T, for Tony.

Now I have to fight back my excitement. It's still such a long shot, I remind myself. So I found a Tony who owns a tat shop.

That's nothing, really. But I abandon the phone booth and get in my car, where I open my map. Trying to figure out where I am in relation to this shop takes me five minutes. It's not all that far.

Driving there, I feel like I'm in a dream. The idea that I might have found Leo's kidnapper is just too much. I feel certain that, in my panic, I'll get in a wreck or otherwise ruin my chance. But I don't. I arrive on the right street safely. And there it is: Tattoos by Tony. When I see a black truck with a design painted on the door, my heart starts to pound.

I park a couple of spaces behind the truck. Turn off the engine. Now what? I can't charge in there and ask if he's a kidnapper. I don't even know if it's the right Tony. I get out of the Honda in what feels like slow motion. I casually stroll by the shop and glance inside.

Oh my God, it's him! It has to be! Late thirties, dark-haired, and suave-looking. Better-looking than Ted Bundy. I try to picture this guy having Leo in a cage, using him for perverse purposes, but I just can't.

Of course, there could be more than one good-looking tattoo artist named Tony in Oakland, but the truck is the kicker, the ace. This *has* to be the guy. My knees are weak and I feel shaky, on the verge of tears or collapse. I wonder if I should find a phone booth and call Inez and tell her I think I've found him.

Then I realize that I didn't necessarily find Leo's kidnapper. *I found the guy who looked at the house in Everett and seemed suspicious to Inez.* There's a huge leap in logic to say he kidnapped Leo. I need to know more, need to actually see or find Leo.

But how am I going to do that? I guess I could wait for this Tony to get off work and then follow him and see if I can catch sight of Leo. I could call the police, but what if this guy has Leo stashed somewhere and he won't talk? What if the police only botch it?

I turn and walk past the shop once again, glancing inside as I do. The guy looks up and I could swear we make eye contact. As I pass by the truck again, I pause. Since he can't see me from where he is, why not glance inside the vehicle to see what I can see? I boldly approach the truck, shield my eyes, and peer inside. Nothing to indicate a kid, much less a kidnapper.

And then something catches my eye. There's a sticker on the back window of the truck's cab. A black paw image with the words PANTHER PRIDE. When I look closer, I see text around the edges: EDNA BREWER MIDDLE SCHOOL. Could this guy have enrolled Leo in school? It seems far-fetched, given we're talking about a kidnapper. And even more unlikely given Leo's disabilities. I know I'm grasping at straws, but this straw gives me tingles.

On impulse, I ask a passerby if she knows where I can find the middle school. She says it's not far. Easy directions. But what if I go there and I miss the dude getting off work? And yet, I doubt this Tony is going to take off from work anytime soon. When I glanced inside, it looked like he had customers waiting their turn. Since I have no better leads, I decide to find the school and wait outside to watch for Leo coming out. The odds that I'd spot him in a crowd of kids pouring from the building are slim.

But it's worth at least a try.

Finding the school is easy. I park and head into the main office, which is right inside an enormous main entrance off the street. I approach the secretary. "I'm supposed to pick up my nephew today. What time does school let out?"

She barely looks up from her desk behind the counter. "Two fifty-five."

I walk back to my car to wait but realize I need to pee. It's only two-fifteen, so I have plenty of time to get back on Park Boulevard and visit one of the cafés I passed. I find a hopping lunch place, and no one seems to notice or care that I haven't ordered anything. But the ladies' room door is locked. Which makes me have to go even worse. While I wait, I check my watch every five seconds. Finally, I try to calm myself down by using some breathing techniques Sharon taught me back in Echo.

It might not even be him. *But what if it is!* I remember Piper's big green eyes. "I'm praying for Leo to come home."

A small, slightly hysterical laugh escapes me. And then, for the first time in my life, I decide to chance it that God might exist. If he ever wanted to convince me, now is his big—perhaps only— chance. *Let it be Leo,* I pray. *Let it be Leo.*

After I take my turn in the restroom, I wash my hands and look in the mirror. I am wild-eyed and my hair—no longer in a braid— looks like a nest for small birds. Instead of drying my hands with a paper towel, I dry them on my hair, trying to calm it down some. I put on fresh lipstick. Then I ask myself the most painful, scariest questions of all: What if Leo doesn't remember me? And what if I'm not sure it's him?

I just don't know.

Back at the school, I'm still early and I get my pick of places to park out front. My plan is simple: If I spot a boy who could be Leo, and he gets on a bus, I'll follow it. Or if he gets in a car, same thing.

My hands on the steering wheel are damp with sweat. Other parents begin to show up. At about two forty-five—ten minutes early—a woman comes out of the building with six kids in tow. One is in a wheelchair, and I quickly realize what's happening. She's letting the special-ed kids board the buses first.

And then I see him. A slender blond boy who looks about thirteen. His hair is long and covers most of the right side of his face. He has a pack on his back and carries a large music case. Could it really be him?

As they get closer, I see that he looks at the ground as he walks and tilts his head to the left. I can't help myself. I jump out of the car and race to intercept the teacher. "Ma'am? Can I have a word?"

She is stocky, a redhead with two inches of gray roots. "Yes?"

I glance behind her. "Can I talk to Leo for a second?"

"I guess," she says warily. So his name *is* Leo! It has to be him!

"Hi, Leo," I call out. He and all the other kids stop walking. I walk right up to him. I get down on my knees as if to pray, so I can look up at his face. "Leo? Do you remember me?"

Leo tries to look at me.

"It's Venus, Leo," I say. "Remember your sister, Venus?"

His grayish eyes skitter across mine and he nods. "My sister, Venus. From before."

I have never wanted to hug a person so badly in my life.

★

PART SIX

Oakland, California; Everett, Washington; February 1986

43

As usual, Tessa gets home first and then waits for Leo at his bus stop. When she asks Leo about his day, instead of his typical "Fine," he says, "I saw Venus."

"What?"

"I saw Venus from before."

Suddenly Tessa feels her throat closing. "Where did you see Venus?"

"At school," he says. "After."

Tessa tries to stifle her panic as she walks Leo the two blocks home. As they enter the house, Tessa looks back and notices that a red Honda is parked half a block away with a woman sitting in it. Tessa swears she is staring right at her.

Inside, she quickly locks the door, using both bolts. She peeks through a crack in the front-room draperies and watches the red car pass. The girl has big black curly hair, and she is staring at their house as she goes by.

Oh my God, could it be Leo's sister? She waits by the window to see if the woman passes by yet again. She doesn't.

Tessa feels flushed with fear, as if she has a fever. She goes to the kitchen and gets a glass of water. Her tongue is stuck to the roof of her mouth. Her knees feel weak. She sits in a kitchen chair. Leo has started playing his cello, even though it's not time to practice. It's a beautiful song, sweet and full of heavy, slow notes.

Her eyes sting. She looks at the clock. How will she pass the hours until her father comes home? What will she tell him? Maybe she should call him at the shop right now and warn him. But it might be nothing and she knows he's in the middle of a busy day, still making up for lost time when he was in Seattle.

She goes to her room. She lays her hands on her statue of the Virgin Mary. She prays, *Let it not be Venus. Let it not be Venus.*

SINCE I CAN'T just grab Leo, I tell him goodbye and that I'll see him in a little bit. I watch what bus he gets onto and then follow it. When he gets off at the second stop, he's met by a pretty Mexican girl who looks sixteen or so. I stay behind, crawling along until they enter a small ranch-style house together. Then I drive by slow enough to see and memorize the address.

Worried I'll forget it in my panic, I pull over a block later. I frantically scour the car for a pen. What if I forget the address and never find the house again? What if it's a dream?

I hurriedly dig around in Inez's messy glove box. No pen, but there's a lipstick. I use it to jot down the address on some receipts that look like they had to do with car repair. I try to picture Inez's face when I deliver Leo back to her.

My lipstick handwriting is shaky, and I need to calm down and think. The house Leo entered was in a decent neighborhood. Maybe Leo is at least being treated well. Then again, what if this house isn't even where he lives? What if that girl was his babysitter or something? If I pull away, I could still lose Leo between there and the real kidnapper's house.

But all my instincts tell me that this is where Leo is living. The way the girl glanced down the street at me, looking worried. With no car out front, and it being afternoon, it seemed safe to say there wasn't another grown-up there.

I guess the next step would be to find a police station. I hadn't thought this part out—what to do when I found Leo. I must not have really expected to find him—especially unharmed and apparently cared for by another family.

I realize the smartest thing to do right now is to call the police and get them involved so they can arrest this Tony guy. Oh, the irony! Once, the police locked me up, and now I need their help to nab someone else. As I drive to find a phone booth, I keep saying to myself, "Oh my God, Leo is alive. Oh my God, Leo is alive."

I'm so excited I'm afraid I'll get in a wreck or something dumb like that and miss my opportunity to rescue Leo. I drive carefully until I reach a busy boulevard, and then I search for a pay phone.

I spot a small diner, which I know will have a phone. The restaurant is dark inside and smells of burned coffee. The pay phone is where I thought it would be, just outside the restrooms. I flip open the front of the book, where you can usually find important community numbers. I should call the Oakland police, but they make it hard to figure out which number you should call. Is this an emergency? I decide that it is. I dial 911 for the second time in my life.

When I state my emergency—my brother was missing and I think I found him—the operator puts me through to a detective. Finally, I'm on the phone with a detective named Cunningham. "My brother was kidnapped in Washington," I explain. "He's been on milk cartons. His name is Leo Miller and he's been missing for six years and I finally just found him here in Oakland."

I come up for air, then hurtle on. "I have the address. I also can tell you where the kidnapper works. What should I do?"

"Calm down, miss," says the detective. "Back up. Take it slow. Your brother was kidnapped from where?"

"From Everett, Washington."

"And when was this?"

"It was in February of 1980. And I just saw him at a middle school and followed him to a house here in Oakland."

. . .

TESSA PUTS ON her apron. She is planning to make lasagna tonight, and she's kind of glad it takes a long time. It will keep her mind off her worries about the girl with the huge hair who might be Venus who might be Leo's sister who might be a person who will take him away.

She starts with a large pot of water on the stove. She puts a pound of hamburger in a frying pan on the other burner. She begins slicing onions. The doorbell rings. Her heart leaps. She lays the butcher knife down with great reluctance. That's how scared she is. In the front room, she glances out the window and sees a squad car. The girl with the black curly hair is sitting in the back. Tessa goes numb with terror. She makes herself open the door. There's nothing else to do.

"Can I help you, Officers?" She sounds like a person on one of those dumb cop shows.

"Yes, maybe you can," says one of them. "Can we come in?"

Tessa opens the door and steps aside. "My dad isn't home," she says. She's so glad this is true. She's aware of the sound of Leo playing his cello in his room. She doesn't want him to stop. She doesn't want him to come out here and see police and freak out.

"Do you know when he will be back?"

"Around six o'clock."

"Do you have a brother named Leo?"

"Well, he's not my brother. He's my cousin." How come she and her dad never talked about what to do if something like this ever happened? What is she supposed to say? She knows she's visibly shaking.

"Can you call your father and tell him that he needs to come right home?" the cop asks. "We'll wait here for him."

Tessa goes to the kitchen to use the phone, but her mind is so frantic that she has trouble thinking of the shop's number. Her fingers shake as she pushes each button. It reminds her of some of her dreams, where she can't dial an important number no matter how many times she tries. But she gets it right, of course. And her father answers.

"Daddy?" Her voice is clearly distraught.

"Tessa, what's wrong?"

She bursts into tears. "The police are here. I'm pretty sure it's about Leo."

LEO LIKES TO play his cello after school. He likes the cello better than Tessa's clarinet and better than other kids' instruments. He thinks the cello is best because you hear it with your whole body, not just your ears. And it makes a warm yellow sound that climbs in your chest and makes you feel like the sun is shining in there.

This afternoon Leo is playing Bach's Cello Suite No. 1. As he runs the bow across the strings, he feels the brightness in his chest. The music thrums like when he hums, only better. Then he hears voices in the living room. Someone has come to the front door, and Tessa is talking to a man who isn't his dad. He starts playing louder and faster to drown out the voices.

After a while, Tessa knocks on his door and Leo stops playing to open it. That is the rule. If people knock, you have to open. "You're interrupting!" he tells her.

"I'm sorry, Leo," she says. "But I have bad news."

"What news?" asks Leo. News is usually on TV.

"I'm sorry. But some people you don't know are going to take you to a place you don't know, and I can't go with you. And Dad can't, either. But it will only be for a couple days, and you're going to see your mother and your sister."

"I don't want to go," says Leo.

"Do you remember your mother?" Tessa asks. "Your sister, Venus? Remember how you just saw Venus at school?"

"I don't want before," he says in his loud voice.

"I understand, Leo. But right now a nice lady and man want me to help you pack some clothes."

"Why are you crying?" he asks.

"Because I don't want you to go," she says.

"I don't want to go, either!" Leo shouts. When Tessa opens Leo's top dresser drawer, he starts to panic. "Not until bedtime!"

"I'm sorry, Leo," she says. She starts putting some of Leo's clothes in a small suitcase.

Leo lunges for the clothes and tries to put them back in the dresser. "No!" he yells. "Not until bedtime!"

But Tessa won't stop. She tells him to stop instead. Then she tells him to play his cello while she packs.

But Leo doesn't want to play his cello. He wants Tessa not to cry. The way Tessa is acting makes Leo afraid. Tessa is always trying to make Leo use feeling words. So maybe if he tells Tessa how he feels, she won't make him go with people he doesn't know.

"I'm scared," he tells Tessa. "My feelings are scared."

"Oh, Leo," she says, trying to catch his eyes. "Me, too." But she still keeps crying and she still keeps putting his clothes in the suitcase.

Leo sits on the edge of his bed and starts to rock hard, maybe even rocking number three, which is supposed to be only for *emergencies*. But Tessa lets him rock as hard as he wants. So maybe this is an emergency. When people make you go where you don't want to go.

44

How am I supposed to just sit here? The detective and his part-ner—I can't remember their names—said to wait in the squad car. Not to come in. But this is driving me crazy.

I look at my watch. I was supposed to call Piper today. Every Friday at 4:00 P.M. she waits for my call, and then she can't think of what to say but she never wants to hang up. This time she'll miss the call, but when she hears why—that I found Leo—she'll be so happy.

It's been almost fifteen minutes since the dark-haired man—Tony—pulled up in the black truck and hurried into the house. I can't sit here in this police car for another minute, not knowing what's going on. What could the cop do to me anyway? Arrest me for not minding him?

I have my hand on the door lever when another police car with flashing lights pulls up in front of me. How many cops does it take? Then I have a moment of panic. What if something went wrong in there? What if the kidnapper pulled a gun? What if Leo is hurt?

Two cops quickly exit the cruiser and head into the house. By now neighbors are standing outside their homes, staring. I feel so conspicuous. It probably looks to them like I am being arrested.

Finally I get out and stride to the front door. I can hear voices; the door is open half an inch, and so I just go in. I see one of the policemen putting cuffs on the Tony guy.

The dark-haired girl—clearly his daughter—is crying.

"Call Uncle Marco right away, honey," this Tony tells her. "Don't worry. It will be okay." The girl is the first to see me standing there in the entry. She wipes her eyes. Lifts her chin in a way that suggests . . . what? She is clinging to her pride, fighting to stay composed. I'm struck by her beauty, her petite features, and her large brown eyes.

"I told you to wait in the car, Ms. Black." It's the first officer, looking affronted.

"I didn't want to wait in the car," I tell him. "I wanted to see who kidnapped my brother."

"We didn't *kidnap* him!" the girl cries out. "We didn't! We took care of him after his dad abandoned him."

"Tessa," says the Tony guy. "Stop now, honey. Don't talk. Just make sure Leo's okay." He says this as they're leading him out the door. I step aside. This Tony guy looks at me as he passes, his eyes pleading for something from me I know I don't have. Mercy? Forgiveness? Help?

"Ms. Black, let me take you to your car," says the cop whose badge reads DETECTIVE CUNNINGHAM.

"What about Leo?" I ask. "I want to see him. I'm ready to take him home."

"That's not possible yet," he tells me. The Mexican girl is listening closely to our conversation. "Officer Pinkerton here will wait with Leo until the folks from children's services arrive. We'll need to interview Leo."

"Children's services?" I can hardly believe my ears. "But I'm his sister! I can take him. Right now!"

"This is policy, ma'am."

"Policy?" I'm yelling at this point. "He's got mental disabilities. You can't just interview him! You can't take just take him!"

Detective Cunningham ignores me and grips my arm firmly. "I'll take you back to your own car, miss, and then you can follow me to the station. We'd like to talk to you some more. Get your mother on the phone, too."

"I'm going to check on Leo," says the Mexican girl, leaving the room.

"You're going to let *her* see Leo? Why can't I see Leo?" I object. I'm dumbfounded.

"He's not cooperative, ma'am. We need to wait for the experts. He has to be checked. You can see him, absolutely. But we can't turn him over yet. . . ."

And then I finally get it. Leo is probably afraid. Terrified, more likely. Police. He must have awful memories. I can't bear to imagine the scene that is about to unfold all over again. Strangers grabbing Leo. Putting him in a strange car and taking him to a strange place.

Only this time, he'll cry for the Mexican girl, not me.

I just know it.

TONY IS SITTING in an interview room at a police station, being questioned by two detectives. He's already told the story from start to finish as best he can, but Detective Cunningham keeps asking Tony the same questions over and over. Somehow, the plain truth is not good enough for him. The other cop, a Detective Torres, is the quiet one. Tony could be wrong, but he seems somewhat sympathetic.

"So why should we believe that you were going to turn yourself in now?" asks Cunningham. "After almost six years?"

He is a heavyset man with rosy cheeks. He looks like you'd expect a cop to look.

Tony is irritated by the "turn yourself in" phrasing. "Like I told you," he says, "I was planning to turn over Leo. I was only waiting until he could perform a solo in a concert at school. It was a big deal. I wanted him to have that before I—"

"So you want us to believe that after almost six years you were just going to give the kid back to his mother?"

"It's the absolute truth. You can believe what you want."

"Tell us again about this Phil Brown fellow you say is the boy's uncle."

"He went by Phil Brown, but I've since learned that he some-times goes by Tinker. I think Thomas Miller is his real name. Like I said, all I knew was what he put on his rental application and what he told me. He said he was the kid's dad. He claimed the mom didn't want him."

"Did he appear to be abusing the boy? Sexually?"

Tony shakes his head. "God, I hope not. I didn't see anything to make me think that. I think he cared about Leo, at least enough to try. But Leo was maybe too much for him, too hard to care for. So he dumped him, I guess."

"He just left one day, drove off? No notice?"

"No notice. I think he knew that we'd take care of Leo."

"So this Tinker could tell you wanted the boy."

Tony's anger flares. "I didn't want him. My daughter befriended Leo. She kept an eye out for him. But it wasn't like we *wanted* Leo."

"But you didn't hesitate to take him?"

"Of course we hesitated—"

A door opens and a woman peeks in. "Mr. Herrera's lawyer is here."

TESSA STAYS AT Marco and Maureen's house that night. Maureen is making her something to eat. Tessa thinks of her lasagna noo-dles floating in water on a cold burner at home. She doesn't know who turned off the stove, but someone did. She checked.

Tessa, along with Marco, was allowed to stay at the house until a man and a woman from children's services arrived to take Leo. The whole time, Leo was in the corner, yelling at the top of his lungs.

What happened next . . . she can't get the images out of her head. Leo being dragged from his room, wailing, "No touching! No touching!"

"It's okay, Leo. It's okay, Leo," she told him over and over.

The man and woman put Leo in a cream-colored sedan, trying to be gentle, but it was way too late for that.

Back inside, the woman put her arm around Tessa. "He's upset now, honey. But we'll be able to help him calm down. He's not the first mentally challenged child we've dealt with."

Tessa didn't want the woman's arm on her shoulders, but she was too polite to resist. The woman insisted on staying until Maureen arrived to be with Tessa. She was annoyed to be treated like a kid but didn't fight it. Where else would she go but M and M's?

It was bad enough watching Leo be taken, but seeing her dad led away in handcuffs . . . She can't stop blaming herself. *All of this is my fault. I was the one who begged my dad to keep Leo. I am the one who should be in jail.*

"How do you feel about potpies?" asks Maureen. Tessa is sitting on Maureen's gold velour couch, hugging a tapestried pillow. She's stopped crying for now. "That's fine," she says. "But I'm not hungry."

Maureen puts her hand on top of Tessa's head. Tessa wonders where she'd be if it weren't for M and M. Would they have taken her away, too—even though she's seventeen?

"Marco found a good lawyer for your dad, sweetie."

"That fast?"

"Well, he knew a guy who knew a guy."

"Is he going to jail?"

"I don't know, Tessa. Maybe for just one or two nights. But when they figure all this out, he won't stay in jail, at least not for too long. They'll have to set bail and then we'll pay to get him out."

When Maureen brings Tessa a potpie on a TV tray, Tessa tries to eat it but can't get down more than a couple of bites. It's chicken with peas and carrots. Leo would never eat it, because the peas should not be mixed with anything else.

BACK AT THE police station, I want to call Inez and tell her the good news first. But it turns out she already knows what is going on. After the Oakland PD had contacted the Everett PD and verified Leo's missing status, they'd called Inez to confirm.

"Oh my God!" she screeches into the phone. "You found him, Venus! You found our boy! Oh, I just . . . I just can't believe it. My Leo is coming home! Have you seen him? What does he look like? How is he, Venus? Did they hurt him?"

"He looks like Leo turned into a teenaged boy with longish blond hair. Skinny, still on the small side."

"He's not hurt or anything?"

"No, Inez. Actually, it looks like they were taking good care of him. A man and his daughter. Leo was even in school. Shit. He was carrying a large musical instrument case when I saw him. Can you imagine Leo playing an instrument?"

"Oh my God, no. I can't imagine it. Did you get a chance to talk to him?"

"Just for a second, in front of the school," I tell her. "I asked him if he remembered me. He nodded and said, 'My sister, Venus.' But I didn't know what to do, because I couldn't just grab him, and I didn't want to scare him or anything. So I drove along behind his bus until he got off and went into a house with the teenaged girl who met him at the stop."

"You're so smart, Venus, just like a detective! I'm flying there tonight," she says excitedly. "Will you be able to pick me up at the airport?"

"Which one?"

"I'm flying into Oakland."

"Where do I go? I don't know anything about how to pick someone up. . . ."

"You'll be there. You will figure it out, Venus. It's what you do."

I don't know how to take that. I motion for something to write with and a cop hands me a small tablet and pen. "What flight?"

"Delta flight one thirty-two. I get in at eleven-forty."

For a moment, neither of us speaks.

"So I'll pick you up. Eleven-forty," I repeat.

I hand the phone back over to the cop, who's been listening at a polite distance. He leads me into an interview room, where I'm asked to tell him and another cop more about my part in how Leo went missing in the first place.

Do I need Betty? This is the first time in years I've had to talk about what happened. I know my rights, and I know that they can't make me do anything. I also suspect they're more curious than trying to be thorough. But I don't want to seem uncooperative, since I want them to let me take Leo home. I lift that old white sheet and share as little as possible, just the stark facts, with the police.

When they finally thank me and say I can go now, I swear to God I sense reluctance on their part. Like after learning what I've done, it feels weird to them that I should be out of jail, walking about free in the world.

Sometimes it feels weird to me, too.

45

Leo is tired from crying, but he can't make himself stop. No matter how hard he rocks, or how many times he counts to fifty, he can't comfort himself. He knows he is rocking number three and banging his head, which is only for emergencies, but Tessa is not here and no one is getting mad at him.

He is in a strange room with two beds. No one is in the other bed. The bedspreads are the wrong orange. There is no closet or dresser. A lady with red shoes was with him in the room for a long time, but she finally left. She told Leo to put on his pajamas. She said to knock on the door when he's done. His pajamas are the right ones. The blue ones from home.

He finally stops banging his head and just rocks. His throat is raw. He loses track of time. Lying on his side, with his arms wrapped around his legs, he focuses all his attention on the ribbed pattern of the bedspread on the other bed. He counts eighty-nine vertical lines from the top of the bedspread to the end that hangs near the floor.

He hears the door open. He doesn't look up, but he knows it is the same woman with red shoes. "Leo, can I help you get in your pajamas?"

Leo sits up and scoots to the corner of the bed. He is afraid the lady will touch him. She sits on the edge of the bed. "I have your toothbrush here. Do you want to brush your teeth?"

"Where's Tony?" he asks.

"Tony can't be here, Leo."

"Where's Tessa?"

"Tessa is somewhere safe," she says.

"I want Tony. I want Tessa."

"I know you do, Leo. But that can't happen tonight. Can I help you with your pajamas?"

"No."

"If I leave you alone again, will you put your pajamas on? If you put them on by yourself, I won't have to touch you. I need you to do what I ask, Leo," she says. That is what Leo's teacher says sometimes. It means she might get angry and use a red voice if Leo doesn't obey.

After the woman leaves, Leo looks at his new yellow watch and sees that it is way past bedtime. Tessa was making lasagna. He hasn't eaten dinner, but he vaguely remembers the lady trying to get him to eat a hamburger instead of a hot dog.

He puts on his blue pajamas. The lady left his yellow toothbrush on the bed, but there is no toothpaste on it. He picks it up. He knocks on the door. The lady opens it. "Good boy, Leo!" she says. "Now let's brush our teeth and go to bed."

He follows her to a small bathroom. She stays outside when he goes in. He shuts the door. He sees that it is the wrong toothpaste. It is not the kind with the red and white on it. It is the wrong blue. It is so wrong that he can't decide. He lays his toothbrush on the counter, because he can't brush with the wrong toothpaste.

He pees. He washes his hands, but there is no towel. There is a metal box on the wall like at school, though. He knows how to use it. He tugs on the edge of the white paper that isn't the right white and one comes out. He dries his hands and tosses the paper in the round metal container.

He opens the door. He follows the lady down a short hall to the same room as before with the beds. She pulls back the covers. She is not supposed to do that. Tessa is. And Tessa should put his clothes for tomorrow on his dresser. He wants to go home. "I want to go home," he says.

"I'm sorry, Leo. You can't go home," the lady says.

"Why?" He tries to look at the lady's eyes. People are supposed to like it when you do that. He can't lock on. His eyes feel the kind of funny that they always do when he's been crying for a long time. Has he been acting like a crybaby? That's what they say at school if you cry too much.

"I can't explain it all to you, Leo. But tomorrow you will get to see your mom."

"My mom?"

"Your mother, Leo. Do you remember your mother?"

"From before?"

"Yes, Leo."

"But I want Tony. I want Tessa. I want to go home." He can't understand why this woman is doing this to him.

TONY IS EXHAUSTED. The metal bed with the thin mattress is almost a relief. He has spent the last hour talking through his situation with James P. McKinney, the defense lawyer Marco found for him. He's a slick-looking guy with eyes that seem too blue to be true—like he stole them off a doll or something. But Marco says he's supposed to be good.

Tony never dreamed he'd need a defense lawyer. He never imagined himself in a jail cell. Often, his customers would reference their drug use or scrapes with the law, assuming that they were in the company of a tough guy. But they couldn't have been further from the truth. Tony was a plain-vanilla good boy at heart.

So how could it be that tonight he'd been read his Miranda rights and arrested and booked on charges of kidnapping? It all seemed surreal. Except for Tessa's tears. The look of shock and fear on her face.

"You are in pretty good shape," McKinney had told him. "They can't prove intent for kidnapping, and we'll be able to prove that Mr. Brown rented a room from you and that he worked at the Burger Bar. Hopefully they'll focus on building a kidnapping case against this guy, not you."

"So what am I looking at?"

"Interfering with child custody is where I hope we can end up. Maybe even a suspended sentence and parole. But they'll start out by charging you with kidnapping, even if they know it probably won't stick. It's hard to say how hard the D.A.'s office will come down. Ironically, you may be in more trouble for knowingly providing false documents—the birth certificate and Social Security fraud. But given the circumstances, I would expect a minimum amount of jail time."

Tony had tried to take it all in. "So can I tell the mother I'm sorry?"

"No contact. Definitely not."

Now, lying in his cell, Tony can't stop thinking about the girl who came into the house just before they took Leo away—the girl the police scolded and quickly escorted out. He's almost positive she's the same young woman he saw walking down Rockefeller near Inez's house last Sunday afternoon on his way out. As he drove by, she was passing under a streetlamp, and her height, along with her head of curly hair, made a strong impression. She'd been carrying a suitcase that looked too heavy for her. He'd almost pulled over to see if she needed a ride.

Now he thinks she may have passed by his shop today, too. This was the girl who murdered her stepfather?

How could she have tracked Tony down from his visit to Everett? He can't put it together, and he finally gives up trying.

He thinks of praying. God, if Maria could see him now. He

tells himself that children's-services people are experts at these situations. They'll take good care of Leo. Tomorrow this whole mess will get straightened out. He tells himself this and many more lies before he is finally rescued by sleep.

IT TAKES TESSA a few seconds to realize where she is. And then the memory of what happened comes crashing in. It is worse than any bad dream she's ever had. Her father in handcuffs. Leo being dragged away by strangers.

She is lying on the hide-a-bed in Marco and Maureen's living room. She hears one of them making coffee in the kitchen. Her eyes feel thick. She has a completely out-of-place thought that she should try coffee for the first time today.

She hears voices. M and M are both in the kitchen, talking. Tessa is not normally one to eavesdrop, but she can't help herself. She quietly climbs off the hide-a-bed and makes her way toward the half door that opens into the kitchen. She positions herself just outside so she can hear what's being said.

Maureen is saying, "Once we find out the bail, can we get it reduced?"

"For kidnapping?" says Marco. "It's gonna be high. Twenty-five thousand is probably a good guess. Of course, at some point—I'm not sure how it works—Tony's lawyer will try to get the charges reduced to interfering with custody."

"What are you saying? That we leave him in there?"

"Well, I'm pretty sure you can get someone out by paying a bail bondsman ten percent, but we don't have twenty-five hundred dollars lying around."

"No, of course not."

"Let's just wait and see," Marco says. "We'll know more after the arraignment. They have forty-eight hours to arraign him, but since that goes into the weekend, it might not happen until Monday."

Tessa hears Maureen say quietly, "Monday?"

"I know, baby. I'm sorry.

"I told Tony when he first got Leo that this was a stupid thing to do. Shit. Why didn't he listen to me? But no. He's gotta do whatever Tessa wants him to do. He can't say no to his precious princess."

Tessa is shocked by Marco's words and the resentment they reveal. She shivers. But she knows he's right, too. It's all her fault. She swings through the doors into the kitchen. "I couldn't help but hear," she says.

They both look startled. "I know it's my fault, Uncle Marco," Tessa says tearfully. "You're right. I begged him. I *made* him do it. I should be the one who goes to jail! You need to tell the police!"

"Oh, baby," says Maureen. She opens her arms, and when Tessa doesn't come, she grabs her into an embrace. "Marco didn't mean it. Come here, baby."

It's too early in the morning to cry, but it's too late to stop now. Tessa sobs on Maureen's shoulder as Marco lays his hand on her head. "I'm so sorry, Tessa," he says. "I didn't mean it, I'm just so worried . . . I say stupid things. You know how much your uncle Marco loves you."

Maureen whispers into her hair, "It's not your fault, baby. It's not your fault at all. It's no one's fault. It was just love. You and your daddy loved that boy, and you did what you thought was best. It's plain old love's fault."

Tessa steps back, wipes under her eyes with her fingers. "Then I hate love," she says. Maureen laughs and Tessa lets a smile slip, too.

"I hate love, too, baby," says Uncle Marco. He reaches his arm firmly around her back. "Please forgive what I said."

"Okay," says Tessa in a small voice. "But we'll get him out on bail?"

She sees Maureen and Marco exchange a glance. "You bet, sweetie," says Marco. "First thing after the arraignment. We'll find a way, even if we have to sell the car."

Tessa walks out from under his arm and grabs a paper towel. Blows her nose, tosses it in the garbage. She takes a deep breath. It's time to think like a grown-up. Act like a grown-up. Be strong for her dad.

"Can I please have some coffee?" she asks.

46

At the airport that night, a big screen tells me that Inez's flight is arriving on time. I take a seat at the gate and pick up a *People* magazine someone left behind. Of course the cover story is about Christa McAuliffe, the teacher who died in the *Challenger*. I don't read the article, because it's just too sad.

Pretty soon I can see what must be Inez's plane taxiing up to the gate. Passengers emerge in spurts, a mix of middle-aged people. A few college kids. Finally Inez appears. She's wearing jeans and a cute scarlet smock top. Her brown boots make her look like a bohemian cowboy. She's in full makeup, of course—carrying a tan leather jacket.

My mother is beautiful.

I can tell she's unsure whether or not to attempt to hug me. She smiles as she approaches. Part of me wants to extend my arms, but I just can't. "How was the flight?" I ask, folding my arms around myself to send a signal.

"It was scary!" she says, a little too loudly. "And I had no idea that they served drinks on planes!" I can smell wine on her breath.

"Do you have luggage?"

"Only this little one," she says. There's a small gray case in her left hand.

I explain to her that we can't see Leo tonight. "They said you should come to the police headquarters in the morning." I offer to take her to the Holiday Inn where I'm staying, and she agrees.

Once we're safely on the freeway, I ask her to look at the map I drew on a napkin to get us back to the hotel. While I drive, she demands I tell her all over again the whole story of how I found Leo. She is giddy with excitement.

I can't blame her for being a bit giddy. I feel a little giddy, too. But I tell her I'm too tired to go over the details tonight. She already knows most of it. And I don't want to mention that there is a sadness to the story that threatens to dampen my joy. The look on the Mexican girl's face. The way Leo was wailing. The feeling that we were breaking up a happy family, which, when I think about it, makes me outraged.

By the time we get to the hotel, Inez is so confident of a new truce between us that she actually asks for the room adjoining mine. I want to object, but how petty would that seem? It dawns on me how hard it would be to get back to my hostile state toward Inez. We've spent real time in each other's presence now, been on the same side of a challenge—and won. And now we're both excited about the same thing.

I just don't want Inez to mistake it all for forgiveness.

As soon as I walk into my hotel room, I see the message light on my phone blinking. I'm guessing it's Piper, since she has my number here. I feel bad, but it's too late to call her back.

I punch the button, put the phone to my ear, and listen to Piper. "Annette, where are you? It's four-thirty." *Clunk. Beep.* "Annette, where are yooouu?" A long silence. "You promised to call and I'm getting mad!" *Clunk. Beep.* "Annette! You promised to call me. So you're a promise-breaker person."

A half hour later, I'm lying in my tightly made Holiday Inn bed, trying to put together the strange pieces of my life. My estranged mother is lodged next door. My long-lost brother is across town in protective custody. A gorgeous man with a beautiful Mexican daughter sits in jail for kidnapping. And a little girl I love thinks I'm a promise-breaker.

Maybe Inez was right before. Somebody should make a movie.

SATURDAY MORNING, INEZ sits in a chair while she looks at a mug shot.

"Do you recognize this man?" asks the detective called Cunningham.

"Yes," says Inez. "He came to look at my house in Everett. It's him." She picks up the photo from the detective's desk and stares at it. "It's the Tony guy." For some reason, she feels a little disappointed. She half-hoped it was someone else.

"If this man had Leo, why did he come to my house in Everett and pretend he might want to buy it?" she asks.

"When exactly did he come to your house?"

"A few days ago . . . It was Sunday, this past Sunday."

"But you'd never seen him before that? Maybe lurking around?"

Inez stares again at the photo. "No."

"Do you know of a man who goes by the name Tinker Miller?"

"Tinker? Sure. Tinker is my late husband's brother. I haven't seen him in years, though. Tinker and our family didn't get along." Inez shakes her head. "He even burglarized us once."

"This man here, Tony Herrera . . ." The detective points at the photo. "He claims that Tinker, going by the name Phil Brown, brought the boy to Oakland and rented an apartment from him. Says the guy claimed to be the boy's father and told him the mother was a heroin addict."

Inez can't believe her ears. "So you're saying Tinker took Leo?"

"It would appear so."

"I don't get it. Why would Tinker take Leo, first of all, and how come this other man had him?"

"Could this Tinker Miller, your brother-in-law, be a pedophile?" asks the detective.

"Oh God! No. I mean, I don't know. I don't think so. But . . ." Clearly she's not a good judge of character, she reminds herself. She never thought Raymond would be a pervert, either. "Oh dear God. Please, no!" she says. "Do you think Leo was sexually abused?"

"That's something we need to evaluate," he says. "That's just one of the things the children's services department will want to explore."

"So how did this Tony end up with Leo, then? I don't get it."

The detective sits up straighter and tucks in his neck the way a fat man might his belly. "His story is that this Tinker fellow up and abandoned the boy."

Well, now, *that* she can believe. Tinker would have had his hands full with Leo. She tries to imagine how Leo would have responded, tries to picture Tinker taking care of Leo with all his picky habits and tantrums and . . . "How long did Tinker have Leo?"

"This Herrera fellow says that Tinker up and took off after a few months. Instead of calling the police to report it, Tony Herrera and his daughter, Tessa, kept Leo. Got him a fake birth certificate and everything."

"So all these years he's been living with this guy and his daughter?"

"That's the story."

"But why? Why would someone do that?"

"He says his daughter cared for the boy." Inez remembers that Venus described seeing a beautiful teenaged Mexican girl at the house where they found Leo. "Apparently she didn't want the boy to end up in foster care."

Inez tries to absorb this. She desperately needs a drink. "So why the hell didn't they first make sure that no one was looking for him? Why assume he doesn't have another family?" She feels her anger rising. "How could they not call the police? They must have known about us, because how else did this Herrera guy come to my house in Everett?"

The detective sits back in his chair. "I'm not sure, ma'am, but in his statements, Mr. Herrera claims that after he saw Leo featured as missing on a milk carton a week or so ago, he realized someone was looking for him and was planning to give the boy back. Apparently he came to Everett to check out the situation. Claims he wanted to make sure Leo was going to a good home."

Suddenly it all makes sense. The reason Tony was more interested in her than in the house. His emotional reaction to Leo's room. She can feel her face burning red. "If he knew I was Leo's mom, then why didn't he say so? Why did he just turn around and go back to California?"

Then it hits her. Obviously, he didn't think she was good enough.

LEO IS ALONE in a playroom with lots of toys. Most of them are for babies. He notices some race cars on a shelf. He picks out an orange one and sits on the floor. He spins the wheels like he used to. He stares into the turning.

When he hears a door open, he looks up, hoping for Tessa.

But it's not her. He sees his sister, Venus, from before. And there's also the one who was his mother. He stares down at the car in his hand and ignores them. He hears their steps coming closer. Then he sees black sneakers with white circles. Brown boots. He wants them to go away.

"Do you remember your sister, Venus?" he hears.

"From before," says Leo. He thinks of the red trucks, the screaming, the silver thing. "I don't want before. I want to go home now."

"I understand," says the voice who is Venus. "Do you remember your mom, Leo?"

"From before," he says. "But I want Tessa. Where is she?"

"Oh, Leo, I'm sorry," his mother says. "She's not here. We're here to take you home." She squats down next to him. "I missed you so much." She tries to touch his long hair, and Leo jerks away. "Don't do that!"

"Okay, Leo. I'm sorry. No touching."

"I see you have a car there." It's Venus. "What if I buy you some new cars to play with?"

"I'm not a baby!" he yells. "I'm thirteen years old!" He starts rocking number two. He can't help it.

"You're right, Leo," says Venus. "You're all grown up now, aren't you?"

She sits on the floor, across from him. "Remember how we used to count the planets, Leo?"

Leo sees a ceiling of stars. The planets hanging in blue light. "Venus is red," he says.

"Yes, Leo!" says his sister from before. "So you do remember your home. Do you want to come home?"

"I want to go home to Tessa! I don't want before!" he yells. He wants to have a tantrum, but Tony says thirteen is too old. Instead, he stands up and looks at his yellow watch. "I need to go to school," he announces. "It's almost time for math!"

Venus stands up, too. "Leo, can you look at me?" He turns his head and tries. His eyes skitter across blue eyes and big black hair. He turns and looks the other way. He doesn't want to see her.

"Go away," he says loudly. "You're confusing me." *Confusing* is a word Leo recently learned. When they still won't go, he stomps across the room, sits down in the corner, with his back to them. He starts to bang his head on the wall like he used to do.

The boots walk toward him.

"It's going to be okay," his mother says in a soft voice. "I love you, Leo."

Tessa and Tony say this a lot, but Tessa has never taught him what he's supposed to say back. He knows other things. Like when

Tessa says, "Thank you," Leo says, "You're welcome." When Tessa says, "I'm sorry," Leo says, "I forgive you."

INEZ IS STILL trying to get through to Leo, but I can't take it another minute. I leave the room, tempted to slam the door. *How did this happen?* I feel like a fool. All my dreams of reuniting with Leo had been happy ones. I'd imagined him being excited to see us, jumping around and making his happy humming sound. Maybe that was too much to expect. But this? *This?*

As I'm headed out of the building, I spot the Mexican girl I saw the other day when they arrested Tony. She is seated in a plastic chair outside an office. This is the Tessa Leo is crying for. I approach her, furious. "Do you realize what you did? My brother has been so brainwashed by you, he thinks you're his family. Now he is so confused, who knows how long it will take to fix this!"

"I'm s-sorry," the girl stammers, clearly afraid of me. "I didn't know . . ."

"*Sorry* doesn't begin to cut it. Wait a minute. Are you here to see Leo? Are they actually going to let *you* see him?"

She looks down at the floor. "They want my help. . . . But I don't have to if—"

"Oh my God. Fuck it all to hell," I say, storming for the door.

ON MONDAY MORNING, Tessa is waiting on a bench outside a courtroom. Marco didn't think her father would want her to see him at the arraignment. She is anxious and resentful. She's practically an adult, and she's pretty sure her dad *would* want her there.

After a while, she wanders down the hall to a water fountain and gets a drink. All the men are wearing suits, and the women are in dress clothes, too. *Professionals,* she thinks. Not the kind of people she grew up around, but maybe the kind she wants to become.

She sits again on the bench and wonders what's happening inside. Could they really charge her father with kidnapping? She has the urge to burst into the courtroom and explain that it's her fault. But she knows that's not how things work.

She thinks about seeing Leo's real sister, Venus. She didn't look anything like Leo. More like his opposite. She was so tall, and with all that curly black hair she struck Tessa as regal or exotic.

Tessa's not sure, but she thinks Venus is probably about twenty. She can't quit thinking about when Venus yelled at her Saturday. She's never had someone get mad at her like that. It was so shocking that she cried afterward. Then she tried to put herself in Venus's place. What if Leo was her real brother and he got kidnapped when he was seven—and when she finally found him he didn't want her?

She couldn't imagine how terrible that would be.

Thinking about it again now, a fresh weight of guilt presses down on her.

She wonders about Leo's mother. Maybe she looks more like Leo. She will be so happy to get her son back. But will Leo even want to go with his mother? After what Venus said Saturday, she doubts it.

"So we meet again," says someone nearby.

Tessa looks up. *Oh my God, it's her! Venus.*

She automatically gets to her feet this time, prepared to run if she has to.

"Do you know if it already started?" Venus asks, nodding toward the courtroom. "Can I still go in?"

"I don't know," Tessa says, surprised Venus isn't yelling at her. "I'm just supposed to wait out here. My uncle Marco says they do more than one at a time, so you can probably go in whenever."

Venus says nothing, but she continues to stand there. Finally Tessa ventures to ask, "Is your mom here, too?" Tessa is even more afraid to see the mom. She has no idea what to expect, but she imagines the woman will lash out at her, maybe even attack her. After what happened with Venus, Tessa wouldn't be surprised.

"No. She's back to the Holiday Inn," Venus says bitterly. "She doesn't want to lay eyes on him."

"Oh," says Tessa. She realizes Venus is talking about her dad, like he's evil or something.

And then it hits her that Venus has no idea she's really to blame. "You need to know it was all my fault!" she blurts out. "The police might not tell you, but *I* should be the one in there," she says, nodding toward the courtroom doors. "*I* kept Leo. I practically *made* my dad keep Leo. It's all my fault, not his."

Tessa can feel Venus looking directly at her. She dares to meet her eyes, blue mixed with a gray the color of knives, rimmed by thick black lashes. To Tessa's surprise, Venus's eyes aren't as angry or mean as she feared.

"You did a terrible thing," Venus says, with a penetrating look.

"I know," says Tessa, determined not to cry. But she can feel tears flowing, the kind you can't help.

"If you had called the police, they would have known Leo was missing and he would have come home! Instead, we lost Leo for six years."

"I know," Tessa repeats. It's all too much, and her legs go weak. "I know. And I'm so sorry. If I could just go back in time and do it differently, I would!"

Tessa feels so wobbly; she sits down on the bench again. And now Venus is so tall and her voice so soft that Tessa barely hears her say, "Yeah. Me, too," before she walks away.

I ENTER THE courtroom just in time to hear the judge charge Tony Herrera with kidnapping and set bail at twenty thousand dollars. I feel angry to be alone, angry that Inez didn't join me here.

"I already met him!" she told me. It was almost like she was embarrassed to see him again.

I also suspect that holing up at the Holiday Inn is less to avoid Tony Herrera than to drink her wine in peace or cry on the phone to her friend Shirley. After Tony Herrera is led away, I stay in the courtroom. I'm in a comfortable daze of some kind.

My mind drifts back to my own arraignment, when I was so in shock, I laughed at the charge of murder one. When the same judge gave me *half* the maximum sentence, I almost didn't care. Five years or seven, my life was over. Or so I thought. Now it hits me in a new way how differently things could have gone. He could have remanded me to adult court or I could have served God knows how long in a real prison. And I can't even remember his name.

I listen to four or five more arraignments. Watching people at the beginning of their journey toward incarceration, I feel my freedom keenly. Something like gratitude flutters at the edge of my emotions. Finally, I've had enough, and I stand and walk back out the big double doors. I glance at the bench in the hall where Tessa had been sitting.

Of course, she's gone now. But something about our exchange took my breath away, totally gutted me. Maybe it was how brave she seemed, the way she took responsibility for keeping Leo. How she apologized so sincerely, the words tumbling out of her mouth without excuse or defense. *It was all my fault. . . . I'm so sorry.*

Maybe I'm jealous of her protectiveness toward her father, the way she didn't want him to carry the blame.

Back at the hotel, I go to Inez's room and fill her in on the hearing. She thinks Tony Herrera will be out on bail soon and allowed to come home until a plea agreement is reached or it goes to trial. If she's right, I'm secretly glad, for the girl's sake. In the meantime, I hate that I can imagine how they will miss Leo. I can just picture how they'll all hug and cry and wonder aloud if Tony is going to prison.

It seems ironic to me now that yet another bedroom belonging to Leo will stand empty.

I leave Inez's room for mine. Even though it isn't one of our scheduled times, I want to hear Piper's voice. Since she moved to

Spokane, I have missed her so much more than I planned. I've longed at times to read a book to her or simply to hear her yammering at me through my closed door. Since she left, we tell each other "I love you" before we hang up, and it feels so natural.

I read the directions by the phone for making long-distance calls and dial Spokane. While it rings without an answer, I wonder if Piper is another reason I was less harsh on Tessa just now. As different as we might be, we have a big mistake in common. We gave our hearts to kids related to us by nothing but love.

47

Monday morning, Tony is released on bail. He has no idea how M and M came up with two grand—and they won't say. That afternoon, Tony shares a quiet lunch with Tessa, when they talk about why they miss Leo and all the funny things he does. Later, Tony agrees to drive Tessa to the Holiday Inn. On the way, he glances at her in the passenger seat. "Tessa, you know you'll have to go in alone," he says. "I'm not supposed to have any contact."

She nods, her eyes serious and dark.

"She might not be kind to you," he warns.

"I know," she says. "I don't blame her." Tony can't believe his quiet, shy daughter is willing to do something so hard. "They might not even give you her room number. And she might be upset that you tracked her down."

"It was Venus who mentioned that Inez was at the Holiday Inn," she counters. "And I think people at the desk will call her room and tell her I'm here."

Tony knows it took Tessa a long time to find the right Holiday Inn. Tony knows because he listened to her: "I'm calling for a Mrs. Inez Black." Tony didn't correct her. It's not Mrs.; it should be Ms.

Tessa has been so brave. Oh my God, how he wishes now that he had told her the truth as soon as he got back from Everett. He delayed in part because he wanted to give Leo his chance to perform with the school orchestra. If he could do it over again . . .

"Dad, are you scared?"

Tony flips his blinker. "Afraid I'll go to jail?"

"Yes. But also are you scared of losing Leo forever?"

Tony knows she asked the question because *she's* scared.

"Of course, honey. But we still have each other and we'll make it through—even if I go to jail for a little while, you'll have M and M."

"It's just so strange," Tessa continues. "I mean, it's only been three days. But all the times when everything is supposed to happen with Leo I know he's upset and is missing us. And school, too."

"He'll be okay, sweetie."

"I don't know," she says.

Tony pulls up at the Holiday Inn. "Are you sure about this?"

"I'm sure." She is wearing one of her dresses, like she's going to church. And she has her hair in a pony with the silly yellow-and-purple ribbon that Leo likes so much.

Tony gets out of the car and pulls the cello case from the backseat. Tessa gets the suitcase out of the other side. "Can you carry both of these?"

"I'm strong, Dad."

AFTER SEEING LEO two more times, Inez feels sapped of her enthusiasm. Seeing him *not see her* had sapped her even more. She can hardly believe that this was the big occasion she'd dreamed of for so many years—when she'd get her son back. She never imagined Leo not wanting her. Leo begging for other people.

She hates them. The man and his daughter. She knows she should be grateful they took good care of Leo, but the fact that they loved him—and seemingly so well—is the part that's actually the hardest for her. *They didn't just take Leo; they took her place. They stole his heart.*

She sits on the end of the bed and sips the cheap wine she

bought at a nearby grocery store. She flips on the television and lights a cigarette. She's tempted to go back and buy a second bottle for later, but she resists. She knows Venus has her eye on it. She needs not to drink so much if she's going to be a good mom to Leo. If she ever gets a real chance.

She tells herself that once she gets him home to Everett everything will fall into place. She tries to focus on the evening news but can't seem to. She wonders when the press is going to get hold of this story and chase them all over the place. She dreads that part, even though it's supposedly a happy ending.

Her hotel phone rings, startling her. She picks it up. "Hello?"

"It's the front desk, ma'am. You have a visitor. A Miss Tessa Herrera. Can I send her up?"

Inez freezes. What on earth? "Just her? Just one person?"

"Just the girl, ma'am."

Inez tries to think. She doesn't want a scene in the lobby. She can't imagine what this girl has to say to her. "What the hell does she want?"

"Ma'am, I wouldn't know. It appears she has things to deliver."

"Fine," says Inez. "Send her up."

She hangs up the phone. She knows this will be the Tessa Venus mentioned, the daughter of Tony Herrera. How does she know where we're staying? What does she want? Is she going to say she's sorry? Oh God, Inez hopes not. Please, no apologies. She's not ready for that. Sorry for making Leo forget his own mother and fall in love with them?

She clears the food tray from the bed, chugs the rest of her wine, and goes to the mirror. She puts on some fresh lipstick. Brushes out her hair. She has the thought that she wants to look like a good mom. But why does she care what this stupid girl thinks?

There's a knock. She takes a deep breath, sets her jaw, and opens the door. "Yes?"

"Hi."

Venus was right: She is beautiful. Petite. She reminds Inez of the Mexican doll she had once, who wore an elaborate outfit but a shy smile.

"Can I help you?" Inez says with deliberate coldness.

"I'm Tessa Herrera. I . . . I have Leo's cello. And some clothes. I thought . . ."

Inez registers what's in each of her hands. "Come in."

Inez is trying to think. She takes the only chair and watches the girl awkwardly set the suitcase and the cello case on the floor. "I just thought Leo might want some more of his things. It might help. . . ."

"How nice of you," Inez says. "To care about what Leo needs— after what you've done."

"I'm sorry, ma'am. We—"

"Don't apologize! How can you apologize for keeping my son from me for six years?" Inez hears herself and is struck by how shrill her voice is.

"I'm sorry," the girl says quietly—and then realizes her mistake. "I mean . . . I know apologizing doesn't change anything."

She is hugging herself, staring at the carpet. Clearly she's terrified of Inez.

"What's in the suitcase?" Inez asks.

The girl hesitates. "Things like clothes that Leo likes. He gets really upset if—"

"You think I don't know about my own son?"

"I'm sorry," she says again.

"Look at me," Inez orders. This is a voice she hasn't used in years, one that comes from feeling her throat tighten with rage. In all her scheming and planning and hoping for Leo to come back to them—and, yes, even in all her praying—she never once imagined she'd get apologies from Leo's kidnapper. In her mind it had been so simple. *You catch the evil person or people who did this terrible thing and then you make sure they rot in jail forever.*

This Tessa girl meets Inez's eyes, her lower lip quivering. The problem is that she looks so damn innocent. Fucking Christ! Leo's kidnapper is a sweet-faced teenager!

"Say what you came to say," she says finally.

The girl takes a breath, looks directly at Inez. "Leo likes pizza now," she says. "He practices his cello from four o'clock to five-thirty. He likes steak now, too. And even lasagna."

When she pauses, Inez says, "Go on."

The girl is clearly trying not to cry. "He wakes up on his own at seven A.M.," she continues, her voice breaking. "He loves math and music. He hates reading and especially spelling. His tooth-brush has to be yellow. His toothpaste has to be white Colgate. He likes to watch bowling on TV. I can write it all down for you if you like."

A small brown hand flashes across her cheek to finally swipe at liquid tracks.

Inez can't believe her ears. "Bowling? He likes to watch bowling on TV?"

"Yes. For hours if you let him. But he hates to go bowling."

"You tried to take him bowling?" Inez asks, disbelieving.

"My dad did. But it was a big mistake. Leo hated all the crashing sounds."

"Well, of course he did!" Inez barks.

Moments pass. "Did you see Tinker with Leo?" Inez asks. Since the girl is here, she might as well learn some things.

"You mean Phil?"

"Tinker. Phil. Whatever. Did he hurt Leo?"

"No, ma'am. Not so that you could see. But before . . . with Phil, Leo never got out of that apartment. His da—Phil kept him locked up in there and he was all alone. So I visited him because I was worried about him. At first, Leo would not answer the door. But I knew he was in there. I would hear him knocking his head on my wall at night."

Inez feels a catch in her heart. He was missing them.

The girl goes on. "I finally borrowed my dad's master key and

I started to visit him secretly. I brought him things. Toys. Or some kind of food to see if he would eat it. He was so skinny. Then Phil let us have Leo over for Easter dinner, and I found out he liked peas." A trembly smile crosses the girl's face.

Inez's head is whirling. She pictures Leo making his pea design on a plate. She hasn't thought of that in years.

"And the cello?" Inez asks.

The girl brightens. "One day I brought home a clarinet, because I was taking lessons at school. And Leo loved it! But he loves cello best. He has an amazing gift for music."

Inez is gladdened by this news but upset she missed such a miracle. "That's great he's made such progress. But when Tinker abandoned Leo, why didn't you call the police instead of keeping him?"

"Phil—Tinker said his wife was a heroin addict who left them. I thought if we called the police that Leo would go to foster care. I couldn't bear the idea of Leo being left with people he didn't know."

"Oh, the irony," Inez says in a bitter voice. Then she leans over and puts her face in her hands.

"I guess I'll go now," says the girl. "But is there any way you could give Leo something to remember me by?" Inez glances up and sees Tessa take a yellow-and-purple ribbon from her hair. "These are his new favorite colors," she adds, carefully smoothing the ribbon on the bed.

As soon as the girl is gone, Inez lets herself cry. She knows what it feels like to beg for forgiveness and not get it.

48

ate Thursday morning, I find myself standing in the hotel park-

Late Thursday morning, I find myself standing in the hotel parking lot, arguing with Inez. Leo has finally been released to us, and we are free to pick him up and take him home. "You have to come with me on the plane, Venus," Inez says. This is the third or fourth time she's insisted. "You have to come with us!"

"I can't," I explain again, annoyed. "Someone has to drive the Honda back up, and I have someone I need to see in Seattle. This weekend is my only chance." I put her small suitcase into the trunk of the Honda. Slam the lid. We're going to pick up Leo first, and then I'll take them to the airport.

"I don't know how I'm going to manage with Leo," Inez insists. "I'm not equipped—"

"Didn't they give you something to help Leo relax on the plane?"

"It's not just that. It's when I get home. . . ."

"It's one weekend," I tell her. "And you have your friend Shirley. You'll be fine for a few days without me."

"You're coming after, though?" She sounds desperate.

"We never talked about what we'd do if . . . Honestly, I'm not sure when I'll be there or for how long. . . ."

"Is it because there's a guy involved? Is it a boyfriend? Are you still moving to California?"

"It's just a little girl, okay? Just a little girl I got to know. But she . . ." I want to say, *needs me,* but that sounds so sappy. "I need some time to figure out what I'm doing," I tell her. "You fly. I'll drive. I'll see you both in a few days. End of story."

ON FRIDAY AFTERNOON, I pull up at the Porters' in Seattle. Piper's aunt Sue decided to go last minute to see friends for a long weekend—so, apart from Mike, I get Piper to myself. It's foggy and cold, but Piper is waiting for me on the porch. She's wearing her green sweatshirt with the hood pulled up.

She rushes to the car when I park. I'm barely out of the car before she throws herself into my arms. "You came! When you kept not calling, I thought you forgot about me. But you came!"

"I came, Piper," I say, pulling her away to look at her face. She looks at me steadily, and suddenly she seems much older.

"What happened? Why did you keep not calling me?"

"You'll never guess."

"I don't want to guess."

"We found Leo."

I had decided to save the news so I could see her reaction in person. Her green eyes are round with surprise. "Your brother, Leo? Where?"

I smile. "California! Now he's coming home to my mom's in Everett. Isn't it exciting?"

I can see her struggle to take in what it means. "California?"

"He was in a house down in California. Some people found him there and decided to take him into their home and make him their little boy. They did it without asking, which was super wrong. But we found him."

"So, he's okay?"

"He's fine. The people who had him actually took pretty good care of him."

"Will you go live with him and your mom now?"

"I don't know what I'm doing, honestly. My mother wants to

sell the house we used to live in. . . . I was going to move to California. But now . . . Oh, it's really complicated, Piper. Since we found Leo, no one knows what they're doing."

Piper thinks about this. "If you move to California, you'll never see me again," she says.

I notice she's been biting her fingernails raw. Her hands are red from the cold. "That's not true, Piper. I would still visit you. But what are we doing, standing out here freezing?" I head for the front door.

As soon as we get inside the house, Piper races to the kitchen and comes back with an envelope. "I almost forgot!" she squeals. "Maybe you won't want to move, because someone dropped off a card for you. I think it's about a boy. But I didn't open it or read it."

I can tell the seal has been opened and licked back shut, but I decide to let it go.

"Well, open it!" she says.

"I don't need to open it right now," I tell her. We're sitting on the couch and she is perched at my arm.

"Open it!" she urges again, bubble gum breath in my face.

The envelope says "Private for Annette" on the front. I pull out a single page of typing paper and quickly glance at the bottom to see that it's a note from Danny. It's written in the same cramped style he used on the napkin that time. When I start to read, my heart stops. He is calling me by my real name.

> Dear Venus, I hope you get this letter. I was sad to learn you'd left the Dipper. I've had some time to think about things and I decided to fess up. You have a right to be mad at me when I tell you that I always knew who you were. I didn't want to scare you off, because you clearly wanted to start over as "Annette." I didn't want to make you lie about your life at dinner, but I didn't want you to think I wasn't interested in you. I worried if I told you that I know who you are, you'd get upset and leave town. I wonder if you

dumped me because I'm a cop. Or maybe because of guys in the past. But I want you to know you're safe with me and beneath my persistence, I'm also the most patient guy in the world. I only want to get to know the *real* you. We could have fun together. I would try to stop flirting with you, even though you're so beautiful, brilliant, and funny.

Your smile is like the stars coming at night, Venus.

If you want to leave our friendship in the past, I have no hard feelings. And I promise I won't ever bother you again. Since I'm a cop, I can't also be a stalker. Ha Ha.

Your Friend,

Danny

He included his phone number again. I tuck the note back into the envelope, unable to hide my smile. But, at the same time, I'm stunned and angry and confused, too. *Danny knew I was Venus Black all along?* I need time to think about this.

"This is really nice, Piper," I tell her. "A letter from Danny—you remember him?"

"Yes! The one you love!"

"I don't love him, Piper," I say, half laughing.

"But why does he call you Venus?" asks Piper.

I sigh. More proof that she's already read the note. I'm hoping most of it went over her head, but of course she'd notice the name. I'm not in the mood to scold her, but I do have to answer her question.

"It's just his nickname for me, Piper. Because I worked at the Big Dipper and he's thinking about stars."

Piper is quiet for a moment, and I can tell she's not satisfied. "But what about—"

"Piper," I say, standing up. "I'm done talking to you about Danny. I don't want to talk about the note anymore. Let's you and I have a fun weekend in Seattle."

I can tell my tone hurt her a little, but she recovers quickly.

That first night, we go roller-skating. It's excruciating and hilarious and wonderful because I'm with Piper. On Saturday, we visit Pike Place Market and bring home some fish for Mike to make for dinner.

When Sunday rolls around, both Piper and I have to go. It's a tearful goodbye, just like I knew it would be. But I had so much fun being Piper's playmate. It was a great relief from having to process all the heavy stuff around Leo.

While I drive up I-5 toward Everett, the sun comes out and the sky clears, and despite it being cold, I roll down my window and let the air rush over my face and let my hair fly. I don't know what to feel. What to do with my life. Where I will live or if I will have any money.

For now, all that really matters is Leo. When I arrive back at the house on Rockefeller, there's a truck parked out front. I figure it must be the one Inez is borrowing from her friend Shirley.

I sit in the car for a moment, contemplating my situation. Finding Leo was as far as I ever got in my thinking—it never occurred to me he wouldn't want to come home. When I phoned Inez from the Porters' house, she sounded desperate and worn out. She begged me to come help with Leo.

I get out of the car and I'm walking toward the house when I spot a tipped beetle on the sidewalk. When I was younger, maybe nine or ten, I used to worry so much about these beetles. I'd walk all over the neighborhood looking for the ones in crisis and flip them back over.

When did that stop happening? Did the beetles stop tipping over or did I just stop noticing them?

I pause now and stoop down to stare at this one. She's shiny, black, and her threadlike legs wildly claw at the air. I wonder how long she's been like this and if she thinks the sky is blue ground and that she's actually getting somewhere. When I can't bear to watch her struggle another second, I gently tip her back onto her belly.

She scurries off, and I wonder if she's grateful to be saved or if she just assumes this is how life as a bug works. You make one wrong move and your whole world gets turned upside down. And then, right when you think it's hopeless, a giant black-haired goddess leans down to tip you over.

49

I go to the front door and knock. Inez doesn't answer, so I try the door, but it's locked. I can hear Leo inside, yelling and crying. I've heard Leo cry plenty of times in my life, but that was when Leo was little. This is the sound of a heartbroken adolescent boy.

When Inez finally opens the door, she looks angry and exhausted. "So. Did you have a nice weekend with whoever?"

"As a matter of fact, I did," I say, moving past her into the house.

"He's not happy," she announces to my back.

"I've got this one," I say. I follow the sound of Leo's crying to his room, where I find him curled up on his old purple blanket in his closet. Beyond the word *Tessa,* I can't understand what Leo's saying, but I think I know what he's feeling.

I sit down near him, just inches away. "Can I pat your back, Leo?" I ask. "Remember, like I used to?"

Since his back is to me, I decide to risk it. I pat in the old way, saying, "One pat, two pats, three pats . . ." When I get to ten, I feel something shift. I keep going, and gradually he begins to quiet. By fifty, he is calm. I pat his back a little longer, drawing strength from Leo for what I'm about to do.

I tell Leo I'm going to stop patting, and I do. Then I leave his room quickly, afraid if I don't act now I'll lose my nerve. I pass the dining area to reach the kitchen and at the end of it, the basement door. It's unlocked, thank God. I practically charge down the steps, like I'm in a rush. At the bottom, I turn left into my old room and flip on the light. I gaze at the stripped mattress, packed boxes, and cleaning supplies.

A piece of art hangs on one wall, a watercolor of a single sunflower that my friend Jackie painted for me in sixth grade. Of course, I know why it was moved here and what it is hiding. I carefully take down the painting and look at the hole behind it. It's larger than I expected, the edges charred and broken, thanks to the blast of Raymond's gun.

THAT DAY, IT was actually Leo who found the hole. He was lying on my bed, naming planets, when he stopped at Saturn. He got up and went over to the wall near my dresser and stood on his tiptoes, reaching for something. The sunlight was slanting through the window just so—and I saw what Leo was after. I put my pinky in the perfectly round hole at the center of a knot in the knotty-pine paneling—and it went all the way through.

Through to what? The more I looked at the hole, the stranger it seemed. I could see nothing through it, but I knew where it led. I told Leo in a stern voice to go upstairs, right then. Fortunately, it didn't spark a trantrum.

I stuck a pencil into the hole, then went out to the garage, telling myself it was probably just a natural flaw in the knotty pine. The garage was unfinished—Raymond used portable heaters in winter to work on cars. His hot-rod calendar on the far wall was jutting out a little bit. When I lifted the calendar, I saw the pointy end of my pencil.

I froze in shock and disbelief as the truth pounded through my brain. Raymond had been spying on me for God knew how long through that hole—watching me dress, watching me walk in naked from the shower, watching my friends undress. . . .

Oh my God. Everything buzzed. My body felt like it burst into flames of shame. It was the worst possible thing I could imagine happening to me.

It was the end of my world.

Panicked and gasping for breath, I shoved the pencil back through the hole and let the hot-rod calendar fall to cover it again. I stumbled to my room and sat on my bed, shaking with rage and terror. I wailed over and over, "Oh my God! Oh my God!"

Raymond was out, helping a friend at his shop. But Inez should get home from work any minute. And when she did, she would see the truth. She would finally throw the bastard out.

The second I heard her walk in upstairs, I ran up and started yelling. "You have to come see this!" While she tried to ask questions, I dragged her down to my room and confronted her with the hole. "He's been watching me!" I shouted. "For God knows how long!"

To prove it, I had her follow me to the garage and lifted the calendar. Inez looked sick, like she'd been slapped. I expected outrage, but instead she began to explain it away. "Maybe the previous owners . . ." she said.

"Are you kidding me?" I screeched.

But she continued to defend him. "I know my own husband, Venus. Ray would never . . . How could you even think such a thing?" Like I was the dirty one.

"You're my mother!" I gasped. "You have to fix this. You have to get rid of him! You have to do something! You can't let him back in this house!"

She promised to fix the hole, and then she said she had to make dinner. I sat on my bed, immobilized. I kept thinking back, putting together the pieces. Surely this was why I had been so revolted by Raymond my entire childhood. Without knowing why, I had always known without knowing, which was the most horrifying part of all.

I don't remember how long I sat there, my rage boiling until it turned into something like a plan. I calmly went upstairs and passed Inez in the kitchen. In their bedroom closet, I stood on tiptoe and caught the edge of a shoe box—the one where Raymond kept his handgun buried under a bunch of Inez's scarves. The silver weapon looked cold and mean against the silky fabrics. I took it out and put the box away.

That's when I realized that Leo had followed me into the bedroom and that he saw what I had in my hand. Quickly I tucked the gun under my shirt.

I hid the gun in my room, in the top drawer of my dresser.

When Raymond pulled into the carport, I rushed upstairs to listen at the door. Despite her denials that Raymond would ever do such a thing, I still believed she'd interrogate him. See through his lies. Kick him out. Instead, she greeted him as if nothing were wrong. Asked about his day. Told him dinner would be ready soon. Surely we wouldn't all sit down at the table like it was a normal night.

Stunned by her words, I went back down the stairs to my room and took the gun out of the drawer and held it. Raymond always taught us never to leave a gun loaded, so I guessed it wasn't something he would do, either.

I was tempted to check the chamber for bullets—but I stopped myself. Because what if it was loaded? What if it wasn't?

When Inez called down that it was time for dinner, I almost didn't go up. I didn't know if I could see Raymond without trying to claw his eyes out. I didn't want to give away what I knew, what Inez knew. I don't remember what Inez served, only that I silently fumed through the meal, careful not to look at Raymond's face. I saw his arms, though. And the thick blond hair on them gagged me so much I couldn't eat.

"I'm not hungry," I finally said, getting up. Surely, now that it was obvious that I was angry and deeply upset about something,

Inez would talk to Raymond. After dinner, she would busy Leo with something and then she'd confront Raymond about the hole. Raymond would probably deny it, but she'd be able to tell he was lying and she'd finally stick up for me, demand that he leave.

But that's not what happened. After dinner, Inez sat at the kitchen table, doing bills, and Raymond watched TV, drinking beer. I hung around, feeling more and more enraged. At one point, I sat at the table and whispered loudly to Inez, "So you're not going to say anything? Do anything?"

She sighed and put down her pen. She looked at me and said, "Can we just stop with the dramatics, Venus? Don't be ridiculous."

"Ridiculous?" I stared at her hard, then got up and went down to my room. No way I was going to live another day with that monster in the house. I took the gun out and debated using it on myself. But I knew I couldn't do it, and besides, there was Leo. Recently, Raymond had gotten more short-tempered and rough than ever with Leo. I'd been allowing him to hurt my brother, one bruise at a time. And if I were gone, God knows what would happen to Leo.

In that moment, I saw as never before that Raymond was a sick, abusive pervert who would never stop hurting both of us. He had to be stopped, and clearly, Inez wasn't going to do that.

At around eight-thirty, she was busy putting Leo to bed, when I announced within Raymond's hearing that I was getting into my pajamas. I went down to my bedroom. Waited. Heard the outside garage door open and shut. A radio came on, and the sequence was suddenly familiar. And with it a parade of mortifying images passed before me. When I learned to masturbate . . . When I paraded around naked, dancing to the radio . . . When my friends spent the night and used my shower . . . Every morning when I came out of the shower . . . right in sight of the hole.

Burning shame and fresh resolve took over.

Slowly, I took off my blouse and hung it in my closet. But when I started to undo my bra, I couldn't do it. Not knowing his eye might be there. Instead, I casually approached the dresser, Inez's words pounding through my brain like a mantra: *Don't be ridiculous. Don't be ridiculous. Don't be ridiculous.*

Okay, I won't be ridiculous. I reached into the top drawer for the gun. It should not be loaded. Raymond's eye shouldn't be at the hole. *Don't be ridiculous. . . .* I held the gun to the hole and pulled the trigger.

The kick was so hard, and the explosion so loud—it was nothing like when Raymond took us out shooting cans in the woods. I heard the heavy sound of him falling, followed by a last gasp of shock or pain—sounds that I would never forget.

I ran past the stairs to the back door of the garage. I got there before Inez. Raymond's body was sprawled backward over the hood of a car, blood splattered everywhere. Weird little globs that reminded me of pink popcorn slid down the car's window, and I realized it must be brain matter. I recall thinking: Who knew it would look like that?

I must have been in some dream state of shock, I suppose.

Inez found me there and started screaming, "He's dead! Oh my God, what have you done! Oh my God!"

"I'll call an ambulance," I said calmly. "Good thing Raymond doesn't peep at me."

I left the garage and went to the kitchen to call 911. I told the operator matter-of-factly what had happened and where I lived. I could tell it was hard for her to hear me over the loud sound of Leo's wailing. Leo! I finally registered his presence, along with the fact that I was still holding the gun.

That's when reality hit, and the strange calm I'd felt collapsed into wild terror and hysterical sobbing.

Somewhere in there, I wet my pants.

. . .

Now I'm standing two feet away from that terrible hole, my arms wrapped around my chest, tears streaming unchecked down my cheeks and neck.

And then I realize thirteen-year-old Leo is standing next to me. I'm frantic to protect him, the way I didn't all those years ago. "Oh, Leo, you shouldn't be down here," I plead, trying to be firm, but gentle, too. "Please go back upstairs!"

I move away from the hole and sit on the bare mattress, hiding my face in my hands, trying to smother my sobs. But instead of leaving, Leo sits down on the mattress near me and puts a hand on my back. To my great surprise, he starts patting, and quietly begins to count, "One pat, two pats, three . . ."

At ten pats, I cry out, "I'm so sorry, Leo!"

"I forgive you," he replies, as if he's been taught to do this. He continues patting and counting while I sob.

I don't know how long I cry or how high Leo counts. Eventually I hear steps coming down the stairs. "Venus?" calls my mother. "Leo?"

Inez stands in the doorway. "I couldn't find you," she says, her voice thin and wavering.

I look up at her then. "Why didn't you fix it?" I ask, wiping my nose on my arm. My words hang in the air, and we both know my question means more than one thing.

"I should have," she says. "I'm so sorry."

"I forgive you," says Leo.

Inez and I look at each other, and smile despite ourselves. "Something the Herreras must have taught him," I say, wiping at my tears.

"Well, it's a good one, isn't it?" she says.

"If only it were that easy," I say, looking away. Leo has stopped patting my back.

"What if it could be?" Inez says. "What if it's not too late, Venus?" Her question is tinged with such raw hope it's hard for me not to weaken. "What if we fix this hole right now," she continues.

"We can do it together. I even bought some of that sparkle shit you're supposed to use to cover it with."

"*Spackle* shit," I correct her, and we both crack up. It takes the two of us a while to plug up such a big, ugly hole. After we're done, we decide to paint the whole room white.

PART SEVEN

★

Sacramento, California; Oakland, California; June 1986

50

It's June 1, 1986, almost three months after my twentieth birthday.

The building I'm looking for is in downtown Sacramento. Even with a map, it takes me a while to figure out how to get there. But I don't mind. I'm in no hurry.

I park the Honda in a large garage in the vicinity of the building. When I get out onto the sidewalk, the air is heavy and warm. I adjust my purse on my arm, walk slower. I check my underarms to make sure there aren't sweat stains.

I cross the street to walk on the opposite sidewalk, where there is shade. I see my image in the windows of storefronts as I pass. I'm wearing a blue linen dress that falls just above my knees, along with huaraches. I think I look pretty. My hair is partly pulled back and clipped. I peek into a children's clothing store. They carry a lot of cute designer clothing—stuff I'd like to buy Piper. I keep walking, knowing I should be getting close. I check the address numbers to be sure they're getting smaller, not bigger. The building itself is unimpressive. A business building that houses dozens of different offices. I scan the reader board in the lobby to find the right one. Third floor.

An attractive man with pale curly hair is also waiting for the elevator. He nods at me, says, "Hello."

"Hello," I say. He's already punched the UP button.

There's a *ding* and the doors slide open. Once inside, the man punches number 4. "Three, please?" I say. He punches the number. He smells good. I look at his hands. They're good hands. Clean. He's holding a briefcase. *Lawyer?*

"Pretty day, huh?" he says.

"Yes," I say. "But hot."

"Pretty girl, too," he says.

I look at him in surprise.

He smiles. "Yes, you."

I blush, look down. "Thank you."

When I step off the elevator, I'm met with a rush of cool air. The office I'm looking for is the second door down a long hall. It opens to a lobby decorated in a modern, fun style. Bright colors, smooth lines. Several pieces of modern art on the walls.

Behind a big peanut-shaped desk is a blond receptionist. She looks too glamorous for a secretary. I approach. "I'm looking for Anna Weir." I didn't make an appointment in case I changed my mind at the last second.

"Is she expecting you?"

"No, not really."

"Okay, well, let me see if she's available." She disappears through a set of doors behind her and I nervously wipe my hands on my dress. I can't believe I'm doing this. Moments later the receptionist returns with another woman. She's dressed in jeans and a black T-shirt decorated with embroidery and sequins. She has light-brown hair, a broad, pretty face with no makeup. Her thick eyebrows make me miss my own. She's thirtyish.

"Hi, I'm Anna," she says, extending a hand. "And you are?"

I only hesitate for a second. "My name is Venus Black."

Two hours later, I leave the office with a manila envelope tucked under my arm. I feel like I have made a new friend. I walk back the same way I came. This time, when I reach the children's boutique, I duck inside. The air-conditioning is wonderful.

"I'm looking for something green," I tell a saleswoman.

"Green?"

"Yes, something green for a girl with green eyes. She's a girls' twelve."

"Well, let's see. . . ."

I follow her to a mannequin wearing a green dress with pink polka dots, a pink ribbon at the waist.

"I like it," I say. "But it's a little too fancy." I can't picture Piper in it.

"I see. Let me think." I follow her to a more casual section. She pulls out a lime-green skirt I don't like.

I shake my head. "Why don't I just look around?"

She nods. "Let me know if I can be of help."

I wander through the racks, pulling out an item here or there. I finally choose a green bathing suit. It is exactly the right green, a cute little one-piece.

I pay for the purchase and head back to the car. It is hotter now than it was before, and traffic is terrible, so I decide to wait out rush hour in a restaurant. Then I start on the drive back to Oakland.

When I get home, it's almost nine, but Inez is still awake, lying on the couch in the living room, watching television. I sniff the air. Inez has supposedly quit smoking, but I don't entirely believe it yet.

"Where have you been?" she asks. She uses the remote to lower the volume of the television.

"Did it go okay with Leo?" I ask. "Bedtime?" I casually glance around for a wineglass. I don't see one.

"Yes. It went okay. And before I forget, Danny called."

My heart does a little flip. I called him while I was still back in Everett. We had a very awkward conversation as I tried to apologize for my rudeness while at the same time scolding him for not telling me the truth—that he knew who I was. "Let's forgive each other," he said, as if it were that simple. And in a way it was. We went on a couple of chaste dates and talked our heads off before I moved away. We laughed a lot, too. We held hands once, and lo and behold, I didn't die. Now we're trying to do a long-distance friendship, but it clearly has romantic overtones. So far, I'm surprised how much you can develop a relationship over the phone. My new therapist says it's a good way to make progress with my men issues.

Meanwhile, Danny has mentioned transferring to the Bay area. But I warned him not to do it just for me.

"So where were you all day?" Inez asks again.

I sit down next to her on the couch. "First I went to the admissions office at Oakland Community College."

She nods. She knows about my plans to attend school in the fall.

"And then I went to Sacramento to see Anna Weir."

"What? Why?" She's startled.

"I decided maybe we should think about doing that book," I tell her. "I actually really liked her, and it turns out she had a rough childhood, too. She even said I could help write it. She gave me an outline and some prompters." I hand Inez the manila envelope.

She stares at me wide-eyed while she pulls out the thin stack of papers. She meets my eyes. "I thought you hated this idea. You really think you're ready for this?"

"I think so," I tell her. "I guess we'll see. Anna says we don't have to be in a hurry. She seems to think our story is important. I never thought of it that way, but maybe she's right."

51

It had been Inez's decision. After we got the room painted white, it still looked really bad, because we didn't use primer and the knotty pine showed through. Even with the hole fixed and the walls painted, I couldn't stay in that room.

For the next couple of weeks I slept on the couch and wrestled with what to do. I knew I couldn't just live there with Inez and babysit Leo all day while she worked. Plus, Leo was not adjusting the way we'd hoped. His therapist said he was traumatized by the move and she suspected he was regressing. He spent most of his time in his closet, hardly ever spoke, and we couldn't imagine him going to school.

One evening Inez sat me down. "Venus, this is no life for you."

"I agree," I told her. "I can't keep doing this."

"Do you still want to move to California?"

"Yes," I told her. "But how can I? With Leo . . ." I shook my head.

"Leo isn't doing well, obviously. And I'm scared for him," Inez said.

"Well, I am, too! But what do you recommend?"

Inez pressed her lips together. "I've made a big decision," she said. "I hope you'll agree. I think you should move to California and get an apartment. I want you to call and see if those people—the Herreras—will keep Leo until I can sell the house and move down there, too. And then we'll work it out. We can have some kind of arrangement where Leo can gradually get used to us again and hopefully, eventually, he can move back in with us. The Herreras could visit all they want. When I ask myself what's best for Leo, that's the answer."

For a moment, I was too surprised to speak. "I thought we *hated* the Herreras! I thought we *blamed* them!"

"There's been too much anger, Venus. I'm so tired of rage and anger. It's Leo who matters now. When you stop and think about it, all of us are to blame in some way. We were all doing the best we could at the time. I think very few people are truly evil."

"Not even you?" I asked.

And she laughed. "Well, I don't know about that. . . ."

"Not even me?" I added, smiling.

"Oh, Venus," she said. "Oh no. Oh, never . . ."

After we briefly hugged—for the first time—I pulled away shyly. "Let's not get ahead of ourselves."

WHEN I FIRST arrived in Oakland, I rented a three-bedroom apartment near the Herreras' and got a daytime waitress job. Almost every evening, I went to see Leo at the Herreras' house. In the beginning, he ignored me. He'd say hello in response to my hello. But all his attention seemed to rest on Tessa. Leo trailed her around the house. And I trailed Leo.

After a couple of weeks of this, Tessa made it a point to run some kind of errand in order to leave me alone with Leo. At first, Leo got upset. But after a while, as I timed my visits to exactly seven o'clock, he came to expect them, to count on them, even.

Once Inez arrived, it took many more weeks to gradually transition Leo from living full-time with the Herreras to here. Some nights, Leo still cries for Tessa. But ever since we convinced him to use the phone, it's better. He calls her and Tony often, says a few words, and hangs up. It seems to help him.

Inez is still not done unpacking, even though she joined me here in early May, after the house on Rockefeller sold. The rooms of the apartment we share are still dotted with boxes—the stuff you can live without, which it turns out is most of what my mother owns.

In the meantime, Inez and I have an understanding. We need each other, and in having a common problem to solve—the problem of loving Leo—we manage to do together what we couldn't alone. Leo is often upset and confused. He's like one of those beetles that keeps tipping itself on its back and then wondering why it's stuck—and we take turns tipping him right side up again.

We have hard days, especially as Inez tries to stop drinking on her own. I keep telling her to go to A.A., but she resists. I think she is weakening, though. I noticed it really got to her the other day when I said, "Haven't you let your pride get in the way long enough?"

Yeah. Pretty funny, me giving Inez lectures on pride.

I finally started reading *You Can Heal Your Life,* and I think it's beginning to make some sense.

I still can't see a future with little miracles like butterflies floating around. But I can imagine being a beached starfish that, given a second or third chance, finally makes its way back into the welcoming sea.

THREE DAYS AFTER my visit to Sacramento, Inez is making me a cake. "I told you that we don't need to have a party, Inez! It's three months late—and that feels dumb."

"I want to have a party," she says, emphasizing *want.* "Heck, this is the first birthday party I've had for one of my kids in seven years! Why can't you stop objecting and go along? It's happening," she says happily.

"Okay, Inez," I say. "But I still don't get it."

"I told you not to call me that," she says. It's a joke with us. She pretends not to like being called Inez, but she knows I'm not going to start calling her Mom at this late date.

"Okay. But let me frost my own damn cake." I take her shoulders and forcibly move her toward a kitchen chair. She lets me. I've noticed she seems really tired lately, but she resists going in for a checkup. It could be that she's just not sleeping, because she's trying to quit drinking and she says without her wine she lies awake all night. I feel bad for her, but she needs to get sober. With all the stress around Leo, when she first arrived in California she was drinking vats of wine and was worthless by 7:00 P.M. every night.

I pick up the spatula. It's the same one from my childhood in Everett. It has a wooden handle with a white plastic top that is slightly bent from being burned in the dishwasher.

"What time is Piper's flight?" asks Inez. I could be imagining it, but I think she feels a bit of trepidation about meeting Piper. Maybe because she can tell Piper is so important to me.

"She arrives at the airport in an hour," I tell her. I still can't believe Piper is coming for my belated birthday. We talk all the time on the phone, but it's her first visit since I officially moved to Oakland back in March.

Leo comes out into the kitchen. "The smell."

"The smell? It's cake, Leo."

"Why?"

"Remember, it's Venus's birthday," Inez says.

"Oh." Leo flaps his left arm three times, a new quirk his doctor attributes to adolescence.

"Do you want to help frost, Leo?" I ask him. Of course he won't. He never does anything in the kitchen.

He walks over to where I am frosting the cake. I see his eyes flit across my hands. "Like peanut butter?" he asks.

I laugh. "Yes, it is just like when you put your peanut butter on the bread and try to cover up all the white."

He keeps staring. "Do you want to try?" I offer the spatula. He considers. Takes it. I am too stunned for words. I look over at Inez. This is the first time since we got Leo back that he has wanted to do something outside his normal routines.

I watch Leo carefully dip the spatula in the frosting bowl. There's about half a cake left to frost. I've done the bottom part. He slowly lifts the spatula with icing on it and touches it on the top of the cake at the very center. I'm guessing that's how he'll do it. Spiraling outward, like he does with peas.

I turn on the faucet and start to clean up. The enchiladas I made earlier are in the refrigerator. I'll put them in the oven when company starts to come.

After the kitchen is presentable, Leo is still working on the cake, and given his rate of speed, it could take all night. I go to my bedroom and change. I pick out a new pair of jeans—the first I have bought outside of a thrift store since I left Echo. They're white, fit like a glove, and they're just the right length. As I pull them on, I flash back to that day of my release from Echo. The weight of my layers from the charity bin. The flash of cameras. How I covered my face and changed my name and tried to escape my past.

The doorbell rings, but we know Leo will answer it. This is a new routine. Now he always answers the door in case it might be Tessa or Tony. It is Tessa. I hear Leo's strange squawks of delight. It still stings a bit that he doesn't do that when it's me at the door.

As WE ALL hoped, the charges against Tony were reduced to interference with custody. He received a two-year suspended sentence, along with probation. The fraud charges—Leo's fake birth certificate and Social Security card—were supposed to cost him six months in jail, but he got out after two.

When Tony offered to pick up Piper, I was grateful because I still feel overwhelmed by airports. But I wasn't sure how Piper would feel about being picked up by a stranger instead of me. She's never met Tony. But Piper didn't hesitate. "I get to meet Tony? Leo's dad?"

"Is that okay?" I asked.

"Yes!" she said. "I want to! But how will I know . . . He doesn't know me."

"He'll be holding a sign that says 'Piper.'"

"Oh! That's kind of cool," she said.

Piper doesn't have a shy bone in her body.

When Tony shows up at the door with Piper, I crush her in a hug, and I take the small package she is anxiously trying to give me.

"Is this for me?"

"Yes," says Piper. "But you probably won't like it."

"Oh pooh!" I tell her. "Of course I will."

"But there's another surprise," she says, giggling and peeking behind her. She goes to the closed front door and opens it again. "Ta-da!" she says.

Oh my gosh. I'm too stunned for words. Danny is standing right in front of me, looking as handsome as ever, in khaki shorts and a dark-blue button-down shirt. He grabs me into a long hug, and I don't resist.

I can't believe he flew here just to see me for my belated birthday.

After Danny's been welcomed, we go to the living room, where Tessa is writing a card, probably to me. She slips it into a book from the coffee table as we enter. This is the first time Piper has ever met Tessa. When I introduce them, Tessa looks at Piper with that soft and probing way she has. I think Tessa's impulse is to hug her, but she extends a hand to Piper instead.

Piper shakes it awkwardly, flashing her gap-toothed smile. "I'm so happy to meet you," she says. And then she giggles like it's so funny.

Sometimes I notice Tessa watching me. We get along well, but she is so quiet and almost mysterious. She's clearly mature for her age. And yet so innocent. At times it seems like she's older than me, even though she's a bit younger.

She's also Leo's favorite person in the world. Sometimes, when this bothers me, I remember the look of naked joy on Leo's face the day I brought him back to the Herreras'. He did this really funny jig, jumping all over. It was both hilarious and beautiful.

Now Inez hands Tessa the box of candles and I watch her carefully arrange them on Leo's perfectly swirled frosting. When Tony leans past Tessa to light the candles, I see him wink at Inez. I think she has a crush on him. As they set the cake before me, I realize I don't know what to wish for. I want to beg them to wait, to give me a few minutes to think.

But it's too late. While they all sing "Happy Birthday," this is what we do: Leo plugs his ears. Tessa smiles shyly across the table at Piper. Inez wipes at tears. Tony leans back and belts it out. And Danny, standing behind me, places a hand on my shoulder. I still can't think of a single thing to wish for. So I fill my lungs with air, let go all at once, and wish for everything.

Epilogue

My name is Venus Black because my dad was Joseph Black, and because on March 4, 1966, my mother, Inez, just so happened to be watching a TV special about the Space Race when her water broke. She named me after the planet Venus.

It was no mistake, my birth. No *chance happenstance*. It had to be me. *This is not something you can trace backward. It's not something you can prove through science. It's just something you know. Something only you can know. It comes to you in moments as simple as finding an eyelash on the tip of your finger.*

The trajectory of my life was always leading me here. I know this when I see the particular green of Piper's eyes. Or when I hear Leo play the color yellow on his cello. I give up trying to know why, and I arrive where I am all over again.

My naked eyes look out at the universe, and what I see is exactly as it appears. Out in the infinite black, a family of stars. Us blinking back at us. The picture in the sky doesn't lie—we are all clearly related.

And God exists. He spies us with his wise eyes. He whispers too softly for human ears to hear. He spins the world like a top, stares into the turning. And sometimes, he rocks.

—Writing sample for Anna Weir

Author's Note

The story of Venus and her family is set in Everett, Washington, in large part because that is where I spent most of my growing-up years—including in a public housing project a few streets over from the Denney Juvenile Justice Center. Back then, we simply called it *juvie*. Both Denney and Echo Glen are real juvenile justice facilities, but changes in their facilities and policies during the past forty years made corroborating details for Venus's experience a challenge. When I was unable to dig up the facts, I let my imagination serve the story.

A key event from my childhood mirrors Venus's, but mostly our stories diverge wildly. Venus is her own character, and she came alive at that surprising juncture in fiction where a writer's efforts end and some kind of magic takes over. More than once, while tracking her story, I thought, *Where did these people come from?*

With regard to the law, in 1977, Washington State passed the landmark Juvenile Justice Act. Among other reforms, the new legislation established standardized sentencing (while leaving judges some leeway), to bring juvenile courts more in line with the practices of adult court. In 1982, amid rising public concern about missing and runaway children, new laws changed police procedures. For example, in the case of a missing child under twelve,

police no longer needed to wait for seventy-two hours before acting on a report. Two years later, in 1984, the National Center for
Missing and Exploited Children was established. Soon after, dair-
ies across the nation began plastering photos of missing kids on
milk cartons in campaigns that became the AMBER Alert Program
of their day.

To the best of my ability, Venus's story reflects both the legal
realities and cultural assumptions of the era. An exception would
be how police responded to Leo's reappearance, and how that
might have played out in 1986. For my telling of that event, and in
the absence of certainty, I took some creative liberties while trying
to keep the story as realistic as possible.

When I asked Leo how it all came out, he said I got the colors
right.

Acknowledgments

I owe an enormous debt of gratitude to so many who helped this novel become a reality.

First, to my husband, Dave, who listened when I got lost, read the manuscript through many times, and regularly offered spot-on advice, I am deeply grateful.

To my sister, Katherine, always my first reader, your honest feedback and perceptive suggestions made a huge difference. When I became ill during a critical time in the revisions process, you stepped in to save me. There are no words.

To my son Noah, who loved an old draft of this story and strongly encouraged me to revisit it and give it another shot—I hope I did you proud. And to my other adult children—Nathan, Neil, Taylor, and Jana—your constant support and avid interest (and impatience to read the novel) meant the world to me.

Where would I be without my fabulous agent, Jane von Mehren, at Aevitas Creative? You immediately believed in this story and made sure it found the perfect home. Thank you. Big thanks also to my brilliant editor at Random House, Kara Cesare, who cared about every line and thought deeply about each character's journey. You're truly amazing. Thanks also to assistant editor Emma Caruso for your great suggestions and continued encouragement.

I also want to thank my mom for always supporting my work, and especially for being brave about some aspects of this story even though they may have evoked painful memories. You're an example to me of how grace and forgiveness can heal the worst wounds. I love you, Mom!

Finally, to all my family and friends who stood by me when I suffered a tragic loss right in the middle of writing this novel— your love and empathy carried me all the way. Your support and tears and heartfelt notes have meant the world, and often brought me comfort when I most needed it. You are living proof that love takes us home.

ABOUT THE AUTHOR

HEATHER LLOYD, who has spent many years working as an editor and writing coach, lives with her husband in New York City. *My Name Is Venus Black* is her first novel.

Heather-Lloyd.com

ABOUT THE TYPE

This book was set in Sabon, a typeface designed by the well-known German typographer Jan Tschichold (1902–74). Sabon's design is based upon the original letterforms of sixteenth-century French type designer Claude Garamond and was created specifically to be used for three sources: foundry type for hand composition, Linotype, and Monotype. Tschichold named his typeface for the famous Frankfurt typefounder Jacques Sabon (c. 1520–80).